The Saber and the Ring

A Saga of Civil War Days

The Saber and the Ring

A Saga of Civil War Days

By

PATRICK BROPHY

BUSHWHACKER BOOKS
Vernon County Historical Society
INC. NOT FOR PROFIT
NEVADA, MISSOURI

Cover Artwork
by Robert Schlyer

ISBN 1-893046-16-8

Library of Congress Control Number: 2004107630

BUSHWHACKER BOOKS
{Bushwhacker Museum}
VERNON COUNTY HISTORICAL SOCIETY
Inc. Not For Profit
231 North Main Street
Nevada, Missouri 64772
Website: www.bushwhacker.org
E-mail: bushwhackerjail@sbcglobal.net

TO MY FRIENDS

(They Know Who They Are)

Above All, TERRY

(Quite Contrary)

Brynhild: I wondered at the man who came in my hall; for I dreamed indeed that I knew thine eyes; but I might not see clearly, or divide the good from the evil, because of the veil that lay heavy on my fortune.

Sigurd: I loved thee better than myself, though I fell into the wiles from whence our lives may not escape; for whenso my own heart and mind availed me, then I sorrowed sore that thou wert not my wife.

Song of the Volsungs and Nibelungs

The Saber and the Ring

ONE

The gunshot rang, muffled but unmistakable in the forlorn street's dusky peace. Just vaulted down from Rustam, his big Mexican bay, young Colonel Starcross swung, alert if unruffled. Yielding the reins to the sentry sprung from the hotel porch's shadows, he stood with Captain Yulee, staring across the meandering ruts at the squat, somehow sinister little brick courthouse.

"You reckon they're shooting each other in there now?" the captain wondered.

"Our luck's not *that* good."

Even as they stared, a single figure filled the dim doorway, peered up and down the street, at last across it. After but a brief pause, righting its skewed shako, it came loping over.

"Colonel, sir—"

Starcross returned the tardy, gawky salute. "Lieutenant. . . ?"

"Klyce, sir. I was looking for Colonel Purinton." The callow cavalier mooted: "Maybe *you'd* best come, sir."

"Not my patch, Lieutenant Klyce. Purinton's the caesar of these streets."

"Oh, please, sir! They—we need a—a cool head in there. They"—voice breaking—"they're going to *hurt* her!"

Perhaps it was the pronoun that caught the colonel's interest; or perhaps just the look of the youthful lieutenant: the look of a well-meaning, *worried* young man, out of his depth, in more ways than one. Prompt, purposeful, the colonel stepped into the street, captain and lieutenant hastening in his wake.

At the courthouse door the latter diffidently gestured not up, toward the offices so lately vacated by the secessionist county government, now Federal garrison headquarters, but aside: into the ground-floor sheriff's sanctum, now likewise serving the latter rather than the former. Well before Lieutenant Klyce could reach and alert the room, the colonel was within.

The handful of militia officers in the clammy, scaly chamber were already on their feet, and their grudging stabs at attention bespoke surprise more than respect. Crouched flanking a yawning strap-iron door, muskets more-or-less at the ready, two seedy troopers made muddled shift to scramble to their feet.

"Carry on!" the colonel snapped, taking in an overall picture of shambling shapes, shifty, sullen eyes, dirty, undone would-be uniforms. Grimly his gaze swept on from doormen to door—out of which, as on cue, fluted a fluttery fanfare of groans.

Drawing closer, Starcross found himself peering down a dim-lit centerway between banks of barred, empty cells. Toward the far end, a third trooper, three makeshift chevrons on his sleeves, lay propped on a rusty bulkhead, his face a mighty, meaty wince, hands gripping a thigh black-red and wetly bright. Beyond his lolling head a last cell door, forming the passage end, stood wide; and half-shielded behind its iron jamb, in the flicker of a bracket lamp, loomed a ghost-white face haloed in short, very red hair and topping a swatch of rent and rumpled blue, a ghost-white throat, the beginnings of a bosom to match, and the big twin muzzles of a tiny pistol in the grip of a white-knuckled fist. Weapon and uniform apart, the ghost-face and the quite unghostly figure it surmounted belonged, clearly enough, to a woman.

The outer room was regaining its heart. "Sir, that—person was stopped by one of our patrols, a would-be dispatch rider; but the dispatches looked—funny. The more . . . intimate part of the impersonation"—the voice oozed prudery and prurience in equal measure—"eluded our preliminary . . . interrogation."

"The sergeant seems to have made good your . . . oversight. Well"—Starcross took a first step into the passage, toward the casualty—"hadn't you best be fetching him a doctor?"

"For God's sake, Colonel!" cried one of the hesitant heroes, "that belly-gun's got lead left for you!"

The colonel paid no heed, merely paused over the sprawled hulk, coldly inventorying stubbled chin, greasy-gray underwear bared by half-undone tunic, soulful, unsoldierly snivel—this last above all. Though bleeding yet, clearly the casualty was in no peril of his life. And then, facing the final figure, there behind the pistol, Starcross reared, for the first time taken aback.

"Why—it's Miss McQuaife!" Gauntleted hand at his hatbrim as all of its own accord, he went on without pause. "You won't remember, but you honored me with a waltz a few years ago at Richwood, my foster-father's place. A few years!" He marveled at it, his smile boyish. "Seems so much more—ages."

"It does indeed, Colonel Starcross—but of course I remember," the woman said, likewise without pause, managing a wan, wary smile of her own. "Though it was some steps from *colonel* then, wasn't it? What's surprising is that you remember *me,* in these circumstances." Real relief belied both the voice and the face behind the staunch persona embodied in the pistol, which she now held out, muzzles punctiliously lowered. She peered past the colonel's shoulder. "To *you,* sir, I yield!"

The sprawled sergeant chose that moment for a histrionic howl. Lieutenant and captain having followed the colonel into the passage, the other officers crowded after. The spokesman—the garrison provost, Starcross reminded himself—less in accusation than in simple amazement, leveled a finger:

"McQuaife—Cathal McQuaife! But of course! The rebel spy! Good Lord—a piece of luck, eh, Colonel?" He all but rubbed his hands, sharing the glory. "A feather in all our caps!"

Starcross cast him a stony glance, true eyes still elsewhere. "You had better come with me, Miss McQuaife. At once."

"*What*?" It was the yelp of the stabbed. "Colonel, you can't be serious! She's—she's *our* prisoner. You've no authority. Not to say, nor any safe, *proper* place to . . . to *hold* her."

"Oh, don't be an ass, Major." The colonel's voice was all the firmer for its gentleness. "We're in the same army . . . I trust. And *my* army does not make war on women."

"Women make war on us," the major smarted, glaring at the particular woman. "This—she's wanted for questioning concerning breaches of security at Departmental headquarters." His pomposity waxed. "She was taken here impersonating a soldier. And she's just done her best to murder Sergeant Tawes!"

"The last point speaks for itself, alas." The colonel grimaced. "As for the rest, I take full responsibility." He held out one gloved hand, pointed the way with the other; and pausing but to pick up her fallen kepi, with all the dignity she could muster—which was much—she accepted the invitation, as to a dance.

Ripples of hostility crisscrossed their path, only to melt away like morning shades. However much the militiamen might resent this regular officer, they respected and, yes, feared him more. His youth notwithstanding, Webb Starcross had a daunting reputation as a fighter, and he looked it, every inch. His stocky, bullocky, burstingly-energetic figure seemed to be forever pawing the earth. Holstered revolver hugged his trim waist; heavy scabbarded saber caressed a scarce thigh with his strides. Bristly blond mustache-ends registered his temper like needles on a dial, rising and falling with his breath, serenely most of the time but menacingly in his aroused moments . . . just now seemingly making up their mind. Resistance crumpled; the militiamen shoaled apart.

"I protest!" The major scrambled to save face. "Colonel Purinton'll—"

"Noted," Starcross acknowledged, mightily ironic. "And your worthy colonel you may refer to me. Gentlemen!"

Cathal McQuaife was a full-bodied woman, not over tall. Her sex, once known, burst from its nondescript, concealing shapelessness with a force that left the observer vexed with himself for ever having missed it. Still, the masquerade had hardly been hopelessly farfetched. In view of the youth of much of the army, in this late fall of 1861, beardless cheeks and even baby-fat were anything but dead giveaways; and Cathal McQuaife's biggish, squarish face lent itself well to a look of pouting, boyish, Byronic firmness—albeit clearly capable too of quite other looks. Webb Starcross was not too otherwise bemused to be bemused by her famous rust-red hair, now sacrilegiously docked, so memorable in more glorious state from that witching hour at Richwood when, a new-minted second lieutenant, he had twirled her in that twice-dazzling waltz; she and her sire having put in their hap appearance at Colonel Colquhoun's festive country evening: the father a distinguished soldier-diplomat, the daughter a distant, princesslike apparition, wreathed in the radiance of a nomadic upbringing in the world's capitals. Now the father, having forgone the old army, was said to be one of President Davis's most intimate military advisors. . . .

The daughter, for her part, had hung on in St. Louis, one of the family's several domestic seats, pursuing her glittering social life in that eerie early-1861 clime that was neither peace nor war—till it grew embarrassingly unblinkable that intelligence from Departmental headquarters was finding its way, likely through the loose lips of sots with stars on their shoulders as well as in their eyes, into ears even more Confederate if rather less shapely than hers. Whether, had she lingered, she'd have been gingerly meted out iron-barred official hospitality was an open question. To Starcross at least it was now clear that her dropping from sight in St. Louis was accounted for less by fear of prison walls than by the wish to render her cause a more dashing sort of service.

"Well, Miss McQuaife"—at last looking her full in the face under the dim doorway lamp—"and does your father know just what you get up to when his back is turned?"

"Not . . . *just* what, I'm afraid." The defensive irony gave way to ruth. "It was my own risk, Colonel, granted. If I hadn't chosen to take it, there could have been no consequences. I do appreciate the fact that you're making them . . . less unpleasant. But I'm fully prepared to face them—consequences."

"Consequences? Oh, you took quite a risk, yes. But you've been . . . lucky. Set your mind at rest. There won't be any consequences"—he actually blushed—"unpleasant ones."

His awkward reassurances only seemed to leave her newly troubled. As side by side they crossed the twilit street her thoughts fluttered about him, palpable as bats. "Aren't you rather putting yourself out on a limb for my sake, Colonel?"

"For honor's sake, I hope; principle's." As they drew near the hotel he slowed their matched pace; Yulee sidestepped on ahead. Starcross eyed the tiny town of Brocksborough huddled all about, lifeless under night's lowering lid. "The consequences," he took up, "may be inconvenient, even if not unpleasant. I'm going to have to take you to my personal quarters. Colonel Purinton's Kansans are the occupying force—and you've just had a taste of their notions of occupation. My own troops are camped outside town. If one of my married officers had his wife along—but we've been a long time in the field, we're as raw as they are, in our own way, and our camp's no place for you. And my only sway here in town rests on the fact they *are* such a raw, daunting lot, my men—as well as unaccountably attached to me. I wouldn't be quartered here myself but to be near the telegraph. So, even apart from *you,* I'm a bit of a thorn in Colonel Purinton's side: He can't get rid of me till I'm ready to go. But on the other hand, alas, neither can I get rid of *him.* Save for a few feet's radius about my person, it's his town. Which is why"—and Webb Starcross wound up on a would-be playful note—"you're going to have to bide close by me."

"Divided counsels in the enemy camp!" The young woman affected glee. "What a pity I'm too tired to care."

"Just what I was thinking." Concerned, he led her on into and through the bare, characterless public part of the small hotel, up the steep, strait boxed stairway. "There should be a bath laid on for me—you'd better have it. This room," he explained, opening the first door at the stair head, "I'm making my office. The sleeping chamber, where the bath—" He broke off, eyes trailing her suddenly-widened ones to the connecting door. In a spooky silence it had opened on a slight, gnomelike figure with long shiny blue-black hair haloing an ageless mahogany moon-face, clad in baggy blue trousers and a purple velvet tunic, silver-concho-belted. In the dim lamplight the effect was eerie, and even with understanding it needed a deliberate act of will to turn the unnatural apparition into a very natural, if very Indian, youth.

"Don't be alarmed," the colonel soothed. "Zurdo is my—well, orderly. And friend. I acquired him in New Mexico—he acquired me, rather, in place of his parents, for whose deaths he might well have held me to blame. Ah, Zurdo"—his voice rose—"this is Miss McQuaife. She's going to be my . . . guest this evening." Delicately he added, "I won't be needing you."

The Indian may have grunted a greeting or acknowledgment; Cathal McQuaife couldn't be sure. At all events, the apparition receded as spookily as he'd come. The amazed uncertainty with which she stared at the vacancy he left was outdone only by that with which she turned back to Webb Starcross.

"He sleeps in the stable," he clarified. "By choice."

"Yes . . . he doesn't look quite tame."

"He won't trouble you—nothing will trouble you. So—please treat the place as your own," he smiled; "and if you'll excuse me for the nonce I'll see if the chambermaid can manage to find you something more . . . er, proper to wear."

Cathal McQuaife gave the cozy, homely room a swift, professional survey, and then her own person, in its "improper" apparel, a closer, more critical one. "You don't seem much concerned with appearances, Colonel," archly—"save mine."

Starcross's tan became a pink. "You'll have to forgive me," he said stiffly. "I've passed most of my late years in the West, among soldiers, frontiersmen, and Indians. My . . . social sensibilities aren't at all what they should be. Still"—sternly he brought himself back to the moment—"with the best will in the world I don't know what I can do else. Your security concerns me far more than your appearance—than 'appearances'—and I've already explained the insecurity you face outside these rooms."

"Understood, Colonel, sir!" Essaying a teasing salute, Cathal McQuaife watched him lay aside his saber and plumed hat. His longish, wavy, taffy-colored hair seemed to light the room like the sun. "In any case, I've yielded to you, haven't I?"

"Have you really!" He donned a wintry smile: the hapless male not merely owning his ignorance of women but fairly taking refuge in it. "Time will tell, I've no doubt at all."

Downstairs Starcross found the hotelkeeper, a stolid German whose moderate Unionism and scorn for the Union's official local emissaries colluded to render the lot of an undemanding regular-army guest seductively congenial. Characteristically he offered no response, not even a lifted brow, to word that a young lady had moved into the colonel's rooms for the night, she might now be found in the bath laid for himself, and she lacked proper apparel; though likely he noted the Spartan young colonel's all-but-tongue-tiedness over his message stemmed less from self-consciousness than from sheer unfamiliarity with such arcana.

Starcross found his aide on the porch, hearing the report of a trooper fresh from the telegraph office. But there was no news; the wires were mute. The town itself lay quiet about them—inordinately so, for while Brocksboroughers had been hunkered low of late nights, their martial keepers by this hour ought to have been well launched on their nightly tipsy tribute to Union, Liberty, or like capitalized toasts. Had word of their headquarters' humiliation percolated down the ranks, wilting the wonted high spirits? Were the unseen heroes nursing their bruised pride, regrouping for the awful counterstroke? If Starcross scented lurking menace in the evening's peace he gave no sign. Focused on his chief, Captain Yulee's antennae twitched, scanned in vain.

At last, unable any longer to restrain himself: "Can I take it you don't want to be disturbed tonight, Colonel?"

Starcross took the gentle tease gently, but typically kept his answer earnest. "You know me better than that, Yulee."

"Well, I always thought so. Zurdo for one, though, finds his dismissal . . . ah, but who can tell with an Indian?" Yulee could be dead-earnest too. "Is it true she's a rebel spy?"

"I couldn't say, I'm sure. It sounds like it, doesn't it? Still, what does it matter? I've never believed spying had all that much effect on our trade. The well-known besotted idiot's babblings in the well-known shell-like ear—if this were the enemy's best we'd have a damned easy time of it, if you ask me. And even if I'm wrong, even if the lady poses us a genuine threat—well, what would you have me do? She's still a woman."

"Of course, Colonel." But the captain sounded less than fully convinced. More than the colonel's, his thoughts were on the unseen Kansans over the way. Hard as it was for the professionals not to scorn such uniformed civilians—yesterday's backwoods demagogues and bullies and layabouts—they felt only too well their inflated sway with the new powers in the land. In the day's revolutionary climate, bull-ox zealotry claimed pride of place over level heads, tolerably well-filled ones. It was too much to expect that the gage Starcross had rather casually tossed down would not in some wise, direct or devious, be picked up.

"Are you afraid I don't know what I'm doing, Yulee?" Starcross glanced back from the doorway.

"Oh, I'd never go *that* far, sir. After all," the captain consoled himself, with a wintry smile, "haven't you always?"

TWO

Complacent or no, Starcross went back upstairs rather like a ship captain returning to the helm in anticipation of a gale. And he'd been there but minutes, idly seated at the table he used as a desk, rummaging the papers and maps spread out over it, his ears as of their own will straining for sounds of bathing in the next room, when the hall door all but burst off its hinges.

"Goddamn your impudence, Starcross, you go too far!" The raging, gaudy figure stalked straight to the table and leaned on it, flaunting a fist. "Goddamn your soul anyway!"

"Good evening, Colonel Purinton." Starcross glanced up, all aplomb. "You're looking remarkably hot for November."

The visitor's "heat" boiled over in a very agony of hyperbole, like a lawyer pleading a weak case; lawyer, of course, being just what Uriel Purinton had been, or been trying to be, but months before, when the Kansas cavalry regiment he'd raised had rather unsurprisingly elected him its leader. Clearly self-designed, the colonel's garish, purplish uniform—blue presumably in short supply—would have pleased the most pompous of bandmasters. Starcross strove to swallow his all-around distaste.

"Want the credit for yourself, eh?" Purinton raved. "Well, you won't get it! Department's going to hear the whole story!"

"How your headquarters heroes managed to battle a lone woman to a draw, near thing though it was?" Behind the lazily lilting leonine mustache Starcross's lip curled. "Yes, indeed, Colonel, it should make . . . titillating reading."

"A woman armed and disguised, who gunned down a soldier of the Union doing his duty! A woman wanted for questioning on matters of gravest military import! Whose secure detention you undid, without an atom of authority! Oh, I'm more than happy to let Department judge for itself! In the meantime—"

The peroration was cut short by a stifled yelp issuing from beyond the connecting door. Before either colonel could stir, the door burst wide and a brightly if slightly covered female figure slid sinuously through. As she sidestepped and braced herself against the wall, primly drawing a scarlet dressing-gown together about her shoulders, Starcross saw through the doorway half-a-dozen of Purinton's harlequinesque heroes converging, irresolutely resolute, muskets at the ready, bayonets winking. At the doorway itself, however, irresolution won the day. Their eyes flew to their commander, seeking guidance—himself about-faced as if fancying *he* were the objective of the assault. He turned back to the table, heartened, it seemed, by neither the reinforcements at his back nor the fact that Starcross hadn't moved a muscle.

"In the meantime, Colonel?" the latter prompted. "Yes . . . I can see what you had in mind for the meantime."

Purinton's mouth worked in fits, fishlike, soundless. Seeking shelter in the room's distractions, he glanced over his shoulder, gradually getting a grip on himself, rediscovering his voice and something of his stilted, courtroom confidence.

"Oh, and likewise, Starcross!" He wrinkled his nose at the woman still struggling with the robe, burying herself in it up to the throat. "I can see, all right; I can see only too well. Ye gods, you must be out of your mind! You honestly think you can get away with this—taking *my* prisoner for your whore—!"

Webb Starcross's mustache spread, twin golden hackles, the wings of an eagle about to take flight. "Purinton"—still he spoke softly—"if those boobies aren't out of these rooms by the count of five, I swear I'm going to notch your ears, if no worse."

Purinton blinked, but managed to muster a scornful snort. "With *what?*" His slit-eyes slunk from the scabbarded saber lying athwart the table to the closed, covered holster belted yet to Starcross's waist. "I think you are outgunned, sir."

"Time will tell." Starcross's fingers twitched. *"One."*

"On top of all else, you threaten me!" Purinton swallowed, with some difficulty. "You wouldn't dare!"

"It'll be interesting to see, won't it? *Two.*"

"Great God in heaven! Headquarters is going to find his hard to believe. I call on these men to witness—"

"*Three.*"

"All right all *right!* Have it your way"—Purinton shooed his men—"for now. Fellow's taken leave of his senses," he assured them, limply. "No reasoning with him!" As the connecting door closed on his routed squad he faced Starcross yet again, making futile fists. "You wouldn't have done it," he gritted.

"You can take yourself off too, Purinton."

"You . . . you high-and-mighty doughface, I promise you, you haven't heard the last of this!"

Webb Starcross wasted no further words. Stonily, boredly almost, he watched the discomfited Kansan carry out his exit with the little huffy dignity he could muster, throwing Cathal McQuaife a malevolent sidelong scowl as he went.

The instant they were alone, Starcross became a different man—up and across the room in a few quick strides, drawing up just short of the woman, arms fecklessly fanning the air, as if keeping from throwing them about her but by the mightiest effort; face full of a chivalrous concern all out-of-proportion to the occasion, as it seemed to her, amusingly, and yet touchingly too.

"Miss McQuaife—are you all right?"

"Quite all right, thank you, Colonel. Never was a bath more welcome, not to say needed." Seeing the subtle irony pass right over his head, she shrugged and soon was as genuinely serious as he. "Yes, perfectly all right; though more than ever troubled by the trouble I'm bringing you . . . building up for you."

"Oh, we've heard the last of Colonel Purinton, I'm sure," he assured her, mulishly refusing to see her larger point. "For the meantime, at least, as he put it."

"Indeed. Other times, though," she persisted—"other Purintons? Your headquarters just might see things his way. I . . . fear for you, Colonel, your future. Not just for *this* but for the side of your character it reveals. You haven't forgotten your manners among the Indians, but I wonder if you've forgotten just how . . .

savage civilization can be. Plains fighting is poor preparation for blows struck from behind—for knives in the back."

He was studying her closely, not in admiration of her astuteness but in ongoing anxious appraisal of her person, as if determined to find damage, and managing to do so—damage done not, however, by Purinton's myrmidons.

"You have committed . . . not treason, perhaps. Worse!" he accused. "The heinousest of crimes—against your hair."

Her mild irritation mellowed in a smile. "A crime that can be undone—that will undo itself. I took my masquerade seriously." But she looked away, smile fading. "As obviously you don't take me. Colonel—I don't do things by halves."

Again her words failed to faze him, as his bemusement with her hair logically led on to his full awareness, for really the first time, of the rest of her person in its much-altered state—of the clingy, suggestive red robe, the matching nightdress beneath, the bare feet shamelessly peeping out farther down.

"You may be right," he murmured, half to himself, "about others seeing things his way, Purinton's. Spaur, the hotel fellow, certainly seems to have done so. I apologize for that—er, apparel, Miss McQuaife. Let me waylay the rascal and set him straight at once. Surely his wife has something more . . . proper."

"Please don't trouble him—them—Colonel. Or yourself." Cathal McQuaife was trying hard not to smile. "It's perfectly all right, I assure you. Perfectly . . . proper."

"Do you think so?" he fretted, all at sea.

"My dear Colonel! You *have* been a long time among the Indians. And yet," mischievously, "I've always been under the impression that *they* wear almost nothing at all."

Again his tan flushed to a pink; but he smiled gamely at his own discomfiture. "You'll find it disappointingly easy to get the better of me in this line, Miss McQuaife."

"Well, we all have our 'lines'—and it's quite easy to draw the wrong conclusions about another's 'line.' In *my* 'line' I assure you it's nothing untoward for a lady to receive a gentleman in *negligee,* that it needn't mean . . . anything untoward."

The colonel's bow would have done a courtier proud. "I reckon there are hidden dimensions in the simplest of us; still I fear you'll find I come tiresomely close to being just what I seem." He spread his arms. "I'm pleased you're pleased with the—er, *that.* If you're quite sure, won't you sit? They should be bringing us something to eat directly." All solicitousness, he saw her to a settee, and then turned away to unbuckle the holstered revolver from his waist and lay it with the scabbarded saber.

"Would you really have used that?"

"Granted I'd have preferred a horsewhip." His hand strayed on to the saber. "I have the eerie feeling our paths have crossed before, Miss McQuaife, more than once." He faced her with the saber in his hands, easing the curved steel from its metal sheath. "You know the story? Your father gave this saber to *my* father on the morrow of Cerro Gordo." The shining Toledo steel ribbon, blue-enamel-inlaid near the hilt, the silver filigree basket handle, caught and propagated the lamplight. It was heavier than most American cavalry sabers, almost a long cutlass. "It was said to have belonged to Santa Anna himself—but then they always said that. Santa Anna had a corner on the spoils market."

Cathal McQuaife sat forward, touched the proffered tip of the razor-edged blade. "Well, of course I know, Colonel. What a modest man you are! Why, everybody knows all about you these days: 'the Modern Xenophon'! And you're starting to make some folks nervous. You ought to have come over by now."

"'The Modern Xenophon'? Dear me." Starcross made a wry face. "I but did my duty, Miss McQuaife. I'm far too dull, too simple a fellow to do more . . . or less."

"Your duty? Even to your superiors, Colonel, your duty just might have countenanced surrender, like Davy Twiggs in Texas. Instead of which," she leaned back, "you carried out a fighting withdrawal through a thousand miles of Indians, outlaws, and Confederates, to say nothing of sand and cactus."

"My duty as I saw it, then," he clarified; "I'm not Davy Twiggs, for a start. Surrender looked to me—shameful, yes, but, to a simple soldier, worse: just . . . inexpedient."

"There *was* a third course."

"Go over?" He turned away, frowning. "Oh yes. But it's no easy matter, changing horses in midstream. When the new war caught up with me I was far afield, fighting the old one. By the time we reached our base, my men and I were bound to each other by bonds that seemed to bind us in turn to the flag we'd just fought so well under. Granted other men have been able to reason themselves into switching flags in such cases, but I, at least, could not. It needed a feat of imagination, a mental gymnastic, quite beyond me. I'm far too dull, too simple. Added to which"—the boyish grin—"I'm ambitious. *You* have all the good generals. There's more room at the top in *this* army."

She was the stubbornly serious one now. "We are your *people.*"

His face went wooden. "I have no people, alas."

She said softly, "I know that too, Colonel. You were a fable throughout the Southwest long before you became the Modern Xenophon. Goodness, does anybody *not* know the tale: how the Yapparika Comanches wiped out your whole family, how you stood them off alone, a boy of ten, till Colonel Colquhoun rescued you with his Rangers and Dragoons? Oh," impatiently, "but you know what I mean! Each of us has his people. You have Colonel Colquhoun, for a start. Colonel Colquhoun, as I hear it, knows well enough who *his* people are." She eyed him askance. "I wonder what he thinks of your going on wearing that coat."

All unhurried, unruffled, Starcross sheathed the saber, laid it back on the table. Slowly he strode back and settled on the snug seat by her side. If her telling of his stirring story had touched him, he kept it hidden. "Colonel Colquhoun and I long ago learned to respect each other's opinions . . . coats."

"And that little girl, his daughter—dimly I seem to remember her from that night; now what *was* her name?"

"Her name," Starcross answered evenly as ever, almost too evenly, "is Candacy Ann. Properly Candace—"

"Candacy Ann—ah yes. How Southern! Oh, and a perfect firebrand of a rebel, too, I've no doubt. What does *she* think, do you reckon—of the color of your coat?"

"I couldn't reckon, to save my life. She's at school back East; I haven't seen her in a coon's age. Why bring *her* up? A mere child—not to say, and my foster-sister."

"Oh, and not a bit of a hero-worshipper of her dashing foster-brother, I'm sure!" Cathal McQuaife's gold-flecked green eyes glinted. "Somehow I picked up the notion of . . . of an old understanding. That's how it is in these planter families."

"My dear Miss McQuaife"—for the first time Starcross's voice betrayed mild impatience—"Colonel Colquhoun has far loftier ambitions for his only child than the hand of a penniless soldier, Modern Xenophon or otherwise. Oh yes, there's an 'old understanding,' all right. It has to do with Chance Buckhannon, the neighbors' son—a soldier, but one as unobjectionable in the color of his coat as in the depths of his purse."

Whether she might have pursued the seemingly touchy subject would never be known. A knock at the door signaled the arrival of the expected meal, borne teetering on the arms of an undersized maid-of-all-work. The hotelman himself followed, stolid, porcine, unwontedly pompous, carrying a bottle.

"What's this, Spaur?" Starcross affected puzzlement. "Can it be you've actually been holding out on me?"

The German grudged his all-purpose grunt.

"Clearly," the woman supplied, "the amenities of the house are custom-fitted to the guest—dull, simple drink for the dull, simple soldier, and so forth."

"I wouldn't be surprised." The dull, simple soldier shrugged, smiled. "And for the red lady, red wine—not to say, and a red robe. What on earth will come next?"

The darkskinned maid having, in several trips, mutteringly, somnambulistically arranged her burdens on a small table drawn up between chairs in the middle of the room, stonily the hotel-keeper plunked down the bottle, herded her to the door, meted the room a microscopic bow, and was gone.

"Do you reckon he's freed that darky?" Cathal McQuaife wondered, casting the closed door a sultry, catty look. "Do you reckon she knows the difference?"

Starcross smiled again. "It's a war over nothing, brought on by hypocrites?"

"Not too far off the mark, perhaps." Carelessly she tossed her head, and spoke what was really on her mind. "We are going to be talked about tomorrow."

He stood waiting behind one of the chairs. "You don't sound too troubled."

"I'm far too hungry." She took the chair and suited deeds to words, eagerly lifting the cover from a casserole, bathing her face in the steam of a fresh-baked chicken. "Besides, as I assured you, I'm steeled for consequences. Not excluding even the loss of my reputation"—with a rueful grin—"if I've got one to lose."

"Yes-s." He busied himself with the wine. "You must tell me about these . . . remarkable doings of yours."

"Ah!" She scarcely paused in her unceremonious assault on the meal. "The interrogation of the prisoner begins!"

"Nothing of the kind." His typical stiffness resurged. "You may make war on me, Miss McQuaife, but you'll find it a lonely pursuit, for I don't propose to make war on you in any sense." Neatly he filled the glasses. "Whatever you may tell me will never leave this room. It's just that I have a natural curiosity."

For the moment his formality proved infectious. She sat staring, lost in thought, holding a chicken leg at untidy half-mast. Then with a shrug she lifted it to her lips, went on eating and speaking with an unladylike economy of movement.

"My story's duller than yours, Colonel; but I've always been a—an unconventional woman. My mother died giving me life. I grew up in a series of temporary homes, all over the world, largely among men, men like my father. I was indulged and ignored at the same time, if you know what I mean. Last winter found us in St. Louis; the secession crisis, building by the day, seemed remote, unreal. Then Father went South, literally and figuratively alike. He'd always been a distant, godlike figure; I'd become very self-reliant. So I stayed on, going right on in the familiar social whirl, the planters' world, the old army. Which all of a sudden was an all-*new* army, troubling but fascinating too, full of interesting possibilities." Impishly she grinned around her drumstick, as in token of things left unsaid, feats modestly unenumerated. "Ah well, but all things come to evensong at last. August brought martial law. The social scene thinned out, like the autumn woods, making concealment ever trickier. It grew clear I wouldn't be leaving at all if I didn't do it soon; and so I slipped out of town and wound up in Little Rock, among *other* old friends."

"And then things got really . . . fascinating"—he topped her glass—"really serious?"

She eyed him through the wine's ruby lens, intent. "Whatever I may feel for my 'cause,' Colonel, I'm hardly one to be content to serve it by rolling bandages. By my doings in St. Louis, useful or no, I had achieved a certain fame—infamy, I'm sure, from your side of the line. There was no lack of gallants in the Trans-Mississippi eager to involve themselves with me—to spoil me, if you will, at my most unconventional. I was a new kind of Southern belle, surrounded by hearts fair begging to be broken. I could pick and choose. You know Jaymie Strainchamps, I think?"

"Strainchamps? Of course." Starcross's glass sagged. "Good Lord, yes. We were classmates at West Point."

"Yes; I thought so." She heaved a sudden sigh. "Poor, dear Jaymie! Convention itself. He *so* wants to marry me."

"Conventional or no," Starcross drawled, all disapproval, "he is criminally careless of his would-be bride."

"Oh, you can't blame *him.*" Her enthusiasm flamed afresh, sparked by his disapprobation. "He took much the line you're taking." Satisfiedly she watched his brows arch as in proof of her point. "I had to talk him 'round. But it wasn't hard."

"I can well imagine."

"It wasn't hard," she repeated, "because it was what he wanted to hear." Leaving off her meal, she threw herself into her words. "Most of our so-called leaders have given Missouri up as well-lost, seeing it as at best more liability than asset. Jaymie disagrees; he takes a broader view. Much is made of the importance of the Mississippi; but, Jaymie argues, it's the Missouri that's vital. If we could hold enough of the state to stop traffic on the Missouri, we could cut the Union in two. Think of it! The Colorado gold, all the West, cut off. That toper fellow Grant wouldn't be invading Tennessee any time soon, to say the least."

"Yes-s." Starcross frowned, lost in thought. "Jaymie always was a sound . . . classroom strategist."

"We now have before us a chance that may never come again. What with Price's Missourians still holding the Southwest, thanks to their September victories—which we foolishly failed to follow up because Missouri hadn't *quite* joined the Confederacy—we have the two-sided base from which a strike at the Missouri River line has every prospect of success . . . says Jaymie."

"You've been reading Jomini yourself, from the sound of it." He eyed her with new respect. "What luck the wrong people are running the Confederate army!"

"Your rejoicings may be premature. They're not total idiots. And Jaymie can be persuasive, he too." Coyly she smiled. "And he too has—friends. A small, snug world, the South."

Starcross went on staring at her in waxing unease.

"They're giving him his chance," she affirmed, "provided he's sure of his intelligence—can assure them we'll have you not only outnumbered but outmaneuvered."

"I see—*begin* to see." In deepening dismay he headshook. "I see *your* part, above all. And I don't *like* what I see."

Matter-of-factly she went on, comradely—manlike: "These nigger- and chicken-stealers, of course, count for little." Casually she waved away the garrison unseen about them. "The Modern Xenophon, on the other hand, with the seasoned timber he fetched out of the wilderness—maybe it should be the Modern Moses, not Xenophon—these were another matter! And we'd lost track of you, Colonel, this side of Leavenworth."

"But now you've found me again. And you know my mind—as well as I know it myself, at least. Only rejoin your Jaymie, and your mission's accomplished."

"Ah. But I'm not very likely to rejoin him, am I?"

"Either way," he scolded, "you've been speaking too freely. First, you shouldn't have given away your longheadedness. You should have stood on your womanly giddiness and ignorance, worked your womanly wiles on me, the ones that seem to have worked so well with Jaymie Strainchamps."

"Perhaps I have; perhaps I am. If womanly wiles are so insidious, how can you be sure when they're being worked or aren't?" She smiled, but with marked impatience. "You protest your dullness and simplicity, Colonel; but I wonder. Jaymie's anything but. He's quick, bright, you'd swear, full of twists and turns. And yet in some strange way, take him all for all—he's all surface. You, on the other hand, plain, simple you, you may present a smooth flat front at every compass point—but a shield, Colonel, hints at something being shielded; a hard crust suggests a soft filling. And one doesn't eat a deep-dish pie like a piece of cake."

"You disprove your own argument by speaking over my head. Which itself may be womanly wiles . . . though I venture the other kind might've been more effective, not to say more fun." Starcross sat back, his bright, beatific blue eyes at rest on her face. As if reaching a decision, he put on a fresh smile, hoisted his glass and held it out. Dutifully she raised her own; the goblets kissed with a clink. "One can never tell," he added, inconsequently.

"Is that a toast?"

"Oh, we can do better than that, surely." Transparently he turned it over in his mind. "Confusion to the enemy," he proposed, like a small boy at play, his mock-seriousness only half hiding a deadly-earnest indeed, "whoever he may be."

"Amen!" They drank, and then grew self-consciously sober together. Starcross broke the spell, leading the return to the settee. "But *Q.E.D.,*" the woman resumed, refusing to be diverted. "A simple man would have no trouble making the enemy out."

"Well, there are simple men and simple men—just as there are enemies and enemies. Soldiers find that out soon enough. Civilians are the 'terrible simplifiers,' unable to tell the mere adversary, out front, from the foe, who may be behind or alongside, with those knives you warned of." He fixed her with a heartfelt look. "You may be my adversary—certainly Jaymie Strainchamps is. But Colonel Purinton is the enemy."

"And there are so many Colonel Purintons! But never mind him—them. Tell me, Colonel"—she returned his look in kind—"do you believe in . . . Fate, shall we call it?" It was a question clearly not to be answered in such naked form, and she hurried to clothe it. "You told me you'd the feeling our paths had crossed before, more than once. Would you believe *I* had just such a feeling that night Father and I came to the dance at Richwood? And I don't mean only knowing that Father had known your father in Mexico, and had given him that saber, or about your boyhood travails among the Comanches—oh, everybody knew all *that.* No: it was more, far more; it was something about *me.* I had the—the fey feeling we'd met before, you and I, all but in some other life, and would meet again, in this one. Here's a man, I told myself, not just who's going to go far, whom we're going to hear much of, but who's going to play a part in my own life."

"All that—of a very backward, very new lieutenant?"

"Backward? Not a bit of it, Colonel. For you felt it too, I flatter myself. You knew just what you were doing, didn't you, where you were going? And you took my measure, in that brief hour, as I took yours. You'd the cheek, backward new lieutenant or no, to assign me, the likes of me, a part in your own future."

"I so flattered *my*self—of course. We're all prone to self-flattery in our youthful fancies. I'm sure I wasn't that night's only frog to fantasize of—of a fairy princess."

Firmly she shook her head. "You weren't flattering yourself, Colonel, and you knew it—know it. The fairy frog, as I recall, was a prince in disguise."

Webb Starcross seemed to turn tardily aware of some eerie barometric change in the room's air now pressing heavily on his eardrums and lungs. He sat warily unmoving there by her side, as if for fear of generating static electricity.

"The likes of you." His azure eyes alone showed life, plumbing her green ones like skylight the glades of a wood. "But what *are* you like . . . apart from fairy princess?"

"There is a way to find out, Colonel. A time-honored way."

"Yes-s." And slowly, surely, as if riding the beam of his gaze, his head descended to hers like the sun itself, following its falling rays. And she no more sought to draw away, nor could have, than the earth from the sun. It was a meeting of spirits, though, far more than of bodies, heavenly or earthly, or even of mere lips. It was a minimal kiss, forthright, elegant as a swordthrust, chaste as the pink of a fencing foil on a stylized heart.

THREE

"Webb." But she added, as if to turn the intimacy, almost the endearment, to mere curiosity: "Why did they name you so?"

Shyly, all prim apology, he sat back. "I'm told it's an old Saxon word for 'blade.' Such a warrior, my father."

"Well, at least *your* father had an excuse: You're a *son. Cathal* means 'eye of battle,' of all things—Celtic."

He laughed. "What a burden. You're doing your best to live up to it, though, it seems."

"You too," she reflected, "the Comanches having left you shouldering yours all alone."

"You, at least, don't *look* hopelessly martial."

"Is that what you are—hopelessly?" She smiled in wonder, both kinds, incredulity crowned by awe. "Orphaned by Indians, you adopt an Indian orphan!"

He shrugged. "What surer basis for a relationship? Enemies and adversaries, remember. Today's adversary may well be tomorrow's ally against the enemy. And Indians I think of yet as adversaries, not enemies. Like Confederates."

"That's . . . very encouraging. Oh, but if we were only on the same side now!"

"Now. . . . There is more than one way it could be arranged."

She threw him a studious sidelong look, intensely questioning, yet at the same time abstract, introspective, less simply questioning than self-questioning. At long last she sighed and sat back, seeming to have reached a critical decision.

"While you were out," she confessed, in tones of mock-penitence, "I took a look at your maps." She gestured at the desk-table. "Out-of-date as they are."

His lips quirked. "My faith in human nature is confirmed!"

"You're not just awaiting orders, Colonel," she accused, in mild tones. "You're waiting for us to make our move—Jaymie's move. And you have expectations of the outcome not unlike his. The opposite of his, I suppose I should say."

The colonel's compact sitting shape unfolded, seemed to turn all thrusting arms and legs. There was noplace for it to go but up. He paced to the table, frowned down at the strata of outspread maps, the image of professional absorption.

"It hardly takes a military genius to see it," he said at last. "Though the would-be military geniuses seem to be failing to see it with marked success. Jaymie's right: the Missouri's the Union's jugular, and a firm, quick hand could take it. If Ben McCulloch had backed Price in September—! But Price still holds the Osage River country, the side of the base." He fingered the uppermost map. "We have troops enough in the state, but what are they doing? Guarding the gorgeously uniformed backsides of political Napoleons!" He roused from his irreverent reverie, glanced around at her, almost in apology. "Your army has all the good generals, just as I said—but they're all east of the Mississippi. The Department awaits a leader . . . on one side or the other."

"A role Colonels Strainchamps and Starcross both aspire to fill, it would seem. One role; two aspirants. . . ."

"You do have a certain knack for your work, Miss McQuaife. You've seated yourself on a seesaw, as it were, midway between the teetertottering counterweights." He smiled, thinking it over. "You might almost be the Valkyrie hovering over the field—'eye of battle' indeed!—she in whose gift lies the victory."

"You grudge me such power?" The young woman rose, came padding forward on her bare feet, a long lissome ripple of red silk topped by rosy face and tousled, cropped red hair. "It's a fleeting power, though. The dull professionals will take over before this war is much older. But perhaps the present hour, as you say, has room for the likes of me. Now—now anyhow—the inspired amateur may make his mark. So I assured Jaymie, at least, when I dined with him at his headquarters at Bosky Dells but a couple of nights ago." Slyly she added, "He too had his maps."

As of their own will, Starcross's eyes slipped back around to his own. "You're not letting the war interfere with your 'unconventional social life,' it would seem."

"If you can call it 'social'—my calling on Private Nameless of the Fourth Iowa Infantry and his many ilk, no longer in need of their worldly goods. Mere sleeping children, sleeping forever. War is so sad!" She sighed, and shook herself. "If only those faked dispatches had been as plausible as I!"

But the colonel's mind had stayed with his maps. "Jaymie will use the Missourians," he told himself. "Courthouse cavaliers, aye, but seasoned now; they've won battles, curbed their ardor." His forefinger made imagined sweeps. "If I were Jaymie. . . ."

Cathal McQuaife broke into his reverie. "You're too proud to have a woman for an enemy—for an adversary even. Are you alike too proud to have one for an ally?"

He blinked up. "I didn't dream I was being proud."

"I would expect no less, Colonel." She drew closer, crooking her head to study the map. "Jaymie was to be guided by my report, of course; but he looked for no surprises from it, and if none there were—will you allow me?" Taking up a stub of pencil she began making firm marks. "He was to leave rendezvous at dawn on the twenty-sixth: two days hence, yes. He was to have two battalions of Texans and Louisianians, along with his own regiment. Price meantime was to draw you out, set you up for Jaymie, coming on at the double quick"—winding up her pencillings with a decisive stab—"to fall on your flank—*so.*"

In the stretching-out silence she peered up and about, to find him staring only at herself, map and its marks disdained.

"Hammer and anvil," she added, for emphasis. "Decision on the twenty-eighth. And if Jaymie does manage to bring it off, Ben McCulloch will move into Missouri in force, changing the whole complexion of the Trans-Mississippi war."

His stare became a frown. "Are you aware—are you *quite* aware of what you're saying, Miss McQuaife? What you're *doing?*" He mulled it, wary, worried. "What *are* you doing?"

Her eyes twinkled. "Isn't it obvious?"

"Yes—it is indeed. Great Scott! I hope you don't think I led you on to these—these improper disclosures." He shook his head as if it ached. "I don't know what to say."

"Lo and behold!" Cathal McQuaife affected peevish delight. "I've gotten the gentleman's attention, at last—I've shocked him into taking me seriously. Horror of horrors, I've broken the rules! When I was little, Colonel, I used to go and stay with my cousins, who'd deign to let me join—on probation—in their boy-games, but then were scandalized when I played by my own rules."

"We are not playing a game, Miss McQuaife."

"*Captain* McQuaife," the woman corrected, with a show of huffiness, almost of anger, "since you *will* be proper."

"What did you say?"

"I have a commission." She preened, played the woman. "A girl doesn't have a general for a father for nothing."

Webb Starcross threw up his hands. "Worse by the minute! Even if it *were* a game, one would expect you to play it by the rules. You don't seem to appreciate that breaking the rules of *this* game can mean being stood up against a wall."

"*You* won't make war on a woman. Can you see those Confederate gentlemen standing me up against a wall?"

"Both sides are likely to do a great many things we have trouble even imagining now, ere this little picnic is over."

"But that's not the point, is it? The point is, I spoil the game, I profane the boys' club! Not a very profound point, Colonel."

He bit back his waxing exasperation. "You want in the club in name only. You want to be a warrior without accepting the dispensation—submitting yourself."

"I never said I wanted to be a *man.* If that's what it takes—all right, I've cheated. You should complain to my father, or Jaymie Strainchamps. *They* let me get away with it."

"And yet," he reproached, "you said something about devotion to your cause."

She smiled. "Did I *name* it, though, my cause? Your soldierly simplicity tries my patience, Colonel, even as my—I suppose—my womanly complexity tries yours. You follow the old flag, you say, out of sheer force of habit. Changing allegiances is too strenuous a gymnastic for your stiff mental joints. Well, it must be nice for your choices to be made for you so painlessly. Granted devotion to causes does seem to come easily to many women; but such devotion, I suspect, owes more to perversity than to heartfelt conviction. When your partisanship carries but little weight, you compensate as best you can by flaunting it. No—women have only one cause: their loved ones, their homes, the familiar life around them, from which they draw security and comfort. And this is the force that holds the world together. To hitch *that* to some far-fetched abstraction whose end effect is to tear the world apart, that were perversity indeed, surely. No: leave the 'causes' to the men, say I." She broke off, her runaway animus expiring in a heavy sigh. "In the end the Colonel Strainchampses are going to lose this war. The little *I* can do is try to see that the Colonel Starcrosses are the winners, not the Colonel Purintons."

"Well put." Starcross's smile was both wry and grim. "So Southernly and womanly put! To reduce it all to personalities. If only the politicians would do as well!"

"I am twice excused, then." Cathal McQuaife returned the smile, but went right on making her point, her case, in all earnest. "I can husband my true devotion for hearth and home. I can find my cause not in mankind but in some man."

Broodingly, eloquently silent, Starcross studied her. "You're being rather hard," he pointed out, "on a certain man."

"Jaymie?" She stood unmoving, ruefully defiant. "Oh, I suppose I can hardly say I never 'led him on,' in any sense at all; but I never led him to betray his trust. If that occurred, it was *his* indiscretion, *his* impropriety, not mine."

The discreet knock at the door broke the spell. Not awaiting leave, Captain Yulee opened the door and strode forward, holding out a cipher telegram flimsy together with its decoded transcript. The colonel took the papers, deigned them a swift, cursory scan, and nodded to the captain, who retraced his steps.

The young woman had moved over to the dark window, affected to peer out. "Your long-awaited orders, Colonel?" With effort Starcross dragged his thoughts back to his guest. He waved the papers and casually let them drop atop the maps. "Colonel Strainchamps has been spied reviewing troops at Bosky Dells. Rumor predicts an early movement in force against the Iron

Mountain Railroad. The Department commander himself means to be there, backed by all his palace guard, to meet his destiny, so long overdue." His heavy sarcasm gave way to buoyant satisfaction. "No—no orders for me. I'm to stay where I am and go on being guided by . . . regional intelligence."

She mused, oracle-like: "Your commander will have a long wait for Jaymie on the Iron Mountain Railroad."

The colonel's mustache twitched like a hungry cat's. The affliction spread to his limbs. "I must go downstairs and—confer." Distractedly he threw a glance back at the woman. "Please don't wait for me. The night will be short enough."

"It would be nice to know what to expect, Colonel."

"Expect?" His distracted, blank look clarified into a smile. "Excuse me; I thought that had been made—rather clear."

"Well, it was; and then it wasn't." Her own smile was teasing, enigmatic. "I'm causing you enough trouble without. . . ."

"Taking my bed? Oh, I'm used to that sort of thing."

Starcross caught his aide up at the foot of the stairs. "Ride out to camp, Yulee, and pass the order—break camp at first light."

The captain, as ever, kept his thoughts to himself. "The Iron Mountain Railroad is a long way away, Colonel."

"Indeed. A good thing we're not going to the Iron Mountain Railroad, then. And show some respect." Only Yulee could have read the humor in the wooden voice and face. "Don't you know you're talking to the Modern Xenophon?"

Yulee looked for no explanation, and none being offered, lifted a hand in hasty half-salute before making off for the shadowy back way leading to the stable; Starcross himself went out the front. The mild night he found void of life but for the sentry at the foot of the porch-steps, standing onelegged leaning on his musket whetting a gigantic knife on the worn leather of his boot.

"A quiet evening, Private."

"Dead as a beef, Colonel." Respectfully straightening, the trooper glared across at the courthouse, still keeping its unaccustomed peace. "They got past me by sneakin' around the back way," he growled. "'Twon't happen twice."

"No; we'll hear no more of them tonight. But keep an eye peeled all the same."

At any other time Starcross might almost have wished otherwise, that more just might have been heard of Uriel Purinton. Activating another had aroused all his native itch for actions of his own. Webb Starcross looked forward to combat, confrontation. But his thoughts, if not quite his eyes, roved from the courthouse over the way to the rooms just over his head. Consummate combatant that he was, in another great realm of life—alike characterized by confrontation, even combat, if of quite another kind—he was far less at home; and with literal battle put off it was into this less familiar list that his energies were surging. He was anything but a man who agonized over his choices, and the simple workings of his simple soul, as he thought of it, but rarely showed on the surface. An onlooker couldn't have told if he were wrestling with himself, striving toward a momentous decision. To all appearances he was his familiar crisp martial self, in whom command was inseparable from execution; to think of doing a thing was for the thing to be done. He was too young a commander, and heretofore too lucky, to have suffered the inherent human weakness for demoralizing second thoughts.

He went back through the hotel's shadowy bowels, emerging in the stable yard. He crossed to the watering trough, splashed cold water on his face and neck, and blotted them dry with his neckerchief. Vaguely he was aware of the leathery masculine odor as ingrained in his body as in his clothes, but clearly there was nothing he could do about it, not on such short notice. He smiled to himself and put it out of his mind. It was the least of his unpreparednesses for *this* campaign.

His sitting room he found livened but by the yellow flicker of the lamp, and lingered but to douse it. In the dark he strode to the connecting door, rapped with the knuckles of one hand while already turning the knob with the other.

"Yes, Colonel. Come in."

The lamp on the bedside table made a radiant halo about the bed head. Its rays bathed the white face and shoulders of Cathal McQuaife, propped high on pillows, bedclothes drawn up under her bare arms; the robe lay discarded on a chair. Starcross drew the door shut behind him and stepped out of the shadows, forward into that beckoning aura not just of light and warmth.

"I hope you're . . . quite comfortable," he said.

"Quite. Oh, I can lie in the bed I've made, Colonel, as I said." Cathal McQuaife took up her smiling—sparring—as if without break. "Certainly one so . . . seductive as this."

He hovered by the bedside, himself unsmiling, full of a self-absorbed look. "You *will* have to forgive me," he said at last. "I *have* been a long time among the Indians, and despite your politeness, my . . . manners *are* rusty from disuse."

"Do you mean there are no manners among the Indians? Dear me. No wonder they're a vanishing race."

"My dealings with them were of the type to call for rather rough manners." Doggedly sober, he went on, "A soldier leads a more sheltered life than you might imagine, Miss McQuaife. He *may* do so, at least. It's the line of least resistance, again." His fingers seemed as of their own will to be setting in to undo the brass buttons of his jacket. "There's little virtue in it. If I never strayed from the line of least resistance, odds are it was mostly because the opportunity never forced itself on me."

"I'm—amazed, Colonel," the woman mused, complacently watching him slip the jacket off and tent it over the chair back, atop the robe. "Amazed, if not flattered exactly—though I suppose honesty may be the sheerest form of flattery after all." Her face seemed to cloud. "And so 'occupation' in the end amounts to the same thing on one side of the street as the other. Xenophon does at a venture what Attila does by design."

"I assure you, when I said I was used to that sort of thing—er, I didn't mean *this* sort of thing. Or perhaps, to paraphrase you, I did, and then I didn't." His glance around at her was unreadable, teasing, like her own, yet serious too, almost frighteningly so. "I hope you haven't let the nickname deceive you. Xenophon won his renown, if memory serves, by retreating."

"A bad habit for a commander." She watched him sit on the bed-edge, against her covered curves, and begin to draw off his boots. "Ah well"—she affected resignation—"to say it again, I can take my medicine, however dreadful."

"Dear lady!"—seeming to take her would-be scruples to heart, he faced her, a solemn new concern in his voice—"I've never dishonored a woman in my life; nor, I assure you, do I mean to start tonight." Brusquely he brought his left hand up, exhibiting on its stubby least finger a chaste, braided golden band. "This belonged to my mother. I watched a Yapparika warrior cut off her finger to get it." And so saying, he wrenched the ring off, and taking her hand up from the hillocked bedclothes slipped it over the knuckle of the bridal digit. He brought the hand on up to his lips and kissed the fisted knuckles around the new addition. "After my rescue, I cut off his to get it back. *He* was still alive."

"Merciful heavens, Colonel—what a bloodcurdling history! It would overwhelm a resistance far more robust than mine." She held the hand up, cocked her head at it; but his bemused face, not the ring, at once had her whole attention, as she already his. He leaned closer, speaking as a stranger, even to himself:

"Thou art the fairest that was ever born!"

"Colonel!" She let the hand fall onto his own, tentatively, tenderly caressing. "What a strange man you are. I fear for you. The world doesn't love such deadly earnest."

"You're still troubled over Colonel Purinton? A pretty serious piece of work himself, yes; but not worth the bother."

"Colonel Purinton! Well, he *is* one side of the coin, granted. But I was thinking of the other." She brought the ringed hand up again, chidingly touched the forefinger to his lips. "That you so casually put yourself in a woman's power."

"The devilish rebel spy triumphs after all, is that it?" He settled himself comfortably athwart her, hands-propped. "Oh, I have more confidence in myself than all that."

"I have confidence in you too, Colonel . . . Webb." Tenderly her hands cradled his tenderly kissing face. "Webb darling! But you're not on the battlefield now."

"Are you sure?" And the tenderness turned to a fervor surprising to them both. He left it off only to add: "I seem to be beholding a Valkyrie for the first time."

"You shouldn't say that," she protested, winced almost: she the truly serious one in the end. "Don't you know Valkyries are beheld only by the dead?"

FOUR

Cathal McQuaife snapped back to herself as matchlight burst into being in a heavy dark. Close before her loomed Webb Starcross's tawny head and white bare shoulders, casting long shadows as he reached the chimney off the lamp, touched the match to the wick. Her squinting eyes watched the room resume its remembered depths, its population of strange shadowed shapes, then moved to the oblong of the window, still velvet-black.

"What is it—?"

"No rest for spies, I'm afraid." Sitting on the bedside, faced back around, he propped an arm across her and leaned on it. "I warned you it would be a short night."

"Far from it—it was the longest night of my life; fullest." Sensuously she stretched, and put her arms up around his neck. Their lips met for a timeless moment. But then ruefully he drew away, eyes boyish-bright. "Must it end so soon, though?"

"We mustn't disappoint Jaymie Strainchamps."

"You've worlds of time. It will take him days to come so far."

He stooped for his trousers. "But I'm not the only one with an appointment with Jaymie, if you'll remember."

She frowned at his back. "I *don't* remember."

On his feet, he turned to face her again, briskly drawing on his blouse and hoisting his suspenders. "As I said last night, my own person is your only surety within our lines. And unfortunately there are other claims on my person. The alternative speaks for itself." He turned away. "You must go out of our lines."

"Oh," wryly, "*is* there such a place?"

"It not only speaks for itself; it suggests further possibilities which I find irresistible." Noting her continued incomprehension he went on to clarify: "You must go back to your friends."

"My *friends*!" She reared on an elbow, bedclothes dropping from her breast. She saw him turn his eyes away. Though he'd had few inhibitions in the dark, visually, as she was finding, he was modest to the point of prudery. Fretfully she drew the covers back up, desperate for his undivided attention. "But—but I've just *left* my friends. My friends are become my foes."

"Well"—the boyish grin—"but they don't know it yet."

Her concern only grew. "I've taken *you* for my friend."

"Just so!" He sat back down beside her, put on a tenderer, more personal look. Gently he took up her hand in both of his, twisted the braided golden band on the ring finger, that seal of their "friendship." "Just days hence, *friend,* I—*we* are going to win a victory." His zeal fed on itself. "Your part is to go back to your Jaymie and tell him what he wants to hear: there's nothing to stop him watering his horses in the Missouri River; the Modern Xenophon's busy agonizing over his *Anabasis*—I leave the embroidery to you." He paused. "It's asking much of you, I know, my love. But a man *may* ask much of his . . . love."

"Oh, Webb"—her eyes sought his—"it's all happening too fast." She lay back, resigned. "You're right, of course. You may ask me anything, and if that's what you ask, it's what I'll do. But not with an easy heart! I said it last night—Fate's played too great a part in our lives already; let's not tempt it. I look back on my past as a long, roundabout road bringing me to you. To go back on that road, to part from you now—the thought fills me with dread." Sadly her head shook. "So many things could happen—"

"I have every confidence in you," he soothed. "In your ability to regain the Confederate camp and play out the game."

"The *game.* And you're the one who said it wasn't!"

"Even a game isn't a game to the true player. There is only one game, my love, and it's very serious indeed."

She made a face. "How can you trust me not to do to you what you see me do to another? How can you set me to deceive, yet be sure you're not yourself being deceived?"

He was untroubled. "There's only one kind of deception and that's self-deception. *I'm* not deceiving myself." He smiled brightly before rising, reaching for his jacket. "I could be wrong, of course. Granted you possess the power to contribute to my downfall just as easily as to Jaymie's, if you so choose. But I think I've judged you more truly than he." Turning back, he caught up her ringed hand, again. "I'm willing to bet on it—my all."

"Oh, Webb!" She half rose from the bed, this time bringing the covers along. "I'm honored by your trust—humbled. You've nothing to fear from me—of course not. But I'm not so sure you have nothing to fear on my account. I have confidence in you; I think you'll do great things; but"—sorrowfully she buried herself on his chest—"I want to *be* there, to—to shield you from myself! Even if not archer, I may be one of the arrows."

"You're still worried about Colonel Purinton? I assure you, on his score, my position will soon be unassailable. *Yours* will be the exposed one. For it's going to become well-known . . . what we've done. After what's going to happen, your friends will know, or at least suspect, that you've . . . left them. They'd suspect even if we'd done nothing. But you have your perfect defense in the truth, blazoned in this ring I've given you." He took up her hand, brought it fisted all the way to his sandy cheek. "It won't kill the accusation but it will disarm it. People won't blame you quite so much while they can blame me. And I can make things right. We'll do it properly. I'll write to your father. As soon as the dust's settled, and it can be arranged, we'll be reunited. And we won't be parted ever again." Squeezing the hand, he let it drop. "I leave you to make ready. You must be away before the town stirs."

In the sitting room Starcross lit the lamp and stood buckling his revolver about his waist. His eyes fell on the sheathed saber there on the table. He gave it a speculative caress, as in invocation, but left it lying, taking up the lamp instead.

Heavy quiet reigned throughout the dark building. Starcross made his way through the service regions, out into the rear yard, over which rose the black apex of the stable against a starry lesser black. Lighting his way into the strawy centerway he came face to face with Zurdo, just emerging from the harness room, though already dressed in his quirky half-uniform, and full awake.

"Zurdo." Lifting the lamp, Starcross looked over the rumps of the half-dozen horses somnolent in their stalls, stout little nondescript beasts bearing government brands, for the most part. "You can saddle one of these brutes, if you will."

Typically Zurdo set to work without comment or sign of curiosity. Starcross left him already leading one of the animals out of its stall. Back within the hotel he turned aside through another door and found himself, as expected, in the kitchen, dark and deserted. He glanced around, lamp held high, and began turning out cupboards and safes, feeling like a small boy again on a midnight raid. Rounding up half a pan of leftover cornbread, a crock of butter, and a pitcher of buttermilk, awkwardly he juggled these on a tray, along with the lamp, back up the stairway.

Cathal McQuaife, once more credibly, if in Starcross's eyes rather startlingly, an enlisted man in the Fourth Iowa Infantry, stood before the shaving mirror eyecockingly adjusting the crumpled kepi over her cropped, rust-red hair.

"I see a great future for you, Captain McQuaife," he told her. "You might even retire as a corporal." Wielding an incongruously wicked-looking sheath-knife he spread butter on a generous hunk of cornbread and proffered it to her. Ransacking the room, he found a tin cup and wiped it out with a towel before filling it with buttermilk. She stood watching, bemused.

"If this is regulation breakfast mess—to say nothing of etiquette—for Federal officers," she observed, making a face, "our war will be lost sooner than I thought."

"It's a—a special occasion." Sheepishly he grinned, as if himself only tardily recognizing the occasion's true specialness.

"Yes," she agreed. They stood in silence for a few minutes, munching the stale cornbread, sacramentally sharing the cup. Nothing had ever tasted so fine to either of them. "Very special. One can have only *one* nuptial breakfast."

"This is hardly a bridal bouquet"—he pulled from his pocket the .51-caliber derringer she'd handed him in the jail, one barrel still armed—"but you'd better have it back."

"Thank you." Licking her fingers, she took the little weapon. "I wonder how Sergeant Tawes is feeling this morning."

"Chastened, I trust." He cast about. "Are you ready?"

Halls and stair lay all in night-dark yet. He took her by the hand and led the way. Outdoors, the lesser dark had lessened further. The stable building made a sharp cutout, softened by the laces of bare branches. The stars were fading, their radiance seeming to drain into the sole incredible pendulous globe of the morning star drooping in the east like the seed of the unborn sun. The two crossed to the other two, Zurdo and the saddled horse. Starcross caught up the reins, starting to lead the animal.

"I'll walk you to the edge of town," he told her. "If anybody sees us, it'll be merely the eccentric Modern Xenophon out for an early gallop, groom in tow."

"You seem to be thinking of everything," she mused, newly dubious. "But how will you account for my absence?"

He put his arm around her, somewhat spoiling the masquerade for which he'd just voiced such concern. "Doesn't it speak for itself? The fiendish rebel outsmarted me and made her escape." He hugged her close, in the highest of spirits. "Seriously I don't expect to have to account for anything. Long before your absence is known, my own will have become a matter of overshadowing concern. What will it matter, save perhaps to Colonel Purinton—and who'll listen to him? Winners, my beloved, like the rare birds they are, are the ones who are listened to."

"And should you be a loser," she pursued, "I suppose I'd be the least of what you'd have to account for."

"If I lose, it but serves me right. I won't call it an impossibility, since you say I'm tempting Fate already; but it's a high improbability. I'm an able soldier, with a veteran command that's like a tool in my hand. And," he added, meaningfully, teasingly, beaming down at her, "my intelligence is superior—or so I'm told."

"Of course." Laughing, she let herself be convinced, once more reassured. "It's a rare moment indeed, one that won't come again. 'Twould be tempting Fate truly to let it slip by. The stars point the way." She looked up at the aging morning star, that fat gem hung tremulous in the brightening east, about to burst. Beneath, the earth lay yet dark; Brocksborough was lifeless but for themselves, the starstruck young lovers amber-caught in their precious moment, embarking on their great adventure. "And even if not, even if you're wrong—my darling, I'd do it anyway."

"If I'm wrong," he echoed, "if I fail, you've but to hold to your story. The gallant, grateful Jaymie will hail you as the architect of his victory. The worst that any clucking tongue can say is that you made the supreme sacrifice for your—er, cause."

"No," she demurred; "the terms are the same, win or lose."

"It won't be lose." He stopped them both, brusquely drew her into his arms. "But, yes, my love—my Valkyrie—win or lose."

She stifled a giggle. "Let's hope no early riser sees the *very* eccentric Modern Xenophon hugging and kissing his groom!"

In eloquent silence they resumed their walk, leading the horse. One road led from the town down to the steamboat landing; but the two wayfarers took the opposite way, which soon led them into a gully wherein a creek moiled beneath a humpbacked stone bridge. Already Brocksborough seemed far behind, for timber's wintry fingers reached right up to the very dooryards, masking the few windows in which dim lights were starting to show. Beyond the bridge, felt if not seen, lay the hinterland, and deep within it, hazy as a cloud, Confederate country.

Starcross drew to a stop on the bridge. "You should have no trouble from here on. Colonel Purinton's patrols are fitful at best; and the denizens are rebels all, covert if not otherwise. You'll soon be putting off your masquerade, I trust."

"My arrangements from here on are well made. I'll be dining once more with Jaymie tomorrow evening."

"Cathal, my dear, my beloved"—he hugged her again, every inch his earnest self—"my heart goes with you."

For once she was even soberer. "You give your heart to an errant female on short acquaintance, Colonel Starcross."

"Nonsense." He stooped and cupped his hand to take her foot. With obvious reluctance she lifted it and let him boost her into the saddle. "We've been as one forever—you said it yourself, have you forgotten? And always will be."

"Then let us be as one in fact." Firmly astride, she reared up straight, but gazed—all-but-yearned—back down to him, her voice at the same time urgent and unsure. "Keep me by your side, Webb! Win your battle without me."

He was unsympathetic. "I don't fight well with an eye cocked over my shoulder. The Roman eagle wasn't just a standard, you know; it was a weapon, cast into the barbarians' midst. You're my eagle." He thought it over. "Perhaps I like to live dangerously; yet I find irresistible the idea of so placing my fate, along with my heart, in your hands. I know no surer way of declaring myself, Cathal—than by letting you declare *your*self, by what you say to Jaymie. And anyhow," more grimly, "you've already done it, committed your betrayal, if that's how you see it."

Clearly his arguments had great force with her, seducing if not quite persuading. "I go under protest," she yielded, though still sagged in a spiritless slump. "I obey a superior officer."

"Protest noted—Captain," he laughed, and catching her by the arm drew her on down into a stoop, to meet her lips with his own. "May God protect you, Cathal."

"And you, Webb. Above all, you."

Reluctant yet, she straightened back up in the saddle as he stood away from the horse; still she seemed unable to make the first move. He smacked the horse's rump. The animal's start became a forward walk, gradually accelerating, first with her resigned acquiecence, at last her active encouragements.

She looked back for a brief last glimpse of him in the waxing daylight, poised unmoving on the bridge, his scarlet-plumed hat doffed in salute; but then her headlong progress commanded all her attention. Resolute, she faced ahead. Soon horse and rider topped the notched lightening skyline, where the rutty road cut between timbered hills, then with eerie finality, as if off the very edge of the earth, dropped from sight and sound.

Webb Starcross stood on there for no more than a minute, though it seemed for far longer, so motionless was he, so outside time, leaning statuelike on the bridge rail as-it-were contemplating the dawning day around him though truly blind to it. Then, somewhere at his back, a cock crowed, answered by the faroff, scrappy breeze-borne notes of a bugle. He stirred, sluggish at first, reluctant, as if awakening from the sweetest of dreams, and then more eagerly, as if recalling that reality too could be seductively sweet, and at a brisk pace set off back toward the town.

FIVE

Major General Webb Starcross stood with a fellow officer on the makeshift street of the Union cavalry headquarters company encampment, bemusedly watching the antics of sundry ambitious others cozying with knots of newspapermen and politicians. A strange trooper drew up before him, saluted.

"General Starcross, sir? I've been all the way over to your headquarters, only to learn—they said I might find you here."

"Well, they were right, Corporal. You've found me."

"Yes, sir. Excuse me, sir, but a prisoner, a high-ranking prisoner, is asking for a—a personal interview."

"With *me?*" Starcross's brow furrowed. "Just who is he, this high-ranking prisoner?"

"I don't know, sir—but he's just yonder." The trooper pointed to a conical tent standing in curious isolation only a few hundred yards along the straggling street. "In there."

"Well, then, Corporal, let's go see what he wants."

"If you'll excuse me, General, I have other messages. . . ."

"Of course. Carry on, then."

Starcross watched the trooper away, nodded to his friend, turned and made for the tent, his curiosity colored by an unaccountable anticipation. The very day bore an uncanny, unsettling character: the day of the Surrender—of the end, almost inconceivably, after so long. It sent the mind reeling back over the road traveled, all those long hard full years, to the beginning itself, that likewise uncanny, exhilarating, now nigh mythic moment.

For Starcross, though, the resurfacing thoughts of that time were not, as doubtless for others, even bittersweetly nostalgic, afforded no note of gratification or consummation when laid alongside the victorious if problematical present. Never in four long years had the thoughts been wholly buried in his head; but the business of war, in which he'd lost himself, had kept the fore of his consciousness filled, kept things past or out-of-view thrust back. His natural bent for focusing on one thing at a time, putting aside all others, had found feasts to surfeit. And now, as the long taut concentration perforce slackened, like racing millstones suddenly deprived of grist, the release came rather as an all-new tension. As birdsong and other old peacetime sounds, so long drowned in the roar of guns, were heard once more, deafeningly gentle, so were those spectral thoughts, long kept thrust back in shadow, starting to stir, threatening to walk abroad again, without their host yet quite being aware of it, unless as that all-over unease.

Which might have been explained by the occasion itself, of course: the thrilling day, so pregnant with history, aptly luminous, atmospheric. In the diffuse, half-cloudy April glare the incongruously new, clean tent fairly glowed before him. It seemed somehow isolated and abandoned despite its thronging surroundings and its sentry, a somehow misplaced or inadequate figure, a mere toy soldier, stood up there for effect, suitably stiffening clockworkslike as the general came and went. The flap was latched open; Starcross stepped through, into the dim.

Well before his eyes could have adjusted, the inward light of understanding broke over him, a thunderous midday dawn.

"Gen—!" A soldier almost before he was a man, Webb Starcross drew up ramrod-straight, brought a parade-ground hand up to his rakishly up-pinned brim. But it was an exercise of feeling as well as of reflex. "General McQuaife—sir!"

The man hovering in the heavy shadows lazily lifted his own gauntleted hand, the acknowledgment irony-heavy. His barrel-like figure, field-uniformed yet immaculately, resplendently so, and fully sidearmed, seemed to fill the whole tent, and suggested anything but a man in durance or otherwise disadvantaged. From the black eye-patch to over-the-knee cavalry boots, he was the Personage Starcross knew well in imagination, and in memory, indelibly from Richwood—"the God of War," as he was called, because of his renown for strategy and his one-eyed, gray-eyed evocation of his Norse namesake; the *wrathful* god for the nonce, before whom one was once more, even as that mythic Richwood evening, the callow, tonguetied second lieutenant. Wracked by rushes of guilty memories, stunned yet by his first shock, Starcross stood in the stretching-out silence, agape.

"Well, you miserable young pup, have you nothing to say for yourself?" The volcano-clap came up strangely muted, as from a seismic shudder deep underground. "You are a trifle late for our interview, nigh four years. By God, I never dreamt a son of Jason Starcross would shirk a challenge!"

The blank of the younger man's face flushed full of pulselike throbs, as of pains—winces as from literal stabs.

"I answered. I went—I waited. All day; the time and place named. You didn't come!" In Webb Starcross's brain the present pains melled with the painful memories, the very parade of them: the Battle of Hungry Ridge that had won him his brigadier's sash and single star, made him the rising man; General McQuaife's challenge, brought through the lines; his reply; and the day, the agonizing wait with Captain Yulee at the tiny country churchhouse deep in the hills in neutral or at least briefly unfought-for country, desperately eyestraining down the road from the south; and the days to come when he'd been a man beside himself, a rogue stallion in need of the curb, ready to resign, to *desert*, and journey south, stayed only by the scoldings of Yulee, and of his newfound friends, the powers in the land, their reminders of his public duty, and the unworthiness of him, the *selfishness* of his navel-gazings at such an hour—and worst of all, the stretching-out silence from south of the line. "Didn't you get my answer?"

"Ah yes, your answer! 'Sword or pistol if you must, sir, but daughter if you will'!" Lieutenant General Odon McQuaife snorted mightily. "A very landmark in the annals of the *Code Duello*!" He glowered. "I was not amused. I was an outraged father, if you'll remember, not to mention an officer on duty. Your remarkable missive caught up with me at Richmond, weeks after the event. It would have made no odds in any case. It was no time for private indulgences, wallowings in adolescent sentimentality; as I told my fine-feathered daughter ere packing her off posthaste, and under close escort, to my place in the Territory."

"Packing her off—? But—but *why*? She must have made it clear: I'd promised—expected—to wed her in all honor."

"Honor!" Another eruption. "A young scoundrel seduces my daughter—nay, fair *debauches* her, for what other word sums up the lickerish gossip that titillated two armies for weeks?—and has the cheek to stand before me and prate of honor!"

"But—" Starcross shook his head, as if to clear it, but to no avail. "You're right, of course." He made motions of helplessness or hopelessness; and then with visible effort took himself in hand, forced his eyes up. "How . . . how is she?"

"Your interest is heartening!" The older man swept the gray hat from his head, as in sarcastic salute, laid it on the nearby camp table, and sank into a folding chair alongside. The baring of his gray head, still like his full beard showing rustlike streaks eerily evocative of his daughter's memorable fiery tresses, left him more vulnerable, or at least mellower, a bit more human; but his face was deep-shadowed still, in both senses—uncompromising still. "Mother and daughter are well, thank you!"

"Daughter. . . ." Starcross reached out to a tentpole, but his fingers found no purchase. "I crave your pardon," he stammered, and slumped into the chair on the table's nigh side, eyes adaze, mind visibly aflame. Mechanically he doffed his own hat, hands threatening to crumple it. "This is too much for me."

"It was a bit much for *her*," dryly, "though you'd never have known it from her."

"*I* should have known—it's all my fault." Starcross writhed. "I should never have sent her away—she didn't want to go. Once we'd reached an understanding, I should've kept her with me, somehow. And yet, propriety, her safety, the morrow, the battle." The words came like winces. "It was to be *our* battle, our victory, the consummation of our plighted troth. To send her back to play her part: the—the temptation was too much for me." He appealed to the older man: "I was—I was playing chess, like your General Lee at Marye's Heights. I was—beside myself."

"Temptation." General McQuaife grimaced. "I know it well. And not only as a soldier. As a fond parent too, oh aye. No, the fault's not *all* yours, General. Not that she asked my leave, ever, but I tolerated her game, her soldier- and spy-playing. Indulged myself by indulging *her,* my only . . . my all. She told me as much, she threw it up to me; it was her defense—that I'd never taken her seriously, none of us had, we men."

"Was it so . . . awful for her?"

"Oh, she was up to it—more than. Her—candor disarmed. What might be said behind her back troubled her not at all; there were no women in the picture, and the army, as you might expect, was far too gentlemanly to cut her to her face.

"The formal 'inquiry' even had its entertaining—its hilarious side, I confess, though I was in no mood to appreciate it. I arrived just as it was winding down, there in a little log schoolhouse lost in the Arkansas wilds: a trinity of braided staff bigwigs, seated heads-in-hands, like a visiting board of education on the glummest examination day in history! And that poor booby Strainchamps all but stood in the corner, wanting only his dunce-cap, miserably pretending to find the army camped outside the window of keenest interest—ah, and throned on the frontmost of the little scholars' backless benches, mere puncheons, gorgeous in a plum-colored riding habit and long red locks not obviously not her own, my daughter, staring them down, the generals, impudently switching her riding crop—oh yes, and there in the back of the room, would you believe it? her Mammy looming, waiting, blacker of brow than of skin: the black brow not for the prosecutors nearly so much as for the defendant, the culprit clearly in for a good, stinging hiding, at least of the tongue, at earliest opportunity.

"*They,* on the other hand, of course hadn't the faintest idea what to do with her. So they cleared the room, adjourned *sine die,* and with undisguised relief left her to me.

"Oh, she made no bones about it. She'd done what she'd done; but what did it amount to? She'd hardly had to tell Strainchamps anything, so yare was he to credit his own illusions. And if we fancied she'd betrayed her cause, well, that was *our* illusion. No, a woman joined no cause but one; and she'd now done so, had found hers. Saying which"—McQuaife headshook, half-outraged, half-amused—"she had the damnable cheek to flaunt that ring on her finger under my very nose!"

"If only I could have been there." Starcross had brightened at this last, but now wilted again. "The Godforsaken war!"

"It has marred more lives than two, my young friend," the older man reminded, sadly. "That's why the two no longer quite so grieve me, perhaps . . . or anger me."

"I can't help the others, sir"—Starcross faced him straight-on—"but if she's still wearing my ring. . . . Four years is a long time. I can't call them back, but I can try my best to make them up. I mean to do so if I can—if she will. One way or the other I go West the minute this—this wretched business is done with." Humbly, earnestly: "I can't decently ask for your blessing—"

General McQuaife waved an impatient hand. "Starcross, I have had half an eye on you for a long while, for more than one reason. I know the sort of man you are. And I know the sort of man *I* am, though that makes it no easier for me *not* to be. And I know my daughter, at least well enough to know the sort of man she'd commit herself to." The iron-gray eye leveled. "My challenge, and my aspersions of your honor, voiced in anger, under provocation, and not from the heart, are withdrawn."

"Thank you, sir. I'm gratified—relieved. My father would be, too." Starcross's hand closed on the hilt of his saber. "When you gave him this blade, those many years ago, you must have done so confident that it would never be dishonored, in peace or war. I think I can say it has not been, in my keeping." He gave the weapon a resolute slap. "That's the other reason I mean to serve henceforth in the West if I can. There once was room for—for honorable service there. There must still be."

"Your first reason—" General McQuaife mused: "Cathal is a proud woman, General. Proud above all since . . . since it happened—*you* happened. One kind of pride, you know, is morbid growth in a wound unhealed: 'Proud flesh,' the croakers call it. I pray you: tread with care! She waits, but for what—who knows? What man ever truly knows a woman's heart?"

Starcross groped for a certainty. "Sir—what of yourself? Is there—is there anything I can do for you?"

The ageless general's smile was spare. "Oh, I've lost battles before, my young friend. I'm a soldier, at home in any military role, even"—he waved about—"even this one."

Sensing the interview was at its end, Webb Starcross stood and took a backward step, put on his hat, composed himself, and repeated his impeccable salute. McQuaife rose too, acknowledged with like formality; and then, as on an impulse, drew off his gauntlet and held out his hand. Starcross stood staring at it for a long moment, plunged in ruth, and then stepped forth, grasped it firmly. Then, all but overwhelmed, in stumbling haste he backed out of the tent, out into the hazy April glare.

Almost at once the weird sensation assailed him as of awakening from a haunting, dizzying dream. As he stumbled away all but in a trance, the conviction assailed him that if he were to turn and reenter that fateful tent he would find it vacant, as deserted and disregarded as from without it appeared. Even the sentry, it seemed, had absented himself, at least from view.

The next morning, inquiring at cavalry headquarters, trying to learn the details of General McQuaife's capture and the likely disposition of his case, with the vague idea of seeking to exert some mitigating influence, if it seemed called for, he found himself unable to learn even the barest facts. The nameless corporal who'd bidden him to the interview could not be found, or identified, to be questioned as to the source or channel of his message—and Starcross found himself unable to remember the fellow's looks, even his unit flashes. Moreover the mysterious tent itself had been struck, if not gone up in a puff of smoke, as to the ever-more-bewildered Starcross began to seem just as likely. The army, he was informed, with an impatience that grew along with his persistence, had no record whatsoever of the capture or detention of Lieutenant General Odon McQuaife.

And indeed, as days passed, the rumor grew rife that, far from ever having been a prisoner at all, General McQuaife was one of the handful of high Confederate officers making their stealthy way southwestward through the disordered hinterland—to Mexico, to tender their services to Emperor Maximilian.

SIX

On another blithe April day, not long after, Webb Starcross found himself happily astride the trusty, veteran Rustam, riding the blooming, unspoiled Maryland countryside east of Washington, kept pace with by Zurdo—a much-grown-up Zurdo—at the reins of a rented horse-and-buggy. The general had returned to his headquarters from Appomattox to find awaiting him not only his requested relief from his command but a letter from his foster-father, Colonel Duncan Colquhoun.

He'd grown used to the tenor of the colonel's letters, filled as they were with uncomplaining litanies of the privations and sorrows of the homefront for a Confederate sympathizer living out the war in occupied country. But this latest letter had held a surprise. He was doubly pleased, the colonel wrote, to learn that Starcross might soon be coming West, coming home.

"Candacy Ann, as you know, is still at her Maryland school. Conditions forbade her return when she finished her studies, but she was able to stay on as a staff member. Naturally I now want her to return as soon as may be; but in view of still unsettled conditions I'm unwilling to allow her to travel alone; and finding her an escort is proving difficult. Aunt Raby's health no longer permits her to leave St. Louis, and Chance, who would seem the ideal choice —poor Chance is only just out of that horrid Chicago prison camp; neither his health nor his purse is in sound fettle at the moment. And then of course Chance would hardly be the *proper* escort in any case, without a female companion.

"The same objection, though, would hardly apply to a foster-brother; and what more perfect protector for a young lady, these days, than a famous major general in blue? If your commitments will allow, Webb, I ask you, *beg* you, when ready to come West, to call for Candacy Ann at her school, which is just east of Washington City, and bring her safely home to me. She is all I have left in the world—but for yourself, I needn't add, who are as dear to me as she. The headmistress's name is Miss Yarrow. In anticipation of your consent I am writing her to expect you."

Starcross found himself easier of mind and lighter of spirits than in months. The encounter with General McQuaife had acted as the lifting of a cloud, whose existence he had long ignored or denied. He felt free to look forward with curiosity to seeing Candacy Ann again. They'd been best friends as children, brother and sister in all but name, through those brief but full young years between his coming to live with the Colquhouns and his all-too-early going away to school. His mind teemed with new-woken images of bright days at blest Richwood, in each of which Candacy Ann held a vital if not central part. With their neighbor friend Chance, he and she had formed a trio that shared unstintingly the doings and dreams of youth. That Chance and Candacy Ann were wordlessly understood to be promised to each other, when the time came, had never troubled the solidarity of the three or Starcross's mind. Complacently he'd accepted himself as the odd one out, the outsider, come late to the scene, the all-but-penniless orphan alongside two children of great neighbor landowners, their destinies logically and inextricably intertwined. It was a pleasing picture of social order that Webb Starcross—really a romantic, like many a would-be-realistic soldier—had no wish to disturb, above all now. If, as seemed all too likely, the war had shaken the dream's worldly underpinnings, all the more reason to cling to the dream itself, to its essence, those twin images; the best of both worlds, the two and the three: Candacy Ann, his foster-sister, and Chance, his friend; and a little to one side, himself.

They'd made rather a late start, Starcross's day having begun with a duty call at the Executive Mansion, with other officers, to receive an accolade from the president himself. For that reason, rather than to impress Candacy Ann or the redoubtable Miss

Yarrow, was he panoplied in his uniform finest. However garbed, he'd had no thought of missing the chance for a ride on the trip out, though wheels would be needed for fetching back the young lady and her belongings. It was a perfect spring day for an outing, and soon, once beyond the crowded capital city's fortified fringes, the country turned bucolic, timelessly manorial, a striking contrast to the scorched, scourged battle zones across the Potomac; albeit in official Washington eyes this too was "enemy country," domain of rebel hearts, if not quite, what with regiments of overwhelming dissuasion so near at hand, of rebel hands or feet.

It was early afternoon as they reached their destination: yet another manor house, as it seemed, and so proved, the bequest of some philanthropic or at least heirless planter. Having cantered Rustam up the boxwood-hedged, raked gravel turnaround Starcross stood down, handed his reins to Zurdo, mounted the low, broad, roofless front terrace, and pulled the bell lever.

Webb Starcross might have been a pound or so heavier than at the war's outset; but days in the saddle and nights in the open had kept his full, stocky frame thewy and supple. Luxuriant long blond hair haloed his broad, square face. The taffy mustache was doubly leonine, in aroused moments downright fierce. The azure eyes still bore all their bright alertness of younger days. The dress uniform fit him in more ways than one. Thick, wide shoulders above trim waist and scarce hips seemed made for the military cut, readily supporting the trappings that would have belittled a lesser man. Red-lined cloak flowed over bemedaled, brass-buttoned, gold-epauletted and -braided jacket. Hat plume nodded literally with panache. Shiny boots reached the knees, the spurs suggestive of a fighting cock. Scabbarded saber and holstered revolver were less accouterments than extensions of his anatomy. He'd ridden most of the way through wildflowery roadside grass, stirring little dust to dull his glitter. Starcross himself only tardily thought of this as the maid who opened the door gave back, all whites of eyes, shying from his *carte de visite* as from a proffered rattlesnake. At once a tall, bone-thin, pince-nezed woman came to the rescue, swooping forward out of the dim entry-hall's depths. Starcross heaped his hat and cloak and gloves on the maid before she could flee, and turned, already bowing.

"Good day, General Starcross. We've been expecting you. I am Miss Yarrow." The headmistress, if not quite awed, was visibly impressed, though she kept even this under stern control.

And before Starcross could respond, a younger woman burst into the hall, through doorfuls of eavesdropping others.

"Webb! Oh, Webb!" The voice's owner fairly swallowed the caller in an uninhibited embrace, surging up on tiptoe to plant on his cheek a not-all-that-sisterly kiss. Then, still grasping both his hands, she stood far enough back to look him in the face. "Webb, is it really you? Isn't he wonderful, Miss Yarrow?"

"It's really me, I'm afraid. The question is," Starcross quipped, albeit half-seriously, "is it really *you?* Candacy Ann? Miss Yarrow, what have you done to her? When last I laid eyes on her she was a—" Uncertainly his hand wavered at about chest height. He flushed, and gave it up. "Well—nothing like this."

"Indeed." Briefly Miss Yarrow tolerated the mutual admiration. "You had best be about your preparations, Candacy Ann. The general is a busy man, I'm sure; and you must allow the two of us a few minutes to become acquainted." More gently she ended, "When you're ready, come and join us for tea in the parlor."

Having noted that he hoped Zurdo might be offered something too, if at the back door, Starcross followed the woman into a room at once cluttered and characterless. Hostess and guest soon sat facing each other from rigid wing chairs.

"Your reputation precedes you, General," said Miss Yarrow, going straight to the point. "And of course I have Colonel Colquhoun's letters. But I confess I still am not *quite* clear concerning your relationship to Candacy Ann and her people."

Starcross stifled a smile. "My own people were massa . . . killed by the Comanches in Texas." Tersely he told the old tale. "Colonel Colquhoun, who was an old friend of my father's, led the party that rescued me. I was brought up in his household—he's been nothing less than a father to me himself. And Candacy Ann a sister." He let a moment pass. "The colonel must have made clear his trouble finding a traveling companion for Candacy Ann. She's expected to marry my good friend Major Chance Buckhannon, late of the First Missouri Brigade—Confederate. But Chance, alas, has had a harder war than I. Both his health and his disordered affairs stood in the way of his coming East himself. And a fiancé, naturally, would have been rather a less proper escort than a foster-brother, an old soldier of no other use to anybody at the moment. And since I'm heading West myself—"

"Of course." By degrees Miss Yarrow thawed, to the point of actually allowing herself a moment of arid humor. "Though Candacy Ann's greeting was scarcely sisterly!"

"It must be the uniform." Starcross laughed, dismissive. "We've not seen each other for so long. If she's as overwhelmed as I by the transformation wrought by the years—by *her* blossoming—it's no wonder. I still can't get over it."

"Yes; Candacy Ann is a very—finished young lady. She's been with us so long—I've been too close to the process truly to see it. We've been most pleased to have her remain past the normal term; she's been such a help with the younger girls. Of course I was well aware that a young lady of her background and expectations wouldn't be making a profession of teaching. But tell me," Miss Yarrow went on, in soberer, more confidential tones, "has her family been seriously reduced by the war?"

"The 'family' is just the colonel now. And me, if I count As for the war, there was little real fighting in that part of Missouri; but the effects, if anything, were all the worse for that—the occupiers have had nothing to distract them from their mischief. The colonel's early . . . outspokenness came back to haunt him.

"And then, Major Buckhannon—his father murdered, himself wounded and captured, their estates seized. Chance has always been almost one of the Colquhouns. As children he and Candacy Ann, and I when I came, were all but inseparable." Shortly Starcross added—mostly, he realized, to himself: "Chance's misfortune makes me rather rue my own good fortune."

"I'm sure it won't matter to Candacy Ann. She's resilient, and true." Miss Yarrow nodded sagely. "And *you,* General—what will you do with your good fortune? As young a man as you are, what of your own future, now that your war is won?"

"*My* war? It was never that. No: give me the other, the older war, the Indian war. That's 'my war', if any. Professionally there's not much left for me but to go back to it."

"'Your war'? You mean . . . because of your family?"

"No no; that wasn't what I meant at all. It was . . . something else altogether. Oh, I hold nothing against the Indians, Miss Yarrow." Suddenly self-conscious, Starcross tried summing up: "I almost wish I *did*. It might . . . make it easier."

"A striking . . . confession, General."

Miss Yarrow's musings were diverted by the bustling-in of Candacy Ann, now prim and pert in a muted plaid traveling suit, flawless, though clearly she'd hurried. A maid trailed her toting a tray. Needlessly Miss Yarrow bade the young woman join them and pour the tea. Starcross, as she did so, found himself watching her closely, still struggling to liken this poised and charming miss to the rumpled, pantaletted playmate of days past. Candacy Ann handed him his cup, together with a sweet teasing smile seeming to hint that she knew just what he was thinking.

But she was unable to curb herself for long. "Isn't he *divine,* Miss Yarrow? Would you believe the first time I saw Webb he was just a rail of a boy, clutching a rifle as big as himself, and that very saber"—she pointed—"looking at us like just a new lot of Comanches? And now—glory be, a major general!"

Starcross's mustached lips quirked. "Major generals are two a penny these days, I'm afraid."

"If only—" Candacy Ann affected to mourn. "He would have looked so fine in gray!"

"Aha, just as I suspected, Miss Yarrow," Starcross made a show of scolding, being careful to smile. "It's a very hotbed of rebellion you're running here."

"I confess"—ponderously Miss Yarrow struggled to reciprocate—"the chief obstacle to study for the past few years has been the prospect of a visit by General Stuart."

"And now comes a general," Candacy Ann pursued, pretending to pout, "only wearing the wrong color coat."

"You should be giving thanks for your—your foster-brother's coat, Candacy Ann. The wrong side turns out the *right* side after all, in our topsyturvy new world."

"You've heard from Chance, I take it." Starcross sought to change the subject.

"Just barely." Candacy Ann managed to turn this too into a grievance. "It's a disgrace how you Yankees treat our gallant prisoners! Even if you allow them the means to write, it takes ages for a letter to arrive." She added, "Papa wrote me Chance was being released. I hardly knew where to write myself."

"Then you'll be pleased to know he's free indeed," Starcross persisted, "and making a steady recovery; though of course he wasn't up to coming East himself—"

"Poor Chance! How does he look?"

"I haven't seen him; but the colonel—"

"What times we live in!" she huffed-on. "A *gentleman* like Chance Buckhannon locked up in a sink of filth and pestilence, denied mere decencies, let alone care; slaves and criminals let run free, robbing and ravaging, actually encouraged—!"

Starcross headed off Miss Yarrow's halfhearted reproof. "All too true. Terrible wrong are being committed in the name of right. The good suffer; the bad run wild and line their pockets. It grieves me too, Candacy Ann. Still, hard times bring out the best in men as well as the worst; I've seen as much of the one as the other in the past four years. This morning," he added, with seeming inconsequence, "I found myself at the Executive Mansion, and actually exchanged a few words with President Lincoln—"

"That old baboon!" Candacy Ann hissed.

"Candacy Ann! Really, my dear." Miss Yarrow's scolding was strikingly mild. Apologetically she appealed to Starcross, "Young people can be so carried away."

"I was never young then, I'm afraid. Certainly I was never 'carried away' by politics. Politicians!" Starcross grimaced. "Yes, the president's one; yet I've begun to think he's the decentest of the lot." But his words elicited no sympathy and he gave them up, let the disagreeable subject die disagreeably.

The talk thereafter moved in trivial grooves and soon wound up. The tea accounted for, Starcross stirred in his chair. He got to his feet; Miss Yarrow and Candacy Ann followed suit, the latter quitting the room at once, the former offering the general her farewell remarks as she walked with him out onto the terrace. There Candacy Ann, in bonnet and cloak, stood supervising the securing of her trunk and bags to the back of the buggy. Zurdo, unregarded, stood waiting at a little distance beside Rustam, whom perforce he would ride back to Washington while the general drove Candacy Ann in the buggy. Increasing numbers of Candacy Ann's fellow students and staff members stepped out around Miss Yarrow to call out their own farewells and see Candacy Ann off seated at the side of her handsome bachelor major general, foster-brother or otherwise; a prospect sure to fuel bedtime gossip in the school for days to come. Candacy Ann took time to embrace and kiss each of them, it seemed, before coming at last, taking Starcross's hand, and climbing in.

"Why haven't you been to see me before?" she demanded, in aggrieved tones, almost before they were underway. "You've been East for ages, haven't you?"

"It would have been nice," Starcross said; "and I would have done so if I could. But the war—even generals have their orders, Candacy Ann; generals above all. I've been on Rustam's back in wildest Virginia almost without break since I was transferred East. This is my first look even at Washington."

As they drove through the greening countryside Candacy Ann chattered happily on, alike exultant in her freedom and in her companion and in the journey ahead, running the gamut of airy topics such as, Starcross supposed, filled the heads of all girls of her years. For his part he found little to say, being content just to listen to her warbling voice, agreeable as mere music, without the lyrics always registering or making sense. But at last, when she touched on the subject of home, his sense of duty, his concern over her obvious illusions, roused him to break in:

"I don't think you're quite aware, Candacy Ann, just how . . . difficult things may be at home. I didn't want to go into them in front of Miss Yarrow—"

"Oh, yes." She took it in stride. "Papa's written and told me —no end. This dreadful war! It's been bad enough for us here. Shortages, skyhigh prices, sassy servants, us girls hardly allowed out of the house, no visits, no parties, no fun at all, everybody pulling a long face. It's the same at home, I'm sure. But things will soon be back to normal now, won't they, Webb?"

"I hope so," he murmured; "though I'm not so sure."

"But—but for Lord's sake, why ever not? The Yankees have everything they want now, don't they? Surely they'll at least leave us in peace. I say let them *have* the niggers. Let them all go away together—back where they came from, niggers and nigger-lovers alike, thieves and ruffians all, there's no odds."

"You must recognize, Candacy Ann," Starcross persisted, in dismay, "the loss of the slaves is having a devastating effect on the fortunes of men like your father. Some people are even calling for them to be treated as traitors, driven out of the country, their lands confiscated and turned over to the freedmen."

"How horrible!" Candacy Ann was shocked and outraged. "How can they even *think* such things? But—but you can keep it from happening to Papa, can't you, Webb?"

"I'll do anything I can," Starcross assured her, none-too-sure himself. "But please—don't overestimate my influence."

"Humph!" she sniffed. "What's the point of being a major general if you don't have influence?"

"I told you—major generals are a drug on the market. Who's going to listen to us now that they don't need us?"

"Don't be so modest, Webb. I'm sure you'll be listened to." Reverent and affectionate together, she stroked the gold stars on his shoulders, and twined their already snugly-linked arms ever more tightly. "It was sheer providence, I'm sure, that you were inspired to join the *wrong* side—to be able to save us from these horrible people now." As if the one thought somehow led to the other, she glanced sideways, and added, suspiciously, "Just what kind of creature *is* that on your pretty horse?"

"He's not a creature, he's an Apache, an Indian." Starcross struggled to explain Zurdo. "I'm worried about him," he went on, mostly to himself, apurpose so, since as he soon saw he was making no impression whatever on her. "He hasn't gotten on well in the East. Since he's grown up and met prejudice he's gone all broody over his identity, his 'Indianness.' I've been trying to talk him into trying the new Indian school at Carlisle Barracks, but I'm sure he means to go straight back to his people." He summed up, sadly, "He won't be with me much longer."

"Well, I'm sure you can do better." Candacy Ann made short work of Zurdo. "Oh, if only *I* could have a servant! I can see it's going to be tiresome being poor."

SEVEN

The loan of a room in fashionable Willard's Hotel had been forced on Starcross by a brother officer as he'd left Virginia. The garish, gregarious establishment held no attraction whatever for him; but he found himself thankful, relieved to have the room for Candacy Ann, himself meaning to spend the night among his kind at one or another of the city's endless military billets. In four years of war, even as rank further distanced him from the need, Starcross had lost none of his attachment to simple living. He could sleep anytime, anywhere he could find a flat spot to lie down, cushioned and covered by only his cloak. He counted nothing as a distraction or discomfort—nothing, that was, but the unnatural noise and crowded confusion of the city.

Candacy Ann, on the other hand, found the chaos exhilarating. She'd been grudged but the barest glimpse of the capital city, she complained, on her coming some five years before, in more peaceful times, closely chaperoned by Aunt Raby and a maid, and saw it as a great, outrageous privation that in all her long years at the school no further glimpses had been allowed. For a lady who might otherwise flout convention—and a brainy, book-learned woman was unconventional by definition—Miss Yarrow had quite rigid, conventional views of such matters. For her, the teeming wartime Federal capital was a sink of iniquity into which her charges were not to venture on any account. Their shopping and other errands were restricted to the nearby county seat, a drowsy, decaying old Chesapeake seaport, its somnolence ruffled only by occasional rumored comings and goings of Confederate spies or smugglers, in spirit as far from nearby Washington as the back side of the moon. The brief ride from the school into Washington's heart had no tiring effect whatever on the young woman. She let hardly a moment pass without some fresh fervid effusion of delight. At these prodigal squanderings of youthful energy in unlikely directions Starcross found himself both amazed and entertained; her enthusiasm was infectious.

For all their differences of temper and habit, Starcross liked the company of the grown-up Candacy Ann, even as he had that of the child. Despite the slight difference in their years, which can loom large in youth, they'd been friends, playmates, comrades. Now that each had taken on a fuller personality, the attachment grew to match. Unsurprised by his own gravitylike pull on Candacy Ann, Starcross was surprised indeed, startled, by the strength of hers on him in turn. The newfound side of her personality, he saw, with some dismay, was that mysterious thing, Femininity—in fact of course no more mysterious than its opposite, yet a mystery indeed to one who'd just passed four years in the company but of other men, rapt in the manliest of pursuits.

Starcross was a physical man, given to bursts of violent action, to forcible impositions of his will on resistant matter or other wills. Resistance attracted him; he found it—logically enough—irresistible. He went straight for the opposition's strong point. And he found it quite difficult to shift to some alternative tactic—say to indirection; or to an alternative strategy having as its end something short of the objective's total obliteration.

A woman, of course, was no objective, no enemy—rather she was part of the defensive base, to be guarded, but for the most part *dis*regarded, while the fight went on. Presence of a woman might not arrest one's accustomed aggressiveness, but it turned it aside from the woman herself. One spared one's left arm for the woman, perhaps, but the right was reserved for the sword, kept ever pointed away from her—toward the dragon. Immured in monkish schooling or riding womanless Western fields through all the years when a young man's blood runs hottest, Starcross had, like many soldiers, let exigency settle into easy habit. He had gone to Cathal McQuaife, spiritually at least, more virgin than she; and for him that night had been far too much the sublime exception to have broken the mold of a life already firmly fixed in other directions. The lovers of his acquaintance made poor soldiers; the reverse, he was convinced, was equally true.

But the soldier who was himself now found himself experiencing the novelty of a holiday from soldiering, actually his first ever. His fibers, long-tautened for fight, had taken their first relaxing twitches, and he was finding it hard, even by the mightiest effort, to tensen them again. The focus had been lost, the bound energy dangerously loosed. He had sensed himself scrambling to make matching mental adjustments. His hurried earlier hours in Washington—notable not least of all for its throngs of fashionable females—had served to remind him that, for some men at least, women were for other ends than being protected. And he had felt perhaps a pang of wry guilt—of regret that, for himself, the commands of manhood had never been commanding enough, or *clear* enough, to trump native inhibition and easy habit. On the drive back to Washington he'd sensed with alarm, for more than one reason, the untoward dimension of his attraction to the blossomed Candacy Ann there at his side. The end of the intimate twosome trip, therefore, he greeted with relief.

In the late afternoon the hotel was even more thronging and raucous than when he'd left it that morning. The throng was little to his liking, but he took solace in the fact that Candacy Ann and he were no longer to be alone together. Their progress through the hotel's public portions, indeed, proved a very gauntlet of encounters with brother officers, who predictably presumed on the tiniest of acquaintances to slake their curiosity—Webb Starcross seen with a woman was cause for curiosity indeed—and be presented to his companion. Chagrinned, Starcross could read the thoughts that passed through their heads—thoroughly unfazed by his repetitious "my foster-sister." *Excellent—so much more original than "cousin," old boy!* leered the knowing faces.

Candacy Ann, for her part, thrilled to the attentions, even the implications. She loved the lively hotel, and clearly had no thought of keeping meekly to the room. When they went up, she seemed to take it as given that Starcross would wait while she settled and freshened a bit, whereafter they would return right into the public eye. His timid suggestion that, after the rigors of the trip, she might prefer early retirement was laughingly brushed aside. Within an hour, then, they were back out on busy Pennsylvania Avenue, strolling the few blocks up to Capitol Hill, while Candacy Ann exclaimed over the sights, the lit-up government buildings rearing in the dusk, still decorated with their flags and illuminations from the successive celebrations of Richmond's fall and General Lee's surrender. Save for answering her sightseeing questions Starcross had little to say. Still, in spite of himself, of his vague unease, he began to enjoy the evening, even as the afternoon.

And afterwards, in Willard's dining room, in the security of bright lights and public chaperonage, he felt better. They dined well, and talked of practical matters. They would travel by train to the Ohio, and the rest of the way by water. The Baltimore and Ohio would have taken them through to St. Louis, but Candacy Ann preferred river travel, with its fabled glamor and luxury, and Starcross agreed for his own reasons. It would take longer but as in the hotel, surely, intimacy would be discouraged.

After the meal, Candacy Ann insisted on another turn around the night-shrouded, gaslit avenue, this time the other way, toward "the Mansion." Activity on the avenue, if anything, had increased since the afternoon, and Starcross, for one, felt a foreboding, fairly a menace, in the careless holiday air. It was a gusty, chilly evening, though the earlier threat of rain seemed to have faded. Despite the mobs milling or blocking the walks, there was no sense of shared lives. Muffled, faceless figures hurried past each other with furtive, wordless glances. Those who stood talking in knots clung to trivial topics. "The Mansion" showed few lights as the strollers passed through the near part of the President's Park, the unbroken sward lying between it and the Potomac's marshy banks. Public paths crisscrossed the park, wove among the government buildings on either side, and here too the avenue's edgy bustle prevailed. In distance and darkness, over the fetid old canal, stood the massive stump of the unfinished Washington Monument. The riverside neighborhood south of the avenue viewed as unsafe, Starcross steered their steps back the way they had come.

They, too, had kept to idle topics; but at last Candacy Ann threw out: "What will you do, Webb?"

"Do? Stay in the army, I suppose. The alternative being beggary. Though I'd almost as soon the latter as more of the former; of what it seems to have become before my very eyes." Heavily, if hopefully, he sighed. "That means the West, the Indians."

"You don't sound too happy about it, even that."

"I find it ever harder to be happy about any kind of fighting. And I'm cripplingly conscious that the Indians are very much like the rebels: people of integrity fighting a lost cause with incredible, quixotic valor. There's no pleasure in beating them, and little honor. But it's the least unpleasant recourse, it seems."

"And is that all? The least unpleasant war you can find?" She turned blunt. "Is there no woman in your life, Webb?"

As Starcross struggled somehow to laugh the question off, she added, "There was a time when I was your best girl."

"And you really belonged to another even then."

"Is that the kind of man you are, Webb Starcross? Huh—how have you ever managed to win any battles at all!"

"The rules of warfare hardly apply. Chance may have joined the Confederacy but I'm not at war with him." In the mellow streetlamplight he smiled at her. "Not that the—alternative might not be pleasant, but I'm afraid I hold friendship higher than—than self-indulgence. *That's* the kind of man I am, alas."

"Not the most flattering thing to say," she complained, half-seriously. "If Chance feels the same way I'm liable to find myself left out altogether. To be surrounded by such warm friendships looks like cold comfort for me."

"I don't see a contradiction—a problem. I don't begrudge Chance your . . . friendship, Candacy Ann. There's even less reason why you should begrudge him mine."

The shadow of the domeless bulk of the Capitol rearing ahead foretold the end of their outing. And as they neared the hotel, and mentally began to rejoin the world it embodied, Starcross at once sensed that the earlier atmosphere of bodeful suspense had erupted into one of seething excitement. The sidewalk was, if anything, even more crowded, figures nervously milling, forming and reforming in murmuring, gesturing clumps.

"Something has happened," he said. He sought out a known face. "What is it, Carnes?"

"It's none too clear, General. Good evening, Miss." In distraction Colonel Carnes touched his brim. "Word went about a while ago of an attack on Secretary Seward. Now the rumor's in the air that the president himself's been assassinated. It sounds like an organized plot against the whole government."

Starcross frowned. "The president's dead?"

"God knows. He was shot in his box in the theater, they say, and carried across the street to a rooming house, unconscious. Secretary Seward was stabbed in his own home; and there may have been attacks on other Cabinet members. General Grant's been sent for, to take charge and defend the city."

"Defend the city? Against whom?"

"Why, the rebels—they're behind it, of course. Oh, Jeff Davis hasn't near emptied his bag of tricks!"

Colonel Carnes excused himself and hastened away. Starcross stared after him as in a trance. He shook it off at last and turned to his companion, so ominously silent.

"Did you hear, Candacy Ann? The president—"

"Good!" She fairly exploded. "It's no more than he deserves!"

Starcross gaped. "Candacy Ann—for heaven's sake, how can you *say* such a thing?"

"Easily enough!" She went on heedless. "It's high time these Yankees had a taste of their own medicine! Did you *hear* that creature? All the rebels' fault; all poor Mr. Davis's doing. As if *he* and his likes haven't been murdering for four years, burning, looting, ravishing, all on the orders of that old baboon! Oh, I hate them all! May they all be murdered in their beds! Webb, Webb—how can you *bear* to wear that uniform?"

Starcross stood stunned, his anger stayed only by his shock. "You don't know what you're saying."

"I know perfectly well what I'm saying!" Candacy Ann stamped a foot. For the first time nearby figures on the walk were diverted out of their separate speculatings to listen and look on in a mutual bemused silence. "They've—they've impoverished my father, you tell me, they've broken my fiancé's health; yet I'm supposed to forgive and forget and sing their praises, help them mourn their sainted leader! Well, I *won't!* I'll say what I think! If *Old Ape's* dead, it's nothing but the judgment of God!"

Still struggling against the shock, the outrage, Starcross strove to mind to whom he was speaking. "You're entitled to your opinions. Your feelings are even—understandable, perhaps. But have the courtesy to consider mine. Candacy Ann, the president's my commander-in-chief. Whatever I may think of him, I won't have you speak of him so, at such a time. It's—it's indecent!"

"It's nothing to do with you," Candacy Ann sniffed in defiance. "If you don't like how I speak, you can take yourself away and leave me alone—spare us both."

"I can't do that and you know it."

"I don't know anything of the kind. You *said* you were going to go away for the night. Well, then—go! Go wring your hands with your bluebellied friends!"

Webb Starcross was left all but speechless. "I'm responsible for you to your father," he managed, at last.

"Oh, stuff and nonsense! I'm perfectly able to be responsible for myself." Candacy Ann stormed away from his side, toward the hotel entrance. "I can find my own way, thank you. You can stay here or—or go to the deuce, it's all one to me." Regally she swept up the steps, at once to be swallowed up inside.

Starcross's staring daze was shattered by a guffaw.

"Whew! Quite a little fireeater you've got there, General. Not many of her kind left in Washington these days."

"She'd better learn to hold her tongue," offered an uglier, female voice, more-or-less female, shrewish anyhow, "if she doesn't want to be stripped and taken a horsewhip to."

Starcross bit off a retort, withered the speakers with a look. Nameless feelings drove their very existence from his mind. He pulled himself halfway together and stalked inside. But unable or unwilling to follow Candacy Ann, he soon found himself refuged in the bustling bar. Anyone who knew him well would have marked at once the dangerous dilatings of the eagle's-wings of mustache: that one unmistakable Starcrossian outward sign of emotion aseethe within, bottled up by castiron self-control.

Starcross was no drinker; but his appearance in the bar saw whiskeys soon materializing before him, treats of acquaintances or even strangers eager for gossip, blissfully blind to his dire unreceptivity. Perversely he downed the drinks as they came, willing to deaden himself to all the world, the gabbling ape-faces, the scarifying clash with Candacy Ann, his own mordant thoughts; but to no avail. The liquor, like the company, aggravated more than it mellowed. At last, the pack diverted to easier prey, he managed to go to earth alone at a corner table.

He had the strange feeling of being at an impasse, at the crux of an awful crisis—a personal crisis, only thrown into starker relief by that other, public crisis of which all the heads and mouths about him were so full. The room, the city, waited breathless for further word of the stricken president; Starcross waited for he knew not what. He felt himself wrestling with a major decision without being clear about its nature. And to such wrestling, to such uncertainty, such indecision—even as to the whiskey—he was cripplingly unaccustomed. At last he recalled that, in any case, there were practicalities to be dealt with, taken relieved refuge in. Newly if deceptively resolute, seemingly clear of head if unsteady of gait, he left the bar, stalked upstairs, and approached the door of the room he'd relinquished to Candacy Ann.

"I must have my razor," he said stiffly, when the door opened.

At once the door swung wide. Candacy Ann, lissomely prim in little-girlish nightgown and robe, her radiant fair hair loose over her shoulders, stood swiftly, dutifully aside.

"Where will you sleep, Webb?" she asked, softly, penitently almost, watching as he veered over to the bureau, touched the little leather case that held his shaving gear, stood there uncertainly pawing his other personal articles.

"Oh, you needn't worry about me. The city's awash in places to sleep; and I can sleep anywhere." Jerkily he turned, faced her. "Unfortunately you'll have to put up with my odious company again tomorrow. All else apart, your father has commissioned me to see you home; and I'm used to doing my duty."

"Of course, Webb." Visibly dismayed, she watched him start back for the door. "No—don't go. Please, give me a chance—I'm sure I owe you an apology."

"Candacy Ann!" Not turning back, Starcross spoke almost in the same breath as she; his words in no way related to hers. "What on earth are we doing? The last thing I want to do is quarrel with you, over—over *politics*, of all things!"

"Yes." She forced out a meek, sheepish little laugh. "But then our quarrels always were about silly things, weren't they?"

"Did we quarrel? Well, yes, I guess we did. As children quarrel. But children get over their differences so easily!"

"Oh, Webb—darling!" She took a step forward. "You were right—I didn't mean it. I don't hate Mr. Lincoln, or wish him ill, not really. It's just that they seem to hate *us,* they do *us* ill. It's hard not to hit back, at least in words. It's just—words."

"You mustn't sink yourself to their level. Words, yes. Just words. That's the root of it all, I sometimes think. If only all the spouters of hard words on both sides over the past ten years had had to live cheek by jowl, as I have for four, with the fruits of their hateful words, with the broken bodies, the festering wounds, the ghastly, meaningless deaths! Oh, Candacy Ann—the sights I've seen! You've no idea." Little by little Starcross had finished closing the gap between them. And suddenly as-it-were for emphasis he seized her by the shoulders, his voice droning on in untypical agitation. Reeling as from a profound physical weakness, not the drink at all, he came to rest much of his weight on her. She might have crumpled beneath it had he not lurched a further step forward, drawing her along, and wound up slumped on the bedside, bringing Candacy Ann down with him in a clumsy embrace. "There was a boy I was especially fond of"—trancelike he was rambling on—"we were standing together under artillery fire. I caught him as he fell. His head . . . the *blood* . . . !"

"Oh, Webb—dear—" But then she confined herself to non-verbal soothings.

"'The general is made of ice,' I heard somebody say, almost with pride." As he faced her his own firm face seemed to shatter like glass. "The general is *not* made of ice."

"He puts up a good appearance of ice sometimes. No—I shouldn't have said that; I take it back." And she hugged him tight. "Not ice now, Webb. No need."

He went on gazing at her in pain, eyes full, mind far away. "I made a mistake, Candacy Ann. I committed a grievous wrong." She had never beheld such pain. "And—and a few days ago a man forgave me and shook me by the hand."

"Well . . . it's all right, then—"

"No! It just made it worse. I could have borne it all, I think, but for that. All but the forgiveness, the hand. The hand I took, without the right—"

"Webb dear, you can't take all the world's guilt on your shoulders. Another did that already." Even to herself Candacy Ann seemed transfigured, exalted to an all-new height of sympathetic understanding. "Put it out of your mind. It's been terrible for you, I'm sure; but it's over. You're safe now, here with me."

"If only!" he mourned. "If only we were still those two children—those innocents!"

"Oh, but we are, Webb, in our hearts; can be. I'm still your best girl, if you need me."

"I'm so *tired,* Candacy Ann. Dead-tired. War—it kills men in more ways than one."

"You mustn't go, not in your state. I'd never forgive myself." She cast about, all womanly practicality. "I—I want to look after you, Webb, not be just a burden, a worry, a . . . duty."

Their bodies touched, side by side there on the bed edge. Soothingly her hand lay on his shoulder, her chin at rest on its back. Little by little he grew aware of her softness, and found it the most natural, most reasonable thing in the world to turn, embrace her, and kiss her with fervor, however still tentative his overtures, still inhibited, still muddled by the unfamiliar, distracting, cross-purposed facts of her sex and their previous tender relationship; still awaiting the word or gesture that would have stopped him, would have arrested his rousing instincts in their tracks. But Candacy Ann did not offer the word or the gesture, simply did not have it at her command. The part of her that knew what was happening wanted it to happen; the part of her that didn't want it to, might not have wanted it to, did not know.

"Candacy Ann! My—my best girl!" It was half a question.

"Yes, Webb. But, yes. Of course."

EIGHT

Webb Starcross shaved with cold water and dressed with care, as for a solemn, formal occasion, a funeral—his own, if his mood were any clue. In the early April morning light he stood critically surveying himself in the shaving mirror, fussily adjusting the last brass button. His eyes were unable altogether to avoid those of Candacy Ann, mute and unmoving on the bed at his back; but it was all to himself that he murmured, at last:

"What have I done?"

Beneath the bedclothes Candacy Ann stretched in sensuous satisfaction. Clearly her thoughts were on the future, not the past. "You didn't do it by yourself," she reminded.

He made himself face, approach her. "It's not the same for you. You may, as you say, be able to be responsible for yourself. But I'm the responsible one in fact." Grimly he shook his head. "What would your father think of me? Or Chance?"

"They need never know."

"*I* know."

"And is that all it meant to you?" Candacy Ann sulked, mildly impatient. "Really, one would almost think you mean you didn't do it because you wanted to do it."

"Of *course* I wanted to do it—that's just what I'm trying to say. I *shouldn't* have wanted to do it."

"Webb, I'm not a little girl any more. It didn't do me any harm to find out what love is, above all from you." She stretched again, and snared his hand in hers. "So that's what it is!"

"I love you too much to want to hurt you. Love!" He winced, and pulled away. "You don't seem to understand the—harm this could do to you, let alone the pain it could bring to others. Think of how your father trusted me—the man to whom I owe so much. Think of Chance, whom I dare call my friend."

"I'm not married to Chance. I'm not even engaged to him, not formally. I might be engaged to *you,* Webb, if you hadn't always been so . . . so backward."

"You're engaged to Chance," firmly, "as far as your father's concerned. As far as Chance is concerned you're engaged to him. As far as *I'm* concerned you're engaged to Chance! I will *not* betray them—betray myself—worse than I have."

"It sounds as if I don't have anything to say about it at all. You can trifle with me just as you please and then cast me aside and wallow in your nobility and self-sacrifice. Like the man always, you can have the best of both worlds—"

"Oh, Candacy Ann—you know it isn't that at all! It's just—I don't want to *ruin* you. Perhaps you're right that what we *did* hasn't done any real harm. But what we *do*—"

"Yes," eagerly. "What *are* we going to do?"

"Nothing, I'd like to think. Nothing more." He sagged on the bed beside her, thankful that her slight though surprisingly full figure was well covered. "We shouldn't have done as much as we've done. I don't understand it. I'm not this kind of man, as a rule. I'll never forgive myself!" He bolted back up. "There's no use saying any more. I'll wait for you downstairs."

To his relief, Starcross managed to lose himself in the ranks of other early risers without obviously having joined them from within rather than off the street. The hubbub of both surprised him till full recollection resurged of the evening's public events, so thrust into the shade by his personal crisis. Now, at least for the moment, the order was reversed, the almighty public concern shrank the private one, made it impossible to be alone with oneself. All talked at once; rumors and theories vied and jangled; yet by this hour there was striking accord on the basic facts. When Candacy Ann came down, not too much later, and he excused himself from gabbling claimants on his ear and joined her for breakfast, he was able to fill her in in few words:

"The president died a couple of hours ago. They say he never regained consciousness."

Candacy Ann bit her lip, showing none of the animus of the evening. "Do they have any idea who did it?"

"Oh yes. Booth, the actor, pulled the trigger. Theater people recognized him. But he somehow got away all the same. The city's in an uproar—a madhouse. It's not just Booth—they're convinced it's a fullblown conspiracy, tied directly to the Confederate leaders." Starcross drew breath. "Whatever one's own feelings, Candacy Ann, I'm afraid the South's lost its firmest friend in the halls of power; while its bitterest enemies have been handed a clear field and the perfect excuse to do their worst."

"Oh dear! What unhappy times we live in." Candacy Ann's hand settled gently, not-all-that-unhappily on Starcross's own on the tabletop. "What does it all mean for *us*?"

"The sooner we're on our way, the better. I won't rest till I'm out of this suffocating place again, in open country."

Events had swept away any thoughts he might have had of traveling as a civilian. Colonel Colquhoun's whole reason for enlisting him as Candacy Ann's escort rested on his rank, and the furor and uncertainty bound to hold sway all about the capital in coming days only honed the point. Already departing civilians were the hapless butts of mindless, lynch-law suspicion, routinely bullied and in some cases detained. At each stop on the short ride north to the junction of the Baltimore and Ohio's main line to the West, squads of ten led by an officer were blundering through the cars, blissfully unmindful of Constitutional niceties; but of course they punctiliously left in peace a two-starred general traveling in his full military panoply, attended by an orderly and escorting a palpably proper young-lady companion.

He embarked on the journey, then, with spirits at last lifting from their nadir, almost with a sense of relief, a sense that he were, if not leaving his problems behind, at least putting off facing them. Even on the crowded, clamorous train, as the greening countryside slid by and the cities gave way to villages and these to virgin hills, an aura of privacy and security seemed to settle over them. Zurdo spent most of his time in the stable car seeing to Rustam's comfort and contentment. Starcross even napped in his seat, and dreamt himself back in the field again, sleeping on the ground and warming himself over campfires; contentedly so.

Even Candacy Ann was far more self-contained than usual, breaking in on his consciousness hardly at all, though she found the rail journey, with all its discomforts and fatigues, as enjoyable as she'd found the capital city. She basked in the curiosity they inevitably aroused, even if largely covert, impersonal, and from afar, the handsome major general and his vivacious young companion. The thought that their fellow-travelers' hazardings as to the real, secret nature of their relationship came uncomfortably close to the truth only added to her excitement.

From the first, Webb Starcross had filled a large place in her affections; now he enjoyed the added, illicit attraction of being the man who'd introduced her to the mysteries of love, of the flesh. She might go on accepting, as Starcross insisted, the premise that Chance Buckhannon was her beloved, her intended; but to the working out of the proposition to its perhaps unwelcome logical conclusion she spared no thought at all. Sufficed it for her that she had taken flight on an adventure of the heart with one whom she had, in one sense, long loved, and was beginning to be convinced she loved indeed, in the truest, grandest sense of all. This, to her mind, inasmuch as she let it wander so far ahead, need not compromise her eventual marriage to another. The following day, perforce spent on the train, was Easter Sunday; but if irruptions of conscience ruffled Candacy Ann's thoughts she soon threw them off. She was a young, healthy woman, just experiencing the first stirrings of her animal nature, backed up by her romantic turn of mind, as well as her womanly knack for the practical. The second evening found them settled, tired and travel-tense, in a Cincinnati hotel, in much the familiar situation, if officially in separate rooms, and faced, it seemed, with the familiar unanswered question of the first evening, back in Willard's. Starcross, though, willingly joined Candacy Ann for a late intimate supper in her room, and afterwards showed slight inclination to leave.

In time she managed to meet the question headon. "I think you're going to—to hate me, Webb."

"*Hate* you?" Startled, he first stared and then smiled, almost grimaced. "I who threw away my honor for you?"

"There! That's what I mean, what I'm saying. I know that's just how you see it, Webb, and what it means to you. Oh," she fairly wailed, "how could you *not* hate me!"

"I may hate myself, Candacy Ann, but not you—never you." Again the wan smile, as grimly he shook his head. "I seem satisfied enough to have you without honor."

She winced at the repeated word. "Temporarily have me? I'm sure you think your honor's gone forever; while what you got for it's anything *but* forever. I'm a bad bargain."

"*Life's* the bad bargain, Candacy Ann. It's no feast of delights we were given, to enjoy as we please, but a crushing weight of solemn duties to others, to things outside ourselves. *Your* duties are to make your father happy, and your husband. Mine are to try living up to your father's trust, and Chance's."

"A downright John Alden you are, Webb Starcross—a glum one, at that. You plead Chance's case more eloquently than *he* ever pled it—certainly than you ever pled your own."

"It isn't only Chance, Candacy Ann. It's isn't only *you*—would that it were!" He gazed off in space. "I have . . . other duties."

She eyed him, unusually intent. "What you mentioned the other night?" She went on at once, seeresslike, insight livening her bright blue button-eyes like water a dry well. "What you *wouldn't* mention rather: The—the woman in your life?"

Starcross made no denial. "That's putting it far too simply. It's more than that: 'a woman.' It's a—a debt of honor."

"*All's* a debt of honor for you, Webb, a solemn duty," she complained. "All save *me.* Don't I come into it at all? Isn't there any way I can figure among your debts and duties?"

"Of course—you *do.* But some duties come before others—literally before. Our duty to each other is just to make the most of this moment and let the memory of it lighten the rest of our lives, while we go on about our . . . our first duties."

"I must be content with the crumbs from the table of duty, or so it sounds." Her eyes rested on him, thoughtful, wondering. "You're so—so *sure,* Webb. If only *I* could be."

"Sure? But I'm not; not at all. That's why I must try so hard."

NINE

Buttoning his jacket, Starcross stood at the smudged window, gazing out on the rooftops of a duskening, backalley St. Louis, listening to Candacy Ann, seated on the lumpy bed at his back, rustling her way back into her mazes of clothing.

For them both, the seeming routineness of their intimacy was overshadowed by oppressive awareness of the turning point it obviously had reached. In the city only since morning, ostensibly they were enjoying a sightseeing turn about town before returning to Aunt Raby's for supper. Having called for Candacy Ann in the rented buggy, however, Starcross had driven straightaway, almost compulsively so, into a part of town bare blocks from Aunt Raby's but in marked contrast thereto, a world apart. The journey had brought them to what seemed to be a rooming house, albeit with no sign owning the fact; neither was there lobby or parlor, no rows of curious loungers to appraise the faces of new arrivals. The entry offered space where a lady might wait, unseen even by the man in charge, while the gentleman arranged the amenities. No servant had led the way upstairs; though almost at once somebody had brought a bottle of wine and glasses to the door and handed them in. The upper hall too was outwardly lifeless yet had the sense of being filled and vibrant with life, teeming if unseen, like the verminous kind Candacy Ann sensed under the drugget.

"I must say, you *do* know your way around, Webb," she murmured, bemused. "One would almost think you'd been doing this sort of thing all your life long."

Starcross shrugged. "One picks up all sorts of useless knowledge; and not just from experience necessarily. Not all my army friends are as . . . unworldly as I. Some of the worldliness is bound to have rubbed off, I reckon—on the surface."

"This is a house of assignation, isn't it?" Candacy Ann looked about at the stained, lurid mulberry-colored wallpaper. "A *maison de rendezvous*—I've often run across the term in French novels, without ever being quite sure what it meant."

"So that's what Miss Yarrow's young ladies got up to, when not waiting for Jeb Stuart to call." Starcross's laugh was spare. "Read French novels! At West Point we weren't allowed to have a work of fiction on the premises."

"And you never broke the rules?"

"I never felt the need. I always seemed able to find fancy enough in fact—romance in reality."

Candacy Ann's face clouded as her mind veered off another way—the familiar way. "You *will* despise me, Webb."

Her reversion to the disagreeable topic irked and dismayed him. He was wearying of protesting-too-much. "Despise—hate you? Oh, Candacy Ann! How could I ever?"

"A woman who goes with you to a house of assignation; a woman who, by your lofty standards, gives herself to you in dishonor? And yet you actually think after I have married another we'll remain just the best of friends—we three—and you'll still respect me, in the glow of the memory of these skulking few days of just us two? Oh, Webb, how could you *not* despise me? I would despise myself." Sadly, "I half do in any case."

"Please." He came and sat beside her on the bed, laid an arm around her shoulders. "You mustn't blame yourself—for anything. Blame *me*. Despise *me*, if you must despise."

"Oh, I know—I know these things are always presumed to be the man's fault, his altogether; but that's all wrong, I know it is. Everybody knows it." She took up his other hand. "*You* know it, Webb. *I* seduced *you*, every bit as much as the other way around, though you're too gallant to admit it—yet—even to yourself. But when you do admit it to yourself. . . ."

"I'm too much of a fatalist for that, Candacy Ann. I can't say I have no remorse for anything I've ever done—quite the contrary.

But I'll have no remorse for anything I've done with you, so long as it's brought you—anyone—no harm."

Again she cast a glance around the tawdry room, and shrank back in sagging dejection. "This is the end, then. That's why you brought me here, isn't it? To make an end."

"Oh, we'll have our time on the boat to Richwood." Hearing the obvious hollowness of his own words, he only grew grimmer. "We knew it would have to end."

"Yes. Oh yes. Given you, dear Webb, it would have to end. But in a room in a—!"

"You make too much of what's around us. What matters is what's inside, in *us.* That we've loved each other, that we always *will* love each other in our way, in a special way known only to ourselves: isn't that enough? Isn't it more, far more than we ever had the right to expect, to hope for?"

"There speaks the man." Candacy Ann spared a wan smile. "Women don't hedge about their hopes—their *loves*—with conditions, rights, *duties*." Arms around him, she drew them close. "We love each other, we'll always love each other . . . *but.*"

"Don't think about it now," he admonished. "Time aplenty afterwards for the *but.*"

Yet the "but," or part of it, pressed on them almost at once. Their time together had been limited, and so hectic, unsatisfying. In minutes the evening's crux had come and gone, the hour was on them to be getting back to Aunt Raby's: back to the world. The long, sweet spring twilight was just fading as they arrived back, in their gloomy silence, at the old townhouse, and face to face—as if their very words had invoked it—with the "but."

Aunt Raby (Arabia, her full name, was seldom heard) and husband Jabez Ament dwelt in a once-elegant neighborhood that had fallen off along with the couple themselves. In his active years a mildly successful broker of cotton and like plantation staples, Ament had been retired even before the war. The storm seemed to have passed right over their heads. Childless, unworldly, both in vaguely failing health, abetted by an aged, bumbling couple of ex-slaves as proof against progress as themselves, the Aments managed to go on living their wonted life of moldy comfort, their wants handily shrinking with their means.

The odds of the Aments' fathoming Starcross and Candacy Ann's guilty secret were nonexistent; and in her and their clannish world it was writ in stone that she must spend the stopover with them. Starcross had withstood their perfunctory invitations, seeking sanctuary rather at the Planter's House as the painlessest way of nudging their liaison toward a decent conclusion. Those days promenading aboard the *Asteria,* the skulking, scanted nights in Candacy Ann's stateroom, seemed stolen from the common calendar, turned timeless, paradisical. Enjoying his first real holiday since quitting Richwood for West Point over a decade before, as tenderly fond of Candacy Ann as ever, no longer had he tried to deny the carnal dimension of that fondness, now that he knew the attraction was mutual and she shared none of his first fear of the liaison as bemeaning to herself. The riverboat idyl had deepened both the addiction, as he saw it, and his desperate determination to bring it to some shadow of a happy end.

As he followed her into the old townhouse entry, Aunt Raby, antique in mildewed, jet-heavy taffeta, came fluttering forward, all unaccustomed agility and animation.

"Candacy Ann! Look who's here!"

Candacy Ann looked. *"Chance!"*

Starcross hung back as she flew forward and Chance Buckhannon came stiffly to his feet and gathered her in his arms. His hug and kiss were cousinly, constrained; her own, Starcross was relieved to note, natural and effusive. The conjunction took only a moment, but it gave Starcross time to appraise his old friend, unseen since before the war. The eerie resemblance between the friends, that had often been noted—more than once they'd been taken for brothers—was less obvious now; for Chance's wound and imprisonment had left him pale and drawn. His youthful stockiness, unlike Starcross's, showed no least sign of spreading into the solidity and gravity of middle age; though his long sandy hair and drooping mustache, darker than Starcross's once, now rather matched them with their faint streaks of premature gray. His infirm look, however shocking, Starcross sensed, represented actually an improvement—Chance must have looked worse but weeks or months before. His frail frame only half-filled his fine but ancient frockcoat, worn over frayed rebel gray.

"Oh, Chance—you're so *thin!*" Candacy Ann stood back and looked him up and down in frank dismay, making no allowances. "What have those Yankee fiends *done* to you!"

"One Yankee fiend at a time." Chance took shambling, swift steps past her, eyes fast on Starcross. The latter stood unmoving, uncharacteristically uncertain, guilty thoughts goading him to see Chance's words and moves as hostility, even assault. But then his friend's arms were all about him at once, his eyes faced over his shoulder, unseen. Starcross found himself happily answering in kind, in relief, to the startlingly hearty greeting. "Well, Yankee fiend? Ye gods, I never dreamt I'd be *hugging* a bluebellied major general! A few months ago I'd have shot at you!"

"Would you, Chance?" Starcross summoned a smile.

"Well-l—probably not quite. But the temptation—"

"I've been learning all about my bluebellied iniquity from Candacy Ann," Starcross jested laboriously, half-serious. "You're the perfect unreconstructed pair."

"Gentlemen, gentlemen," protested Jabez Ament, with all his wonted denseness taking them seriously indeed. "The war's over, or so I'm told. Leave us not break it out again."

Chance snorted. "Who's warring? Webb and I were never at war. *Were* we, old man?" Before Starcross could assent, Chance went right on: "If I'd ever found Webb in my sights, my trigger finger'd've gone plumb palsied, I'm sure."

With more effect, however indirectly, Aunt Raby disposed of the war by bidding them all in to supper. Chance, walking firmly if with a marked limp, naturally and it seemed without thought or plan paired off with Candacy Ann. Starcross offered Aunt Raby his arm, leaving her husband funteringly bringing up the rear, alone. As the meal was being served by the Aments' two servants, as vague and doddering as themselves, Starcross cut into Candacy Ann's chatter, cautiously to probe his friend:

"I wondered—I was starting to think you must have made straight for home, Chance."

"Home," Chance echoed, going grim. "There's not much there for me to go to—nothing like as much as here for me to wait in agog anticipation of." He fairly beamed from one newcomer to the other. "And then I've had to spend time going from doctor to doctor and lawyer to lawyer, trying to reclaim my health, of both kinds, material as well as physical."

"There's been some progress with the latter, at least," Starcross ventured, "according to Colonel Colquhoun."

"No thanks to the quacks; I seem to be mending just in spite of them. Took a minié in the leg in a skirmish near Atlanta—a victory for us, they called it, but not for me. Woke up in Yankee hands. Then some kind of mortification got in the wound. I'm a tough customer, they tell me, or I wouldn't be here."

"And the . . . and the other?"

Chance sighed, glancing at Candacy Ann there by his side. "Treen," he intoned, "is gone." Treen was the Buckhannon plantation, grander than Richwood, alongside it, broad acres of fertile, once richly remunerative bottomland. "Colonel Colquhoun tried to pay the taxes in my name, a gesture he could ill afford, but the offer was refused. The bayonet-elected officials wanted the land, not the money, and they got it. Some pal of the scalawag sheriff, a St. Louis cobbler turned factoryman, who made a pile selling your army cardboard boots, picked the place up for a song; then, when he found it couldn't be worked at a profit without the slaves, who'd all run off, those that hadn't been herded off like livestock by humanitarians, he lost interest and went back to St. Louis. Squatters broke into the house and made themselves at home. One night it burned to the ground around them."

"Oh dear!" Candacy Ann shook her head. "How unspeakably sad! Is there no end to the litany of our misfortunes?"

"In any case," Chance went on, "I'm told there's no hope of my getting the land back, at least not till some kind of sane, normal government gets back in power, and that isn't likely for years to come—the political climate's darkening, not brightening.

"And all the same, I'd be in the cardboard boot king's boat. I don't have the wherewithal to run a plantation, not without the slaves. Not even, not to say, to fight for it in court."

"It's horrible," Candacy Ann commiserated. "But don't be downhearted, Chance. We're all going to be poor now, or so Webb tells me. All poor together."

"You don't *sound* all that downhearted," would-be-cheerfully Starcross pointed out to Chance.

"How could I," Chance queried, "having just been reunited with the two most precious things in my world? When so many have lost even their friends, that we three have lived for this moment is something one can't be thankful enough for."

"Amen," Starcross seconded.

"We three *friends,*" Candacy Ann sniffed.

"Candacy Ann's jealous," Starcross hastened to note.

"Jealous?" Chance puzzled. "What am I missing here?"

"Well, it seems, if you and I are to be friends, Candacy Ann aspires to be something more than a friend. She's jealous of you on my account, and of me on yours."

"The former's understandable enough," Chance laughed, and closed his hand over Candacy Ann's. "And the latter's nothing new, if memory serves." He let go her hand and turned his own palm upward. "Remember, Webb, when we did our rather messy blood-brotherhood rite? See—I still have the scar."

"*I* remember," Candacy Ann huffed. "I remember how put out Mr. Buckhannon and Papa were with the pretty pair of you. They bled whole bucketfuls, the fools," she told her aunt. "The doctor had to be called from town."

"What *I* remember," teased Chance, "is how put out *you* were, my dear, when we wouldn't hear of you joining in."

"Fancy," Starcross added to the teasing, "a *girl* blood-brother!"

"I could have been a blood-sister. But oh no—it was too solemn, too important for a *girl.* Is it any wonder I'm jealous?"

"Solemn and important," Chance agreed. "Altogether beyond a woman's grasp. You prove it by your very words."

"Well, thank you very much, Mr. Blood-brother!"

"Why, Webb and I would *die* for each other. If he'd sent for me in the thickest of the war and said 'I need you; come,' I'd have gone; deserted and gone to him. Maybe he wouldn't have done the same for me—it's harder for generals to desert."

Starcross didn't know the answer. "I'd do anything for you now, Chance. Unfortunately, though I have my health and my rank, neither is a fungible asset; and of other assets I have little. More than you perhaps but not enough to save you."

"And to aid anybody, even a blood-brother, I'm even worse equipped. Still—we both have our sword-arms."

"Does that mean—? You have plans, Chance?"

"My plans are—I think the term is *fluid.* Sword-arms are little in demand at the moment, in this country anyhow. The only prospective employer is your army, and it seems to be firing more than hiring. Besides"—surveying Starcross wryly—"it would take me a while to overcome my sartorial aversion to blue."

"Surely your plans aren't so totally 'fluid,'" prompted Candacy Ann, impatiently. "On *all* fronts."

"Of course not, my dear," Chance assured her. "I must go home, if for no other reason than for the time-honored interview with Colonel Colquhoun. I must make absolutely certain he fully understands my bleak prospects."

"Yes," Starcross put in. "We must travel together."

"If Papa's going to make bleak prospects an obstacle," Candacy Ann pouted, "I'm doomed to die an old maid."

"Oh, I don't know," Chance tweaked. "There's Webb."

"The colonel too has that aversion to blue," Starcross was quick to point out.

He had sat all on edge through the tabletalk, and took the meal's end as his cue to escape, saying he'd matters to attend to, hinting that Chance and Candacy Ann deserved an evening alone together, time to catch up with each other's lives and renew their intimacy—start the courtship anew. And hoping the arrangement might extend through the next day, he promised, when pressed, to look in again in the evening, and took his leave. As he hoped, his going seemed to be taken as a matter of course. Only Aunt Raby sided him to the door. Candacy Ann and Chance, however effusive in their farewells, kept their seats, and—with satisfaction Starcross saw—relapsed at once into twosome talk.

Starcross's protestations of preoccupation were not wholly invented. The middle of the next day he spent courtesy-calling on Blake Frear, the local leader of the coterie of movers and shakers who'd taken him up after his splendid little setpiece victory at Hungry Ridge in 1861, during those darkest early days of the war. Their influence he had often sensed operating from afar, behind the scenes, though direct contacts had been few and never of his doing. He had, however, met the older Frear brother Morgan, the Cabinet member, the gray eminence, in Washington.

The junior Frear was a small, weedy man of early middle age, with a drooping mustache far too large for his narrow, foxy face. But his unimpressive figure radiated energy, and seemed larger than it was. Starcross had met him only the once, in 1861; but the politician greeted him familiarly as he was shown into the parlor of his modest but well-appointed townhouse.

Agreeably overshadowing the parley with the politician himself, Starcross found an even more familiar figure in the room. Huell Yulee, his good right arm in the days on the Plains and early in the war, had emerged as Colonel Yulee. But Frear kept the two from indulging their pleasure in their reunion for long.

"General Starcross," he marveled, "the invisible man! They called him Xenophon once, but I see him more as Lohengrin or the ghostly like. He swoops down out of the clouds and saves the day. You look around to thank him, and he's not there."

"It never occurred to me that thanks were to be looked for," Starcross mused, discomfited, "for doing one's duty, being given the opportunity. It's I who owe the thanks, surely."

"Still the innocent!" Frear smiled at Yulee. "And the exception. Some of your peers look for thanks all the way to the presidency." The politician turned more serious. "Yet, as I recall, we once had more than a little difficulty persuading you to do your duty, to seize the opportunity you were being offered."

Starcross's discomfort redoubled. "Our personal problems overwhelm the best of us at times."

"Oh, it's nothing to apologize for. I remember the story well —discreetly, of course."

"I always wondered how you knew so quickly, sir. Of course the tale got about in time, was bound to, thanks to the worthy Colonel Uriel Purinton, whose favorite person I was anything but at that point. So soon, though . . . ?"

Blake Frear's vulpine eyes eased over to Huell Yulee.

"I'm the guilty party, General," confessed the latter. "I took it upon myself to bring the—er, the problem to the attention of one of Mr. Frear's military confidants."

"You had no right—" Starcross muttered.

"He had every right," Frear put in. "Not just as an officer but as your friend. He saw things clearly—that you were about to commit professional suicide, just at the moment when the army and the country needed you. He believed we must know the facts in order to make the most persuasive case to you."

"And so you shamed me, between you, into sticking my duty as a soldier to the betrayal of my duty as a man."

"Most of us have been 'shamed' by the war—surely not to *betray*—to *put off* our private duties. I think putting off was the thought in your case? Nobody dreamt, of course, four years ago, that the putting off would be for so painfully long."

"Yes. And time can make such a difference."

"But you still have hopes of doing your—your private duty?"

"I mean to try my best. That's the chief reason I resigned and came West so soon. If anybody's of a mind to *thank* me they can help me get a Southwestern command."

"Put in your application and be sure to let me know," Frear rejoined. "I have to tell you, though, there will be precious little call for major generals in the Southwest."

"Lord! Make me rather a lieutenant with a saber in my hand and a foe before me than a general—driving a quill."

"Good generals are scarcer than good lieutenants; and the army ever more does its fighting with quills. Are you sure, General, this isn't just the wish to be your younger self again?"

Starcross hardly knew what to say. "It isn't that I don't relish command; I just don't relish it to the exclusion of execution, which rank seems to entail. If it comes to a hard-and-fast choice, I'd almost rather carry out commands than give them."

"Hardest of all is to carry out one's own commands," Frear said. "The whole military idea rests on dividing command from execution, lodging them in separate breasts. For *self*-commands are the hard ones. The commander knows all the doubts qualifying and underlying the orders he gives. They would inhibit, even paralyze him, were he himself their executioner; while to the one he passes it to the order is clear, unqualified; unconditional. An order, pure and simple, to be carried out."

"I never thought of it so. Nor did I ever have any noticeable trouble carrying out my own orders, as it were. Still, the war having brought home to me the possible longterm effects of the most offhand of orders, I can well see what you mean."

The politician prevailed on his guests to join him for the midday meal, and they lingered long over a well-laden table, and then, in the late afternoon, took their leave together. Yulee turning out also to be putting up at the Planter's House, they returned there together, renewing their acquaintance, rediscovering their old compatability, and exchanging their personal histories of the war. Entering the old hotel they found themselves drawn into the early-evening crowd gathered in the bar, Federal officers for the most part, in place of the merchants and planters of old.

They had been there hardly half an hour, albeit Starcross was already on the point of excusing himself when, happening to glance up, he saw Chance Buckhannon standing just within the door, flanked by two companions. And he was visibly a very different Chance from only the night before. A walking stick was in his hand, but when he came stalking on forward, stiffly, it was without its aid—rather he waved it in the air as a cudgel; and he was dressed not only in last night's worn uniform trousers but as well in his gray jacket, tentlike over his wasted frame though impeccably brushed and pressed and—defying his parole, a clear, apurpose provocation—complete with the banded gold of rank. Chance had reopened the war. Starcross's jaw started to move but the greeting reflexively forming on his lips expired under the double brunt of Chance's person and words:

"You cad!" Like a lightning-stroke Chance's knuckles came crashing into his jaw, with far more force and weight than one would have judged the uncertainly convalescent Chance capable of mustering. "You—you unspeakable swine!"

TEN

Taken off-guard, Starcross went reeling backwards, all but toppling like tenpins the several tipplers ranged along the bar behind him. In his first splitsecond of regained self-possession he found himself sitting, or rather sprawling, supine on the gritty floor, propped half on the brass footrail, half on an anonymous pair of legs. Bewildered he gaped up at Chance, now looming right over him, fair atremble and for the time being speechless, his face wracked and stormy with his rage, his walking stick raised high, though whether as a would-be bludgeon or merely for dramatic emphasis remained unclear. His two companions seemed as startled by the assault as the rest of the room. They moved forward on his either side as if to restrain him by main force, one actually if ineffectually grappling with the cocked arm.

"Chance—" Starcross began.

"Yes, Webb?" Chance sneered. "Why don't you say something? Let everybody hear what you have to say!"

Starcross closed his mouth; touched a hand to it and drew it away dripping red. The room was coming alive; the men behind Starcross fumbled fecklessly to help him to his feet, others milled in uncertain hostility, gabbling without sense.

"What the devil—?"

Chance scorned them all. "We took you in, took you to our bosom," he raved. "And how have you repaid us? Oh no, I won't say it." He writhed in his companions' grasp. "Get up, Goddamn your rotten soul—take your punishment like a man!"

The room's hostility was approaching an ugly coherence. Chance's friends renewed their efforts and at last he relented, let them draw him away. The invading forced backed off and then at the door turned and vanished. Shakily Starcross struggled to his feet, impatiently brushing the would-be-helpful arms aside. The hubbub of talk turned on the assailant's identity.

"There's one damned reb let out of the stockade much too soon," growled a political general, far gone in drink. "He should go back in forthwith. Does anybody know—?"

"No." Starcross's voice was low but sharp, thunderously so.

"Can't have a madman running around still fighting the war."

"It's nothing to do with the war. Nor with *you,* General." For the first time betraying feeling, his expression discouraging further curiosity or comment, Starcross broke from the ring of onlookers, started unsteadily for the door. But he stopped by a table in the emptier end of the room and slumped down. He touched his handkerchief to his mouth, bemusedly studied the results. The others took the hint, turned back to the bar, their tones hushed, as if somebody had died. The lone exception was Yulee, who soon drew near the table toting a pair of neat whiskeys.

"If you'd rather be alone, General. . . ."

Indifferently Starcross waved at the facing chair, gratefully accepted one of the whiskeys.

"Packs quite a punch for a convalescent," he muttered.

"You know him, then?"

"*Know* him?" Starcross stared at Yulee, stricken. "That man's my best friend. *Was.*" He upended the drink and then added, sadly, as if to himself: "My blood-brother!"

"Then . . . I take it you know his . . . grievance."

"Oh, I know. He has one. A point. A case."

"Ah. But don't be too fair," Yulee admonished. "General, you must think of yourself."

"No. Not so. There are . . . others involved."

Starcross looked up with a start. A somehow familiar figure had materialized at his shoulder: small, slim, swart, dandified in gaudy frockcoat and billowing necktie. Long, well-waxed mustache-ends spanned his sharp face. Tardily Starcross knew him: one of Chance's moments-ago companions.

"General Starcross." Came a sweeping bow. "Captain Hugunin, sir, representing Major Buckhannon. I am commissioned to tell you, sir, that if you do not mean to call out Major Buckhannon, you are to consider yourself called out."

"Chance is wasting no time," Starcross mused.

Yulee stirred in his seat. "I am at your service, General."

"This is madness. I don't want to fight Chance."

"He may not want to fight you either, at heart. But it's clear he feels his honor has been impugned—and he has certainly managed to impugned yours." Yulee drew dreath. "Added to which, I'd hazard he's not likely to give you any peace short of satisfaction. So-o, unless you *do* mean to have him arrested—"

The threesome parley had reawoken the room's curiosity. The star-spangled politico reeled a step forward.

"Only thing to do!" sharply he cut Yulee off. "And this—this Creole popinjay in the bargain. Dueling, challenging, *is* against the law, even in this rebel sinkhole."

"Summon the police to my rescue?" Starcross spoke to the problem, not deigning even to notice its articulator. "That's the Yankee shopkeeper's answer, I'm sure. No—no. Rather madness than—than dishonor." He smiled, all ruth. "Honor, or the *look* of honor. I never dreamt what a burden it could be."

Yulee glanced at Captain Hugunin. "Then shall I—we—?"

"Oh, by all means." In despair Starcross flung his hands up. "Since we're being mad, let us be *right* mad."

He sat on alone, if not for long; only idly glanced up at Yulee returning. "The captain's as ignorant of the grievance as I, but he's convinced reconciliation's out of the question."

"Yes; I'm not surprised."

"There was no point in delay," Yulee went on, businesslike. "'Twould only be inviting interference from the likes of our Yankee shopkeeper friend yonder. We agreed the . . . interview should take place at dawn tomorrow on Bloody Island. Knowing the city, Hugunin will engage the other players. I chose pistols, General, assuming that would be your preference."

"Yes. Perfect. Chance is an excellent shot." At Yulee's lifted brows, Starcross added, in earnest, "Thank you, Yulee. I can't tell you how much I appreciate your support."

"Shall I call at your room at around—let's see, dawn is sixish at least—at around four, then?"

Starcross went up to his room, but only for long enough to apply alum to his lip, brush his jacket, and wryly, ruefully eye his otherwise presentable image in the looking-glass.

Out on the dusky street, he hailed a cab and directed it to the Ament home. He was rather taken aback to find the Aments and Candacy Ann just rising from the table. Between his distraction and the lingering light of the April afternoon he'd totally lost sight of the hour, even as of hunger. The evening was warm as well as bright, and it was no trouble at all to draw Candacy Ann apart by suggesting a stroll in the lozenge of iron-fenced garden slotted in between the Ament house and its neighbor.

Candacy Ann at first noticed nothing of his distraction, nor even his scabbed and swollen mouth. She was far too full of her own day, made up, it seemed, of wistful rounds of couturier shops far beyond her means. Only her complaints of neglect at last penetrated Starcross's own head. Chance had been expected to join her, she said, but had failed to appear; and, all indignation, she'd tired of waiting. Starcross cut her chatter short.

"Chance's mind was elsewhere. He has challenged me."

Candacy Ann's eyes rounded, first just in incomprehension, then in dumbstrickenness. "To a *duel*?" For the first time she seemed to *see* him. "Webb—your face!" Suddenly she was a different woman, sober, acute. "How did he find out?"

"Oh, Candacy Ann, don't be childish." Starcross paced before the iron seat onto which she'd sagged. "This is just what I've tried to tell you from the beginning. Such things are always found out. If he had the least suspicion, I'm sure he'd but to look at our faces for confirmation. And then, out of all the people on the boat with us, odds were overwhelming that at least one would know *us* without our knowing *him;* know who we were and what we were doing, and know Chance and see it as his duty to tell him."

"And we thought we were being so clever!"

"I never once thought I was being clever," Starcross snapped. "I thought—I *knew* I was being incredibly stupid." He headshook. "I simply didn't know how to help myself."

"Well," stiffly, "I'm sorry if you have regrets."

"Regrets! Of *course* I don't have regrets, not for yesterday. I only regret tomorrow." He grimaced. "The consequences."

"Well, if you feel that way . . . just because he challenged you, you don't have to accept. He can't make you, can he?"

In the fading light he looked long at her in disappointment, even though her reaction came as no real surprise. So total was her incomprehension he could see no way to begin to enlighten her—to explain himself. He moved on to more practical matters, areas in which she'd likelier understand and agree.

"Chance, even *this* Chance, is too decent a man to wish to do *you* harm; but he might do so just by inadvertence, or out of spite and anger—he's *very* angry—were I to deny him satisfaction; if I *could.* The one way to be sure to forestall that is for me to meet him and get it over with as quickly as possible."

She appealed up to his pacing form. "What will—happen?"

"That's just what we must have the—interview to find out." He ceased his restless circling, sagged beside her. "Don't worry. The cause may not remain a total secret, but it needn't become public knowledge of the sort to—to ruin you. Even if Chance no longer wants to marry you, he wouldn't spoil your chances if he could help it—if he's not too much beside himself."

"If he no longer wants to marry me, for God's sake where's the problem? Why does he want to *fight* you over me?"

"Not over you, or not just." Starcross was finding her view of the affair incredibly, disappointingly self-centered; but he quelled the thought, charitably minded himself of her youth and inexperience. Wasn't self-absorption an expectable, venial peccadillo in a young woman? "A principle's at stake. I've traduced a woman's honor, in Chance's eyes, and by extension his own, since he had a claim on the woman. And so he's traduced mine, in public, and by extension yours, in private. Neither of us has any choice in the matter, he for the sake of his self-respect, I for the sake of my public respect." Grimly: "I no longer *have* any self-respect."

"I'm *so* sorry, Webb—in more ways than one. What you say makes no sense to me at all, but I know it does to you; it means everything to you." She caught his hand. "Oh, it's all my fault, I'm sure, somehow; it must be. You wouldn't have done anything you did without my encouragement; and you can call it principle if you want, but if it wasn't for me you and Chance wouldn't fight, either of you." She looked at him in all earnest. "When I asked you what would happen I wasn't thinking of my reputation—I'm not quite *that* shallow, Webb. Good Lord, you might be killed, either of you, or even both, or seriously hurt." Her fervent words embraced both men, but her arms only Starcross. "I don't want that; I—I couldn't live with it. Oh, there should be *some*thing I could do, since I'm the cause—to *stop* it, I mean, to stop you."

"Maybe you're right—maybe you *are* the cause, in a way. There was always a rivalry between Chance and me, you know, in all things, though it was a friendly rivalry, or seemed to be; and maybe more often than not it *did* have to do with you. We—*performed* for your eyes, for your approval: Chance the possessor defending his own; I the challenger unable to resist teasing him onto the defensive. And Chance, I daresay, hastened off to his quixotic war with at least half an eye on the smiles of his beloved back home. Maybe something like as much could be said of me, too, though I was gone long before, when you were still a little girl in my eyes. Maybe, even in sticking with the 'wrong' side, and carrying on a career more humdrum than quixotic, maybe at least in some corner of my heart I always hoped my childhood sweetheart was looking on, and would—understand."

"Oh, Webb, that's very sweet! I did, and I do, I understand. I'm not as heartless as I may seem—the contrary. I have room in my heart for both of you, I assure you, for you and for Chance. I just pray nothing happens to either of you."

"I just pray he kills me!"

"Oh, Webb, don't *say* that! Why on earth—?"

"Because I don't want to kill *him*. *He* may have managed to overcome his faith in blood-brotherhood, but *I* haven't. Though that isn't my only reason, or all of it." Sadly he shook his head. "*He's* done nothing to deserve to suffer for—to suffer more."

ELEVEN

Despite his troubled thoughts Starcross slept well and woke himself in the darkest hours before the dawn. Yulee found him impeccably groomed—uniformed. His brow creased.

"I have no other clothes," Starcross told him. "And this is war, isn't it?" Downstairs Starcross stopped before the front desk and roused the nodding night clerk. He produced a single sheet of foolscap, penned his signature at the bottom, and bade Yulee and the clerk add theirs as witnesses. He sealed it in an envelope and left it with the clerk. "My will," he muttered as they left the hotel, "leaving my all to Chance." Yulee's brows rose, wrinkling again, but characteristically he kept his silence.

A carriage hired by Yulee waited out front, and the two rode in a stillness broken only by their own clattering wheels over cobbles, through ghostly, gaslit streets to the darker waterfront depths of North St. Louis, and at last onto a lonely levee where a boatman waited in the misty, crepuscular chill.

The river spread out vast before them, felt more than seen, breasting with implied menace though for the moment tame, a hibernating beast not yet warmed back to life. Their Charon showed no surprise to be ferrying a major general. The mightiest man, after all, sooner or later must cross the Styx.

While he oared them, seemingly with more seaward than forward motion, over the broad placid main channel, itself not palpably moving at all but in truth moving like the sun in the sky, inexorably and irresistibly, they sat in the bow watching the city stirring from its sleep behind them, soon all but lost in the mighty littoral where it lay, with the spring dawn starting to break along the horizon all around. They had to crook their heads, though, to see the long, low, willowy sliver of Bloody Island moored barge-like near the hinter shore, sundered from Illinois only by a chute, or small back channel; technically an *accretive* not an *avulsive,* protean child of the river, not seriously claimed or policed by either state, and so St. Louis's longtime locus for discreet gentlemanly "interviews," its insensate sands and scrub soaked and stained with a sanguine history. In earlier, more spacious days, duels, often as-it-were between giants, had been fought here in the full sight of approving public eyes; but to modern, "progressive" minds the old notion of trial by combat had grown ever more alien, and ever more its practice had labored under the righteous cluckings of peevish, puritan tongues, backed up by laws. The "interviews" took place far less frequently these days, and under furtive conditions, distracting thoughts always having to be given to possible dishonorably hasty flights from honor's field.

It was a large, long island; but the "field" by hoary custom was a shallow-cuplike portion of the flat sandy center plateau on the cityward side, half-screened from the river by scraggly willows, this April day saffron-twigged, asmoke with new leaf. Stepping ashore, Starcross and Yulee saw other boats not far downstream, one already put in and quitted, the other just putting in. Parting the willows, they found the officiants already in their places, somber in their frocks and tophats, the physician marked by his bag, the referee by his solemn, Vandyked air of authority, his undersized flunky by the bulky pistol-case he held flat like a tray.

Then, farther along, Starcross saw Chance Buckhannon—uniformed, of course—fair bursting from the willows, trailed by Captain Hugunin, who moved into the lead. Yulee left Starcross's side; together the two seconds joined the referee for the ritual reciting of the rules. From their facing distances the principals looked on like bystanders as the seconds, overseen by the referee, stepped off and pegged the distances, and then returned to watch the referee open the case and charge and prime the pistols. Yulee, representing the challenged, offhandedly picked up a weapon, Hugunin the other. They parted, backtracked to their principals, who stepped forward to meet them at the designated places. As from the beginning Starcross was struck by the sense as of Fate, as of predestined events unfolding inexorably, inhumanly as clock-works. Or rather, like the precise, stylized, if all-too-human gyrations of a dance, which indeed it was: a death-dance, devised to hedge the unbearable within bearable bounds.

As-it-were rousing tardily, reluctantly from dream to reality, good to bad, he found himself standing thirty paces from the gray, tense, willow-thin, willow-limber stalk of Chance, the gleaming, antique twelve-inch, crook-handled hairtrigger smoothbore pistol heavy in his own hand. As from a distance he heard the referee, in jaded, perfunctory tones, inquire of Chance for a last time if he wouldn't entertain the thought of reconciliation.

"Just let's get on with it!" Chance snarled, frail frame almost visibly atremble with its inner turmoil.

The referee announced and began his count.

On the instant of the count of three Chance eagerly leveled his weapon and discharged it. Starcross's own came up more slowly, unwillingly, as but of its own accord. Chance's ball went whining past his ear like an angry hornet. He waited a suspenseful few moments, as if to let Chance's dismay have its fullest effect. Then he turned his weapon to zenith and shivered the unoffending, peaceful inverted bowl of the saffron dawn.

"That won't save you!" Chance blew up in an outraged howl. Haplessly Hugunin hovered, fought to quell the fitlike fury. The referee reproved; the doctor too chimed in that honor had been satisfied. Chance calmed down a bit at last, *ran* down rather; but after much consultation Hugunin glanced bleakly about, shaking his head. The pistols were brought in, recharged, exchanged, and returned. Sinews stretched taut yet again, nerves strained to the breaking point, like the springs of the guns.

On the second count of three, Chance aimed and fired with more deliberate care; but the result was the same. Unscathed, beneath the second singing, singeing hornet, Starcross once more lifted his pistol upright and emptied it into the air. Again Hugunin closed with Chance, imploring; again the referee expostulated, pontificated—and again Chance scorned them all. Furiously he bespoke Starcross, past Hugunin's head:

"We'll stand here shooting till the crack of doom, damn you, if that's what it takes!"

Watching the referee and his assistant again recharging the pistols, Starcross, deep in the sea of his despair, began to feel stirrings of impatience—exasperation. This was a strange Chance indeed, a Chance he'd never known; not at all the whimsical, easy-going, irresolute fellow he *did* know. He was being worse than unreasonable. *Twice* had Starcross offered himself for the ritual sacrifice, for the expiation of his sin. There was a limit, even to guilt, to the price reasonably to be paid for it.

Weapon in hand yet again, three-count yet again come and gone, yet again he held his fire, allowed Chance the first shot. He felt his sleeve twitch under the grazing whine of the ounce ball. Glancing down at the marred fabric, ridiculously vexed, he faced back forward and with utmost indifference brought his shooting arm up and jerked the hairtrigger. Ruth overwhelmed him at once as he saw Chance start, stagger, and sag sideways on his game leg, the emptied pistol slipping from his grasp.

His own weapon adroop, Starcross took an anguished step forward, but the referee's voice stayed him. "Keep your place, General!" The doctor joined Hugunin, already knelt over Chance, whose curses droned lustily on: He'd have yet another shot; he had arm enough to shoot down a dog, and so forth. But his gun-arm had taken the ball; the referee was adamant; the interview was over. Again Starcross stirred, yearning toward the tableau thirty paces away; but Yulee's hand stayed him.

"General—you must leave the field," he reminded, glancing anxiously around at the waxing daylight. "There are patrols, and our coming was no secret." His eyes rested on the uniform. "It—it wouldn't do for you to be found here."

"I must know how he is."

"I'll make sure and meet you at the boat."

Unwillingly Starcross nodded, let Yulee take the forgotten pistol from his fingers. He turned and trudged back through the grassy sand and the willow screen onto the damp, fishy beach, soon joined by their boatman, who, clearly, with his fellows, had enjoyed the show, the upper-class madness, from the vantage of the underbrush. Yulee soon caught him up.

"Not too bad," he reassured. "He took it in the armpit, but it's a clean, through wound, nasty but not dangerous—quoting the doctor. He'll have a stiff arm for a few weeks, but he'll mend without difficulty—barring the unforeseen."

"Did he . . . say anything?"

Yulee seemed to reply only as a duty. "He said you haven't heard the last of it—of him. He promised you."

"Well"—Starcross shrugged with hollow cheer—"sufficient unto the day. . . ."

Indeed it was a glum, untypically distracted Webb Starcross who went back, first in the boat, then in the waiting carriage. Dropping Yulee at the hotel, he grasped his hand in gratitude, saying—superfluously—he had a call to make.

At the Ament house he had a maddeningly long wait before the seedy old manservant, startled and sleepy-eyed, unlocked the door to his repeated, persistent rings. He thrust past the man with explanatory half-sentences: He *must* see Miss Candacy Ann, he knew where to find her, no announcing was called for, the household need not be roused. In his stupor the man stood agape, making no move as Starcross took the graceful, turning steps in twos and threes. Candacy Ann, he knew, occupied a little suite overlooking the garden. The outer or sitting room's double doors opened at his touch; Candacy Ann, as he'd known she would be, was there, hunched over a silver coffee service at a table in the window bay, framed by chintzy white swagged curtains almost matching her dressing gown. Her figure was composed, hair and gown, though her face less so, at least underneath. It bore no hint of sleep, sequel or anticipation. Her eyes flew up and about at his brusque entry; the rest of her followed at once.

"Webb—oh, Webb! Oh, thank God!" She closed with him and embraced him, buried her face on his breast. "I've hardly drawn a breath all night. What happened?" She looked up, made her eyes meet his. "This doesn't mean—?"

"No," he assured, explaining as briefly as he could without leaving out any key thing. "He'll be all right. He's a tough customer, as he said." He made a face. "I too, I reckon. Three shots! Of course those old smoothbores are wildly inaccurate—still, if Chance hadn't been literally shaking with rage—"

"Thank God for his rage! Oh, Webb, Webb"—her embrace grew more fervid—"you're *mad,* stark mad, both of you. Chance certainly, but you too. Just to *stand* there—!"

"Oh, quite. I couldn't agree more." Gently he eased past her and slumped in one of the chairs at the table, not just to keep her at a distance but because suddenly he was too weak to stand. When he spoke, it was to himself more than to her. "I did my best—my worst. It wasn't good enough, I'm afraid." He lost himself in the memory. "He might've kept us there forever. I had to wound him, you could say, just to try and end it."

"Well, it *is* ended, anyhow." Candacy Ann came and stood by his side, arm on his shoulder, cheek at rest complacently, fondly on his taffy hair. "And you're safe. *Both* of you."

"That's just it—it *isn't* ended at all." Gently he disengaged. "It just made him madder. Understandably, I reckon, being bested so easily, seeing me walk off all unscathed. He promised me as much—that I hadn't heard the last of it, of him."

"But what does *that* mean?" Candacy Ann seemed at last to face the full implications, not to say the momentary inopportuneness of displays of affection. She circled to the facing chair, her hands, if not her mind, busying themselves pouring him a cup of coffee. "Surely he won't make you fight again."

"I don't know what he'll do. No no, not that. I've been thinking it over, trying to think what *I'd* do. . . . He's so unlike me, though; so unlike *himself,* the man I knew. I don't *know* this man he's become, this blood-brother who'd shed my blood. If I were *that* man, were that *mad—*" Gloomily he pondered, picking his words with care. "He'll head straight home and tell your father, that's what he'll do. That's his next move."

"Oh no!" Candacy Ann's face paled. "Chance wouldn't do such a thing, wouldn't stoop so low. You said it yourself."

"This isn't Chance any more, *our* Chance. He's my enemy, not my friend. *Your* enemy too maybe, who knows? Think about it, then. That being the case, it's his logical next line of attack. If he can't kill me one way he can kill me another—in the eyes of the man whose esteem he knows means more to me than almost anything else on earth. And then, he'll have this new wound to account for. The colonel's bound to get wind of the duel in any case, sooner or later. Chance can confess in a good cause, in all innocence, letting one reluctant disclosure lead to another. Oh, I'm not saying he'll be scurrilous, or even explicit at all, call you bad names—he won't have to. The barest hint, a quick gallant retreat into stout gentlemanly silence, and it's done."

"Oh dear, oh dear." Candacy Ann cast all about, lost in her despair. "Oh, poor Papa! It's all very well for Chance to punish *us*—but *Papa?* It's—it's too much."

"Chance might well be the one to say that, Candacy Ann," he reminded. "That's something else to be remembered: *he's* in the right. You weren't just his by solemn understanding, you were all in all to him. I saw it the other night. Now that he'd lost all, all else, all save you, and in a way me—oh, don't you see? And then to lose you and me both, all in a twinkling, and in the most painful way, by betrayal. We *betrayed* him, Candacy Ann, his beloved and his blood-brother alike. Is it any wonder he's over the edge? Oh hell!" Starcross's air of understanding of, even identification with Chance gave way to incomprehension of and disaffection from himself. "If I'd just let well enough alone, let *you* alone! When all my finer feelings were crying out to me—"

"I know what you mean, Webb," she assured, in a faraway voice that left it clear she didn't at all; "but it's hard to be told that what I feel for you with such conviction, and you for me, if I'm not presuming too much, is—is *wrong.*"

"If you know what I mean," he said, "you know that's not it. It's not right against wrong—that would be too easy, too simple; and life's never that, as I've found out the hard way. It's right against right. You and I, we have our right, in our feelings for each other. But Chance has his right too, and his comes first. If we deny that, Candacy Ann, we're left with a moral chaos in which our own right is just as deniable, just as meaningless."

"What will we do, then, Webb?"

"It's not for us to do anything, anything but what we would have done in any case. Go on, go home, as if none of it had happened, nothing had changed. If Chance chooses to hurry ahead and prepare our coming, that's his affair."

"You know what I meant really. *Has* nothing changed? The only change I seem to fear now—oh, you know what it is!"

"No; the important things haven't changed, Candacy Ann." Starcross closed his hand over hers on the tabletop. "I—I shot a man a while ago to keep them from changing. It would make no sense for us now to change them ourselves."

She sounded unconvinced. "When will we go?"

"The sooner the better—tomorrow. I'll find a boat today." Leadenly Starcross dragged himself up. Halfway to the door he stopped, keeping his back to her, making fists at his sides. "No point putting it off. We can't put it off forever."

"If only we could!" She let a pregnant moment pass; he felt her stir, and steal close up behind him. "*Couldn't* we?"

He half turned back, tried to smile. "I don't think so."

"Oh, Webb! Do we *have* to go home?" Her faltering eyes sought strength in his. Her hands wrung each other. "We—we could run away. I'm of age. I don't have to marry Chance, even if he still wants me. Why immolate ourselves?"

"Our 'immolation' doesn't require our presence, Candacy Ann." Sadly, adamantly Starcross turned away from her again. "Your father would know just the same."

"Yes—but we wouldn't have to face him."

"And not just that, there'd be *worse* for him to know: that we were cowards as well as traitors. That would be 'immolation' for me indeed, whether I faced him over it or not." His jaw set like concrete. "I'm hardly in the habit of running away, Candacy Ann. I may have betrayed my best friend and my foster-father, but I won't run away from the fact. I may have violated the spirit of my obligations but I won't violate the letter as well. I'll make my own hard choices; I won't make Chance's for him."

"Oh, I'm sure you're right, Webb—dear Webb. It just seems so—so *unfair.* What did we *do,* so awful, to be so punished? Why do there have to be such consequences? Oh, why does life have to be so complicated? Why can't it all be just as it was? We were such *friends,* you and Chance and I. Even the other night, to hear you two tell it, nothing could ever have parted us."

"We were children, Candacy Ann—*you* were, even then. You were trying to go on being a child. Chance too, in his way. I may have my own lapses, but for the most part I stopped being a child when I watched my parents and brothers being cut to pieces by the Comanches." Heaving a sigh, he drew her to himself. "From that moment I knew *loss* as just the human condition. Sooner or later we lose everything, even ourselves."

"Tell me, Webb." Her voice quavered. "What if Chance does still want me, after all? What then?"

"For you and me, you mean? You want me to say nothing'll change, that what's between us will go on regardless, nurtured in secret? Oh, Candacy Ann! What I feel for you, my love, will go on the same, yes; but it will be, will *have* to be, love from afar." He grasped the door-pull. "I couldn't bear to live near Chance."

"Yes; that's just what I would expect from you, Webb—my Galahad!" Visibly, mournfully she shriveled into herself. "Today, then, tonight, is . . . will be the last?"

"I'm hardly in the mood for it. Still, I reckon we can scarcely worsen our guilt at this late date. If we're going to be 'immolated' one way as well as the other, I suppose we might as well wring whatever consolation—commiseration—we can out of deserving it. And anyhow, one ought always to live as if each day or night of one's life were the last." His would-be cheer gave up the ghost. "Something I learned long ago on the Texas Plains."

TWELVE

"Nothing has changed," Candacy Ann murmured, seemingly unconscious of the irony, as the small sternwheeler *Wakanda* rounded the exquisitely familiar river bend and the proud, white, pillared face of Richwood house glowed miragelike in the April morning sun high on its hill like a Greek temple, and at river level beneath it the smudged small speck of the private dock, and the smaller specks waiting upon it, steadily enlarged.

"Only we." At the promenade deck's rail, Starcross moved closer to her side, laid an arm around her shoulders. When she looked around, his smile was typically bleak.

Her own look was even bleaker. "I'm starting to know how a criminal must feel on the way to his hanging."

"Take it as it comes," he reminded, reproved, though he felt the same. "Such a pleasant morning for a homecoming."

Starcross had spent his last free hours in St. Louis seeking to trace Chance Buckhannon. It had proved difficult at first. Chance had told almost nobody where he was staying, for reasons Starcross could well understand when, at last, he found and scouted out the run-down boarding hotel in a sleazy district, spoke to the manager, and had his hunch confirmed: Chance had surrendered his room suddenly around midday. His arm being in a sling hadn't seemed to interfere with his haste or resolve. He could have taken an earlier boat or else the train to Jefferson City, therefrom by ferry and stagecoach the brief remaining distance home, either way arriving well before Starcross and Candacy Ann.

Starcross had kept none of this from his companion, though it could only add to her gloom, as to his. Having dined a last time with the Aments, they'd paid the *maison de rendezvous* too a last homage—done their best to eat, drink, and be merry for the time-honored reason, but with ill success. And on the voyage itself had communed hardly at all, he paying her stateroom no clandestine call, their shared anxieties seeming to sunder far more than unite them. Now Starcross found the strained young face there by his side as eerily unrevealing as a mirror-image.

This last leg of their long pilgrimage was relatively, mercifully brief. The *Wakanda,* bound for Fort Leavenworth, stopped on signal at private docks like Richwood's, albeit such privileged traffic was much reduced since piping prewar peacetime. Their boat moved all but alone in the vast river where once it would never have been out of sight of other vessels, or hearing of their shrill salutes; Richwood's dock would have teemed with ebon forms chanting as they heaved tobacco and hemp bales. The fields in the background, now fallow and under siege by the roundabout wilds, would have worn a manicured, bountiful look. It was anything but true, then, that nothing had changed. The house, from afar, might look timeless, but almost more as geological outcrop than life-sign. And biding river and bluffs but threw the human changes into sad relief. As the *Wakanda* neared, and Starcross made out Duncan Colquhoun and the two servants waiting on the dock beneath the signal staff, eerily he was taken back all the way to his first coming here—far longer ago, it seemed, than fifteen years, the colonel at his side instead of before him, himself the scrawny, forlorn youth of Candacy Ann's evocation, the images of his butchered family still aflicker in his eyes and in the white knuckles of the hand that gripped the saber it gripped even now, knuckles as white as then, if for rather another reason. Well, he chid himself, if a ten-year-old could live through the loss of nigh his all, a man could live down the loss of what was left.

The moment came at last. Briskly lines were passed to the dock, the gangplank went down, deck crew scurried, shouldering the heavier pieces of Candacy Ann's luggage. The passengers disembarked toward the waiting faces on the dock, and almost before the bewildering first brunt of meeting and greeting was begun, hands and gangplank alike had withdrawn back aboard, and with a gay whistle-adieu the *Wakanda* backed toward mid-channel and turned upstream, battling the sluggish seaward surge on its long, labored steam to the edge of the prairies.

"Webb—dear boy!" Taken up with his daughter while Starcross lost himself seeing to the luggage, Colonel Colquhoun spoke over her shoulder. He moved forward, bringing her along, and grasped Starcross's hand. Then, dissatisfied, he took his other arm from around her and wrapped both around Starcross. "Listen to me!" he laughed. "I should be saluting and saying 'Sir'!"

"I must get out of this uniform," Starcross muttered.

"Don't be in a hurry. Let folks hereabouts see you first."

Starcross could only respond in kind to the colonel's fond embrace and friendly, bantering words; for his affection for the older man was real and deep. His every instinct was to read reserve in the colonel's effusions; though even if real it might've been but weariness, the toll of creeping eld. For this was what struck Starcross with most force. Not since leaving the state in the first year of the war had he seen the older man, and the changes in him were dismaying. His once tall, heavy, wiry frame moved with a steady stoop and with seeming difficulty. His hair, luxuriant yet, had turned snowy. Deep lines scored his kindly face. Still, his exuberance endured. Starcross turned to trade greetings with Mammy Tirzah, who it seemed had changed not at all, calling him "Masta Webb" as if years hadn't passed; and with her overawed simple son Zadok, grown startlingly in body if not otherwise. But Colonel Colquhoun soon reasserted his ascendancy.

"How grand to have you home, you both!" Placing himself between the two arrivals, he looked from one to the other. "Isn't our Webb something to look at, daughter? Dip him in bronze and he'll be ready for the courthouse lawn!"

"Better a bronze coat than the coat he's wearing," perfunctorily Candacy Ann sniffed.

"Speaking of something to look at"—Starcross nodded at *her* —"why, I'm not even in the running."

"Indeed." Her father eyed her closely, affecting uncertainty. "Are you *quite* sure you've brought me back the *right* young lady, Webb? That hoyden I sent away so few years ago?"

"So few?" Candacy Ann heaved a sigh. "Oh dear. It seems a thousand. Another life."

"Yes," echoed the colonel. "It does. Was."

"And we were just saying nothing has changed!"

Starcross could rein in his curiosity no longer. "Chance," he asked, would-be-casually, "Chance has reached home?"

"Oh yes," said the colonel absently. "Only yesterday, in fact. He called—I tried to prevail on him to put up with us, but he's staying in town. You'll see him this evening. I've laid on a little get-together," the colonel added, "a homecoming party, so to speak, for Candacy Ann—for us all. It won't amount to much by the standards of the old days, I'm afraid. Things are a bit . . . pinched at present; but we'll do the best we can. It's a grand day, after all, a time for thanksgiving—in more ways than one."

The colonel's words, blithe yet cryptic somehow, more than ever confirmed Starcross in his foreboding. Chance had come out of his way to call on the colonel—and then taken himself off, as it were not to have to face Starcross and Candacy Ann till the time and place of his choosing—his and the colonel's.

As they walked up the steep path to the house, however, other sensations, the paradoxical impressions of homecoming, equally dismaying in their own way, assailed and distracted him. At every hand sad signs of change jarred and warred with heartening images of spooky familiarity. Unkempt grounds, untended fields, quarters and outbuildings lonely and run-down—Richwood was the wartime South in little, a South with which Starcross was all too familiar: the hands driven off by their "liberators" or straggled off in their wake; the homeland's spirit conscripted to the cause, the defense of the substance, and vice versa, even the spirit lost in the end. Mammy Tirzah and Zadok—the latter bringing up the rear bent double under Candacy Ann's trunk—were the only ex-slaves, confirmed the colonel, who'd stayed on out of choice; the handful of aged and infirm counted only as debits. Starcross withheld comment—time enough for *that* unpleasantness too. Clearly the colonel was content enough just in the hour, in the reunion with his daughter, whatever estranging knowledge he might harbor. Let him be the one to let himself down, choose his moment. For Starcross, a marked feeling of relief was surging like a countercurrent against the tide of his anxiety. However poorly, he had discharged a duty, discharged it to the letter at least, and to the best of his abilities and character. Nothing was left for him to do, then, but stand at ease if he could, for the first time in so long, and await the colonel's pleasure—or otherwise.

And he was able to do so in his own company, retreating following the sparse homecoming meal to his room, his own bedroom upstairs, where he'd lived as a boy and where, eerily, many of his belongings still reposed, almost just as he'd thrown them down on his last day before going away to school. The nostalgic stirrings only worsened his sense of loss and exile. And buried beneath his present, secondary anxiety, of course, was that *first* anxiety, however little allowed up into consciousness of late. Happily habit let him rest even under the most trying of circumstances. Sprawled on the big tester bed he lapsed into deep, dreamless sleep and awoke refreshed, startled to see how far the slanted sunbeams had stolen over the floor, how blue the shades had turned. His valise had been unpacked, his military best reverently pressed and laid out—the household's standards might have fallen off but, thanks to Mammy Tirzah, they hadn't collapsed. Starcross abluted and dressed himself with care, a man resolved to cut the most imposing figure he could at his hanging.

He found the colonel sitting on the veranda overlooking the river, where, before they'd managed to exchange more than a few superficialities, Candacy Ann joined them, fresh-faced from her own siesta, and where Mammy Tirzah soon served tea, doubtless doled out of a precious and dwindling stock. Late-afternoon tea was a time-honored rite at Richwood, lavish and often supplanting supper altogether—as perforce would be the case this evening, since the house's resources no longer ran to entertaining a large company at table. The tea, augmented by the dregs of the wine cellar, would simply be stretched, in both time and quantity, to accommodate the guests, the first of whom soon began to arrive, in their patched antique partying best, on a motley assortment of wobbly wheels and broken-down steeds.

For Starcross it was a strange evening, at times approaching total unreality. The forced, frenetic gaiety of guests and hosts contrasted grotesquely with his own inner state. Surrounded by figures most all familiar and friendly, he felt hopelessly isolated and alone, though not because he wore the uniform of their recent enemies. To these tatters of the county plantation gentry, men and women who had survived the war but at great cost, Webb Starcross remained above all a local boy who'd gone away and made good; if not quite still one of themselves not quite a renegade either, the enemy, in his imposing if disliked uniform. Little of the loud partisanship that had echoed over these opulent, rolling hills back in 1861 was to be heard nowadays. Indeed, the talk of the evening hardly rose above a murmur, and was mostly of who had survived the war and in what condition; and even the brightest voices bore strains of sadness, being unable to remark the survivors without remarking the absent, the myriad young men now filling lost, shallow graves in Tennessee or Mississippi. Whether in deference to Starcross's allegiance, or simply as an effort on the colonel's part to face reality, a handful of Union men had been invited, not only longstanding residents of known character and tolerated politics but outsiders too, started up out of the local mudsills or newly arrived from more Northern climes, unsavory creatures perhaps but of too vital importance to the neighborhood's immediate future to be snubbed.

"You expected Chance, you said—" Starcross ventured.

"Oh, he'll be here, I'm sure."

Several older men had brought musical instruments, and the broad ballroom forming one side of the house was thrown open and illumined with precious candles; but even while the homespun festivity seemed gratifying to the rest of the gathering, to Starcross it only added a further note of despair. It helped none that images of *another* festive evening in this very room—images centered around the haunting image of a face—kept forcing their way, in spite of him, up out of his very depths.

The long, serene spring evening had given way to full dark when, with a little fanfare, the players broke off their sequence of dated musical numbers, and Colonel Colquhoun moved to the head of the room. As the assemblage fell silent Starcross, stranded more or less in the middle, started to turn full circle to take stock of the motley forms and faces around him, only to find himself frozen in mid-turn at sight of Chance Buckhannon framed in the open veranda door, walking stick grasped in his left hand, his right arm in a sling. But before he could react, could move, even if he'd known which way to move, the old colonel was speaking. With a feeling of being beset from both sides at once Starcross tore his eyes away from Chance, finished his full turn.

"Good friends!" The colonel's exuberant manner soon had the room's full attention. "Welcome to Richwood. This is a great, solemn day for me, and I want to share it with you all. Most every one of us is burdened by thought of those who would have been here with us on such a night in times past; but surely our proper homage to them is to give thanks that the terrible war is over at last, and, while never, ever forgetting those who are with us no more, to bear ourselves with humility and forgiveness one toward another. Let us rejoice in those who have been spared, as in the season's assurances all about us of life going on.

"I ask you in particular to join me in heartfelt thanks for the safe return home of my daughter Candacy Ann—the child I sent away five long years ago, now returned to me a finished young lady, hardly recognizable, I confess." Laughter laced the flutter of applause. "But I invited you here tonight, my friends and neighbors, not for that alone. It would be too much to expect that a young woman of Candacy Ann's years and maturity of judgment should not by this time have made the most important decision of her life. She has, and she has made it known to me. It comes as not quite the complete surprise to me that it may to some of you. Even when appearances suggested otherwise, I think I always knew, deep down, that Candacy Ann would make the choice she has; and no choice could be more profoundly gratifying to me; for her young man is one whom I hold nearer and dearer than anyone on earth save only herself. As well as the love of a father for a son, I have the highest regard for him as a man. In his chosen profession he has covered himself with honor and glory beyond my poor powers to tell—it needn't be told in any case; you all know the story as well as I. While he and I haven't always seen things alike, never, *never* has a harsh word passed between us; and never have I been so reminded that love, friendship, mutual regard are the essence of life, its very foundation, while opinions, 'causes,' even the wars they breed, are but passing phantoms.

"To most of you, of course, it will come as no surprise that I refer to my foster-son, the son of the oldest, closest friend of my greener days, who came to live under my roof in sorriest circumstances when he was but a lad of ten." The colonel beamed, savoring his words. "And tonight I have the grateful opportunity and the *right* at last to call him, not just foster-son, but *son* indeed, and for more than one reason. Friends, neighbors, guests—it is my great honor and pleasure to announce the betrothal of my beloved daughter Candacy Ann to my beloved foster-son—my *son*—the renowned Major General Webb Starcross!"

Through the long speech, Starcross had stood riveted, his sense of bizarre inevitability increasing along with his understanding, which seemed to fly right ahead of the colonel's words themselves, anticipating them, if only just. A thousand contradictory impulses surged through his breast. Dimly he was aware of the room around him starting to react, a first reaction essentially similar to his own: *Well, but of course—it's just what we should have expected!* Remotely he felt the murmuring figures closing in on him with their well-wishings and hearty outthrust hands; but they had no real existence for him, no meaning. Unable to move, he turned in place, readying to search the rear of the room near the door for a further merest glimpse of Chance, half-expecting not to see him—for him to have faded back into the night.

But he was being unfair to Chance. Chance, it seemed, even as the colonel held all eyes and ears, had made his steady way forward; for the half-turn brought Starcross face-to-face with him: with the man he'd last faced at thirty paces over pistols, and the last before that at the point of a fist in the Planter's House bar. It may have been all his imagination but the crowd seemed to back away from the two of them, leave them alone together there at the room's heart, as if to give them space for the about-to-be *pas de deux,* if not put themselves out of the way of its possible violence. Chance, indeed, had his stick yet in his left hand; and his face was unreadable. As for Starcross, he still had recovered his powers neither of movement nor of speech. Had the stick started to descend toward his head he couldn't have moved out of its way. But when Chance stirred it was only, by a deft sleight, to shift the stick to the fingers of his other hand, his right, where it thrust useless from the sling. And then, after only a brief if breathless moment, he thrust out the emptied left, upturned.

"Let me be the first to congratulate you, Webb," he said gently, breaking into a wry, wan grin, glancing genially around at the watching faces. When the eyes came back to Starcross they were more serious—a bit more. "Looks like the only way I'll ever be the 'best man,' so I'd better make the most of it, eh?"

The crowd, animated by these noble if cryptic utterances, would be denied no longer, pressed forward with its handclasps and hearty backslaps, its cheek-pecks in the women's cases, separating the two men. Starcross soon gave up his bootless struggle to keep Chance in view, to hold onto that sense of desperately desired contact in the hope of elucidation, enlightenment. In the turmoil his eyes, *all* eyes, inexorably were drawn yet again to the head of the room, to the now side-by-side figures of Colonel Colquhoun and Candacy Ann, themselves besieged by well-wishers. As his powers of movement seeped back he began, if only by sheer reflex or instinct of duty, to force his way forward to join them, as so clearly was called for, the colonel and his daughter being an eloquently incomplete group at such a moment; and indeed Candacy Ann's delighted, exultant eyes brightly, mindlessly beckoning him over the intervening heads.

Still, Candacy Ann's face lacked for him the reality, the all-embracing importance it just then ought to have had. Even as he fought through to her side at last, linked hands with her and the colonel alike, then turned to face the throng—the captive animal of the occasion, publicly displayed by the captors—even as he leaned to kiss her, that other so clearly called-for action, and then gazed into those eyes, desperately questing, and found no recognition in them, no sense of mutual predicament, only a dreamy, heedless bliss, it was not *her* face he beheld at all, that bright, beaming, shallow face. For superimposed over it, for him all but bodily, was another face altogether—that ghostly if unghostlike face out of the exquisite past: the fiery-pink, jade-eyed, pensive, protean, profound face of Cathal McQuaife.

THIRTEEN

"I hope it wasn't too tremendous a shock for you last night, my boy," the colonel said apologetically. "An old man must be indulged his little whims." They sat facing each other over breakfast in the colonel's tall-windowed, sunny study. The hour was early. Candacy Ann had yet to come down.

"It was a . . . surprise, I grant." Starcross chose his words with care. "You might have given me a hint, at least."

"In more leisurely days, certainly I would have done so. So many things we'd do differently in other, more settled days." Delicately the colonel cleared his throat. "Delay, a more . . . measured approach, I trust, would have made no difference."

"Oh, no, sir. Of course not. It's just that—you gave me no chance to remind you: I'm a relatively poor man. You may have lost sight of that, what with so much else on your mind. I was amazed recently to notice the government's actually paying me eight thousand a year; and of course the little bit my father left, which you so wisely invested in New York, is safe and has grown, what with the army supporting me in my simple style. Still, by Richwood standards it isn't much. I don't even own a roof over my head. The most I can ever hope to offer Candacy Ann, sir, is a Spartan life in a series of officers' quarters, likely in some of the roughest posts in the West. She's used to gentler, grander things; she deserves better than I can give her." He looked penetratingly, almost appealingly, at the colonel. "It's hardly a secret she once expected better—that you expected better for her."

"'Better?' The colonel waved the quibble away. "There *is* no 'better' any more, Webb—not for our likes. I need hardly remind you of the tragically reduced fortunes of our neighbor and friend, who, indeed, once figured so intimately in Candacy Ann's 'better' expectations—and, oh aye, my own."

"Well—just so you understand," Starcross fretted, "though I wonder if Candacy Ann does." He and the colonel were not exchanging confidences, he sensed; they were sparring with each other. "For that matter I wonder if the lot of an impoverished gentleman, hero of a lost cause, isn't equal to that of a middling general officer whose little glory, whatever it amounted to, lies behind him. The army, you know, Colonel, will shortly undergo a drastic contraction. I'll be lucky to be just a colonel again, and in future operations out West there'll be few openings for advancement, as well as ferocious competition for them."

"Ah, you're such a modest fellow, Webb. Need I remind you—Candacy Ann may be used to easy circumstances, but she comes of sturdiest pioneer stock. Her grandmother enjoyed an equally gentle upbringing in Virginia, but she did quite well on the Kentucky frontier, a rougher place than any Western post in our day. Women are tougher, more adaptable than we fancy. Candacy Ann will adapt—nay, thrive. Above all women want security, not drama and adventure; and security is just what the army in peacetime amounts to—I speak from experience." The colonel smiled. "It might almost be said to be *made* for women. *You're* the one apt to find it unrewarding, chafing, Webb, not Candacy Ann at all. I can just see her presiding over your string of frontier posts, consort of the commandant, the war hero, the man of her choice, her heart's desire; mistress of all she surveys! Dear me, yes, it's the fulfillment of any woman's dreams."

"I trust you're right, sir." Starcross gave back the smile.

"Your frankness becomes you, Webb," the colonel resumed, fidgeting in his chair, "and certainly I owe you frankness in return. You warn me of your comparative poverty. It's my sad duty to tell you of my absolute poverty. There will be no jointure for Candacy Ann, no dowry. It will strain my resources even to give her the kind of wedding she's always expected and that I'd always meant for her. My sort, you know, have been badly damaged—nay, ruined, by the war. My own bad judgment made it all worse. My active days, you know, were spent in the army. My father ran Richwood while he lived; and afterwards I hired an overseer and bemused myself with politics. Times were good, the land was rich, and seemed able to keep me rich without my attention.

"Then the times turned ugly; Mr. Rattery—my last overseer, you know; he was a Yankee, and he went home. I resolved to run Richwood on my own, though I was no planter, no businessman. After only one or two seasons I was in difficulty. Added to which, I wasn't cynical enough to put self-interest—nay, self-preservation —before partisan loyalty. My investments in the Cause, in that heady air of early 1861, were cast in limbo almost at once, and sank ever deeper as the war went against us, and above all as the new men who took over made it clear their objective was to ruin us, the planter class, the old governing class, once and for all. My early outspokenness made me a special object of their attentions. My taxes were doubled, and doubled again—the assessors and collectors and law enforcers being prewar odd-job-men, cobblers and the likes, if not mere layabouts, failures with a born hatred of success and its rewards. At the same time Jayhawkers and our own militiamen divided their time between sheer theft, pillage, and agitating and forced 'liberating' among the slaves. My hands and those of my neighbors drifted or were driven away, at first by twos and threes, then *en masse*—the slave patrol, of course, died along with the old government. Slavery wasn't ended by law till January of this year, but for all practical purposes ceased to exist years ago. One can hire the hands back—in theory; but they've been given the pernicious notion they need no longer work at all; on top of which, few of us have left the wherewithal to pay them. For the third spring I'm having to sit at these windows and watch my fields lie fallow, going back to wilderness. And the house, kept up or no, is a millstone 'round my neck. When the taxes come due again, in the fall, and no crop made, I'll be bankrupt. I may well lose it, every acre. And with all the county in much the same embarrassment, it will pass at a bargain price to some damned mudsill who turned his coat at just the right moment, or some scoundrel of a Yankee who made his fortune outfitting your troops in shoddy or feeding them weevily bread!"

"I wish there was something I could do," Starcross said with feeling. "I did what I could in the South to prevent outrages against the people, and punished those who committed them. But I'm not here at the head of an army, and I don't think my mere word would carry much weight. Still, if there's anything—"

The colonel headshook. "To the self-righteous pirates in the saddle hereabouts, you're as good as one of us. It makes no odds you've spent the past few years making the world safe for their likes. Just as it makes no odds I took the oath."

"Needless to add, my mite is at your disposal."

"You'd just as well toss it down a well. I'd far rather see it husbanded for Candacy Ann, for your future together."

Starcross could put it off no longer. "Colonel, you've mentioned Chance's . . . poverty. But that wasn't his reason, or his only or chief reason, for—for withdrawing his suit."

"Well—" His eyes faltering, the colonel dabbed at his mouth with his napkin.

"I must go and see him. But first I need to have at least some sense of—of what passed between you." Starcross pressed, "You said you owed me frankness, sir."

The colonel nodded. "Oh, it's nothing to be kept from you. Chance was the soul of delicacy. His first impulse, he said, he being only human, was to accuse you of dishonorable behavior. Of course I'd wanted to know about his arm. When he told me, my first thought, aside from relief, was what a prize pair of fools you'd been, you both, but above all he—he agreed. Yet it was the duel itself, he said, that brought him to his senses—the shock and pain of the ball, oddly, killed both his anger and his illusions; he saw clearly the fool he was being. Clearly Candacy Ann had made her choice—Chance knew you well enough to know that must be the case. And anyhow, what had he any longer to offer her? Their 'understanding' had never been more than implied, never a thing of passion; and there was no passion, he said, in their reunion. The passion lay elsewhere, clearly, and he simply couldn't stand in its way, at the cost of two precious friendships. The only decent thing for him to do, then, was to bow out with grace—to hurry home and explain to me why he must, and make clear that no blame attached to you or to Candacy Ann."

"I can't agree," Starcross mourned. "I betrayed you both."

"Nonsense," the colonel boomed, his hearty self again. He bounded from his chair. "Yes indeed; go and see him, by all means; let there be no lingering lack of understanding between you—no more than between you and me, my dear Webb. You'll find him in Bolton Green, at Mrs. Hogsett's. We've precious little left in the way of real horseflesh, but old Jethro, out in the stable, will find you something at least with four legs."

Not waiting for Candacy Ann, Starcross set off straight after breakfast, mounted on a bony, broken-down but willing old nag led out of the great, gloomy, ghostly stable and rigged with worn saddle and patched leathers by an abjectly apologetic, equally-broken-down old Jethro. Wryly ruing Rustam, waiting with Zurdo in St. Louis, Starcross walked the old horse through the peaceful, greening countryside, so full of the images of his youth, at first feeling his spirits lift, his misgivings recede.

But the familiar, again, lay in too jarring contrast with the strange. The old was too much overshadowed by the new, none of it pleasant. At every turn of the road, it seemed, lay an untilled, brush-grown field, a tumbled or burnt or vanished rail fence, a home, cabin or mansion, untended and untenanted, or the place that had *been* a home marked now but by a forlorn chimney, or perhaps, more forlorn still, a little mound of raw earth topped by a rude headboard scrawled with a familiar name.

The panorama of little tragedies culminated, for Starcross, at the stately gateway to Treen, the great Buckhannon plantation, the mighty Greek Revival mansion that once had reared Olympuslike on its low hill amid its glades and rich fields. He sat there letting the old horse rest, looking on the chipped, blackened Corinthian columns and the ragged roofless gable apexes, sadness assailing him like vertigo, till he could bear it no more, and reined away and rode on, trying to lose himself in the biding assurances of nature resurgent all about, the birdsong and the verdure and the bloom. Nature, at least, endured; albeit it was raw, wild nature, not underpinning or ornamenting or complementing the world of man, as in memory, but the contrary, swiftly effacing its every trace, blotting the very remembrance of it, creeping over the forsaken fields and into the dooryards, covering the crumbling walls.

Between his scant luggage and an old wardrobe in his room Starcross had managed to dress for the country and the occasion, though quite aware that his military bearing shone right through rough corduroy breeches, cowhide boots, and planter's hat. Most of those he met along the way knew him for what he was, and *whom* he was, knew him above all as Colonel Colquhoun's prospective son-in-law—for news of that momentous development clearly had spread with the usual rural speed.

Never a large or a lively place, Bolton Green seemed to have shrunken in the years since he'd seen it last. Purposely sited at the county's center, as its seat, stirring to life only during court sessions, it had never shared the busy life of the older settlements and plantations along the river. Complacently it awaited the railroad that must surely, without effort, make it a great city. Clearly the railroad had yet to come. A lone row of false-fronted stores amid little clusters of tree-shrouded homes, it wore a dilapidated, half-deserted air. Those few figures out and about seemed frozen in place, like the pixilated denizens of a fairytale village. Starcross walked the horse slowly along the dirt street, aware of unseen eyes following his progress. At the farther end of the business block he vaulted off and looped the reins on a canted hitching rail. Here, a few feet back behind mighty, ancient sugar maples, stood Mrs. Hogsett's, a rambling frame wrapped in a veranda, a village landmark, its best pretensions toward a hostelry. Crossing the broad veranda, entering the parlor, he met no sign of the landlady; but a guest, from behind a skimpy newssheet, directed him; and when he climbed the stairs and knocked on the designated door, "Come in, Webb," Chance's voice called out at once.

He sat before the front window, carelessly clad in trousers and a rumpled robe, a glass in his hand, a nigh-empty unlabeled bottle on the small table close by his side.

"You were looking for me, then?"

"Saw you ride up, on your mighty steed." Chance gestured at the front window, spilling a few drops in the process. "But, yes, I was looking for you, I reckon. Sit down, Webb. And pardon me for not getting up—it's an undertaking."

Starcross gave the spare yet cluttered room a covert cast about. He took a pile of clothes from a straight chair.

"You rather rushed off last night," he said. "You were there, and then you weren't."

"Hardly wanted to steal the principals' thunder." Blearily Chance smiled. "Drink?" The offer politely declined, he topped his own glass. "A bit early in the day to get drunk, aye, but the leg's giving me holy hell this morning. Last night's ride out to Richwood, I reckon, on a bag of bones to match your own."

"And the arm? I see you're not wearing the sling."

"Well, I'm not hitting anybody in the jaw this morning either." Chance made a wry face. "Oh, it's mending. Stiff, sore, but mending. Takes more than an ounce ball in the armpit to do down a bullet-riddled old campaigner like me."

"Thank God for that—and no thanks to me."

"To *me,* you mean. I was out of my mind, you know, Webb —plumb out of my damnfool wits."

"I wish I could offer as good an excuse."

"Excuse? What is there to excuse, in your case? But *me!* Those things I said—inexcusable; unforgivable. I'd like to think that wasn't *me* talking, Webb, the real me. But that's asking too much. I must own it all, all I said and did."

"I had faith it wasn't the real you, Chance. We all have more than one self in us, the best of us has a devil as well as an angel. But I must say, Chance—*your* angel and devil certainly come and go, blow hot and cold. I can't keep up with them."

"Oh, we cavaliers, you know," Chance laughed, "we wear our hearts on our sleeves—and chips on our shoulders, too, half the time. Quick to war, quick to peace."

"That augurs well for the future of the country—our forcibly reunited country."

"Well, I couldn't say about that. I was arguing *ad hominem.* We're good at it, we bonehead cavaliers. But I'm not so sure as much applies to society." Grimly, "One can harbor a social grudge without begrudging any particular person."

"You have every reason for harboring a grudge against this particular person, Chance."

"Oh, Webb, that's nonsense. Thank heavens I came to my senses and saw it. Oh, I was outraged at you, all right, and I won't deny it was on my own account. But believe me, chiefly it was on

Candacy Ann's account. My reaction was just what you'd expect of a bonehead cavalier. You'd dishonored her, egad! You'd done her wrong; and not just *any* woman—though I trust I'd have been properly outraged in any case—but one over whom I'd fancied myself protector, of a sort, if not quite proprietor. I was just too blind-angry, too outraged to see, to face up to the obvious: that Candacy Ann had chosen for herself. She isn't quite the fragile flower we sometimes like making her out. I'll wager *she* had as much to do with . . . what happened, as you did."

"I don't know," Starcross confessed. "I'm not all that clear about what *did* happen, any of it. All I know for sure is, I had no intention of letting it happen—anything. Candacy Ann was yours; and you were my friend; and that was that."

"You were being too generous, too selfless, as ever. Our little 'interview' brought it right home to *me,* on the other hand, that the real wrong, the real dishonor, would be for me to try to hold Candacy Ann to some vague childhood pledge, a thing she clearly had no heart left for. And what did I any longer have to offer her, but a broken pocketbook and an all-but-broken body, a fellow without a trade or a prospect, who drinks to ease his pains—" Chance's smile turned a trifle less grim. "Tell me, how does it feel to be a famous major general on the winning side?"

"Unreal." Starcross shrugged, bemused. "*Sic transit gloria,* etcetera. What profit it a man to gain the whole world and so forth—it's all true after all. But, Chance," soberly, "Candacy Ann wouldn't have forsaken you just because of your—your misfortunes. She too has her angel and devil, and I trust the devil isn't quite so in the ascendant as you hint. At least," he laughed, "we can be sure it wasn't the uniform that swayed her!"

"It was the uniform that was your undoing in another sense. I can't say I had any real suspicions, though Candacy Ann's brightness toward you was hard not to notice. She's not as good at keeping her feelings hidden as you. But then a man came to see me, a grubby little busybody out of our mutual past. Probably you wouldn't have known him, but he knew you. It was on the boat from Cincinnati. Everybody on board, it seems, was full of the Yankee major general and his, ahem, foster-sister. What did I do? I hit him with my stick! He wasn't offended; went away actually still expecting I'd redirect my wrath and get around to rewarding him. Well, and I *did* redirect my wrath, didn't I? Deny it as I might, I knew it was true; and the evidence—St. Louis isn't *that* full of damnfool major generals walking into houses of assignation in uniform! I was cut to the quick. I went off and got drunk. I was drunk that evening in the Planter's House bar, I hope you know that. God A'mighty, speaking of damn fools—!"

"You didn't look anything like the fool that I felt," Starcross muttered, grimly shook his head. "It was the lowest moment of my life. I just prayed your aim would be true."

"My rage undid me, or more correctly saved me, saved us both, above all after you threw away your first shot. That really sent me over the edge. It wasn't till afterwards, till the pain in my arm overcame that in my heart"—Chance's voice faltered—"that I knew what a mistake I'd made, or come damned near making, faced up to my damnfoolishness. *Knew* I didn't want to shoot you over Candacy Ann, over her honor or my own." From his depths, shyly: "Didn't even want to stay at outs with you."

"You're a forgiving, generous man, Chance. All heart."

"No—all head, I'd say. For once!"

Starcross thought it over. "And does your head have anything to tell you about your own future, early wedlock being out?"

Chance shrugged. "There's no future for me here, at least. I'll soon have to go back to St. Louis and look for a living, I reckon, selling shoelaces or the like. I can't *do* anything, you know, anything in demand. I'm a planter without a plantation, a soldier without an army. And there's aplenty of both about."

"But your a resourceful, resilient man, Chance. I'm sure you'll find something. If I can help you I will, it goes without saying. Tell me"—Starcross switched subjects—"what of Colonel Colquhoun? He confided in me this morning. Tantalized me."

Chance grimaced. "To be brutally frank, I don't see any way out for the colonel. There's nothing *you* can do, for a start. You've no idea the kind of men on top of the heap hereabouts just now. And since martial law ended there's no way of bringing pressure on them from above. Our so-called state government answers to no one, and it's just the upper echelon of the county despotism—the higher-up highway robbers, so to speak."

"What a prospect! Makes me wish I'd gone abroad ages ago, never heard of the accursed war." Starcross smiled wanly, wryly. "Candacy Ann fancies my taking the 'wrong' side was heaven's way of making the world safe for her and hers."

"Dear old Candacy Ann! What a blessing, a solace she won't have to go down in squalid ruin with the rest of us—with me. It would be so much harder, sadder for her."

"You won't go down, Chance. We won't let you, Candacy Ann and I. We're still three, as ever, not just two. Through it all I've never been able to look at her without guiltily asking myself, 'But what about Chance?' I still can't."

"Oh, Webb, you blithering fool. You're the grimmest, most diffident triumphant suitor I've ever crossed paths with. 'Guilty'? What *is* it with you? Just cold feet? Or . . . or do you have doubts after all? About—about Candacy Ann, I mean."

"I have more on my conscience than Candacy Ann, Chance."

"Ah"—Chance's bleary eyes grew clairvoyant—"a woman! That's it, isn't it? Another woman."

Starcross's nod was lost in his headshaking wretchedness. "You've heard it, surely, heard whispers of it. It must have been the most public 'private' affair of all the war." Tersely, confessionally he told his friend the whole tale of his encounter with Cathal McQuaife. "I reckoned without a father's wrath—another cavalier—not to say the war's worse wrath."

"I *did* get wind of it, much garbled—I was a long way away at the time. My amazement knew no bounds. I remember thinking in a way it sounded like you up and down, the Webb Starcross I knew; yet in another like anybody on earth but."

"Yes." Starcross went on, words dwindling to winces: "In Virginia I met General McQuaife. We . . . reached an understanding. I meant to pick up right where I'd left off, if I but could. We shook hands—he shook my hand! And then. . . ."

"Ah"—Chance sat forward, all understanding, himself feeling the other's anguish—"yes. And then Candacy Ann. What a rotten piece of luck! I didn't dream, old man. If I had—"

"No. You couldn't have done anything, anything different, shouldn't have." Starcross was all sudden self-blame. "I'm the one who should have . . . done something different."

Chance tried turning him to the irony of it, the other, ever-present comic side of the tragic human coin. "Huh, any other man but you, Webb, would've done something very different indeed—smelt what was coming and made himself scarce while he could, if his heart lay where I suspect yours truly lies."

"I couldn't do that. You know I couldn't."

"Yes. You weren't any other."

"I had no choice. The choice was made for me, by sheer proximity. The claims being equal, the nearer had to prevail. I've never believed in 'reasons of the heart', though I feel their power. No—my heart must go with the rest of me." He stood, turned to take his leave. "Heart? I must have no heart!"

"Far from it—you're all heart. You, not me. I *do* come to my senses sooner or later; my head takes over. I wonder . . . I almost wish it hadn't." Chance too struggled to his feet with some difficulty, heartfelt himself. "Webb, this is terrible."

"Indeed. Having betrayed you, I've now betrayed *them*. The difference being, to them I've no hope of ever making it up."

Chance seemed ready to go on doubting the prognosis, only to give the effort up at last. Between his thoughts, his game leg, and the whiskey, he stood swaying, in more ways than one. "'All heart' you called me! Webb, Webb, you put me to shame." Mellow, maudlin, tongue thickening, Chance held out his hand; Starcross took it; they traded thoughtful, feelingful looks.

At last Chance said it: "This won't do."

"No." Starcross caught him by the elbows. As with one will they embraced, almost overcome by the mutual muddle of their feelings. Most strongly of all Starcross felt the druglike relief of his sudden sense that, after all, he still had at least one real friend, one who could share his inmost thoughts—aches.

"It's getting to be a habit with me," Chance laughed, smacking him on the back, "this fraternizing with the enemy."

"The *late* enemy, make it, at least," Starcross corrected, hope-springing-eternal. "Or, no, not even that." Memories stirred, eerie, ambiguous, troubling. "The late *adversary.*"

FOURTEEN

Webb Starcross sat alone on a sun-warmed iron bench in the tiny center park of the little health resort improbably named Thermopolis, wedged in a steep, strait Ozark valley and mounting the surrounding timbered slopes. For half-a-dozen mornings had he so sat, digesting his hotel breakfast, going through the motions of reading his newspaper or his mail, more truly just watching the world pass by around him, the odd, cosmopolitan spa-town world, and in looking back; finding himself with leisure for looking back, it seemed, for the first time in more than a year.

There was much to look back on. It had been the fullest year of his life—hardly fuller than the war years, perhaps, but fuller of a greater variety of experiences: his marriage; his taking his temporary (he hoped) staff position at Departmental headquarters in St. Louis, setting up housekeeping in officers' quarters at Jefferson Barracks, the sprawling army camp on the city's southern fringes, beside the Mississippi; by stages easing Candacy Ann into military life, at the same time letting her be relatively close to her father; Chance Buckhanon's looming on the bourne of their life, working in a street-railway office and living alone in the city, socializing too little, as Starcross saw it, and drinking too much; lastly the blessed advent of Webb Starcross, Junior, fairly coinciding with the anything-but-blessed advent of Colonel Colquhoun—a wasted, palpably failing colonel, hobbling off the boat like the dazed survivor of a shipwreck, the image of the breakup of the ship that had been his world, his very life, the good ship Richwood, scored in his face;

the vague cluckings of the post physician and his prescription, at last, of a health resort, his chance suggestion of Thermopolis, a place of modest note for its would-be restorative waters, and of burgeoning renown since the war as a fashionable though still comparatively inexpensive summer social refuge from St. Louis's muggy river heat and metropolitan bustle.

Starcross had happened to have leave coming; and so had willingly brought his mushroomed ménage—Zurdo had gone home to his people, and traveling in mufti Starcross forwent an orderly; there was just Zadok, turned up as the colonel's appendage (Mammy Tirzah, feeling her years or likelier just resistant to transplant, had stayed behind with friends in Bolton Green), and Shuthelah, the maid Candacy Ann had found in the city—by rattling railroad and bonejarring coach over the hills to Thermopolis, and settled down in a hotel: a boxy brick edifice mellowed with New Orleans-style iron-grilled balconies, fronting the winding road that formed the town's main street, though at the same time by virtue of a crazy geography it also managed to overlook it from the hilly outskirts, and was fairly cut off from it by woods.

From its veranda, short, steep paths wove through the trees, past many small springs in their gingerbread gazebos, affording exercise along with the waters, onto the street and on down to the town's hub, where springs and the bathhouses clumped together around the little park. Here, due to some geological quirk, the waters bubbled from the earth at very high temperature, leaving clouds of steam ever hanging in the cool mountain air. Walkways were well furnished with benches, where the infirm might catch their breath and quaff their ration of the waters. Strolling entrepreneurs hawked cups of assorted materials and workmanship for rental or purchase, while from upper windows all about screamed down the blazoned names of healers of every persuasion, offering in all their ways to initiate the sufferer into the mysteries of balnealogy as well as kindred -ologies and -iatries.

Thermopolis, too, notwithstanding its tininess and isolation, was a crossroads. Every class, every corner of the continent, it seemed to Starcross, contributed to the crowds that wandered through the park on any given day. Himself a private, self-contained man, he was quite content to pass long periods reft of the close company of his fellow-creatures; but the spectacle they afforded, seen at a distance and from without, in his otherwise unoccupied hours he found entertaining enough.

And he had found himself with more than a few such hours since their coming to Thermopolis. Candacy Ann's energies were more than accounted for by the problems of keeping a hotel household in working order, added to the further concerns of motherhood and her special and waxing concern for her father, who had stepped, almost had to be lifted, from the coach, pasty-faced and nigh comatose, his soiled white suit tentlike over his wasted frame, and had not since responded to the waters, ever more spending his days in his room, if not in bed.

Although Starcross now saw himself as settled, thoroughly domesticated, in fact a twelvemonth of marriage had managed to make him no more domestic than ever. Candacy Ann foı her part seemed to see him as an impediment, less a helping hand even than Zadok to proper household or child- or invalid-tending operations; and he was content to leave these esoterica in her able hands, keep himself well out of the way, unless expressly called upon. Thus, perforce likewise deprived of his work, he found himself wholly on his own, and likely to remain so. Thrown back on his inner resources he tended to find them manifested, first, as noted, in looking over the new, strange place and its denizens, subjecting them to frankly military appraisals, laying out likely strategies and troop dispositions for taking or holding the position; second, again as noted, in looking back, mentally catching up, or doing his best, with the happenings of the past year and more, which had crowded on him too thick and fast to be coped with, threaded into the fabric of his life, as they'd come.

Yet the conclusion to which these reflections seemed to lead was that they just could not be. The past year was no seamless continuing of the warp of the years gone before, but a patch-on, of jarring color and pattern. There had been a complete break, a stark, violent splicing of one fabric on another.

The break itself, however, had had about it no whisper of violence. Even to the bridegroom it had been a most felicitous occasion, the wedding of Miss Candacy Ann Colquhoun and Major General Webb Starcross, taking place on a fine June morning in the same bare ballroom at Richwood where the betrothal had been announced. Colonel Colhuquon, as he'd himself foretold, had strained his resources to give his daughter a proper festive sendoff, and by and large his exertions had been crowned with success. All the world around had been invited, and had come to see and share the happiness of the bride, radiantly triumphant in her old and new, mostly old, in lace and train that lost nothing for having been pieced together in poverty and haste, alongside her leonine soldier in his dress blue, banded and braided and sashed with gold, tasseled saber scabbarded at his side.

But their eyes, had they managed to look under the surface, might have focused rather on a different couple—not the properly complementary principals but the bridegroom and his best man, between whom even in their so unlike attire there was so marked a likeness. Chance Buckhannon had begun to regain the flesh lost in prison camp; his face once more was nigh as full and square as his friend's; his light-brown mustache almost equally leonine. His gait had regained something of its old quickness, and he'd put aside his walking stick if not quite his other, more discreet crutch, whose continued use might have accounted for at least part of the fullness and hearty flush of his face. The itinerant photographer the colonel had found to memorialize the occasion, posing his subjects on the veranda, had contrived, by cutting the maid of honor in half, to include the whole of the best man—to frame the three figures, not the two, at his finished image's center. There they stood, then, for the ages, the smiling side-by-side figures, the three and the two of Starcross's memories, and of his ideals: the same three, if by no means the same two.

Candacy Ann, if surprised or puzzled by the wholehearted reconciliation of Starcross and Chance, had said nothing about it. Indeed, serious topics seemed to have flown from her thoughts altogether. Her bemused husband had trouble reaching her on any deeper plane, and found himself trying ever less.

Candacy Ann was bright enough. She could be serious if compelled, Starcross long knew or had learnt that; but in the absence of compulsion she shrank from the effort. And lately it was as if she saw all practical problems as solved, as having miraculously solved themselves, all the unhappy inconvenient compulsions of circumstances felicitously left behind. His continued efforts to ready her for army life, as a drab Spartan dispensation, elicited little interest or were dismissed out of hand.

Nevertheless, as the honeymoon gave way to more homely arrangements, of her Starcross found no cause to complain. Effortlessly she adjusted to their household situation, even as to the accompanying social life at Jefferson Barracks—or adjusted it to herself. The intimate aspect of their union, of course, held no surprises for either. It went on much as before, in Washington and on the journey West, albeit with predictably diminishing intensity. Now that it was a regular, reliable thing, no longer bearing that hectic, furtive, illicit urgency, it began to take on the nature rather of a familiar periodic comfort, taken for granted even though relished still, like a tidy, satisfying meal at the end of an appetite-whetting day. Candacy Ann in particular, Starcross sensed, was steadily losing interest, though she contrived to keep up a convincing wifely pretense. It was no more than he expected, and a matter of no great concern to him. His own energies were content to go on being sidetracked into other channels.

The army being still in the throes of shrinkage, Starcross had known that there might be delay in getting the desired field command in the West. But his marriage had not only made an early field assignment less desirable, it had removed the reason for that desire—though this was a train of thought he found uncomfortable to follow, and so eagerly, and guiltily, let himself be diverted from following. When offered the interim post of chief of staff to the commander of the Western Department, accordingly, he had accepted; the operative word, to his mind, being *interim.*

Still, his would-be-provisional new life had soon taken on a settled character, dismayingly conventional. He slept at home every night, took most of his meals there, and by day sat at a desk, moving about on paper the real soldiers of the real Western army —meantime struggling against the gravitylike force visibly overtaking so many about him, the seductive pull of security and ease. In self-defense he hewed to his old habit of taking daily rides on Rustam's back. Even as Candacy Ann, he adjusted well enough, though in his heart of hearts he felt like a wild animal being inexorably, insidiously tamed, broken to harness.

The feeling was added to by the birth of his son, in the post infirmary on a cold, raw, gray January day. Starcross wondered if Candacy Ann was as conscious as he that the child had to have been conceived on one of those memorable April nights in Washington or Cincinnati or on board the *Asteria.* It was a subject they seemed not to have occasion to touch on, and odds were would not have touched on in any case. For a decided propriety had sprung up between husband and wife that had not been there between mere man and woman. Webb Starcross, Junior, a big, hearty baby, seemingly came into the world under the luckiest of stars. The Department commander himself was his godfather. It had been a difficult birth for Candacy Ann, but she recovered satisfactorily, and in good time to preen and pose in her triumph. She proved able to nurse her baby, and to Starcross's surprise actually insisted on doing so; it was far from the fashion among ladies of her class. Again, Starcross could not complain.

The birth, in fact, had a far worse effect on the grandfather than on the mother. Arriving but weeks ahead of the child, already worn down by the trial of Richwood's dissolution, through which the Starcrosses had been unable to support him, the doctor having forbidden the very *enceinte* Candacy Ann to travel at all, Colonel Colquhoun further wore himself out in hectic anticipations of his grandchild, nervously darting to and fro during the last hours of suspense then the first ones of rejoicing. It had not been said, in so many words, that he was to stay on with his son-in-law and daughter, but events conspired toward that end. The colonel squandered the residue of his limited strength fecklessly fetching and carrying for new mother and child, running needless errands and the likes, then afterwards joining in the late-night drinking party in the new father's honor given by his brother officers. Next morning he declined to get up from his bed; the post physician had to be called in; and directly Candacy Ann was up from her own bed attending on her late attendant. So had it gone for six months. The colonel settled in as a regular, semi-invalid member of the household. The physician pontificated confidingly, in unwitting self-mockery, of "a gradual ebbing of the vital forces"—an ebbing, if unlikely to be stayed by submission to the spa regimen, at least perhaps to be better endured amid its distractions.

Starcross's other and growing concern was Chance, who within weeks had followed them to St. Louis. He arrived looking fit, almost his old self, and full of his news: By way of a fellow officer in the late Confederate army he had found a place in the offices of a streetcar company. And had entered on this all-new phase of his life in all cheer, it seemed, neither bitter nor regretful. While he lived at a distance, in modest rooms, he was a regular evening visitor in the Starcross parlor or dining room, and to all appearances the three-cornered childhood friendship flowed as serenely, timelessly on as the Mississippi out the window.

But it soon grew only too clear: all was not well with Chance. Starcross's efforts to draw his friend into wholesome social channels, including him even in the clannish, ingrown life of the post, to undo any sense of abandonment, came to little. Handsome, impoverished ex-Confederate officers were a drug on the St. Louis social market. Relations between the late enemies could be awkward, and Chance made scant effort to ease them, to meet the other side halfway, to make himself congenial. In company he drank too much and grew either brooding or over-excited and bellicose. He just didn't seem to be *interested;* indeed, seemed to grow ever less-so. Keeping more and more to himself, as well as Starcross could tell, he hewed to a quiet, nay dull routine, divided between his work and his rooms, drinking even more, and to worse effect, in his own company than in others'.

Starcross's concern for him, his efforts on his behalf, oddly got scant encouragement from Candacy Ann. Welcoming and affectionate as ever while he was in their home, effortlessly she put Chance out of her head once he was out of her sight. Any more there was room for but one man in her life, and even he, he noted, tended to become for her more an edifice than a personality, a landmark rather than an object of affection. "My husband" became "the general," first in her social talk, then in her babytalk to her uncomprehending son, even between themselves. "You know best, General," was her watchword, voiced all vaguely, her mind on the child in her lap or her father in the next room, whenever he sought to air some thought, say, on the score of Chance, his well-being or future, subjects in which she seemed able to muster no real interest. And so he gave up airing them.

Such was the narrow round of Starcross's wedded life, as of his thoughts, as he sat on the Thermopolis park bench, a year into that new life: his wife; his baby son; his failing father-in-law; his troubled friend. One person was conspicuously absent from the round, from the thoughts, but it was an absence so total that he simply had no way of being aware of it. But he was to be reminded, and with a force, an urgency that would sweep all the others before it, shrink them to insignificance.

Some of the park's walkways lay at acute angles to each other. The benches in some cases thus stood nigh back to back. Starcross, beguiled by his thoughts, and by the agreeable ambiance in general, remained only vaguely aware of its particulars, including the bench behind him, but yards away, and the strangers sitting thereupon, the scraps of their conversation. The memorable albeit buried name, therefore, when it reached his ears for the first time in more than a year, when it came, on a stranger's voice, seemed to come quite without context: not the subject or object of a sentence, a complete thought, but rather as an invocation, a reproach—the cryptic, awful utterance of an oracle.

"Cathal McQuaife," the voice said.

FIFTEEN

On the long, two-stage coach ride from Thermopolis to Fort Smith, on the Western Border, Starcross had ample leisure to live it over, indeed nothing else to do, nothing to distract or calm his inflamed mind. The words overheard in the park, incredibly but hours since, echoed and reechoed in his head:

Cathal McQuaife? The rebel spy?

None other. Old General McQuaife's daughter. The general's had that place for years, you know—big house, sprawling ranch-land leased from the Indians.

But isn't he in Mexico yet, a fugitive?

Just so. They'd have an easy time of it, they reckoned. Well, they were reckoning without the daughter—her father's daughter in more than name, as they found. And then she's got a daughter of her own—a she-bear defending her den and cub! She wasn't alone either, she had friends with her, renegade Indians, rebels—outlaws, the army calls 'em. There could be but one outcome of course, but it was a stand-up fight while it lasted. The troops had a run for their money; took casualties, which didn't help their humor. Oh, it's not funny, of course; yet there is *a certain humor in the thought of their frustration, those men not used to being flouted, who've gotten away with so much. Their behavior won't bear close scrutiny if it ever comes out. Which of course it won't. Oh aye, it's rebels they're up against, McQuaife and the daughter and her friends; but I don't hold with this—this barefaced plunder of the beaten. We didn't beat them for that.*

But what did *happen? To the woman, I mean.*

Well, it was just yesterday, remember. When I left, the troops were in possession of the house, nothing to be seen or heard of the woman, at least not by mere passersby like me. Which bodes her no good at all, if you ask me. Those pretties would do anything to get their hands on that property by right as well as might; and she's all that's standing in their way . . . if *she's still standing. And even if she is, I wouldn't give much for her chances.*

Surely they wouldn't . . . do away with a woman in cold blood.

Oh, they would. It's a rough, lawless country, where anything can happen—does *happen, day after day.*

Well, it's an outrage, whatever sort of woman she is, rebel or harlot or both together. One ought to do something—report them to the proper authorities, at the very least.

My dear, benighted friend, they're *the "proper authorities."*

The interval after the two men had risen and drifted off, still talking, for Starcross was a blur. He'd remained frozen to his own bench, gazing sightless straight ahead, paralyzed not so much by the burthen of what had been said, paralyzing enough in itself, as just by the name—*her* name. It had run his heart through like an arrow, bringing as it did the dizzying recognition that he'd buried the barest memory of it, of *her,* the first women he'd ever loved; that he'd hardly allowed himself to behold her face even in his inmost mind's eye, since his marriage to another.

But the moment, in all its urgency, had soon asserted itself. His old awakened guilt surged through him as, fairly without willing it, he left the bench, found himself back at the hotel almost without awareness of having made the trek. About him, the quietly bustling hostelry seemed grotesquely unreal. Its air of complacent contentment, when he'd left it hardly hours before, had evaporated, together with his own inner peace.

Ever the man of action, Starcross never once thought to do other than he was doing. Instantly his mind had digested the intelligence, drawn the tactical conclusion therefrom. The enemy had broken through; and but one force lay at hand to be thrown into the breach: himself. The place, the McQuaife leasehold, hard by Fort Cressup, in the Indian Territory, he knew lay not far west of the Border, but a few days' ride from Thermopolis. He could go there, see with his own eye, do what must be done, and be back before his absence had been noted: a secondary consideration in any case. His first impulse was to tell Candacy Ann all; but time hardly allowed; nor was he in any fit state to sit quietly, patiently baring his breast. Moreover, his return to their suite earlier than expected she hardly even seemed to notice, her mind being as ever wholly taken up with her now bedridden father. He had trouble getting her attention even to impress on her:

"I'm going to have to go away for a few days."

"So soon, General?" Unruffled, scarcely fazed at all, she leaped instantly to inflexible conclusions. "Goodness me, can't they give you a week's peace, at least?"

Their parting embrace and kiss were distracted on his part, perfunctory on hers. "Well, don't be any longer than you must, General. Why, what if Papa—?"

After a sleepless night's stop, the second leg of his journey set him down late on the second day at Fort Smith. The place had for long been no real fort, merely a brawling Border town, threshold and jumping-off point for the Indian Territory stretching beyond. While civilization had held sway east of the line for fifty years, not for another fifty would the same order and security prevail to its west. And inevitably, some of the lawlessness backwashed into the town, through which fugitives from justice—from somebody's notion of justice—passed on their westward flight, and to which, rather less frequently, they were forcibly haled back for trial and disposal. Fort Smith thus was a place used to strange faces, used to ignoring them, in the interest of health—for Starcross's purpose, perfect. He hunted up a dumpy, out-of-the-way hotel and grudged himself a meal and a fitful few hours' sleep.

When he descended well before dawn next morning, his appearance had undergone a marked change. Already in mufti, even in Thermopolis's eye but an anonymous civilian, he was now at his most nondescript in faded relics from faded times at Richwood, brought away for some inertial or sentimental reason. The limp brim of his stained, ancient hat slouched far down toward his turned-up collar, leaving his face in shadow, eyes but two points of light like a cat's in a dark cavern. And low on his thigh in an open holster, oiled and use-honed, rode his Walker Colt, one of the first of that famous family of revolving pistols and still one of the best, precious legacy from his father, who had taught him to use it with deadly accuracy, a skill he had kept up by steady practice during the war. Passersby were at pains to pay him no note, but with wry satisfaction he noted his effect on those who had no choice: the hotelier, the livery stable hostler. Leaving a deposit, he hired a tough little buckskin who likely had begun life running free in the mountains or on the Plains, a horse with whom, as a born-and-bred Southwesterner himself, he soon established full rapport. Crossing the river by ferry at town outskirts and heading on west along the well-defined, well-traveled military road leading to and linking the Territorial forts, he rode through the day, and right on through the following mild, bright June night.

Toward dawn, still in hilly, timbered country, he stopped at a "half-faced" cabin to buy a Spartan breakfast for himself and his mount, and sound out the lie of the land ahead, from a halfbreed couple already astir at his approach, the white man chopping firewood, the Indian woman stooped witchlike over her outdoor cooking fire. Starcross still had no notion what he would do; it hinged wholly on what he would find.

The sun was well up in the sky at his back when at last he found himself on the crest of a gentle hill at the edge of heavy timber looking out over a broad valley toward a farther hill: a high, meadowy slope with a large, two-storied sandstone house at its summit, against another timber-fringe, all but within it. A rail fence enclosed the foot of the hill, just beyond the near-waterless little watercourse on the valley floor, where the road crossed by a shallow ford. Gateless sandstone gateposts broke the zigzag sweep of the fence; and just within, a blue-coated trooper sagged slackly on his musket. Eyes and mind already hurrying on, Starcross made out the heavier figure of a noncommissioned officer boredly pacing the house's shadowy broad front gallery.

Minutes later he forded the creek; and well before the sentry awoke to his coming he was between the posts and past. Horse and rider were fast fading up the rising lane toward the house before the man managed to get his musket unslung.

"Hey!" he yelped. "What—where d'you think you're going?" Biting his tongue, he set off running in dusty pursuit.

Easily leaving the man behind, Starcross reined up before the spacious, columned gallery, beside a tethered horse and buggy and a blooded chestnut regally accoutered in a shiny dragoon saddle, blue-and-gold blanket, and gleaming leathers. The sergeant —for sergeant he proved to be, of a sort—loomed forth out of the colonnade's shadows, into the midday June glare. Starcross knew the type well, at once: jowly, world-weary face, overweight figure bulging out of blowzy, sweat-stained, idiosyncratic apparel only loosely making a uniform. All complacency, the sergeant hooked grimily gauntleted thumbs through his belt.

"And what d'you reckon you're doing here, Mister?" He was all biting sarcasm.

Dismounted, Starcross brought daunting eyes to bear. "Why don't you answer first, Sergeant—since you were here first?"

"Ho—a joker, eh?" Right hand dropped from the belt, down toward the low-hanging holster. "And a rebel too, if I don't miss my guess. Answer my question, Goddamn you, Reb! Who d'you think won the bloomin' war, anyway?"

"I'm beginning to wonder myself any more, Sergeant," Starcross mused, with a grim smile; but then he grew deadly serious; peremptory. "Where is Miss McQuaife?"

The sentry at this point came huffing up, woefully winded, anxious to make up for his lapse. Irritably the sergeant waved him back. "Never mind, Sloan, I'll handle this." Thoughtfully he stared at Starcross, waiting pointedly till the trooper had retreated out of earshot. Vague doubts were gnawing at his confidence. "Miss McQuaife, is it? And who wants to know?"

"An impatient man, Sergeant"—impatient indeed.

The sergeant's eyes wavered between the visitor's own and the revolver at his thigh. Clearly his ears took in the unmistakable tone of command, difficult to disdain even on an enemy tongue. The sergeant, Starcross saw, was one of that soldier species for whom soldiering lay not in daring and deciding but in moving with the tide, leaving the daring and deciding to others. He roused, turned, striving to cover his shortcomings with heavy sarcasm. "An impatient man! Let me announce you."

"That won't be necessary." Starcross thrust his reins in the meaty hands. "I'm used to announcing myself." He mounted the gallery steps, casually turning his back. As he'd expected, the sergeant just stood, holding the reins, agape. And then at the open door Starcross found himself facing a second figure.

"What's going on, Sergeant? Who's this?"

The contrast with the sergeant could not have been more marked. The figure was a civilian's, but the voice belonged to a combatant, if of quite an unmilitary type. After the outdoors the inside of the house was dim. Starcross saw only the man's outline, a cadaverously thin outline, with holstered revolver tied low, right hand at ease on the butt as if that were its natural resting place. The sergeant started up some stuttering plaint of explanation, but the animated cadaver paid scant notice.

"All right; we'll see," he said. "Step in, friend, by all means. Let's have a look at you."

Inside, with grotesque hospitality he motioned toward open double doors giving off one side of the entry hall. Unhesitantly Starcross went before him into the room: a large, high-ceilinged parlor with two wing chairs arrayed before a cold fireplace, on either side of a low table bearing a cut-glass decanter. In one of the chairs, glass in hand, sat a paunchy, beet-nosed personage with an eagle on the collar of his rumpled blue uniform; in the other a small, middleaged, ferret-faced man with grizzly mutton-chop whiskers, clad for city streets in a Prince Albert coat, top-hat in his lap. Starcross knew neither man, but it was an easy guess that the officer was the Fort Cressup commandant, Colonel Chievous. The civilian had the look of a petty clerk, or perhaps petty criminal, somehow soared above his station.

The *third* man, however, the cadaver who had come to the door, Starcross had known at once: not just the type but even the individual, under sundry names on dodgers all headed *Wanted.* It was on this man that he kept his real attention, even while seeming all-absorbed in the seated duo. These two for the time being said not a word, scarcely even moved, merely blinkingly gave back his stare. Clearly his coming had caught them in the midst of an exchange of questionable confidences.

"What are you lot doing here?" Starcross, like the fighter he was, pressed his initial edge. "This isn't a tavern, it's a private home. It belongs to General Odon McQuaife."

"It belongs to the Indians," the civilian corrected, his confidence rebounding as if he had found the intruder's weak spot. "General Odon McQuaife indeed! Trespasser as well as traitor. His titles are invalid. His lease is being terminated."

"And Mr. Gaunce should know," contributed the colonel in jovial, slurred tones, upending his glass, reaching for the decanter. "He's the Cherokee Indian agent."

"And I take it your case against General McQuaife has already been adjudicated by the United States District Court or before a duly constituted military tribunal?"

Officer and agent exchanged a glance. The latter kept his silence, grown suddenly, newly cautious. The colonel, in contrast, went on sputtering, blustering, heedless: "Old McQuaife long ago lit out for Mexico; that's 'adjudication' aplenty for me. And for 'duly constituted military tribunal' I give you this!" Affectionately he patted the covered holster belted to his ample waist. "This is war, after all, y'know. It's not *near* over yet."

"Indeed; I have heard tell of your war." Starcross's tone grew uglier. "I ask it once and for all: *Where is Miss McQuaife?*"

Again the two men traded glances, furtive and unsure. The colonel opened his mouth, but in haste the agent overrode him. "Upstairs, as far as we know," he said. "She hasn't made our . . . difficult duty any less difficult. And now," all heavy sarcasm, "if we've satisfied your curiosity, perhaps you'll return the courtesy. The crying question just now, after all, is Who are *you?*"

For answer Webb Starcross whirled, cocked revolver magically in his hand, finger squeezing the trigger. The third man had sloped in after him, around the room's edge, to confront him from the flank. As the report died he crumpled to the floor, slow-motionlike, his own weapon—drawn with lightning speed, by dying reflexes—spilling from his fingers. Agent and colonel started to their feet together, though the latter took far longer to reach them and had trouble keeping them when he had.

"Murder!" he burbled—exclamation more than accusation.

Starcross finished his turn. Drawn by the shot, the sergeant had come bursting into the open doorway. But the moment his gaze took in the smoking revolver in the stranger's hand, his own hand fell hastily away from his holster.

"Sergeant," Starcross told him, "there are warrants outstanding, military and civilian, against the . . . draff yonder on the floor. Departmental headquarters will confirm." He smiled, all irony. "You will want to report his—apprehension."

The sergeant looked to his colonel, but found anything but help. "I reckon," he muttered. Still getting no guidance, he did what came naturally and heeded the voice of command, oozed back out of the room, all but with a salute.

"And as for the pretty pair of *you*"—Starcross swung back around—"I propose to look upstairs. If you're still here when I come back, I just may shoot you both. I may come after you and shoot you anyway, depending on what I find."

Colonel Chievous, starting to sag back in his chair, suddenly changed his mind. He seemed still to want to bluster, but his crony managed to convince him that for the time being discretion might prove the better part of valor. The latter's compliance hardly hid the hint that there would be other times.

But Webb Starcross ignored the implication even as the men themselves. Dismissing them from his thoughts altogether, scornfully he showed them his back. Out in the hall, already bolting up the sweeping stairway, he was only distantly aware of agent and colonel making-haste-slowly in the other direction, out the front door, the latter impatiently steadying the former, the sergeant springing forth to assist his tipsy commander down the gallery steps and up into his saddle. Yet Starcross still had his revolver gripped in his hand, swinging as he climbed.

Over his head the large, rambling house seemed to yawn off in all directions, its farther reaches fading away in dense shadows. The silence was oppressive, sinister somehow. The heavy stone walls fairly killed all sound from out-of-doors, leaving the upstairs corridor utterly cut off, tomblike. One anomaly, though, drew Starcross's attention. All around the head of the stairs, a scattering of bulletholes, raw and new, scarred the plaster.

Close by stood a closed oaken door. Starcross moved over to it, tried the knob, found it unlocked. Slowly he shoved it open, cautiously stepped over the threshold.

The fore of the room was dim, though ample light poured in behind from long windows, throwing into nimbused silhouette a shimmering, ghostly form hovering, fair floating, just within. As the door swung back from between them the figure lifted a wavery arm—and Starcross heard the dry *snick* of a revolver's hammer falling on an empty chamber. His own right arm in the same split-second came up by reflex, even as the figure brought the empty revolver on up and then back down with force like a club. Starcross caught it against his own weapon, parrying the blow like a swordsman. At the same time—the last of its strength seemingly spent in these throes of ultimate defiance—the ghostlike form swayed, and then slumped forward in a heap right up against his legs. The revolver went clattering away over the floor.

"Cathal," said Webb Starcross.

He slid to his knees beside the fallen form. Her eyes were wide but the glaze on their surfaces told him she did not see him. His own eyes dropped on at once from her ravaged, fevered face, swept down over her body, clad only in a long full undergarment, and had no trouble making out the cause of her distress: One whole side of the shift was more black-red than white. She had been shot in the edge of the chest, almost in the armpit. How much blood had been lost was impossible to tell; but the wound, Starcross saw in stricken dismay, had had no care; its lips wore an ugly, ominous look. And there was no exit wound; the bullet was still lodged somewhere deep in the flesh.

A vast canopied bed filled the middle of the room. Carefully Starcross lifted the limp body, an arm under the shoulders, another under the knees. As he carried her to the bed and laid her on it, she stirred feebly and strove to speak; but the sounds were indecipherable, meaningless—the maunderings of a distracted mind. At last she grew quieter. Starcross turned, taking in the rest of his surroundings. The room had a disorderly, denlike air. From the windows could be seen only the sloping front grounds and at the foot the Indian agent's buggy passing between the gateposts, the colonel's horse trailing after it in the dust, the teetering colonel barely keeping his saddle, and the sentry standing gaping first after the routed pair, then back toward the house.

Turning back into the room, Starcross laid his revolver on a marble table beside the bed. A candle stood there in a holder, beside a near-empty pitcher of water and a full basin. Lighting a match and touching it to the candle, he bent over the unconscious woman and tore her garment, laying the wound bare. He gazed long, appraising in the dim, wavering light the grim prospect that confronted him. He took off his jacket, and from his waist, inside his shirt, drew his big scabbarded knife: another accessory from other times that he had donned as a matter of course, along with the Colt, and unsheathed the long, thin, razor-edged blade. He went back to the windows, and this time stood looking, not outside, but solemnly, ruefully at the knife as if offering up a prayer, or mustering his courage, or both. At last he strode back, and perhaps heeding some obscure intuition held the blade in the candle flame. Turning around and sitting on the edge of the bed, he took a deep breath and bent to his task.

SIXTEEN

The candle had burned down, guttered out; daylight came into the room at a steep slant, and shadows were deepening. A drained Webb Starcross slumped in a chair beside the canopied bed, eyes only for the sleeping woman. To a stranger he might have looked in more serious condition than she of his concern. Blood streaked and stained his sleeves and shirt-front; his stubbled, sunken-eyed face wore the look of a sick man just passed through a crisis whose outcome was still unsure.

Cathal McQuaife, on the other hand, following the earlier thrashings of her pain, or of her fevered dreams, rested in peace. Several times had she seemed to waken, had looked him in the eyes, but never with lucidity, with any hint of recognition. It had been an ordeal, a near thing, for him more than for her. His hopes for her recovery remained high. He'd done his best, and his best was very good indeed. A son of the frontier and a soldier who'd had to be his own medical officer after more than one brush with Apaches, and who had seen men blown beyond medical help at his very side, Webb Starcross was as prepared to face calmly and cope effectively with a serious injury as any man of his day. Once his knife had cut the bullet out, the ravaged flesh had bled freely enough to cleanse the wound, yet not so freely as to bring shock. She needed stitches; but he had found clean linen for a compress and bound it firmly in place with strips torn from her garment. Her nakedness he had noticed hardly at all as he worked, her bare breasts as he drew the strips over and under them. But at last he did so. It was less the sight that moved him, though, than the memory. Delicately, in both senses, he drew sheet and patchwork quilt all the way up over the supine form. And in his so doing his sight caught on her hands, casually crossed at her waist: on the golden band agleam on one of the fingers.

Tenderly he took the hand up in both of his, touched the ring, pierced to his very heart's core. His movements had brought him forward out of the chair. Now suddenly his long-maintained iron control gave way. He knelt—crumpled—at the bedside, elbows on the edge, wracked face cradled in his hands.

"Cathal. Oh, Cathal—"

But she did not stir. Still he gazed on the ring and fondled the hand that wore it, a man torn, divided between duties. Or rather a man who knew his first duty well and yet rued and would delay the denial of the other which it decreed.

"I cannot"—he might have been speaking to the woman or only to himself—"and I must. Forgive me, Cathal . . . again."

And as if but by an act of supreme will he eased the ring from the slender finger and, after a brief qualm, slid it back on the one from where he had taken it over five years before. That Cathal McQuaife had gone on wearing it, as in memory of that long-ago night, despite its disappointments—its betrayal—left him feeling a thief as well as a cad. All but overwhelmed in his wretchedness, wearing an utterly shattered look, he kissed the now pathetically naked hand and replaced it, and drew the covers on up to her shoulders. On impulse he bent forward and kissed her beaded brow; and then, taking a deep breath, he regained his feet and at least the shadow of his wonted self-control.

He picked up the great .56-caliber cylindroconchoidal bullet, turned it over and over. A close or knowing watcher might have noted the all-over tightening of his muscles, the quiver of his mustache like the throb of a heart. The bullet had come from an army musket. He laid it back on the table and picked up his revolver. Having replaced the spent load and cap, he moved again to the windows. The prospect out front, save for the now more shallowly slanting daylight, remained the same, the sergeant presumably under the gallery roof, out of sight, the would-be gateman down at his post. Beyond, the road stretched empty away.

With a last silent look at the woman in the bed, Starcross went out of the room, drawing the door closed. He turned aside from the stairs, though, along the shadowy hall, opening doors on empty rooms as he went. Beyond a right-angle turn, the hallway ended in a steep, boxed-in service stair. Going down, revolver ready in his hand, he found himself in pantry regions, untenanted as the rest. A back door gave onto a rear gallery from which a flagged walkway led off over a ragged enclosure to a sprawl of outbuildings: summer kitchen, smokehouse, sheds, stables, and, farther on, a double row of cabins, from some of whose chimneys smoke fingered up into the windless, brassy blue.

As he stood watching, a blue-clad soldier sprang out of the maze of outbuildings, musket slung over his shoulder by the barrel, his free hand holding a fried-chicken leg up to a busily munching mouth. At sight of the grim, bloodied stranger he froze in mid-stride, making no move to bring his weapon about.

"Get out of my sight, Private," Starcross bit off, with mildness, so he thought. But judging from its effect it was a mildness more menacing than any thunderbolt. "I've got no quarrel with you; but I'm a very quarrelsome man just now."

"Gettin'—goin'!" Leerily the soldier sidestepped, avoiding quick movements, limbs frozen in their awkward positions. At last he broke and fled around the house-corner.

Starcross ventured on among the buildings, from whence the soldier had come. Instinct assured him other mortals were about; common sense alone told him Cathal McQuaife's servants and dependents, however terrorized, scattered, would not have fled far. As he entered the smaller enclosure formed by the buildings, ducked under the summer kitchen's low gallery roof, he glimpsed through the open door the bulky figure of a woman in apron and headrag, standing with her arms about a child, a girl half embracing her protectress, half turned as at bay. The woman's face was earthen; the child's stark-white. Recognition flooding him, tinged with ruth, Starcross's gaze fastened on the little girl's hair, pale blonde with just a hint of red. Like a sleepwalker he stepped over the high threshold, for-the-nonce his guard down.

Instinct resurged just in time to save his life. As the shadow descended from the side, his gun-hand shot up seemingly without his willing it. The revolver took the swooping, inertial force of the long knife against the cylinder and parried it. Then, before his attacker could either arm-cock for a second slash or close and grapple, Starcross kneed him between the thighs. Backing off, he found himself gazing down on the crumpled, writhing figure of an Indian, his hair in braids albeit the rest of him clad in nondescript white man's clothes. Anything but permanently injured, he was well out of action for the time being. Trucially Starcross brought the revolver down and turned to the earthen woman, statuelike throughout the clash, stolidly returning his look.

"You fools! I mean you no harm." He found it beyond him to stay his anger. "Why aren't you with your mistress?"

At long last, the woman answered in a word: "The soldiers."

"Surely they wouldn't stop you attending her."

"She—*she* send me away before, to bring the child away. She tell Buckchita"—nodding at the floored man—"and the others to go away before the soldiers come. They kill them all if they stay, she say; but not kill her if they could help it."

"They almost couldn't help it," Starcross gritted.

"We thought she *was* killed. We see nothing, hear nothing. The soldiers, they run wild, threaten, warn us out. They were many. We afraid. Our menfolk—who did stay, who fought them —some were wounded. One was killed."

Starcross glanced at the vanquished Buckchita, recouped to the point of propping himself on an elbow. His open eyes were slitted and fixed on Starcross, thoughtful, though quite without menace or even malice. Clearly the woman was his senior in their quirky hierarchy. Her forthright talk with the daunting stranger seemed to legitimate his presence and stay the reflex of defense. Starcross's eyes went back to the woman.

"Your mistress isn't dead, but she was shot. She's feverish and out of her head. I've dressed her wound, but she needs care, constant care. See to it. The soldiers will trouble you no more; of that you may be sure." He saw the cautious doubt deepen in the woman's round brown face. "What they have been doing, I assure you, is not according to law, and when their superiors learn of it they will dismiss and punish those who ordered it, and carried it out. And I mean to make sure they learn."

"Yes, sir. . . . Who are you, sir?"

"Just a passerby." Starcross smiled. An idea sprang up in his mind, from what uncanny depths he knew not. He hesitated only briefly before embracing it, offhandedly uttering the fateful formal words: "You may tell your mistress, when she is herself, that Major Buckhannon called, is most distressed to find her indisposed, and perhaps will call again. Can you remember that?"

"I think so, Major, sir. Major Buckhannon."

"Just so." Starcross gave the woman a stiff nod, the Indian another. But before turning away he let his eyes again rest long and thoughtful on the quiet little girl, penned yet in the woman's arms. She was a comely child, with very light-blue eyes and fine-cut features—fairer than her mother, the hair almost ash-blonde, though with that fugitive tinge of red. Her gaze met his with a steady intensity that likely was only childish curiosity but that his fancy swelled to eerie, uneasy recognition.

"And what's your name, child?"

The girl hesitated only briefly. "Star."

"*Sir,*" the woman scolded.

"Star, sir."

It was too much for him, literally—far worse than facedowns with guns and knives. Starcross turned and fled.

Back in the house he measured the long center hallway past the parlor door, beyond which still lay the bloody corpse, disregarded. Through the open front door could be seen the back of the bulky, blowzy sergeant, buttocks leant on the hitching rail. But the presence sensed at his back, his head came craning about. He sprang upright, backed away from the rail, arms well out from his sides, a wary but easygoing, wheedling grin on his face.

"I was ordered to stay here, Mister," he plainted.

"And a soldier always obeys orders, doesn't he?" Starcross nodded. "So long as they don't outrage his conscience."

"Right you are, Mister." Slowly the sergeant untensened, and then grinned again, eyeing the other in frank, wry admiration. "By God, if you aren't a cool customer!"

"No, Sergeant. At the moment I'm an extremely *hot* customer." He turned, glanced up at the house-front. "Have you any idea what's been going on here?"

"Not for my likes to have ideas, Mister. Fellow don't survive in this army by havin' ideas—nor a conscience neither, as you call it." Briefly the sergeant glanced off toward the distant road. "I wouldn't have missed it for the world, though." His toothy grin broadened, turned less fawning, almost comradely. "If you don't mind my sayin' so, the most interestin' part may be yet to come—seein' what Lieutenant Klyce and a Dragoon squad make of you. Oh, and t'other way 'round, of course."

Again he glanced. Starcross did likewise, and made out the dusty wake being thrown up by the file of mounted figures crossing the valley floor, now fording the creek. And even as he and the sergeant watched, the lead horseman led the way between the sandstone gateposts. The droopy sentry undrooped, stiffened to life, as if heartened by the reinforcements.

"And all in my honor?" Starcross mused—and then frowned in thought. "*Klyce,* did you say?"

The sergeant nodded, the grin still in place. "Damned good officer, the lieutenant, a real soldier. You may find him a tougher nut to crack than . . . well, than some."

"I have a notion you're right, Sergeant." Having given the oncoming troopers a final glance, however, he seemed to lose interest. He unhitched his horse's reins from the rail and started aside with him, nodding at a well and a wooden watering trough a hundred yards or so from the side of the house, in the shadow of a great fieldstone barn. "I must water my horse," he said, matter-of-factly. "Tell the lieutenant I await his pleasure."

The sergeant offered no objections as Starcross strode leisurely out over the yard. The buckskin at the trough, Starcross hoisted a bucket up out of the well and watered himself. He splashed water on his face with his hands and stood wiping them on his neckerchief, blissfully indifferent, it seemed, to the scene at his back, the thunderous coming of the horsemen, the puzzled parley of the lieutenant and the sergeant. Then the creak of leather, the clink of metal, the scuffle of heavy footfalls signalled the approach of the musket-bristling troop down the gentle slope. Starcross glanced about just fully enough to satisfy himself that Lieutenant Klyce strode well in the lead.

"All right, Mr. Troublemaker—" the latter began.

"Your prisoner, by all means, Lieutenant Klyce." Minimally Starcross raised his hands, turning half about to show his profile. "The troop will not be necessary." With gratification he noted the lieutenant's lightning-stroke of astonishment, his gaping seesaw between two contradictory habits. "Nor the salute."

"You—!" gasped the lieutenant.

"A word in private, Klyce?" Starcross prompted.

The lieutenant shook off his daze. His perplexity vented itself in officerly aggravation as he swung on the men falling all over each other as they braked in his wake. "Go back! Wait at the house! *I'll* deal with this." He stood waiting till the mystified troopers had absorbed the order, sorted themselves out and straggled back up the slope toward the gallery corner, where the sergeant stood, hands on hips, alike mystifiedly taking in this fresh turnabout. When Klyce once more faced about it was to find his "prisoner" strayed a few steps on into the barn's shade, seemingly wholly rapt in the arcadian valley vista. Hastily he caught up. "General—" he began. "It *is* General Starcross, isn't it? Good God, you're chief of staff at Departmental headquarters."

Starcross nodded. "A mere private citizen, at the moment." Klyce had matured, satisfiedly he saw; the raw youth of '61 had seasoned. Damned good officer, as even a sleazy sergeant could see—and still a decent one. "And what of you, Klyce? How has the war treated you? In the regulars now, I see."

Klyce grew self-conscious. "Can't say the *war* did much for me, sir. And I soon had my fill of the militia. But—well, I reckon I picked up a liking for the footloose army life. I transferred quick as I could, though I had to give up a captaincy to do it."

"You did the right thing," Starcross assured him. "A regular soldier belongs in the regulars."

The lieutenant's face fell. All belated anxiety, he spared a glance back over his shoulder. "The regulars ain't exactly a Sunday school picnic either—not all the time anyhow."

"No, indeed. . . . What did they tell you?"

"Just—some unknown, unregenerate rebel had shown up and shot Mr. Gaunce's man and was plumb terrorizing the place. I was to fall out a detail and tend to it . . . him. That was about as clear as he made it—*could* make it, the colonel."

"Klyce—just what's been going on here?"

The lieutenant made a face. "I only wish I could tell you, sir. Me, I've just come in off the Plains with a patrol. The bachelor officers' mess was rife with talk, but it was hard to make much sense of it. It's a damned thorny problem we've got in this neck of the woods, I have to tell you, what with outlaws and Indians, wild and tame, plus more renegade rebels than you can shake a stick at. And Miss McQuaife's hardly helped herself—openly, defiantly befriending some of the worst of them. They've been spotted coming and going around this house. The official line this time seems to be that shots were fired from it at innocent passersby, and troops were sent out from the fort to put a stop to it. There's no civilian law hereabouts at all, of course."

"And you credit this—this official line?"

"Oh, there's *some*thing in it—if you swallow some folks' idea of 'innocent passersby.' If I'm not misinformed, you fired a—a telling shot at one of them yourself."

Visibly Starcross turned it all over in his head. "I can see you don't want to name names."

"Well, it ain't exactly the easiest thing. It's not a problem a junior officer can do much about on his own. Thank God *you're* here. This isn't a good post, sir!" Klyce eyed the house. "Oh, but tell me, is—er, is Miss McQuaife all right?"

"Well you may ask." Starcross's mustache twitched. "I found her barricaded in her bedroom, defending herself with an empty revolver, out of her right mind and with a bullet in her breast—an army musket bullet, Klyce! I cut it out, did all else I could. The post surgeon must come and have a look at her."

"He won't get near her if she's in her right mind, sir," Klyce said, apologetically. "Miss McQuaife is a very stubborn, contrary young lady, and she makes no secret of her hatred of us all. The troops who were ordered to take the house took casualties. The fact didn't inspire their chivalry, if they had any."

"They seem to have contented themselves with taking over the downstairs and keeping the servants out—a serious enough matter in itself, considering. I take it Miss McQuaife held them out of the upstairs till their minds wandered or their zeal lessened and they simply put her out of their heads. All very reasonable, I'm sure. They couldn't be expected to know *she* would be so unreasonable—so *contrary,* as you put it. But I'm feeling rather unreasonable and contrary myself at the moment, Klyce. I arrived here to find U.S. soldiers making free of the place, a besotted colonel and a reptilian politician parked in the parlor drinking the house liquor, bodyguarded by a fugitive from justice, and the mistress upstairs weltering in her own blood!"

"A damned outrage, I agree, sir," Klyce said. "I didn't know. And even if I had—"

"Yes. Not much a junior officer can do, you said. Don't be too sure, Lieutenant. Now—there are two courses of action open, as I see it. And the choice rests all with you." Starcross drew breath. "I shouldn't have to remind you, Klyce, you of all people, of my—my earlier encounter with Miss McQuaife."

"No, sir." The lieutenant disciplined his deferent smile into a grimace, restrained himself from noting aloud that the "earlier encounter" spoke for itself in every twitch and fiber of Starcross's face, betrayed itself as not a thing only of the dead past. "Not that I ever knew the whole story, the *true* story," he qualified. "But I never believed what Colonel Purinton—"

"There may have been truth in what he said. I wouldn't have cared, *don't* care, for my own part. But I'm a married man now, Klyce—a happily married man."

"Of course, sir. Say no more, sir."

"Now then: I can come back with you to the fort and we'll have the whole thing thrashed out at once. I wouldn't mind that the least bit, for my own part; indeed, I'd relish it. But—well, I don't much relish taking the chance of subjecting my wife to the inevitable malice of clucking tongues, if it could be avoided at all. With that in mind, or on some unaccountable impulse, I left the servants here with the name of a friend instead of my own. I have a bit of influence in the halls of power, a bit of unspent credit in high places. I can assure you, as soon as I get back to civilization and send a telegram, Klyce, certain things are going to happen hereabouts; and even failing that, even if I have to see to it myself, the fur is going to fly, and guts too, it just may be." Starcross's voice grew more gentle, his eyes on the younger man. "It would mean leaving you in a rather awkward position for the meantime.

You'd have to embroider some plausible explanation why you returned without me. But if you can manage it, you'll have earned yourself that captaincy, at the very least."

Klyce stiffened. "You don't have to reward me for doing the right thing, General."

"No; of course not. But virtue deserves to be rewarded, and a favor for a friend inspires a favor in return. You've no idea what a favor you'd be doing me."

"What about your . . . your other friend? Whose name you said you borrowed?" Again Lieutenant Klyce stifled his smile. "Will he appreciate the fact he's just paid the Territory a visit and, so it seems, rescued a—a damsel in distress?"

"I see no problem. He's a bachelor, and since the war the very epitome of your frustrated slayer of dragons and rescuer of damsels. It's just the sort of thing to appeal to him. All he has to do, anyhow, is not give me away." Starcross paused. "*You're* the one to worry about. You'd be under intense pressure."

But Klyce, likewise, seemed to be finding it just the appealing sort of thing. "What can they do, clap me in irons?" he asked, eyes bright. "It wouldn't kill me if they did. Oh, I'll be all right, sir. You can count on me indeed. Why, I think I'm going to enjoy it. Anything to give this post the turning on its ear it needs."

"It's going to be turned on its ear, Lieutenant, if I have to come back and turn it with these hands. But I won't have to." Starcross proffered one of the hands. On both sides the clasp was heartfelt. "Klyce, I can't thank you enough!"

SEVENTEEN

Webb Starcross climbed Thermopolis's steep main street from the stage station toward his hotel, carpetbag in hand, ruefully rubbing his fingers over his stubbled chin, stayed from wondering at the rumpled, disreputable appearance he must present only by his obsessive reflection on the lengthy telegram he'd sent back at Fort Smith. The return horseback ride he'd spent composing the message in his head, the night in the Border town putting it in the private cipher Blake Frear had fairly forced on him and that he'd never before used, or looked ever to have occasion to use. The communication's tone, he was only too painfully aware, had been uncharacteristically shrill. He'd threatened, or at least implied the threat, to take private action, of a namelessly dramatic, indeed violent nature, if his "requests" for official action were not quickly and fully and satisfactorily met.

Thoughts therefore on anything but his trudge up the street and the town about him, he remained altogether oblivious of the figure materialized right before him till he all but collided with it. Halting abruptly, he brought his eyes up.

"Webb!" Chance Buckhannon spoke with pleased surprise, grasping Starcross's hand in both of his own. "Candacy Ann told me you'd been called away."

"Chance." With like pleasure, if even greater surprise, Starcross looked his friend up and down. "What on earth—?"

"Just passing through, old man. From nowhere to nowhere. Let my address be henceforth just 'G.T.T.'" Chance shrugged in careless, massive, sober self-deprecation. "You know—Gone To Texas. Or the devil, if there's a difference."

"Oh, Chance!" By degrees acute dismay spread over Starcross's face. "No—you don't mean you've thrown over the job? But—but I thought it was working out."

"You *would* think so, old man. Never could see what was right in front of you, if it wasn't down a gunsight." Chance shook his head, grew rueful. "For the right man it might've worked out, I reckon. But I'm not that man, Webb—the sort to sit in an office day after day, not after all I've been through, the life I've led. I just couldn't *take* any more, just couldn't help myself. I simply lost all patience, provoked a quarrel with the boss—it wasn't hard. He invited me to leave and not come back."

Starcross glanced on up the street toward the looming hilltop hotel, naggingly conscious that duty awaited him there, in the shape of Candacy Ann. He was just as conscious, however, of that other duty that confronted him here. Moreover, that mad, amorphous idea that had haunted the back of his mind for the past couple of days kept insinuating itself forward.

Nearby stood a dingy little doggery that served stronger drink than spring water. Chance was looking longingly that way, so Starcross waved hospitably, led the way inside. In the small, thronged room they found privacy at a corner table. Starcross was about to call for beer, but Chance made it whiskey.

"What will you do, then?" Starcross asked. Chance, he saw, was looking seedy, unusually, worryingly so. "Seems I'm always asking you that. Texas, though—?"

"A big, brawling country, or so they tell me," Chance said, all mock-cheerful. "No place for clerks and quilldrivers, but a place for the likes of me, maybe. Somewhere," he added, less cheerfully, "there must be such a place."

"Well, it's good to see you all the same, Chance." Starcross pondered, began nerving himself. "Opportune as well. There's—there's something I've got to tell you."

"Tell away, old man. No secrets between us two, eh?"

"No-o. . . . But I'm dead serious, Chance." Starcross drew a long, heavy breath. "You remember, don't you, what I touched on last year, back at Bolton Green?"

He remembered. "The . . . the woman. The 'other woman'?"

Starcross nodded and hastened on, bringing the story up to date, as briefly, if as fully, as he could: "Though I'd gone there incognito I was fully prepared to see it through under my own name, if need be. A matter of indifference to me on my own account, you understand; but Candacy Ann—you *do* understand? For me to have been involved with another woman years ago is one thing; but for me to have just paid that same woman a secret visit—well, when the moment came, Chance, I didn't give my own name, I just couldn't." Haplessly smiling: "I gave yours."

"Mine?" Chance puzzled over it. "You said you were *I?"*

"I can't explain it, Chance. I'm a poor dissembler. I think I was afraid I couldn't say a made-up name with any conviction at all. Or perhaps I was thinking of how we look so much alike, you and I—I could impersonate you easier than anyone else, to my own mind at least. Certainly it wouldn't do *you* any harm. I had the whimsical notion the business just might appeal to you, tickle your fancy. Just the sort of derring-do one would expect of Chance Buckhannon, that famous frustrated cavalier and knight-errant—to swoop down and knock the villains on their ears, rescue the dragon-beset enchanted princess, and ride back off into the clouds! And then, when, so fortuitously, Lieutenant Klyce turned up, the whole thing left the realm of fantasy—"

Waxing interest, almost intrigue, had slowly replaced the blank incredulity in Chance's face.

"I'll be blowed," he laughed. "Playing matchmaker, are you? That too, not just dramatist?" His tone changed. "I don't need a keeper quite yet, though, old man."

"Of course not. But I'm not trying to do anything but cover my own tracks. You don't have to *do* a thing—just not give me away. If it's ho for Texas—fine; it'll never matter one way or the other. I thought you should know, though. If you're ever asked, you were in the Territory these past few days, being Galahad."

"Still"—Chance peered thoughtfully into his whiskey—"the Territory's pretty much the same as Texas, from what I've heard tell. As good as—for running away to."

"Better even, perhaps, in your case. It wouldn't be running away, for you. The very opposite, in fact."

"I'd be returning to the scene of my derring-do?" Chance laughed. "It's a nice notion—oh, but I couldn't get away with it, Webb. Why, you must have been seen by—how many?"

"But seen as what, whom? What do people ever see but what they expect to see? They saw an ex-Confederate turned drifter, if not outright outlaw. And remember, the ones who matter most aren't going to be on hand much longer. If you were to show up playing the part . . . and you'd really only have to convince one person, you know. And *she* didn't see a thing, not really. She was right out of her head the whole time."

"You're overlooking the bigger picture. If I were to show up playing the famous part, Webb—first thing of all I'd be clapped in the Fort Cressup guardhouse."

"I don't think so, Chance. I've just sent a wire guaranteed to give the command at Fort Cressup other things to think about than a dead outlaw or even its own humiliation. The climate out there is due for revolutionary improvement."

Chance shook his head—not in negation, simply in amused amaze. "Blast you anyway, Webb. I'm put in mind, painfully so, of many a time when we were kids. You were so good at coming up with fancy campaign plans, that somehow called for you to be in command and me to do the footsoldiering; like the Battle of the Bee-tree, remember? *I* was the one who got stung!"

"Chance"—Starcross forbore to smile—"if it weren't for Candacy Ann I wouldn't be telling you this. I'd be—well, you know what I'd be doing. Oh, but don't you see? I *can't.* I—I honor-bound myself to Cathal McQuaife—and then found myself honor-bound to Candacy Ann; and Candacy Ann was there by my side while Cathal McQuaife was out of sight, out of reach.

"Still, I'm honor-bound to Cathal McQuaife. I must do what I can for her, within my constraints, which speak for themselves. With her father a fugitive, herself in shaky possession of something coveted by a gang of outlaws masquerading as the law, as the *army*—rendered still more vulnerable by the fact that, thanks to me, her reputation is blackened, she's a husbandless mother, a scarlet woman, fair game—she needs a champion, Chance, a friend—a *man.* Clearly, I can't be that man. I don't know what else I can do but recommend her to *my* best man."

For a long moment Chance said nothing, visibly touched. "She doesn't need your recommending, if memory serves. I was there too, you know, that night at Richwood, all those long years ago. She had a bit of a 'reputation' even then—colorful, if not quite black or scarlet; but the thing was, it made no difference—*makes* no difference. She's a woman in a million, everybody always said so." Chance mulled it over. "The thing that *does* make a difference, as I see it, is—*you* think so too."

"What? What do you mean?"

"I mean you love her. You love her still."

"Please, Chance. Have mercy. I love my wife."

"Oh, quite right, old man. Of course." Chance laughed gently. "Forgive me. 'Nough said."

"And I ought to be showing it." Starcross stirred. "Won't you come back to the hotel with me? Candacy Ann would like you to dine with us, I'm sure."

"I don't think so, Webb; though thanks all the same. I said my goodbyes when I looked in on her earlier. So I'll be on my way. There's a late afternoon coach; my luggage, my worldly all, awaits me at the station. And my finances don't run to lounging about swank resorts, like some I could name." Genially Chance grinned. "If I'm ever to mend my purse, I've got to get over into outlaw country and lift somebody else's, turn road agent or cattle rustler or—or imitation Galahad, who knows?"

"Are you serious? I mean about the country?"

"M'm—well, we'll see, won't we? As I said, it's more or less the same direction."

They parted outside, Starcross worrisomely watching his friend wavering down the steep street, then himself turning the other, uphill way, eyes hurrying on ahead toward the hotel visible through the trees, bulking against the afternoon sky.

Their talk had had at least as profound an effect on Starcross as on Chance. Not a man who allowed his feelings much latitude, when they did break through Starcross was apt to be seriously swayed. He now seemed to see his life, after all, as a whole—a tragic whole. Chance was right; but so was he. He seemed fated to go on forever cherishing one kind of love, the desperate longing for a passionate albeit ideal woman beyond his reach, in secret alongside or behind another kind, an everyday affection for a very real, quite down-to-earth woman all-too-much within his reach. About the latter, the frank exchange with Chance had left him feeling guilty, and almost maudlin. For his ideal love he could do nothing, nothing *more*. For the real one he could do something, and accordingly he must. His marriage meant much to him, more than he'd been able to tell Chance. Surely his duty to it outweighed his other duties. From the outset he had gone through the motions, hewed to the letter. Now he must rededicate himself to fulfilling the spirit. Somehow he must find anew with Candacy Ann that understanding, as he fancied he remembered it, of their earliest days. He had few illusions; Candacy Ann was that down-to-earth, practical, *typical* woman, with that womanly knack for reducing life to its commonplaceness, its trivia, and being quite content therewith. But didn't that mean just that it remained for *him* to make good the lacks—the spirit, the *passion?*

She met him at their sitting-room door, stood on tiptoe to kiss his cheek—wrinkling her nose at the sandpaper she found there. Just as when he had left, she was full of her father, her child, her other concerns, and would not have really looked at him at all, he thought, but for the unfamiliar experience of his stubble.

"I've decided to grow a beard," he hastened to explain, preparing to lay out his reasons; but Candacy Ann quickly cut in to make it clear she required no reasons.

"You'll look ever so distinguished, I'm sure, General." Smiling perfunctorily, she lapsed back into her wonted objectification of him—martial monuments *were* bearded. "It's good to have you back. I'm ever so worried about Papa."

"I'll just look in on him, then." Thoughts very much elsewhere, Starcross started for the connecting door. "I've . . . got something to tell you, Candacy Ann," he said, with a distracted glance back at her. "I met Chance on the street."

"Oh, did you? Good. Yes; he was here, looking for you. He wouldn't stay. Poor Chance!" She heaved a sigh. "Whatever is to become of him?" Inconsequently she chattered on as Starcross peeped through into the colonel's bedroom.

"He's asleep, it seems." He drew the door closed and came back. "Where are Zadok and Shuthelah?"

"Oh, I gave Shuthelah leave to go down to the colored bathhouse for the misery in her back." Candacy Ann smiled at her own generosity. "Zadok, I reckon he's wandering around somewhere. I swear, that boy grows more worthless every day."

"We can talk without being disturbed, then."

"Talk? About Chance?" Candacy Ann's eyes at last came to rest on him. "General, you're behaving almost like a jealous husband. Chance is as much my friend as yours."

"Not about Chance. Candacy Ann!" Starcross's voice rose in impatience. "Will you please sit down and be still, *listen?* What I have to say is going to take a while. It's not going to be easy; and it's terribly important . . . to you and me."

Her attention arrested at last by his stern tone, Candacy Ann dutifully backed down on the edge of the room's little settee and then, rather more reluctantly, leaned back in it, that she might gaze up at her husband. Faint frown-lines of concern or puzzlement formed on her brow. Starcross, however, found himself unable to sit beside her or even go on facing her. He began pacing in jerky little circles there on the carpet before her.

"Years ago," he began, speaking with great, almost physical difficulty, "before I ever thought of you as anything but my foster-sister—I hinted at this back East; but I don't think you truly took it in; it didn't mean so much then anyway, to you and me—years ago, I say, I was involved with a . . . with another woman."

"Webb—" Taken altogether by surprise, Candacy Ann let her characteristic formality slip. "I'm not *that* possessive . . . *that* jealous. That's . . . that's *your* business."

"No—that's my point. It isn't—it *wasn't* just my business. It was public knowledge, a bit of a sensation. You must be one of the few people who'd have to be told."

By steady degrees Candacy Ann was growing rather heavily hushed—ominously so. Her repeated protests began to bear a perfunctory ring. "You don't have to tell me."

"Yes, I do. Please don't interrupt. I'm finding it hard enough as it is. But I must tell you." As briefly and painlessly as he could, Starcross sketched what had happened between himself and Cathal McQuaife that late-1861 night in Brocksborough. "It was much as with you and me in Washington—only with her I *meant* it to happen. I meant to marry her—I gave her my mother's ring." He took another pacing turn, headshaking sadly. "But I made a mistake. I sent her back to her friends to complete the deception her coming to me had made possible. And then, between the war and her father's outrage, we were unable to be reunited. I was beside myself, ready to desert, seek her out; but my friends reminded me—*shamed* me—I had the war to fight.

"She," he went on miserably, "she was disgraced. Her father sent her away to the Indian Territory, where she gave birth to a child—my child. I'd never forgotten, though I learned that part of it only when I met General McQuaife in Virginia—it was just days before I came for you at your school. I told him I meant to finish what I'd begun, to right the wrong if I could, once I was free. He —he shook my hand," sickly. "I told you.

"But I was never free. Nobody ever is, it seems, not in this life. There's no such thing as freedom, as the late slaves are starting to find out. Oh, you know what I mean, Candacy Ann," Starcross appealed it: "You know what happened next."

Candacy Ann was staring, round-eyed, the eyes transfixed on his face. "You . . . you came to me, though pledged to her? You married me, though you . . . loved her?"

"No—no! It's—it's nothing so simple as that," Starcross protested, in the tone of a man who knows he is misunderstood, perversely blundering on all the same, clearly only making matters worse. "My love for you has nothing to do with what I feel—*felt*— for her. No," he corrected, beseeching her understanding: "*feel.* Oh, I'm sure I should have ceased to feel anything for her as soon as I felt something for you. But I couldn't. *Can't,* even now." He paused, and then took the final plunge. "For, you see, it's a bit more than something that happened long ago."

Passing a fretful hand over his brow, he went on with it, telling once again the story he'd told hardly an hour before, for Chance's edification, with judicious omissions, or at least adjustments of emphasis: how that day in the park he'd overheard, all anew, the name of Cathal McQuaife; how his late absence had taken him into the Indian Territory, and what he'd found there; and above all *done* there. In conclusion he thrust out his hand, held before her eyes the braided-gold ring on the little finger.

"She was still wearing it," he said, from the abysses of his misery. "I—I took it back. It was the hardest thing I've ever done in my life. But of course I had to do it."

"Webb." Candacy Ann began to stir. "I don't know what to say." And for once in her life this seemed to be literally true. Her uncertain, withdrawn look drove Starcross on to renewed efforts. He wrenched the ring from his finger and held it out.

"Here. It belongs to you by right."

A trifle mollified, she let him slide the ring on her finger, atop the wedding band. She lifted her hand, thoughtfully appraised the addition. "I don't know whether I want to wear it or not," she murmured. "It has such an unhappy history, as you tell it—recent as well as ancient. It didn't do *her* much good, did it?"

"You needn't wear it," he told her. "You *shouldn't,* for that matter. I've told you all this in the strictest confidence, of course. Nobody must ever know, above all about the ring. It would be a gratuitous blow to her pride, to learn it was I who took it from her, which I've done my best to obscure. I went there incognito, you see; I called myself by another name—by *Chance's* name. And when I saw Chance a while ago I told him the whole story, so he wouldn't contradict me by inadvertence, if the matter ever came up. He just might go there himself, in fact, out of curiosity if nothing else, and garner the credit. Who knows what might come of that? One way or the other, for us, it's over."

"Doesn't Chance have troubles enough of his own?"

"I think that, as much as anything else, was my motive for putting the idea in his head. Chance—surely I don't have to tell you—has been spiritually adrift since the war. That's his 'trouble,' nothing more. He badly needs a preoccupation, a cause. For his sheer salvation he needs a—an anchor. And Cathal McQuaife is anchor enough for the most unmoored of men."

"I never knew you to be so—so calculating, General."

"I'm not telling him what to do," Starcross argued, fretful; "it's wholly up to him. If he passes it up, goes his Texas way, it won't matter one way or the other. And if he should decide to visit Fort Cressup—*revisit* it, as the stranger who routed the intruders from Miss McQuaife's house and bound up her wound, it won't do him a bit of harm that I can see. The contrary."

Candacy Ann was untypically cynical. "It won't do *you* any harm either, will it?"

"Not just me. *Us.* Candacy Ann"—with a deepening sense of desperation, of failure, Starcross struggled to put across what was in his heart, to make her understand, perhaps even just to make himself understand—"there was no way for me to undo my involvement with Cathal McQuaife. The best I could do was try and put a decent period to it, as decent as humanly possible, without letting the world know I was doing so, giving it grist for malicious gossip, which could hardly do *you* any good, us any good—*us,* not just me. I hoped, *prayed* you'd understand. I haven't enjoyed this—this disrobing. Certainly I didn't do it as an indulgence. And if putting myself through it has not made clear my underlying feelings—well, then I despair. Of *us.*"

"Well, but of *course,* Webb—darling!" Candacy Ann caught his hand, drew him around to face her, smiling soothingly, dismissively, as to an irrationally upset child. "You must think me an awful woman if you think I *don't* understand. You've taken me by surprise, that's all." Again she held up her own hand, solemnly appraised the ring on her finger. "I reckon I'm as jealous as any woman with a husband she prizes," she confessed, the smile still fixed in place like a mask. "It's . . . unsettling enough suddenly learning he ever cared for another woman at all, let alone that he still cares *some*thing for her, enough to undertake extraordinary personal, risky, *secret* actions on her behalf. But I *do* understand, my dear, I do." She rose, closed the gap between them, the smile filling with real warmth, at last. "And we won't say any more about it, will we?" she ended. "We won't have to."

EIGHTEEN

That evening, following a strained supper, Candacy Ann hurried back to her father. Left to his restless self, Starcross went for a walk in the hotel's woodsy grounds. The fateful talk, however satisfactorily concluded, as it seemed, left him feeling grimly dissatisfied. The confession had drained him, physically almost, and left him with the feeling it had all been for nothing, that Candacy Ann *hadn't* understood at all, indeed might just be incapable of understanding. Starcross knew he knew little about women, about the workings of their minds; but knew enough to sense that such understanding probably was impossible, and its lack no failure of his or even of Candacy Ann's. Other men, he knew, made no effort at all toward such understanding with their wives. But he was idealist enough to have hoped for a fuller relationship with his; which was why he'd simply *had* to share his mind with her. Yet the would-be cathartic conversation had left him feeling not just harried and disappointed but haunted by the suspicion that his good intentions had done more harm than good.

He lost all track of the time; for when Zadok's drawling voice jerked him back to himself, the long June twilight, he saw with a start, had all but faded from the dense trees; and the voice, lazing as ever, all the same bore an urgency suggesting that much time had flown and his return was overdue. "Missus General" wanted him, was the message. Accompanying the childish young man back to their suite, he found Candacy Ann frantically pacing the sitting room. In relief she surged forward.

"General! For goodness' sake where have you *been?* It's Papa. He's—he's taken bad. The doctor was here. He said there was—just nothing he could do."

Starcross eyed the connecting door. "What is it exactly?"

"Oh, I don't know. The doctor made no more sense than ever. Something must have happened, he said, something *inside.* Oh, Papa's rational enough, but so—so agitated. It came on him all of a sudden. And he's been asking for *you.*"

"For *me*?" Starcross absorbed the surprise, nodded. With Candacy Ann following, he stepped through into the next room. Shuthelah, sitting by the bedside, sprang to her feet. The old man was awake, lying pillow-propped. He looked paler and frailer, Starcross thought; but his eyes were bright as ever.

"Webb! Webb, my boy, my dear boy! Candacy Ann"—relief strengthened the frail voice as the colonel accosted his daughter—"Webb and I must have a little talk."

"Of course, Papa. Whatever you say. Webb—be sure to call me if—if you need me." She gave up the effort to be reassuring—to reassure herself. "Come along, Shuthelah."

The women withdrawn, Starcross took the chair beside the bed, drew it closer. Colonel Colquhoun struggled to sit up, but then helplessly sagged back on the pillows. Starcross stayed his own forward motion, so clearly helpless alike.

"Don't tire yourself, Colonel—please."

"Webb!" Feebly grasping Starcross's hand on the bed edge, the old man eyed him with urgent intent; still he seemed unable to speak his mind at once. "Don't coddle me, Webb. I haven't time for it. And I've got to—to unburden myself."

"Do you want to see a minister, sir? This Reverend—what is it?—Gazaway, the one Candacy Ann's been talking to—"

"Damn Reverend Gazaway! I'm not the man for it, that sort of thing. Oh, I'll see the worthy reverend, if there's time, just for Candacy Ann's sake. But you're the priest for me, Webb. Oh, don't you *see*? But of course you don't—you *don't* see. That's just it, the very thing. That's why I've got to tell you."

"I'm sure it can't be as serious as you seem to think, Colonel, as terrible." Starcross tried not to be "coddling," but found it hard. "Few things are, when all's said and done."

"Forgive a weak, frightened old man if you can, Webb. I—I couldn't face it, just couldn't face it, that's all. I wasn't used to being poor and powerless. I didn't mind for myself, of course, not at all. But for Candacy Ann—I couldn't bear for her to be denied at least the shadow of the life I'd imagined for her, and that she'd imagined for herself; denied it by my failure, my final failure. I'd failed in all else; and that I could accept. But to have to admit that final failure—it was more than I could bear."

Starcross tried to quell his uncomprehending frown. "We've been through this before, sir. And I've assured you—"

"We *touched* on it before," the colonel conceded. "I hinted at it. But you didn't pick up on the hint, not really. And I didn't have the courage to make it clear."

"I can't see how you could have been clearer, sir. Anyway," cheerily, "what does it matter? It's all worked out for the best. Candacy Ann and I are perfectly happy."

"Never mind Candacy Ann. Oh, it's all worked out well for Candacy Ann! *She's* happy, I'm sure." The colonel smiled grimly, confidingly. "I love my daughter, Webb. But I have no illusions about her. And I love and respect my foster-son, my son-in-law. And the thought I may have wronged the latter for the sake of the former—I can't go to my grave without owning it, facing up to it, even if it means now . . . wronging the former." Starcross stared, wanting to break in but unable to speak. "Webb, Webb—oh, you *must* see it: You were *tricked.* We—we *trapped* you."

"No, I *don't* see, Colonel," Starcross insisted.

"We set a trap for you, and you let us do it. You let yourself be trapped, because you're the man you are." The colonel shook his head sadly. "And the bitter irony of it is, you'd have let yourself be 'trapped' all the same, without the trap."

"Colonel, I assure you," Starcross soothed—"coddled"—"I don't know what you're talking about."

"Maybe it wasn't wholly conscious, coldblooded; but there it was. Could I *honestly* have asked you to see Candacy Ann home without harboring the ghost of the thought—what a perfect banishing of my nightmare if only *you* were to take Chance's place at her side, not for the journey only but for life . . . if something were to blossom along the way between the two of you?"

Stunned, Starcross strove to muster his wits. "If our idlest thoughts, our fleetingest dreams, are criminal, Colonel, we're all guilty. Guilt lies in actions, not thoughts. And I'm the one who acted. Trap? It would be truer to say I trapped myself. But it's better, surely, that we don't think in such terms at all, traps and trapping. It demeans what we have, the happiness we have from it, despite all. Suffice it to say I did a wrong, but it was the kind of wrong that's really only a misplaced right, and so I was able to make it up, make it right. It grieves me that you ever had to know. I don't know what Chance may have told you, Colonel; but you must have been sorely disappointed in me."

"Chance." The old man brushed this aside. "Chance told me very little; he was the soul of delicacy, of decency. Of course he had to tell me his real reason for withdrawing his suit—not his poverty. Not the poverty of his purse, that is, but the poverty of his passion—of Candacy Ann's. And then he had to account for his initial anger, for the duel, which even apart from his injured arm couldn't have been kept from me for long. He said just that Candacy Ann had made her true feelings and wishes perfectly clear, as you had yours. Leaving me to fill in the particulars for myself: that the only obstacle to a happy outcome was himself; that you, once that obstacle had been removed. . . ."

"Would be sure to do the right thing." Starcross was recalling Chance's words: Any other man, any other but he, would have smelled what was coming, scented the "trap," and made himself scarce. And whose trap? The colonel's only?

"Please—you mustn't blame Chance," the colonel hastened to add, as if reading his mind. "He *was* my co-conspirator, in a sense. He helped me set the trap, spring it, or at least handed me the opportunity; but it wasn't truly a *knowing* conspiring on his part. And he was moved only by the most selfless, most beneficent of motives. To trust you to do that right thing, without compulsion, that was as far as Chance's contribution went. The rest, the 'compulsion'—for that's what it amounted to—the haste, the unwillingness to confide in you, to *trust* you, ye gods—all that was *my* doing, mine alone. I've owned my motive, tried. I was a man bedeviled. Candacy Ann's homecoming brought me face to face with it, my last, worst devil: the chortling imp of my failure of her whom I most loved. And there at her side stood *you*—Lohengrin, swooped down from the clouds and, alas, destined to ascend soon again to the clouds, leaving us mere mortals in our coil of troubles. You were a lifeline, Webb, and I grasped it, frantically, without thought, almost without will, by sheer reflex. Between my fear and my pride, I couldn't *ask* you to come to my rescue. So-o, I stooped to tricking you into doing so—forcing you."

Starcross at last managed, "And what of—what of Candacy Ann? Was her part conscious or unconscious?"

"Candacy Ann was no part of my—deceit; my co-conspirator in no sense. She volunteered nothing, and I didn't press her. Only asked her if what Chance had said were true: that you, not he, were the true object of her affections. She said—"

"Yes. But for all you know—for all *she* knows herself even, she may have been playing her own little part."

"Playing the part a woman always plays, oh, undoubtedly. If she'd made up her mind she wanted you for a husband, she'd have had her little ways of pursuing, realizing the desire, giving it every opportunity of realizing itself; nothing any woman in such a position wouldn't have done, nothing to be held against her. But what *I* did, Webb, did to you—unconscionable."

"My dear colonel, you didn't do anything. Because you knew you didn't have to. That I'd have wed Candacy Ann all the same, once it was clear Chance no longer—"

"Just so—that's the rub, the thing, the worst of it. You would have, and I knew it in my heart, I was sure of it, of you. But I was beyond reasons even of the heart. My desperation fed on itself. I couldn't leave it to hap. Any instant you might have been called away. I didn't dare do what I'd have liked: simply sat by and let nature find its own way, let things between you and Candacy Ann go on blossoming of themselves. Instead, I stooped to the trap—the most needless trap in the history of venery."

"And the most toothless—the most painless." Starcross soothed, "coddled," in all earnest. "There was no trap, Colonel. You distress yourself over nothing."

"Noble of you to say so, my boy. Just what I would expect. Of these last months, you know, I've had a great deal of time for reflection, on many things. Thanks wholly to you, Webb, I've been able to live out my last days in ease and outward happiness. I've been able to put aside the scheming selfishness that drove me to assure that end; and what has emerged, Webb, is renewed and redoubled respect for you. You are the son I would have had if I could. My God! And how have I repaid your sonship? Is Candacy Ann worth such a price, is she worthy of such a husband? You would have wed her all the same, you say, and naturally I believe you; but now neither of us will ever know for sure. It may be wrong of me to burden you with all this at this point, when in any case nothing can be done about it; but I've *had* to do so just for my own peace. And moreover, I think I've said nothing you didn't already know in your heart. I think you have had a nagging doubt about your marriage, without knowing why. And so I've only clarified your doubt, perhaps even helped you exorcise it. If not, if I've merely added to your grief—well, then I can but ask you to forgive me, if you can, *that* too. And it's such a little thing alongside the other—a trifle. If you can forgive me for deceiving you, you can forgive me for telling you you were deceived."

"If there is anything to forgive—Father—it is forgiven."

"You mustn't call me that," the colonel said, sadly and sternly together. "Your father was my good friend, and a good man. I'm sure you remember that as well as I do."

"I remember—I remember much." Webb Starcross did remember, and he fancied that for-the-nonce they remembered together: the now old man who at the head of his Dragoons and Rangers on the Texas Plains had come on the wagon train beset by Yapparika Comanches, and driven the attackers away only to find the bodies of Jason Starcross and his wife and two children; and the other man who that day as a ten-year-old boy behind a rifle had stood up amidst the shambles and stolidly greeted his father's old friend. "But a man may have two fathers," this latter man said. "If any man has, *I* have had two fathers."

"Thank you, Webb. Thank you." With the greatest effort the colonel raised a hand and held it out wavering, to be grasped in Starcross's. His tired eyes brimmed. "Son!"

His own eyes as full, Starcross withdrew quietly, leaving the old man in seeming peace, in a fuller peace at least than he had found him, hardly half an hour before.

But Starcross himself was anything but at peace. It was as if the colonel's "confession"—it had been a day for ill-starred "confessions"—had merely shifted his burden to younger shoulders, strong but already overburdened shoulders. Myriad contradictory thoughts and feelings vied for attention in Starcross's mind as he passed into the sitting room where Candacy Ann sat waiting; and the sight of her brought to the surface and renewed an even intenser wave of that letdown, or even disappointment, that had followed his own "confession." The colonel's disclosure simply confirmed for Starcross what he had already begun to know: that in "confessing" he had immolated himself for nothing. At great emotional cost he had striven to maintain his marriage on a sublime level of mutual honesty and trust; and it had now been brought home to him that honesty was a thing never truly to be known between Candacy Ann and himself, that his marriage had been raised on a teetery foundation of dishonesty, and that consequently trust as well must be diminished.

Candacy Ann stood, smiled vacuously, and expectantly, as if to let him share with her what her father had shared, if he would; and then, when he wouldn't, matter-of-factly, the smile fading, slipped past him, back to her father's bedside.

To Starcross it was painfully emblematic. What her father had shared with him he could never share with her. Never, ever again would he be able wholly to confide in her, for fear that she did not confide in him. The colonel had been at pains to exonerate her; yet as the colonel himself had said, with that honesty of one seesawing on the brink of eternity, he had revealed nothing Starcross had not already known in the depths of his heart. Ever had there been a canker of doubt in the back of his mind, doubt of the root of his marriage, fugitive doubt even of Candacy Ann herself. The colonel's confidences had cast glaring light on the question of her motives on the occasion of their reunion in the East. Now that canker of doubt would linger forever, afester.

But Starcross was accustomed to meet troubles manfully, confront the reverses of personal life even as those of the battlefield, and ever keep his own counsel. An onlooker would have noticed no difference in him in the days following his seemingly unnoted absence from Thermopolis. The emotional upheavals that accompanied or ensued it were known to no one. Chance Buckhannon, of course, knew just what had happened in that absence; but Chance was himself absent. Candacy Ann knew; but Candacy Ann would be the last person on earth to reveal it. And Colonel Colquhoun knew that an element, at least, of deception, trickery, had entered into the making of his daughter's marriage. But only Starcross himself knew all these things together. He, who had been alone for most of his days, and contentedly so, newly cut off from all other souls by burdensome knowledge, began to feel in coming days an unfamiliar pang of loneliness.

Colonel Colquhoun failed to recover from his late turn for the worse. Only hours after Starcross's visit, he grew newly agitated, prey to irrational fears and alarms. The household spent an anxious, sleepless night, unblinkable as other than a death-watch. The early rays of summer dawn were breaking over Thermopolis's wooded hills when Colonel Duncan Colquhoun, his loved ones gathered about his bed, regained his composure for the last brief time and then peacefully breathed his last, his daughter prayerfully on her knees against the bedside; his foster-son and son-in-law statuesque at the foot; on the off side, in Shuthelah's arms, his heedless grandson, fetched in for his final blessing; and in the background Zadok, moaning-on choruslike.

Candacy Ann bore her bereavement bravely, soon putting visible sorrow aside to confront the countless practical problems of a death in a hotel far from home: mourning wear to be selected and fitted, strangers to be consulted, even relied upon, affidavits from Dr. Limpus and others to be collected to make the colonel's demise official and so assure payment of his modest insurance. In these, as well as more spiritual matters, the Reverend Gazaway proved himself very helpful, unobtrusively seeing the Starcrosses through the trying steps of preparation for funeral and interment. Candacy Ann quickly acceded to the impracticability of returning the colonel's remains either to Richwood, now the property of strangers, or to St. Louis. Thermopolis's lack of railroad service and the burgeoning heat of the season called for a local, early interment. On a steep hill overlooking the town, all but lost in the dense woods, lay a little burying ground where others who had failed to find their lost health in this venue of health-giving waters found at least their earthly rest. It seemed but right for Colonel Duncan Colquhoun to be added to their ranks.

Candacy Ann had found time to befriend other visitors; and moreover there were a handful of eccentric Thermopolitans who made it their connoisseurlike avocation to salute the misfortunes of visitors by attending their funerals. Colonel Colquhoun's graveside service was well-attended, therefore, much to Candacy Ann's gratification; though for Starcross the onlooking faces had no reality or meaning. His surroundings as a whole, he noted with dismay, for him any more had ever less reality.

As they reentered the hotel following the burial, the bell captain bore down upon him bearing a tray on which lay a telegram envelope. Candacy Ann had invited the minister to join them for supper, that the meal might have something of the formality and dignity of a funeral repast; and Starcross, letting the two go ahead into the dining room, tarried to read his telegram.

As he anticipated, the long message was in cipher. He found a writing desk in a corner and sat, taking the key from his pocket notebook. The code was quite a simple one and he transcribed it quickly; though from long habit he forbore trying to take in its burthen as he went. Not till he had finished and the whole communication lay written out before him, in his own blocky hand, on a white page of his own notebook, did the words and letters and phrases cease to be mere marks and take on a coherent import. The impersonal words were Blake Frear's:

With difficulty meeting your requests. Lt. Klyce promoted captain, Col. Chievous suspended, disposition pending your inquiry. To wit you are appointed command Southwestern Subdepartment headquartered Ft. Cressup directly commanding there pro tem. Situation there your responsibility but remind you War Department has no authority Indian affairs or agents. Must also advise political climate throws in doubt ability your friends oblige future. Your orders on way by usual. Your prayer answered. Congratulations or commiserations as case may be. Regards and luck.

Starcross sat staring at the paper till the words blurred. Yes: his prayer had been answered, and it had turned out a mixed blessing at least, if not quite, as per the old saying, a curse. He had been granted his heart's desire, a Western command, where he might be at least *close* to real soldiering, if not directly joining in it. But the sunny boon had been overcast by undreamt-of clouds. For the first time ever had he flexed that muscle of "influence" which he had so long ago acquired; but the motion had in a sense recoiled on his head. For he had sought not just to mend the situation he had found at Fort Cressup but at the same time to distance himself from it. Toward that end had he bared his breast to Chance, and to Candacy Ann. Yet now he and she, if not Chance as well, ironically were caught up in it together.

First of all he faced the unsavory duty of breaking the news to Candacy Ann that he and she now were to go and dwell hard by that other woman his attachment to whom, he had assured her, was a thing all of the dead past, though to whom he had just seen fit to pay a clandestine visit. She wouldn't object, of course, or even question, any more than he himself would question or object to his orders. But already he could see her looks, and even read her thoughts. This new development, he foresaw, could only worsen that division that had been growing up between them. Untypically he found himself facing the future with near-dread, with a nameless foreboding gripping his heart.

Ruefully he took up the transcribed message, read it through another time, and then drew a match from his pocket, touched the flame to both cipher and transcription, crushed the carbonized remains in his hands, and scattered the ashes.

NINETEEN

The first days of the new commandant at Fort Cressup were crowded, hectic, full of seismic shocks in the public eye; yet none ever quite as real to himself as the rumblings rather of his private life—e.g. his reunion with Chance Buckhannon.

Not for many a year had Fort Cressup been a fort indeed, or observed conditions of strict security. No longer an outpost, it was rather a nerve-center and distribution point for the real outposts, farther West. And locally it had become in essence but the center of the surrounding settlement—the inexorably exploding white community in a land supposedly forever reserved for Redmen. The road through the military reservation, as outward peacetime returned to stay, had begun to serve also, indeed mostly, as the conduit for nonmilitary traffic between "the States" and the Plains. Indians, wild and tame, found loafing and napping places in the shade of the fort buildings, blockhouses ignobly reduced to mere offices. Civilian whites afoot or ahorse came and went along the dusty or muddy track. Starcross, one deskbound afternoon chancing to glance out his office window in Headquarters House, easily made out the showy rider showily prancing the splendid blooded black up to the hitching rail and vaulting down.

Horse's and rider's fine accouterments alike clearly told that Chance's fortunes had undergone a marked improvement since their last meeting in Thermopolis, but months before. Of course the full story of that improvement already had reached Starcross's ears in detail. Well aware of Chance's mission, he told his orderly that the visitor was to be admitted, and stood waiting. Soon the friends were once more, first, grasping hands, then shoulders. Starcross made a point of letting the outer office staff witness the hearty reunion before closing the door and gesturing to the chair fernent his desk, and then circling to his own.

"So"—breathing a note of disbelief—"you came. And stayed."

"*Veni, vidi,* anyhow—the *vici* already taken care of, so to speak." All broad grin, glancing at the closed door, Chance went on lightly, if more seriously too: "You put me onto a good thing, old man. The . . . merchandise, if I may be crass for a moment, was every bit as advertised. Mrs. Buckhannon, as she now is"—mock-loftily, self-mockingly—"looks forward to welcoming you to the neighborhood. We're a mite disappointed, for that matter, both of us, not yet to have been given the opportunity."

"Much on my mind, Chance, as I oughtn't to have to tell you. Besides—" Visibly Starcross altered what he'd been about to say. "I congratulate you, Chance. You work fast—when you *do* work. I . . . I hope to God it all turns out for the best."

"No reason why it shouldn't." Chance grew still more confiding, more serious. "I understand your . . . your old agony now, Webb. A . . . a remarkable woman, Cathal."

"Yes-s. And she received you as—as—"

"Her savior?" Chance smiled a wry affirmative, but at once turned sober yet again. "We were married within weeks, as soon as she was fully on the mend. Oh, I'm a living legend hereabouts. The Galahad, the Lohengrin who came back!"

"No suggestion of the guardhouse, then?"

"Oh, anything but. I'm untouchable, 'twould seem. Not to say, miles in your debt, old man. Or in your power, if you would. You can undo me, you know, with a word."

"My dear Chance, I couldn't. You know I couldn't; not without undoing myself. Besides, if you're in my debt, or my power, it's no more than turnabout. I was in yours—*am* in yours; and, in the face of great provocation, you chose not to undo me. I sincerely hope I'll prove, am proving, as—as true a friend."

They found themselves bandying heartfelt looks like hot potatoes. At long last selfconsciously both looked aside at once, forced their minds together into manlier channels.

"I didn't ask for this assignment, I hope you know that," Starcross muttered. "I don't relish it at all. It's going to be damned awkward. That's part of why I've—avoided you." He hesitated. "How is Cath—Mrs. Buckhannon taking it?"

"The new commandant?" Chance thought it over. "Cathal and I confide on most subjects but not all, and above all not *that*. Outwardly she's indifferent. I can't tell you what goes on under the surface; but I'm sure I don't have even to *try* to tell you Cathal's a resilient, indomitable lady. She'll meet you with the same grace and pride and reserve she'd meet any other prominent man. Fort Cressup will never know from her—" Chance stopped, pondered again. "Oh, it knows already, of course; but *that* lies too far in the dead past any longer to matter. The gossips are tired of it. For them it's nothing to do with the present."

"If only it were so for me! If only I could expect so well of myself. That I'll never betray the past by my present." Starcross stirred, unwontedly uneasy. "And—the child?"

"Star—that's her name." Chance's voice dropped, took on an even more delicate tone. "Cathal's never dissembled being an unwed mother—though *your* name's never passed her lips. It's none of her doing the girl's paternity's an open secret, one of those things all know but none speaks of. Cathal herself keeps silence, and since in such cases the world condemns the woman while excusing the man, the open secret will, I feel sure, remain more secret than open. The putative father's return to the vicinity of mother and child, after so long, may furnish grist for the mills of a diehard bilious tongue or two; but most people, even the bilious, have less farfetched scandals to savor."

"You're most encouraging, Chance . . . I think!" Starcross laughed, though with effort. "Tell me, though: what of the—the trouble that first brought me here?"

Chance gave a delicate cough into his fist. "That's what I came to see you about—second, of course, to welcoming an old friend." He frowned, rapt in thought. "Cathal and I haven't truly confided on that score either. She's volunteered very little—and of course I have to be careful in my curiosity, not to give away the potentially fatal fact that my own knowledge, for the most part, comes very much at second hand."

"Yes-s. Well, *my* curiosity suffers no such constraint."

The biting tone, full of hinted menace, left Chance looking anxious. He leaned forward. "I pray you, Webb—back off a bit. You've been raising holy hell around here."

"I vowed to turn this place on its ear. I'm keeping my vow."

"And what is it gaining you—apart, I presume, from some private, some *selfish* satisfaction?"

Rather to his own surprise, Starcross took the barbed words anything but amiss. He was too much struck by their irony—by the fact of his private anything-*but*-satisfaction.

"Indeed," he conceded. "Raising hell may have its perverse satisfactions but it's not necessarily productive. I arrived to find Colonel Chievous, my predecessor, away in New Orleans, urgently consulting a medical specialist. Far from being fit to face an inquiry, he's had to proceed straight to the quiet and seclusion of a seacoast and begin a long rest-cure. Lieutenant Colonel Rollow, who would have taken over, already was on leave, a leave from which he has yet to return. There was the sense of rats and the sinking ship. My hell-raising perforce has been confined to the small fry, and that's proved frustrating in its own way. Captain Eadred Coonce, who commanded the detail that assaulted and occupied the McQuaife house, turns out a decent soldier only obeying the commands of his superior with little information by which to judge them. I could only respect him for the way he stood up to me and explained and defended himself.

"That leaves only the agent, Gaunce, and his faceless ilk, whose name seems to be legion, and over whom, as I've been reminded, and not only by him, I have no authority. The swine—would you believe he had the gall to call on me and, if not in so many words, offer to 'cut me in' on what he isn't doing?"

"I'd believe. And—and he didn't . . . *know* you?"

"Oh no. Thanks be for small blessings. Gaunce, as I soon found, is nearsighted. And even apart from that, he saw what he expected to see: a bewhiskered, dandified general, not a shabby, fugitive rebel with a stubbled chin and a rather unnerving way with a revolver." Starcross grimaced. "'Authority' or no, I warned him I'd have my eye on him; and if he ever ventured back in this office I'd take pleasure in personally, bodily throwing him out."

"The bull-ox in the Fort Cressup china-closet!" But Chance's smile soon faded. "If only the right things get broken! Webb—you can't break the Gaunces of this world. Forget him, can't you? Forget it all! Some messes are better left be."

Starcross stared, perplexed, dismayed. "Chance—I found Cathal with a bullet in her breast and that scoundrel in her house, thick as thieves—fittingly—with men of the command I now head. I tell you, the holy hell is only beginning!"

"But that's all of the past now, Webb. By all means, shake up your army all you please—but not on Cathal's account. Must I remind you, she's no longer your responsibility, in any sense? If that's still an issue, it's for her and me to deal with—"

"I can't agree with you, Chance. I can't leave it to you and Cathal—to private vengeance, or no action at all, or whatever it is you may have in mind. I can't and I won't."

"Would you bring the same righteous fervor to your crusade if the victim were some other woman?"

"Righteous?" Starcross stared. "I'm not going to answer that, Chance—nor quarrel with you. But I *will* do my duty."

Chameleonlike, Chance melted in hearty laughter—laughter at himself. "Honestly, can you believe it? In three short months I've turned into a jealous husband! And showing it toward the last man on earth to whom I've any right to do so!"

"You have every right, Chance. Cathal is yours."

"Aye; just so. And my feeling—my *fear,* Webb, is that more of your shaking-up and holy-hell-raising and turning things on their ear just might prove embarrassing not only to your army but perhaps, through some of her friends, to Cathal."

"Chance." Starcross sat forward, earnest, concerned. "Old friend—don't mince words! What am I missing? What do you know that I don't? That you're not telling me?"

"It's no big mystery, Webb. We've just come out of a bitter war. Not all those on the losing side accept their undoing with the kind of amiable complacency you see sitting before you. This Territory's a refuge for many—wild spirits to start with—who personally have never surrendered; and the Civilized Tribes—they never liked the Yankee government anyhow, and most of them bolted and backed the South. And atop all else, the ugliest specimens among the winners swarm the land like righteous locusts. You'll find it all boils down to the simple, sordid, timeless, turkey-buzzard squabble—to *war,* in a word, o'er the spoils of war. You—'I'—walked in on a skirmish in that war."

"And Cathal's . . . 'friends' . . . ?"

"The McQuaifes and the Tribes are friends, yes, from before the Removal—I don't know the whole story. And then, any old Confederate, however reprobate—yours truly, for one—is Cathal's friend. And Cathal stands by her friends."

"Against the enemy, anyhow." Memories stirred; Starcross stirred too. "'Whoever he may be.' Oh, I know the lady—if man ever knows woman! As—steadfast a one as ever breathed."

Chance's smile came and went yet again. "*Stubborn*, some might make it, if not something even less polite."

"Spoils of war! There'll be no spoils—there'll be no *war,* unless I do the waging of it, while I'm in command here. I won't abide lawlessness from either side."

The smile fled Chance's face altogether; he shook his head. "There may be forces at work too ramified, too complex, for you or any other one man, however mighty—"

"*What* 'forces'? What do you *mean*, Chance?"

"Oh, don't be simple, Webb. What do you think I mean? I mean human greed, human pride—human*ness*! Do you honestly fancy you have a chance against them?"

Starcross frowned. "No-o . . . I can't drive the devil out of the world, *his* world—I'm not quite *that* simple, Chance! But I fancy I can drive his minions out of my jurisdiction."

"If you can make them out in the first place: there's the rub! There's a bit of the devil in each of us, along with the angel, as you once reminded me." All wry grin Chance roused, came to his feet. "Well, I mustn't take up any more of your time—devil-downing's a time-consuming business. And *I'm* the devil, or at least one of his minions, to most of *your* minions. They looked daggers enough at me coming in; I don't suppose you noticed. Untouchable or no, I'm not a popular figure in these august premises, you know, and not just for having fought on the 'wrong' side, but for going right on doing so. For throwing in my lot with the local devils . . . deviless. For wiving the 'Queen of the Outlaws'."

The term brought a grimace. "We must change all that, you and I—we four. Just the place to start. Candacy Ann and I are holding a reception in two nights' time. I'll expect you and Mrs. Buckhannon, along with everybody else who *is* anybody in these parts—guns and bowie knives left at the door. Any who don't come willingly, I swear I'll send a squad for them."

"But of course we'll come, Webb," Chance rejoined. "With pleasure. And till then please give dear old Candacy Ann my very warmest regards—from the bottom of my heart."

"It would hardly be proper for me to be so . . . fulsome; but my best wishes to Cath—to your good lady, Chance."

The other memorable event, most memorable, undoubtedly, for Starcross of his own Fort Cressup "initiation" was of course the reception he'd mentioned to Chance—or at least the exquisitely private side of that would-be very public occasion.

The introductory gathering held by the new commandant and his lady wife on a warm October evening was, would have been in any case, a landmark in Fort Cressup's languid social calendar. What scant "society" the area boasted was rather a plural, "societies"—a ragbag of clans and cliques, that never functioned as a unit, indeed did each its damnedest to avoid the company of the others altogether. Invitations, then, in the accepted sense, had not been issued, merely an all-inclusive, broadside bidding that might well have been taken as a command, albeit anything but an unwelcome one; every faction, as it turned out, being eagerer to take the measure of the new commandant, and of his relations with the others, than to snub those others for an evening.

The blanket invitation having of course included the Indian agents, even Caughlin Gaunce was there, doubtless taking measures of his own. Agent and general acknowledged each other's presence—existence—in the main by scorning it.

Most of the downstairs of massive boarded-over squared-log Headquarters House (the Starcrosses lived upstairs) had been taken over for the evening, its workaday furnishings of desks, chairs, and cabinets moved back to the walls and at least mellowed, if not quite hidden, with patriotic drapery. At one end, a uniformed group made music with piano and strings; while at the other stood tables with brimming punchbowls and a surprisingly sumptuous standup feast. Hard by the entrance stood the general and his lady, she at the height of her glory in a fashionable peach tulle gown, he perhaps more glorious still in his gold-encrusted dress blue, complete to gold-tasseled saber.

For both, the evening was historic: for Candacy Ann an unrelieved triumph; for Starcross an auspicious if merely dutiful routine—at least till a stir at the doorway marked the coming of the Buckhannons: an event to all, it seemed, but to Starcross the all-overshadowing event. As if all-unexpectedly he found himself trading looks, through the milling coming-and-going unregarded others, with the woman with whom he had last so traded looks in a glorious dawn on the humpbacked bridge at Brocksborough in the first year of the war. His own riveted attention drew little note, since she commanded all the room's attention, not only for her beauty, which Starcross was seeing for really the first time since that landmark *first* time, that antebellum, nay antediluvian night at Richwood: the famous rust-red hair, full-grown, framing the firm, full, fine-cut face fairly radiating health and seemingly unfazed by the years and their travails, offset by a plush gown the very green of her eyes; commanded attention not only for that beauty but as well because of her delicate relationship with the fort, not to mention her yet-more-delicate unmentioned, indeed unmentionable relationship with its new commandant. It might have been the latter's fancy, but to him it seemed the room's hubbub of other converse tapered off in suspenseful expectancy.

"Ah—Webb, Candacy Ann." Chance's formal introduction might have taken them both in, or only Candacy Ann. "Let me present my wife, Cathal."

Candacy Ann acknowledged, as if for both, with matching formality and perfect grace, and then unbent in a warmer if somewhat saccharine smile: "We must become fast friends, Mrs. Buckhannon. We have so much in common."

"Have we, Mrs. Starcross?"

Candacy Ann neatly, mildly turned the mild rebuff. "After all, as I'm sure I needn't tell you, it's by bare hap *I'm* not your handsome husband's wife." She beamed at Chance. "And we share such like backgrounds, you and I; *and* Chance"—playfully scancing her own man. "Webb's the only Yankee among us."

"Webb, a Yankee?" Chance scolded, alike playful. "Don't be insulting." As for his wife's edification, however needlessly, he added, "The three of us grew up together."

"Then *I* am the stranger," mused Cathal Buckhannon.

"No no—we adopt you. The Three Musketeers are become four," Candacy Ann reassured, with all the social sweetness at her command. "Our lady D'Artagnan!"

The Buckhannons moved along, among the other guests, inevitably if imperceptibly drawn to their own, unreconstructed kind, among the others: the Radicals; the would-be neutrals, Dr. Cripliver and merchant Mr. Cheatle and their desiccated dames, the Reverend Captain Yonderly and his fat one, stock dealers, commission merchants and like transients; even the stolid delegation of Indians whose entry, very fashion-plates in impeccable frocks and cravats and top-hats, set rippling almost more of a stir of breathless suspense than the Buckhannons' own. These were not blanket Indians, but cultivated, educated men who had spent time in European capitals as well as Washington and Richmond. Chief Rayne, for one, was famous for his ambiguous allegiance. His tribe had formally seceded, and Federal hopes of rallying the rank-and-file about him in a rival tribal government had come to little. Starcross made a try at stroking the old chief and his stone-faced entourage, mouthing the proper if vacuous words, promising an early visit, a parley; but he found it heavy going, not least because his own thoughts were so cripplingly elsewhere.

His one interval alone with those thoughts' subject came on the heels of her own more-than-friendly exchange with the Red-men as they moved along; and he seized on this bridge over the awkward silence as he took her empty punch glass and absently passed it to the parade-dressed soldier server.

"You enjoy the confidence of the Indians to a remarkable degree, it would seem," he ventured.

"To the army's envy? Its chagrin?"

"To its puzzlement, at least—to mine, I should say; I'm not the army." Starcross groped for the right words. "Which seems to have trouble earning that confidence for itself."

"Then the army must change its behavior. One hopes that's what you've come for, General." Cathal McQuaife Buckhannon's regal smile was cool, fairly glacial, as she took back her refilled glass. "The sympathy between the Indians and me and mine is soon accounted for, by our similar experiences. They, too, have been harried out of house and home, had those homes besieged, entered, and plundered by heroes in blue, and themselves been maimed and murdered with impunity."

Starcross hastened to say, "Nobody regrets the—the outrage of last June more than I. I'm doing all I can to find out just what happened—how it could have happened."

"Don't put yourself out on my account, General, please." She smiled wryly—or was it grimly? Electrically their eyes met. "My words have an eerily familiar ring."

"Cathal—!" Starcross caught himself in time, however, let the fateful, heartrending reminder pass unpursued. "Not on your account—or not just. On the army's account rather; for its own good. For"—still he groped—"for principle."

"Principle." Her lips quirked. "That word too has a familiar ring. It takes me back. . . ."

Starcross swallowed, uncharacteristically discountenanced. "But to succeed," he persevered, "I must have help. You must help me; help me more than Chance, it seems, is inclined to do." He cast about. "We must talk about it later."

She too glanced about, saw Candacy Ann standing between two fawning officers, beaming from one to the other.

"Your wife is very beautiful—that classic blonde beauty." She brought her eyes back to Starcross—two green gimlets. "And I seem to remember a sort of prophecy I once uttered." Ironically, "I seem, indeed, to be full of memories."

"Cathal," he agonized. "I pray you, understand—"

"Shouldn't it be Mrs. Buckhannon to you, General? Well, but please believe me, there's nothing for me to understand. There's nothing to do with me that you need concern yourself about. I am happily married to a gallant gentleman who is perfectly capable of looking after me and my interests—who's proved it, I'd say. I don't want to—to risk that happiness by dwelling on the past," coldly, "whether the recent or the remote."

"Cathal—*damn* Mrs. Buckhannon! I don't believe you! Happiness in the present can rest only on understanding of the past.

You *don't* understand, and you *aren't* happy; it's all over your face. And you hold *me* to blame—as of course you should."

"You flatter yourself, General," she retorted, the jade eyes flaming in sudden, simmering anger.

"Oh, Cathal, Cathal, I beg you—"

"Whatever he begs you, Mrs. Buckhannon," Candacy Ann cut in, suddenly materializing at his elbow, grasping it, "don't oblige him! We spoil our menfolk as it is. They require firm management, like children—and judicious denial."

Cathal Buckhannon more than rose to the uneasy occasion. Her smile was paper-thin, but serene.

"I fear it's oftener the other way around."

"Not in *this* family, I assure you," Candacy Ann insisted, gazing up at her spouse with a casual fondness securely rooted in proprietorship. "Oh, I have the general well trained!"

"I'm afraid I couldn't say that about my husband . . . or that I would ever wish to. But then perhaps, my father being who he is, I've a different notion of what makes a man. Oh, and that reminds me—please let me offer my belated condolences on your own father's passing, Mrs. Starcross." The irony was almost iron indeed—a subtle stiletto. "Such a sad case, his reduced circumstances at the end, a fine old gentleman."

In desperate haste Starcross broke in, like a referee: "What news of General McQuaife?"

"Yes—indeed. One *does* hope he hasn't been waylaid by bandits," Candacy Ann riposted—almost with a smirk. "Just my point. Imagine! Allowing a man, husband *or* father, to wander off to perilous foreign parts at the drop of a hat!"

"Unfortunately, when you live by principle, you must be prepared to face uncertain and unpleasant consequences. And *my* definition of manhood certainly involves living by principle—as does your husband's, or so he's told me." Slyly Cathal turned to Starcross. "I thank you for your interest, General. My father, when last I heard, was fairly wallowing in the hospitality of Emperor Maximilian. Why, he may even have seduced a lady-in-waiting or two by this time." With a dismissive shrug she turned again to Candacy Ann. "There are no bandits in Chapultepec Palace—not yet." Viciously: "The bandits are harder by."

At that moment Chance Buckhannon, clearly enjoying himself more than the other three, appeared beside his wife, flushed of face, to snatch up and upend another punch, make a few inapposite and not altogether sensible remarks, and then claim his wife for a reel being organized in the far end of the room. She went along without protest, if also without noticeable enthusiasm. Starcross glanced at Candacy Ann, only to be rewarded with her hallmark social smile, saccharine and vacuous.

Why, he fretted, was he filled with forebodings of disaster? Why did these two women—the two women in his life—who, outwardly at least, had hit it off with each other as tolerably as *any* two attractive ladies, each accustomed to being the center of all attention—why did they strike him rather as two preening, posturing, circling cats on the verge of a deadly spat?

TWENTY

Thinking it over afterwards, Starcross found himself puzzled —troubled—by his wife's catty friendship for Cathal Buckhannon far less than by Cathal's in return. Candacy Ann was just unable to resist, however subtly, flaunting her triumph: She'd supplanted the other not just as parochial social queen but in the arms of the man, the better man. More still, secretly she knew just how total was her triumph: that her rival had not an inkling of the thoroughness of her defeat, the extent of her weakness: that she had wed *her* man under a drastic, disastrous misconception, crediting *him* with the prowess of Candacy Ann's own man. Small wonder, then, that Candacy Ann was willing, *eager* even, to be friends with Cathal Buckhannon . . . to deign to be friends.

Cathal's own seeming willingness, as time passed, was harder to fathom. She as well might feel confident of her own coign of vantage. She was after all the same ravishing woman as ever, still commanding the fascination if not quite admiration of all, female almost even as surely as male. But clearly Cathal was too canny not to feel—intuit—her weakness as well as her strength. The complacency with which she had taken the blows of her fate was too unlikely to command belief. A woman loved and left, left with a child, was little likelier to forget than to forgive. And that Cathal had *not* forgotten, Starcross had the evidence of his senses. Her formality, her *glacialness* toward himself, her wry pretense that nothing had befallen between them ever—her whole mien belied itself. Her father's warning, voiced in that eerie Appomattox tent, came back: Cathal was a proud woman, and proud flesh grew in an unhealed wound of a proud spirit. Till he had had an intimate interview with her he would know no rest. Fortunately, as he'd warned her, he had his pretext. The confrontation was as needful to his public duty as to his private peace.

Making no secret of his call, neither did he go out of his way to draw attention to it. Used as he was to a few solitary hours in the saddle several times a week, familiarizing himself with his new realm, there was nothing strange in his sending for Rustam, a few mornings after the reception, forgoing any escort, mounting, and riding out of the compound. He glanced back at the upstairs windows of his living quarters, ready to wave at any flick of curtain, of life, but none was to be seen. Candacy Ann as ever was deeply about her housewifely and motherly business.

Fort Cressup fairly marked the margin of the prairies. A river traversed the flatlands nearby; but it was a shallow, seasonal stream, evidenced but by a wavery line of stunted cottonwoods, and anywhere easily forded. Eastward of the fort it veered off in a northward loop, parting company with the military road, which headed straight on east through low, timbered mountains forming the western limits of the Southern Highlands. Small wonder, Starcross mused, that Southern Highland culture had put down hardy taproots here, in layers: first the sedentary Indians, then the backwoodsmen and hardscrabble farmers—squatters in law, perhaps, but well-entrenched possessors in fact. And lastly, the war had brought in a more restive, more troubling folk. Born wild spirits, made wilder, hardened by hardship, unable to reclaim the ways of peace, found these hills the ideal sanctuary. Locals red and white alike, full of their own resentments, tended to see the worst such newcomers as but fellow-sufferers, to be tolerated if not actively abetted. No easy, simple task had been set before him, Starcross recognized, to disentangle the rights and wrongs—or rather rights and rights—of this new land.

It certainly was a lovely one, above all in late autumn. Near at hand, smiling slopes seesawed between green and golden, while oaken crests wore copper crowns. And in the background the low but rugged mountains loomed like ships lazily moving through a bemusing blue fog. Human intrusions were few. Starcross passed only an occasional rude log cabin with a smoke-tendril rising straight up from its cat-and-clay chimney. Few of the denizens showed themselves; and those who did, of whatever hue, were wary of the anonymous horseman in blue.

McQuaife Haven, as it was formally known, lay a mere five miles from the fort, in the extreme northeastern corner of the wild, sprawling ranch realm General McQuaife had leased from his old Indian friends. The house itself, as Starcross remembered all too well, looked east from atop one of the gentle, glady ridges so characteristic of the country, down on the little seasonal watercourse where the military road meandered across. He paused briefly to let Rustam blow, and ponder the look of the great hilltop house sitting as if spellbound in the midst of a wilderness.

Never a deep thinker, Starcross was not disposed to think beyond the problems of the moment. The bittersweet memory of his *first* visit, now so dissimilarly if eerily being repeated, fretted him only in that the one grew out of the other. At Thermopolis he had fancied he had detected a pattern in his life, and the same sense assailed him now—that for years he had been confronting essentially the same problem, making dogged sallies at it, only to find it worse-confounded by each bull-ox lunge.

A coffee-colored girl, looking scarcely twelve, hove in the open doorway as he was hitching Rustam. Mounting the deep-shaded gallery, essaying pleasantries, he garnered not a syllable of acknowledgment. Sighing, he offered the child his *carte de visite,* wondering if she would know what it was for.

The soundless vastness within swallowed her up. She was gone for long, but at last reappeared and with a minimal handflick motioned him in. Still without words he found himself left in the long side parlor where he had surprised Colonel Chievous and the Indian agent, Gaunce, and had shot the gunman. He looked that way long and hard, as if for leftover bloodstains. He found himself unable to sit in one of the wing chairs the interlopers had occupied. Restively he paced, his eyes inventorying the room though his mind not truly in it at all. Still the house gave off no stirrings of life around him; but at last, soundlessly, Cathal Buckhannon stood in the doorway. He stopped his pacing.

"My husband is away," she said stonily.

"It's you I came to see; I gave you fair warning." He made a bullish rush toward her but stopped just short, searching her face, beseeching it. Distraught, he passed a hand over his own face. "Cathal, I'm not here by choice, either at the fort or in this room. I'm not here to make you uncomfortable, or myself either, though the Lord knows I'm achieving the latter. For the past I have nothing but regrets; but I can't undo the past.

"Since I *must* be here," he went on, "since we must be thrown together willynilly—please, let us be friends. Already it's well-known that we're not strangers. You can't go on with this—this charade that we are. It's—it's unnatural!"

"Perhaps we *are* strangers, really," she murmured, pensive, maddeningly withdrawn. "Our . . . acquaintance was very brief. Perhaps we 'knew' each other only in the Biblical sense. Clearly enough, you don't know me as I am now."

But he was by then altogether in the past. His voice, tremulous as his mustache, betrayed unwonted, almost unbearable feeling. He had to turn away, begin again. "I wrote to your father, I named the day, the place. I was there; I waited, all day, till I could wait no more. Oh, Cathal, why weren't *you* there!" The question was rhetorical, since he knew the answer.

"Why did you send me away?" *This* one was unanswerable.

"It was a mistake—I own it. But it was a—an honest mistake. I was still thinking in terms of peacetime, as we all were then. It hadn't yet forced itself upon me that the war would turn out such an insuperable obstacle. And apart from that, it hadn't occurred to me—it wouldn't have in a thousand years—that your father would prove such another kind of obstacle."

"That surprised me too," she conceded, candidly. "I never realized he . . . loved me so much . . . to be so jealous. No: my—my misgivings were entirely intuition."

"I should have bowed to your intuition. I should have done a thousand things; should have resigned my commission, *deserted,* gone searching for you. But the silence! I wouldn't have known where to go, where to look. And I was not free. The war closed over my head. I resolved to do my duty to the army, and then my duty to you—I never dreamt it would take so long. I hid it from myself—I *had* to—but it never changed. When I met your father in the East I told him as much. He was mollified and in effect gave me his blessing. And then Colonel Colquhoun, Candacy Ann's father, charged me to see her home from her school." He faced back around. "The rest speaks for itself, surely."

"The whole story speaks for itself, General. Eloquently. You upset yourself over nothing. You've said you want me to understand, *begged* me to, and I've assured you there's nothing to be understood. I don't know what more can be said."

"I don't upset myself—the upset forces itself on me. Never in all the years have I been free of it; but above all since I've come here and seen you, it's become—more than I can bear. Your look for me, the very wall you build against me, belies your mask of unconcern. I can't blame you if you hold me responsible for—for our mutual misfortune; but at least be candid about it. Let us be honest with each other, even if not friends."

"Your pain does you honor, General. You must admit that our 'mutual misfortune' looks rather *un*mutual on the surface. Still, your pain, I'm perfectly willing to concede, may have been just as great as mine; yes; perhaps even greater."

"No matter." He brushed it aside. "Certainly I feel no honor for my pain, I ask no credit for it. Mine ought to have been greater, just because clearly your real suffering was the greater. And so I suppose our feelings now must be just as lopsided. I suppose, were I the woman, I would hate me too. But being the man, I find it hard being hated after having done my best."

"Hate?" For the first time her look grew gentler. "But I don't hate you, General. That look you say I have for you, that wall, my reserve, whatever—it stems not from hate, but merely from the fact that a woman finds it hard to discuss her dishonor even with the man with whom she dishonored herself—with him above all. Since *she* did the dishonoring. He meant none, just as he said." Opaquely she went on, "Worst of all is hating oneself. You're at risk of doing just that, I think, General, and you mustn't." She headshook. "And aren't you taking another kind of risk, coming here like this? What would your Candacy Ann think?"

"I come in the line of duty." Starcross got the better of his feelings at last, turned all business. "As I told you, I mean to do it, and I need help—*your* help. Furthermore, I must give you a word of warning. To the objective newcomer, reasonably objective, it does appear that all the fault may not lie on the other side, that you yourself may have been behaving rather, shall we say, unwisely, at least in your choice of friends. It's no easy matter for them to criticize you to me; yet they dare tell me you give aid and comfort to outlaws, that you play games with them—us, the army—falling back on your prominence and your sex—"

"Outlaws?" wryly. "Dear me. The other night it was bandits. Let's have a definition first."

"That's not the question; it's begging it. The war settled that. *Vae victus,* sad to say. The vanquished, if they don't submit to the judgment of the sword, go on living by it, they're the outlaws; *that's* the definition, for better or worse. And if the winners, or some of them, are themselves behaving as outlaws, if not worse, there are right ways of calling them to account. That's my mission, self-imposed if not officially imposed: to make it unnecessary to flout the law even if the law flouts itself." He faced her square-on. "Who is it, Cathal? Who's behind it? Is it only Gaunce?"

Cathal Buckhannon's smile was scornful—pitying. "You are an innocent, General—*simple*, as I recall you once put it yourself. Not Lohengrin after all, perhaps, but Parsifal, the pure fool. It's a wonder to me you got so far, though I reckon your masters had need of fools and innocents in the late unpleasantness. They make good soldiers, as some hundreds of thousands of dead or maimed ones eloquently attest. They don't need suchlikes any more, your masters. War is simple. Peace, if you can call it that, what we enjoy, civilization, as I once warned you, is a more complicated business, in which innocence, simplicity, is an inconvenience, an embarrassment—nay, a peril."

"Agreed, agreed—give me war any day. But my 'masters,' whom you revile, so rightfully, have given me peace, or what passes for it, and I have no choice but to keep it as best I can. I confess my unfitness. Why else do I ask for help?"

"I don't know how I can help you."

"Name me names. Name me their crimes."

"You don't need me for that, General. You just named one yourself. And his crimes? It would be quicker to name those he has so far overlooked. If a way exists to rob the Indians, Gaunce will find it. Oh, but why bother singling Gaunce out? The Indian Bureau is simply a collection of Gaunces, an organized enterprise for robbing the Indians—and the taxpayers."

"The Indian Bureau is outside my reach, even if were possible for an individual to fight an organization—a simple individual, your pure fool"—wryly he bowed—"versus a much-ramified and, I gather, diabolically clever organization. Well, but organizations are themselves made up of individuals, and some of those individuals, in this case, just may fall within my reach. If Gaunce's machinations have army connections—"

"Your army, General, is a machine for making the world comfortable for Gaunces—and itself, of course."

Starcross opened his mouth to protest but then let it close in a drawn-out, pregnant silence. Chance Buckhannon had materialized in a doorway at the back of the room.

"Don't let me interrupt this obvious council of war," he joked, cryptically sardonic.

"What a soundless house this is," Starcross marveled.

"Yes. Ideal for sneaking about keeping an eye on one's wife." Chance switched on his easy grin, came forward. "Didn't I advise you to let it alone, old man?"

"You did indeed, Chance. But I never promised to take your advice. I cannot."

"Oh, investigate to your heart's content." Chance's mood shifted again. "You've all the Territory to do it in—thousands of square miles. Just leave us out of it, can't you?"

Starcross picked up on the subtle hostility. "If only I could! Nobody wishes you well with more fervor than I do, Chance—the two of you. You know that."

"Yes; I know it well. Of course. Sorry, Webb. Forgive me." Chance finished with a shrug: "I've said my say. I won't repeat myself. And you must do your duty."

Starcross excused himself and left the room quickly before Chance could react again. Cathal too continued to stand unmoving. As the sound of hooves faded from out front, Chance turned back to his wife. His grin became a grimace.

"If it were any other but old Webb, I'd be worried."

"About your husbandly honor?"

"Don't be ridiculous. You know about what! My love, it's time you took me full into your confidence. I don't propose to be one of these feckless fellows who blusters, drinks, and visits a painted lady, while his wife wears the pants"—his petulant tone gave way to concern, to deadly earnest—"and rides a tiger."

Cathal too turned from arch to serious. "It's so . . . obvious, then, the tiger?"

"Great God! I've got eyes, ears. Buckchita and Chusto are closemouthed—almost as much so as my wife—but they've begun to trust me. And I *do* have friends at the fort—Webb isn't the only one." Pregnantly: "And the others aren't Webbs."

"I can see you have an alternative proposal," she mused—"in the way of riding tigers."

"I can tell you when and where the next Agency train moves. Webb, bless his innocent heart, as I don't have to tell you, called off Chievous's routine troop escorts."

"Indeed?" Cathal again turned arch. "And Agency freighting news should be of interest to me?"

"Buckchita seemed to find it of keenest interest."

She studied him closely, and at last smiled. "Then why don't you go and ask him to join us and discuss it further?"

"When one's been robbed, one tends to think of robbing the robbers. We know the feeling well, don't we, my love, both of us?" Chance caught her hands in his and leaned over, kissed her lips. Fervently he finished: "I won't fail you, Cathal!"

Her laugh was less fervent, but real enough—loving enough. "Fail me? Why ever should you? You've done marvelously so far, haven't you?"

TWENTY-ONE

A few mornings afterwards, Candacy Ann was telling her half-attentive husband of a proposed excursion of herself and *Cathal* —they were on a first-name basis, almost cloyingly so—to Fort Smith, the local ladies' shopping resources having been long since exhausted. Starcross's eyes reared from his breakfast.

"I'm pleased you get on so well, you and Mrs. Buckhannon," he said, and smiled. But it was a puzzled, troubled smile, almost a disguised frown. "Pleased—and surprised."

"I'm not so sure we do, really." Candacy Ann's frown was undisguised, effortful with thought. "I do the best I can, try to give the appearance at least . . . as one of my wifely duties."

"Well—thank you; though I regret it requires an effort."

"It does. And Cathal makes very little effort herself." Candacy Ann's face clouded in minor martyrdom. "I think she's the—the haughtiest woman I've ever known."

Now it was her husband finding thought a labor. "You must make allowances. By hauteur I take it you mean pride; and pride can be the consequence of hurt, suffering. And surely I don't have to remind you what Mrs. Buckhannon has suffered."

"The last thing she'd want is pity, *my* pity."

"Of course. Pity's the last thing one must feel—show." He could not match her offhand tone—or fathom it, either. "Just . . . understanding, my dear, that's all I ask."

"That's difficult enough; but if you can be friendly with her, 'understanding,' I suppose I can as well."

"I have no choice, Candacy Ann, as well you know. My duty compels me to be friendly with everybody hereabouts, whatever my personal feelings. My duty required me to call on Mrs. Buckhannon. And unquestionably it will again."

"Of course," Candacy Ann allowed, if still with that martyred air. "And I venture I know my duty as well as you."

"Indeed you do, my dear. It's just that I regret that you find it —well, a *duty*. My own duty, I confess, is onerous enough, heavier than I'd dreamt. I didn't ask for this assignment, as you know. I would rather we lived on the far side of the world from Mrs. Buckhannon; I would prefer never to have to see or speak to her. But I have my duties, my public duty, and then, on top of it, my—my private duty. As I told you in Thermopolis, I bear such a measure of personal responsibility for her misfortune. . . ."

He trailed off at her vexed look. Clearly she would not have this part of the past repeatedly brought back—in this, at least, wife and other woman were as one. While Starcross was mulling the irony, Candacy Ann added, cryptically, "Cathal seems to have quite a knack for turning her misfortunes into fortunes."

"What on earth do you mean by that?"

"Doesn't it speak for itself? Out of her old—misfortune she finds the mightiest man about for her secret protector. Out of her new misfortune she finds a second—second only to the first." Perversely: "She's mated better than she's worthy of."

Starcross wanted to dispute, to refute these troubling cattinesses one by one, but confined himself to reasserting his original point. "I wish I could agree—about her 'fortunes.' I'm very much afraid her contentment's a matter of appearances only—that in her heart of hearts she's a bitter woman who resents and disdains her husband, her 'secret protector' even more; and who's letting her bitterness lead her down dangerous paths."

"Well, far be it from me to excuse everything she may do; and yet I fancy, Webb, if I hadn't married you, if I'd married Chance, or someone like him, I might feel much the same."

"You've lost me," he sighed. "I thought you were counting Chance as one of her . . . fortunes."

"I thought *you* were," she riposted. "After having so triumphantly played the matchmaker, you don't seem to be putting much faith in Chance's steadying influence, his power to protect his wife, whether from others or just from herself."

"I did *not* play matchmaker." Vexed, he sensed he protested too much. "Even so, they *do* seem suited and happy on the surface." He thought it over. "Well, but you're right. I'm beginning to be afraid Chance isn't the man to save his wife from herself. He has his own resentments, his own bitterness."

"Didn't I try telling you that, back at Thermopolis?"

"It wasn't so then—or not so much so." Again he sighed. "He's changed since he came here."

"Why wouldn't he, for heaven's sake? After all, isn't he living a lie, living under false pretenses every minute of his married life? Living on the credit of *your* deed!"

"Candacy Ann! You mustn't even *think* such things! If Cath—if Mrs. Buckhannon were so much as to *suspect*—"

"I can't *help* thinking it—*thinking* it, at least. I'm a wife, after all—jealous. I can't help taking pride in my husband's prowess, even if I'm the only one who knows of it."

"You and Chance," he murmured. "And I. All of us but she."

Once again Starcross was more mystified by Cathal's motives than by his wife's. Candacy Ann readily told little white lies; still her protested reasons for cultivating Mrs. Buckhannon rang true. But what were Cathal's reasons? He entertained no illusions of true liking blossoming between the two women, the two circling, preening, posturing cats. In a way he found it a relief to have his actually simpler professional worries to turn to.

Starcross had been fortunate indeed in having an at-loose-ends Colonel Yulee to bring out as aide in his Subdepartmental capacity, and in managing to keep on the newly-Captain Isham Klyce as his good right arm in his other post as commandant of Fort Cressup proper. Otherwise he had had to make do with the materials at hand, albeit it seemed to be working out better than might have been expected. The hidden hostility clearly cherished by some of the "old guard" probably amounted to no more than the time-honored resentment of any brisk new broom. Eadred Coonce, at least, was turning out a willing, able ally in the formal inquiry Starcross had set going, behind which smokescreen, of course, he was pursuing an inquiry of his own.

He was starting, in fact, to look on the official investigation with mixed feelings, as a monster of his own creation, once begun unstoppable and out of his own control. However culpable might have been the doings of Colonel Chievous and other officers, not to say of the would-be-untouchable Indian agent Gaunce and his ilk and their minions, the inquiry, as such inquiries will do, and as Chance had warned, had a perverse way of straying off onto the equal if opposite sins of their opponents.

Such ruminatings ought to have prepared him, descending the outside stairway from their quarters, fresh from the breakfast talk with Candacy Ann, rounding the gallery corner and entering the outer office, for the news that awaited him in the grim faces of Yulee, Klyce, and Coonce, all three; but it was no less unwelcome, an inauspicious beginning for the new day.

"Outlaws attacked an Agency supply train last night"—Klyce was spokesman. "Teamsters were hurt, one killed, the wagons made off with—into thin air." Making for the big Territorial wall map, he tapped it with a forefinger. "Hereabouts."

Starcross fisheyed the wall as if the map itself were to blame. He led the others into his own sanctum, away from clerkly ears, fisheyed the three of them. "Gaunce's goods?"

"Government goods," Klyce corrected—"gospel according to Gaunce," dryly. "Annual allotment goods on their way to one of his subagencies for distribution. The problem is, nobody can make head or tail of Gaunce's maze of overlapping enterprises save Gaunce himself. We're left to take his word for it, so long as his own superiors won't investigate—don't care."

"Which is beside the point anyway, sir," Yulee reminded. "Gaunce is shrieking for troops—his chief clerk was in my office when I came in, at daybreak. There's going to be tremendous pressure on us to resume the escorts."

"And heat on me, you might as well go ahead and add, for calling them off in the first place."

"Well-l, such attacks *are* something new, and there're those eager to blame the change of command and policy—yes, *you*. But nothing's truly new—just the tactic. Gaunce's trains moved fairly bristling with escorts thanks to the obliging Colonel Chievous, and the outlaws still found ways to pick them clean."

"Troops are useless against pilferage." Coonce took it up. "Indians are master pilferers; and they're Indians all right. Pulling the troops off just turned the robbing more blatant—and violent. Hardly a change for the better, of course."

"Indians," Starcross mulled. "Just 'Indians'? No names?"

"They wore masks. Some of the teamsters, though, claim to have recognized Chusto." Coonce hesitated, coughed delicately. "I don't have to tell you who *he* is, sir."

Starcross shook his head in dismay. He spoke as if alone. "The fools! What do they think they can gain this way?"

"Pardon me, sir," Huell Yulee put in, "but you're being too generous. *Indians* are what you and I used to fight—fight fair, both ways. *These* are outlaws—highway robbers."

"I'm not excusing them." The general threw up his hands. "Gaunce is robbing *them.* They're just getting their own back, a little, as they see it. By the very worst means, granted."

"It isn't only Gaunce. There are five principal agents in the district, all men who have influence in the East, else they'd never have gotten their appointments. Each has his subagents and clerks, a sheer army of dependents. And since *our* army gave up the sutlers, often the agents have taken their places, holding contracts for beef and hay and other commodities, not just for the reservations but for the army itself. Fortunes are involved—sums sufficient to tempt the decentest army officer."

"And all within the letter of the law," Starcross growled.

Yulee shrugged. "Agents tend to grow rich even within the letter of the law. But being human, and beset with temptations, many give way to greed. Officers, as I don't have to tell you, *don't* grow rich within the law . . . and we're human too."

"Let's hope so anyway," Starcross said, with a wry smile. "If not necessarily in that sense."

"Still"—Yulee hewed to the point—"if wrong's being done there'll be evidence, bound to be, things even the Bureau can't ignore. If we can only lay hands on it—"

"But that's in the long run," Klyce fretted. "Our problem for now is"—leerily eyeing his commander—"the other side."

"The outlaws—say it." Starcross heaved a sigh. "I want the teamsters' statements sent at once to the United States marshal's office. If he finds grounds for arrests, and applies for troops, we will of course furnish them, but only under strictly limited conditions, with care taken that the officer commanding any such detail understands and agrees with those conditions."

The others nodded; yet Starcross sensed their thoughts were rather more negative. He went straight to the issue.

"What's been done about this Chusto?"

"Nothing, sir—yet." Klyce's face was wooden. "We were sure you'd prefer to—to look into it yourself."

"And you were right. It's the first thing I'm going to do. I read your minds, gentlemen, your misgivings; but I assure you I'm as concerned for . . . impartiality as all of you."

"Of course, General." This from Yulee, the one with the most standing, in more ways than one. "I think what you're reading is rather our concern for your own safety. You—you've been making enemies right and left. Take an escort."

"The rickety, squint-eyed Mr. Gaunce is going to waylay me?"

"He has his hirelings. Like that one Major Buckhannon shot. His replacement, so to speak, has arrived; no paper out on him. We could send him packing all the same, of course; but he'd just be replaced by another, perhaps unknown to us."

"And that's not all, sir." Klyce waited till the general turned to face him. "An old friend of yours—using the term loosely—has blown in from points north: Uriel Purinton."

"Purinton!"

"Himself. Late of the Jayhawkers. Late of a court-martial conviction and dishonorable discharge for his wartime heroics. A bitter man, with perhaps a long memory."

"*And* a coward. No, gentlemen. The troops have better things to do than guard my backside while I ride five miles from town, calling on old friends." He cast about a last wry look of amiable defiance. "I may wind up arresting the Buckhannons, but they're my friends, and I will *not* call on them at the head of a regiment." Adamantly: "Even behind bars, they'd still be my friends."

Within minutes Starcross was galloping Rustam out of the fort compound, repeating his previous ride the five miles to McQuaife Haven, if far less leisurely, less at peace, certainly far less appreciative of the countryside, or even aware of it.

His reception at his destination, however, was fairly a duplicate of the prior one. Once again he found himself standing in the long parlor, face to face with Cathal Buckhannon. Her words too were much the same as before—as cold.

"Again, my husband isn't here." As on impulse she added, "I suppose that pleases you."

"No. This time it was both of you I wanted to see."

"We both told you we didn't want to see *you.*" The icy Cathal Buckhannon thawed as it were in spite of herself, accosted him with kindling heat. "That we didn't want you here."

"It isn't a matter of what you want, any more than of what *I* want. No longer, if ever." His grim glance all about returned to her face. "Where is he, then, your husband?"

"Far away, and for the night, on business." Snidely, "We *are* a cattle ranch, you know."

"God, how I wish that were a complete statement: the whole truth, as the law likes to put it. *Cathal*!" desperately. "One of your Indian friends was *seen*—recognized."

"Then do your duty. Have you brought the manacles?" She thrust her arms out, the wrists bared. "Or are the troops to follow, to do the dutiful general's dirtywork—?"

"The dutiful general is trying—hard—to do *both* his duties."

She went on heedless, heated. "Keep his clean hands spotless? Clear out the nest of thieves once and for all?" The bathetic voice turned vicious. "You have a precedent."

"Cathal, for God's sake—!"

"The dutiful general is trying hard, yes, to do *one* of his duties, at least—the imagined one." The voice softened a little; but it was a hard softness, almost pity. "It's for that you're here. If it were only the other, merely my friends, you wouldn't be here at all—those troops would be. *You're* here, General—"

"Enough 'General'!" The words burst from him like cannon-rounds. He moved on her fairly with physical menace. "Must you be as bad as my wife? You know my name."

Unruffled, standing her ground, she shrugged. "What's in a name? You're here, *Webb,* like this, alone, because you think you owe me something, protection, whatnot, because of what befell, or didn't befall, between us long, long ago."

"What's in a name indeed? Oh, my own never sounded so sweet!" His eyes closed, as if to shut out all the unsweet present. "I wonder . . . But, yes, Cathal—of course."

"It becomes you to think that, Gen—Webb. But it wouldn't become me to agree. You owe me nothing."

"To say that, to say I owe you nothing, is to say nothing *did* befall between us. And that you *cannot* say."

"I *can* say it. I *do* say it! The past defines the present, perhaps, but by the same token the present defines the past. We're nothing to each other in the present; therefore we can have been nothing to each other in some past, lost moment."

"Cathal—*Cathal*!" Suddenly, roughly, he seized her shoulders, shook her—hard. "If you're nothing to me, why am I a—a living dead man, alive only in being cut to the heart, all but bleeding real blood, at your denial of me, denying me even the memory? I was half-alive while I was parted from you by miles. Now that you part me from you worse, keep me at arm's length even as I hold you in mine, I am *all* dead." As if to bridge the hopeless distance or plunge headlong into it, the yawning-gap of the spirit, he crushed her to him, made them one, sank his face in her hair there against her own face, just the red strands between them. "I loved you more than life—I *do* love you—I *will*!"

"Webb! Stop it! You can't, you mustn't. I'm another man's. And you're not the man—the thief—"

"I *am*—a thief and worse. I would do murder, self-murder, gladly, to wipe out my worse-than-murder, my *theft* from you. But it wouldn't—you're right. It can't be wiped out; the past can't be called back, made right." But his actions—the iron embrace from which she could not escape, the brusquely seeking browsings of lips on cheek, of lips on lips at last—belied his words, that flowed now fairly as tears. "Nothing was, as nothing is."

"Oh, Webb, Webb, you shouldn't, you mustn't"—words as halfhearted as her struggles against his clutch, against his lips . . . against herself. "You must stop because I cannot. I can't keep it up any longer. *I'm* not right, no—*you* are. I lied. I told the truth before." Their passions, so long parted, as-it-were rejoined, burst into bloom. "I said it was the longest night of my life."

"It never ended, Cathal. Not for me."

"The longest, and the shortest, as you forewarned—though you little dreamt *how* long, *how* short." Pliant now in his arms, still she mourned—agonized. "Only a night, Webb, however long, however full! A night, and ships that passed in it!"

"Yes—and yet, *no.* I said we would be together forever. We have been. As little peace as it's brought us—it's brought us truth: You are my wife, not his. I love you. I *will* love you."

"I can't stop you—I don't want to stop you. I tried—pretended I wanted to—only to have it over and over brought home to me—the man you are—the *only* man ever, for me." She broke off her giving-back kisses but to laugh, shedding tears literally of joy. "Now you know why I didn't want you here!"

"That's why I *am* here. Because I did know it, without quite knowing. Because I felt just the same."

"Only a night, Webb, a long brief night; but no, it never ended. I've never forgotten it, I've never stopped loving you. Before God, I am your wife." And this time the embrace was hers. "'Though the world be lost, and the heavens fall.'"

"Another long brief night," he mused, and cast his eyes about the empty cavern of the house. His irony sloughed away in deadliest earnest. "Thief indeed, and worse. I'll betray my friend for it, for this other long brief night; I'll betray my lawful wedded woman, betray myself, for an instant of your love, even your mere regard. I don't think I can go on without it—I, the dull, dutiful, *dead* soldier, starved for a crumb from the feast once spread before him and thrust aside! Scorn me, Cathal, *hate* me—tomorrow." Indeed it was a dead man's plea for life. "Just love me now."

"I'll love you to the last!"—accepting his hand, as it were an invitation to a dance. "As for the rest, I'm not a seeress, not quite. And love, alas, is blind. But maybe it's better so."

TWENTY-TWO

By midmorning, the puzzlement at Headquarters House had turned to real anxiety. The general had not expressly stated his intention to return at any certain time; but that he would let himself be benighted but five miles from his own comfortable board and bed—and wife—seemed unlikely, many as were the reasons he might have tarried with his problematical friends at McQuaife Haven. Casually, carefully feeling out Mrs. Starcross, Colonel Yulee found her—though an absentminded frown flitted across her brow—blissfully unconcerned about the general's safety. She had sensibler things to think about, thank you. The general knew what he was doing. The general was invincible.

His officers might have been less sure; still, their anxieties were relieved when word relayed in of the approach by the eastern road of the familiar big bay horse with its familiar solidly-built, golden-bearded rider—leading a second horse bearing an eyecatching burden. In no time horses and all were right before their eyes, a buoyant Webb Starcross was drawing Rustam up to the rail, even as most of the office staff came out onto the gallery to gape. Other figures, military and civilian, issuing from the length and breadth of the compound, crowded about.

Tied over the little claybank's saddle, on its stomach, legs stiffly waggling, arms and head limply adangle, was a very dead body. Dismounted, starting forward, Starcross breasted the shoal of his officers—surprised, it seemed, at their surprise; only tardily recognizing that explanations were called for.

"Ah, this, I think"—waving over his shoulder—"must be the problem mentioned yesterday."

"A problem now resolved." Captain Coonce stepped out and lifted the dead head by its hair, put a name to it: "Bogan Dark. Aptly a dark enough name in the rougher cowtowns."

"The good Gaunce is going to find himself with a manpower problem," mused Isham Klyce, dryly.

"Obliged to raise his wages, at least," contributed Yulee. All eyes were on the hole neatly drilled between the two dead eyes. "For God's sake, General—don't keep us on tenterhooks forever! We were getting damned worried."

"And not without reason, clearly," footnoted Coonce.

"Yes." Again their commander's high spirits struck them all. His idle shrug was massively dismissive. "You gentlemen spoke very much to the point yesterday. I'd say he was charged to take me unawares; but that was too much to ask of a man with a reputation." His smile was wry. "He had to have his victim know by whom he had the honor of being dispatched."

"Generals are not supposed to be so—so quick."

"I wasn't always a general." Starcross's eyes had strayed. The others' followed his on along the street. "Ah, lo and behold. We won't have to send for the knacker."

One of the original fort buildings, but a couple of doors down, had been turned over to the Indian Agency. And among the staring figures on the boardwalk before it, clearly just emerged, was unquestionably that of the stooped, sticklike, perhaps deceptively decrepit-looking Caughlin Gaunce, Esq.

"Invite him over," said Starcross. "By main force, if need be."

Swapping eyebrow-raised glances with his fellows, Captain Coonce detached himself and hastened the few dozen yards. He returned almost at once, followed by an obviously not unwilling Gaunce, never one to shirk a challenge, and his poor eyesight clearly no bar to his full perception of the situation. The gold-headed stick he flourished was an aid not to locomotion so much as to ostentation, even as his diamond stickpin.

"Come and claim your property, Gaunce," Starcross greeted, still in the highest of spirits. "I can't imagine such a creature has any such thing as next-of-kin."

"I can't imagine what you're talking about, General," Gaunce protested, with no effort whatever at sincerity. "*You* brought this fellow down? My salute for your marksmanship. And my thanks. It *does* seem he's stolen a horse of mine."

"Take it back, then, by all means—but not without its cargo."

They appraised each other. "You play a good hand with the Fates, General. The drawback is, *they* win all the same, later if not sooner. Marksmanship, moreover, makes a man a *mark* in these benighted parts. And there is always a better."

"Yes; I've been warned of the Fates before." Still Starcross's mildness surprised and puzzled his subordinates. "You may be right. I'll try and go down in a blaze of glory."

Yulee trailed after him as he started away, out of earshot. "Still—admit it, General, damn it: The varmint does have a point. Oh, great shooting. But some dumb luck too."

"Another name for the Fates?" Starcross laughed. "Well, I seem to have been dealt more than one helping of it, whatever it is. And all true soldiers are fatalists, I should think."

"I've never seen you in better spirits, sir," Yulee marveled, himself inspired. "Still, shooting a man, a man who *needs* shooting—it does that for you, I reckon."

"Indeed." Starcross flushed, his own humor dampening. "Unless there's something urgent, Yulee, I'm going up long enough at least to remind my wife she has a husband."

As the general went on alone up the wooden outside staircase, a close observer would have noticed the further dampening of his spirits with each upward tread. Nothing could have better set up a healthy, relatively young man than a night spent in the arms of the woman he loved—nay, for whom he entertained, as he now knew, a grand passion—this followed almost at once by a facedown with a minion of Satan, emerged from victorious, almost effortlessly so. The former event of course meant by far the more to him; was cause for high spirits though alas, paradoxically, for low ones too. The nearer he drew to his own door, the more was he again not his new self but the all-too-familiar old one: that half-dead man, alive only in his anguish, his self-division, and now his guilt; unable to look at his wife, or think of his friend, without it. Reunited with the former after the night's absence, routinely welcomed with a kiss and a budget of domestic news, ever louder he seemed to hear echoing in the hollows of his heart those words he had once avowed: *—and forsaking all others—*

He found his thoughts by turns soaring then sinking; not at all taking in the new day, with his wife at its center, but stealing back, reliving the night, the wee hours, that other long-brief night: waking by Cathal's side, able to close his mind to the bed they lay in—the bed he'd left her in alone in June—but by dint of the reminder, the eerie likeness to that *other* bed they once had shared, that other long-ago awakening; sacramentally breaking his fast with her before taking his leave, wryly complacent at thought of the unseen hands, with eyes to match, seeing if unseen, that had conjured the meal—this other, second bridal breakfast—likely in his confidence that the servants they belonged to were Cathal's, not her husband's. And those few words they'd exchanged, at the table or at their parting, as unable to speak of the future as he was even to think of it now; the very most to be hoped for, the thought they seemed to share, if not in words, was that matters might go on more or less the same, might turn no worse. Their parting, if not quite their parting words, bore a dismaying likeness to that other parting, there on the humpbacked bridge, in the same afterglow, perhaps, though lacking the same high hopes.

Starcross saw it almost as a relief to have the other question, his other duty, that awaited him downstairs, to turn to: the other matter that had taken him to McQuaife Haven, taken him back to Cathal, as he had told her, but then which he had sadly neglected, to his chagrin yet his peevish satisfaction too, to pursue with her. Heart had claimed precedence, head had yielded; and then head and heart together turned and fled. If he had worrited, still worrited, the heartache, though of course anything but resolving it, to the headache he had failed even to face up. . . .

Himself unable to face up to it, save fatalistically, Webb Starcross's future, his Fate, had he but known, was being mooted, or *plotted* perhaps were the better word, in more than one quarter through the rest of that day. Caughlin Gaunce had gone fuming away from the facedown before Headquarters House, stalking along with all the aroused, resolute if not quite yet resolved, purposeful stride of a far younger man.

Rather than reentering his own official preserve, though, he paused but long enough to command a gaping clerk to send some menial to claim the horse, and, yes, even its unsavory burden, and dispatch others with cryptic messages in sundry directions. Then he stalked on, out of the old fort compound into the would-be *town* of Fort Cressup, now little more than a cluster of stews and dens. Reaching an inconspicuous, nondescript building giving off an alley, Gaunce stepped in as if he belonged, took a bottle out of a desk drawer, poured himself a wee dram, and sat back, thinking more than drinking. Within the hour he was joined by others one by one; grudgingly shared about a few drops. One arrival above all seemed to fire his stinginess and disgust.

"I wasn't aware blithering idiocy was an actionable military offense, Purinton. The courts-martial must be kept busy."

"Bogan Dark's idiocy—" protested Uriel Purinton, still the pettifogger, disbarred or otherwise back home, busily, slipperily distancing himself from a letdown of a client.

"He was your man, in more ways than one—you should've known. And hammered it into his head: He was to remove an obstacle, not, ye gods, indulge in a joust."

"How was I to know," Purinton plainted, "that—that star-studded quilldriver was so quick?"

"That, too, you should've known—old friends that you are."

"This is getting us nowhere," broke in one of the others. "The issue is, do we sit here wringing our hands while this lucky fool goes on putting us out of business, or do we put *him* out of business? Find the man, or men, up to the job?"

"Purinton's the man," suggested another. He seemed to find obscure high humor in the thought. "He's the only one here to whom it's more than just business."

"Purinton's anything *but* the man." Gaunce eyed the said man in distaste. "It's a time for cool heads, not hot ones. Besides" —he tented his fingers, rapt in thought—"I've a notion the end of the fool's luck lies not here at the fort at all."

The others waited, eager to batten on the keener mind.

"But not far away. A bare five miles, in fact."

"The devil! McQuaife Haven? Hell fire, he's thick-as-thieves with those . . . those thieves."

"Just so. Mind the old saying—set one to catch one. . . ."

The other place where Starcross's Fate was being mooted, in a farfetched sense even being decided, if all-unbeknownst, was at the heart of his own circle, the circle of his friends, his very family circle. Might there even have been a starry crossing point, a conjunction: the trolls and the gods . . . goddesses?

"Why, oh why didn't you tell me?" an indignant Candacy Ann upbraided her husband over their evening meal. "About last night; or I reckon I mean this morning, don't I?"

Starcross all but gave himself away. Just in time he remembered Candacy Ann's fixation on surfaces, immediacies.

"I didn't want to worry you over nothing."

"Nothing! You might have been killed, for heaven's sake!"

"Well, I wasn't. What *might have been* is nothing by very definition." He almost flinched from his own irony, and took refuge in a diversion. "Still, I'd feel better myself if you put off your excursion with Mrs. Buckhannon, just till—"

"You're being inconsistent, General. Nobody's going to trouble *us,* not with two of Cathal's menservants along. Besides, the farther east, the safer, you've told me so yourself, more than once. And moreover, it's the perfect opportunity for me to do my duty." Before he could express his puzzlement, his unease, she added to it: "What with you befriending her—in the line of duty—surely it will look better with me doing so socially."

With effort he conjured a complacent smile. "Never mind the looks of things. If you're not easy befriending Mrs. Buckhannon, Candacy Ann, you'd best give up trying."

"Are *you* easy befriending her?"

"Certainly not—anything but." Seeing his inconsistency, conceding the charge, he gave up his own trying. "All right, my dear," he sighed. "Use your own judgment."

The relationship between the women still left Starcross at a loss; only now it was Candacy Ann's attitude that baffled him the more. *Cathal* was the one with the new secret, the hole-card in their feline game, their undeclared women's war. Why, then, was Candacy Ann, too, so buoyed, so gaily-grimly game?

The women made their trip to Fort Smith. Though it was out of the way, Cathal at her own insistence called for Candacy Ann at

Headquarters House in surely the Territory's most splendid private equipage, replete with Indian driver and footman, guard, or whatever he might be. At an early hour they were on their way, and all went agreeably, without incident, even their talk, which remained trivial and desultory. Only a very acute eavesdropper could have discerned any pattern in it, or any rise in its level of tension, at least till toward the end. All the little practicalities and distractions at last behind them, the anticipations, the shopping, the suppertime retrospections in the gossipy boarding place kept by a McQuaife connection, only well on the way home the next day did the talk take on coherence, or turn, bluntly, to the point.

"Tell me, Candacy Ann"—Cathal made the first move—"why do you . . . disapprove of me? Your husband must do so officially of course; but *you*—was it only to please him that you said, at the start, we must be friends, we'd so much in common?"

"I—'disapprove'—of you?"

"You *don't like me,* then. Is it just because of—of him?"

"My! We're being honest indeed, aren't we? I should ask the same thing then, I suppose: 'Because of him'?"

"I suppose so. Yet it's not really *you* I don't like. I dislike in you the things I find in far too many of our sex—dishonesty, hypocrisy, 'respectability.' And I think what you don't like in me is their lack. In more than one way, I'm not 'respectable.'"

"Obviously you think you have higher standards. But no: it's not your 'unrespectability'—though perhaps it's a related concept. It's your *superiority* I don't like. Your hauteur."

"Hauteur—that's a widespread 'woman's complaint' too, as the doctors say; one we both suffer, perhaps. I recall how our first meeting turned into a sparring-match over our menfolk; how you made my father out a fugitive—from justice, by implication—dodging bandits, likely little better than a bandit himself."

"*You* made *my* father out a failure." Candacy Ann was getting her stride. "As if fleeing with a price on one's head, hiding behind a foreign popinjay puppet, counted as success! But I was not aware of making comparisons. Indeed, comparisons are just out of the question. Your husband—I've known him longer than you, my dear Cathal, and I like him still, the old flame that never quite died. Still, there can hardly be a comparison."

"Certainly not. Chance was wearing the purple when your Webb was a penniless orphan, taken in by your father."

"One of my 'failure' father's successes? Cathal, you are being ridiculous. Have you forgotten there was a war? A cruel thing, war, and yet an honest, unerring winnower. Not to say it's poor Chance's fault he came out of his war broken and intemperate, saving himself only by a—a lucky marriage."

"Ah, but isn't that to say, neither is it to Webb's credit that he came out of *his* war a hero who alike 'saved himself'—*lost* himself rather—let himself be lost, *stolen* into marriage? Webb Starcross is a man among men, a hero, yes, none would deny it, above all not I; but Chance—your broken, intemperate Chance faced down your husband's whole army with ease, and saved *me*. You won't condescend to him before me, Candacy Ann."

The latter's pale blue eyes glittered. "And yet you will do as much to Webb? Damn him with faint praise? A mighty man, a great hero—though no thanks to himself? As if any could dream of such twisted things but a deluded, bitter woman."

"Are you sure? 'Deluded, bitter'—it might better be said of Webb himself; might be *just* the thing to be said of him."

"I repeat, you are ridiculous. You little dream—"

"I venture your dislike of me has nothing to do with politics, or with fathers, or with my hauteur or yours; or my dislike of you. You dislike, you *hate* me because you feel the truth. Know it or no, you're haunted by it; hagridden. Webb Starcross is a great, a mighty man, oh yes, a hero . . . but not a happy one."

The knives were full out now. "What makes you think so?"

Cathal was her "haughtiest" self. "That *he came to me.* He may have spent his morning brushing aside an assassin, but his night he devoted to another kind of derring-do. He came to me, your contented man, for what he could not find at home."

Candacy Ann stared, flushed with anger, and yet strangely showing no real surprise; showing rather the first kindling flickers of a look of absolute triumph. "Oh, you're quite right, my dear Cathal—in part, at least. Yes, I 'feel', I know. More than *you* know! More than you dream in your wildest dreams!"

Cathal's fugitive frown belied the massive shrug. "You may explain or no; I don't care."

"Mark this, Cathal: I don't want to explain. It grieves me to do so. I would have preferred to be your friend, for always; but you spurn me. Never mind the other things. One thing is enough: You throw it in my face. Not just my husband's lapse—worse: all his years of guilt and anguish for what once befell between you and him, his yearnings to atone." As she said this, Candacy Ann was tugging from her left hand the stylish white mitt, unremoved, in Cathal's presence, in all their two days together. She held out the bared hand, the fingers splayed, exhibiting inches from Cathal's eyes the two rings on the bridal finger: the modern sculpted, be-diamonded wedding band, topped by the worn, plain, braided golden circlet. "You have seen this before, I believe."

Cathal Buckhannon's jade eyes were fixed on the ring as on the return regard of a diamondback rattlesnake coiled to strike. For a time—for an eternity—there was neither animation nor comprehension in her face, even as visibly her mind strained like an overtaxed engine. As the other waited, watched, steadily the high color, life itself, trickled away, leaving the queenly face as that of a corpse, skull-white, speechless, even mindless.

Candacy Ann furnished the speech, the presence-of-mind. "Oh, he came to you, perhaps—but more than that, you see, *he saved you,* my Webb. Rescued you not once but twice: first from a fate worse than death in the Brocksborough jail, then from death itself in your own bedroom.—My goodness!" she spoke with mock normality, glancing out the carriage window at the twilit fringes of Fort Cressup first creeping into view then falling away. "We've reached our destination; home at last. *So* kind of you to bring me to my very door." Deftly she let herself out the moment the coach lumbered to a halt. "Oh no, don't stir, my dear. You're eager for home also, I'm sure—home and husband"—mercilessly ironic. "Your fellow will hand down my bundles."

"You are a wicked woman," murmured Cathal, barely audible—barely alive. "A cruel-hearted woman."

"I am a woman." Candacy Ann beamed back in the coach window before turning, flouncing away. "We do what we must. You will agree, I'm sure. Goodbye!"

TWENTY-THREE

Even had the thought occurred to him, Starcross had hardly had time to contrast the several descents of Chance Buckhannon upon his office since the beginning, or indeed the successive avatars of Chance himself. His comings always were precipitate; yet even sooner than usual, it seemed, this morning's Chance was within, seated, the door shut behind him—the same Chance, even as the same blooded black horse tethered out front. And yet *not* the same at all: the pomaded hair all rumpled, the elegant clothes slept-in-looking, the handsome face tormented into ugliness, looking as though it hadn't slept in nights. The eyes and nerves were those of one jumpily coming off a binge.

"For God's sake, Webb—something to drink!"

Refraining from some feeble joke concerning the earliness of the hour, Starcross dutifully produced his private bottle, poured a measure, dismayedly watched it disappear.

"It's Cathal." A stranger might have taken this for a medical bulletin: Chance's revelation of his wife's contraction of a deadly disease. Starcross knew better, without quite knowing that he knew, or *what* he knew. "I was . . . out late—most of the night," Chance began his effort to explain, having helped himself to a second drink. "When I got in, the bedroom lamp was lit, so I went in, went about the usual, man joining wife for bed. It was a time dawning on me, the—the state she was in."

He ran feckless fingers through his tousled hair. "Oh, I don't mean only the clothes, the rumpled nightgown, the red haystack on her head, though obviously she hadn't slept a wink; looked worse than *I* must look. Not *her* looks but the look she had for *me,* coming up on an elbow and fixing me with it, the look of a snake for its prey, a *vicious* look; there's no other word for it. I thought she must be drunk; but when she spoke it was with withering sobriety—and murderously withering sarcasm.

"She said—*sneered*—'What did you do with it, that ring you took from my finger?'"

Starcross jerked forward but then at once slumped back. There was no call for surprise, or for elucidation; neither was there a thing to be done, nothing but sit exchanging dismayed, despairing, pained looks with his friend; who, it only tardily dawned on him at last, was running on, beseeching:

"You . . . you gave it to your wife." It was half a question, though only half.

"Candacy Ann." A lament, not an answer—no answer was needed. "How *could* she?" But again, no answer was needed. The answer lay in his own last pilgrimage to McQuaife Haven, Starcross was thinking, not the women's to Fort Smith.

"Webb—Webb, what am I going to *do?*" Chance was slumping over the desk's edge, all but weeping into his drink. "I *love* Cathal. Despite the strange way we came together, I love her. I was nothing. I was at the end of my tether, and she saved me. Or you and she saved me between you. Suddenly I was something after all, someone a splendid woman looked upon with admiration, even if not quite love. And now she despises me." He fought back his sobs. "She forbids me her bed."

"But why does she blame you? You didn't do anything."

"Yes! Isn't that just it? I didn't do anything."

"All my doing," Starcross acknowledged, ruefully. "My fault."

"I'm not carrying on like this for *me,* Webb. She's done her worst to me. It's—I'm afraid of what she may do to herself."

Starcross sprang up. "I'll go and see her."

"Yes!" Chance grasped at the straw. "That's why I came to you; not that I reasoned it out—sheer instinct." Wanly he smiled at his own helplessness and wretchedness. "Webb's the one, the only hope. And it's true, Webb. You're the only one. Me, I'm no use to anybody. I'm going to go get dead-drunk!"

Leaving the office but minutes after Chance, Starcross was even less alive than usual to the world going on around him: the hum of military routine that ought to have been his own prime concern; the wife upstairs (it never crossed his mind to go up and confront her with her deed; what would be the use? They were well past that point with each other); the comfortable bulk of Rustam brought ready around at his bidding, and then between his legs taking the familiar way out; the familiar smiling countryside. Even as Chance's descents on him, his own pilgrimages in the other direction formed a declining, downward succession: the series of his blind bull-ox lunges, with ever-failing strength, at the insoluble problem which was his very life.

The situation at the house, likewise familiar, likewise little penetrated his awareness. He had never made the effort to sort out the domestic staff, if it could be thus dignified, of McQuaife Haven—the place bore a paradoxical air of teeming emptiness: abandon manned and watched over by unseen souls—he simply dealt with whatever improbable guardian spirit happened to confront him, red or black or white. "She want to see nobody," objected the woman who this time materialized out of the yawning, lonely gloom, once he'd let himself in.

"She's going to see me."

He swept past the woman and up the stairs by twos and threes, neither noting nor caring whether she went on objecting or made shift to follow. Again, he let himself in the door at the head of the stairs, that memorable oaken door.

The whole scene was memorable: the room every bit as disordered as the first time he'd opened the door on it; the denizen every bit as *dishabille,* and as distraught, though now sprawled on the bed, not first facing him in arms then dropping at his feet; and in her right senses—more in them, at least, than then.

"*You.*" She seemed equally unsurprised and uninterested, though that vicious, venomous, coiled-serpent look of Chance's dazed description was instantly, unerringly evident. "You dare show me your face—after showing me your treachery?"

"It's not a time for etiquette," he said, as if her words alluded to the proprieties. "You have been—*cruel* to Chance. *Mine*'s the treachery, just as you say, not his. Blame me."

"Yes—oh yes; there is blame to go around." Her laugh was grim, grotesque, as she lifted and looked at her naked finger. "I always reckoned one of the soldiers stole the ring. Well"—eyes streaking back—"and one did, didn't he?"

"Cathal!" His hard tone melted, became one of supplication. He glanced about the room, summoned his first time in it. "I was a—a married man. The ring—God, I don't know. A man gives his ring to his wife. And you were my wife before God; but before the world—and we live in the world. I spoke Chance's name just to *not* speak my own—to spare my wife, my worldly wife. I didn't dream—" He broke off, beseeched: "Chance came, and made you a good, decent husband. He loves you."

"I don't love him. How could I? I love another. Even when I loved *him,* I loved that other, don't you see?" Bitterly she smiled at her bitterly nice way of putting it. "He was an imposter. I loved the one he impersonated." She sat full up, half on the bedside, the better to face him. "I *do* love him, I *will* love him, even as I lately told him." She bespoke him at last in the first person—"I love you and I hate you"—even as her eyes came to rest again on her bare finger, on the ring not there. "I went on wearing it, at first, thinking—no: *knowing*—you'd come, sooner or later. Even after you'd wed another. . . . And then you did come, but like a thief in the night, and fittingly enough stole back the ring—and gave it to *her*." She shook herself, faced him. "You killed half of me all those years ago, that other time you 'didn't dream.' Now you kill the rest of me. Worse: you give that witch of a wife of yours the means to kill me. I can hear her mocking me even now!"

Unable to cope with this, he strove to put it out of mind, to focus his wits where he might hope to cope.

"What are you going to do?"

"Nothing that's any concern of yours. Get out of my house. I told you—I don't want you here. I've told you why."

"It was a mad reason."

"Was it? I'd say events have made it sane, if it wasn't before." Briefly her madness made *her* sane. "I can take only so much. I mean it. Get out. I never want to see you again."

"All right, Cathal. All right. But first"—and he matched stares with her—"first I want to see my daughter."

"Oh—*your* daughter?" Her lip curled, seeming to say a thousand unsaid, unsayable things at once.

"All right—again. We won't mince pronouns. In view of all the rest, they hardly matter. *Your* daughter," he corrected, backing firmly into a chair. "I still want to see her."

She kept up the war of looks for a bit, but then shrugged. She caught up a little bell from the bedside table. The man, an Indian man, clearly as much bodyguard as servant, must have been hovering hard by, for he entered almost as the bell tinkled. Once he had withdrawn, all wooden reproof, Starcross essayed:

"What does she know?"

"She knows Chance isn't her father—of course." Cathal was all sarcasm. "She doesn't know *who* her father is." As in relief—their wait wasn't long—she turned from Starcross to the opening door. "Perhaps it *is* time to put that right, that much—that little." Her hard face mellowed. "Come in, Star."

Starcross drew to his feet as the little girl came in, trailed by a woman: the coffee-colored woman he'd encountered with the girl that fateful other time, in the summer kitchen.

It was the girl who held his eyes, though, as Cathal called her on to herself and then turned her, pointed her at Starcross, who'd sunken back into his seat. Even as that other day he found himself all but overcome. The girl's ruddy fairness was so perfectly, poignantly the embodied meeting of her mother and himself; as even her name, bestowed by a happier, hopefuller woman than her yonder on the bed, seemed to proclaim.

"Star"—trundling her forward—"this is your father."

Dutifully the girl came on, all the way, suffered his tentative, tonguetied touch; even broke his silence.

"I saw you before . . . sir."

"The general at the fort—" carelessly her mother prompted.

"Before." Firmly the girl bespoke Starcross. "I saw you before you were the general."

"Yes," he managed; managed even a wry smile. "You saw me before. Before I was the general."

He looked for curiosity, questions: Why didn't he live with them? Would he live with them? Would she see more of him? But the girl's curiosity seemed to satisfy itself simply by sight. Her blue eyes fully, fair literally took him in. Verbally she contented herself with pursuing the memory. "You had no beard."

"Children are harder to fool than the rest of us," laughed Cathal. "Well"—all impatience—"are you satisfied?"

Starcross bent forward, grasped the girl by the upper arms, touched his lips, and the wiry beard, tenderly, to her satiny cheek. "Yes"—and sighed out what might have been his soul itself—"though you know that's anything but the word."

Girl and woman duteously withdrawn, all of Cathal's venom seemed to resurge. "Yes. She saw you before. *I* saw you before, too. Only I couldn't quite make you out." She spoke as if still it were the case. "In a dream I saw you; your eyes—"

"Cathal"—heartsick, he sprang to his feet—"I meant what I said the other night. *More* than I said. What does this change?" He took a charging step toward her. "Come away with me! We'll go to Mexico, to your father. You and Star and I."

"This is so sudden, General!" She feigned vaporishness, her sarcasm withering; but swiftly turned all serious. "*You*—desert? Desert your precious army, your precious worldly-wedded wife, your precious friend, your precious *principles?*"

"You said it yourself: 'Though the world be lost, and the heavens fall.' *You* meant it too, I took it, take it." He looked back—lost himself in looking back. "I can hardly do worse. I'll undo all else to do it. A man can be true to but one thing, it seems, one other soul. You were my first choice to be true to." He was all but on top of her. "You are my last, if you but will."

"I *won't*"—facing away, there at the bedside—"I won't have you." And back, fiercely. "No. Nor any other!"

He stood swallowing at it like a not-too-unsavory fatal dose; fell back on that fear of another fatality that had brought him, that still he might forestall. "What *will* you, then?"

"For one thing, say no more. *Go,* I tell you. Get out."

"Cathal—" He closed the last gap between them, reached out as-it-were to lay hold of her, but found himself facing the black maw of a revolver, drawn from under the bedclothes, full-cocked. He glanced down, body-shrugging, soul-sick. "Go right ahead"—bringing his eyes back up, bared to hers, those other, deadlier bullets—"pull the trigger. It might set it all to rights."

"Is there no other way I can get you out of my sight?"

"Oh, I'll go." He laughed his despair. "The mood I'm in, I wouldn't at all mind being murdered. Still, I *would* very much mind making you a murderess—even of me."

It would be difficult to say which husband went home the sadder that night, though Starcross's homecoming was far and away the less dramatic and momentous.

The day was far from over when he arrived back at Headquarters House. There he asked half-heartedly, absentmindedly after Chance, but learning nothing soon forcibly put him from mind. His humor was not improved by reminders of the gaggle of senior officers and politicians due to descend within days, looking to bask in the reflected limelight of the scheduled review of troops heading for Southwest service and others homing from their own, to be bemedaled, promoted, and forgotten. Earnestly Starcross wished himself one of the former, heading out simply to shoot at honest men, forthrightly shooting back.

At the usual hour he went upstairs to his usual familial supper and evening. An onlooker would never have known anything was amiss between husband and wife. Dandling his son on his knee, half-heeding Candacy Ann's routine tale of household triumphs and tragedies, Starcross found it hard to believe himself.

He broke into her flow: "Have you seen anything of Chance?"

She mustered her scattered thoughts. "Chance? No-o. . . . You were expecting him?"

Starcross spoke matter-of-factly: "He came to see me. He's at his wit's end. Cathal has taken to her bed."

"Oh, *that.*" If husband had looked for wife to fall into fits of jealousy, or even surprise, he was doomed to disappointment. "*Every*body's heard that. Even Indian servants are gossips."

"I wonder if your 'everybody' knows the cause."

"She has only herself to blame. She has a better man than she deserves. But that's not enough for her." The pettishness turned deadly-earnest. "She wants *mine.*"

"Seemingly not. She's turned her face against me too."

"You went to find out, did you?"

"At Chance's urging, I went. Candacy Ann, I don't think you realize just how serious—"

"Webb—I don't seem to realize *any*thing any more: just that I love you. I would even *share* you with her, if that's what you want, if I'm not enough for you. But I won't let her take *all* of you away from me. I'd do *any*thing to stop her."

"Yes." More bemused than surprised by her candor, still he found candor in return, for once, beyond his powers. "You've proved it, I'd say. I should be flattered, I suppose, that you still find me worth fighting for—even half of me."

"Oh, Webb—" She spoke with sudden motherly patience. "You're the only one who doesn't see your own worth! *I'm* the worthless one. But I can't help it." She frowned with the unaccustomed effort of thought; but with no hint of tears. "More than once you've spoken of . . . *her* pride. I have mine, too. Love me, if you can, however little. But at least don't hurt me."

Starcross's bemusement, his detachment, his sense of unreality, persisted right through the wrenching plea and the shallow, routine reconciliation that followed. His own mind was beyond him, his own feelings too much for him; hers were as of another world. Crazily he found himself trying to see Candacy Ann as a Confederate spy, as the "Queen of the Outlaws"; but *her* deadly earnest was of a different, homelier kind. His affection for her, homely to match, was far from dead; her shortcomings were anything but strange to him. He was married, like most husbands, he knew, accepted, to a bland, trivial little woman, whose lovable moments far outweighed her hateful ones, yet whose trite ones outweighed them both; able to tame and trivialize the tragic, to turn life's sublimest heats and depths tepid and shallow. He would have found this sufficient, known and sought no more, had not another kind of woman long ago crossed his path, cometlike—or rather filled his sky like a new fixed star.

Crazily too, conversely, he found himself trying to see that other kind of woman as able to content herself with only half of him, prepared to share him with another, a hated rival—content with mere appearance, with the proprieties. That was the whole thing, wasn't it—the difference between the women? Cathal was reality, in the highest sense, Candacy Ann but its shadow; or in a still higher sense Candacy Ann was the real; Cathal was surreal, ideal—and, it followed, alas, out-of-reach. . . .

Chance Buckhannon, for his part, went home, at last, with trepidation, trembly literally and otherwise, already sobered from the binge that had filled or rather blotted out the heart of his day. It might have seemed strange that he should go home at all; but there was noplace else for him to go—there were no painted ladies, at least, among Chance's solaces—and it was far too much to expect that he could keep away for long from her whose regard, esteem, if no more, had become life itself to him. Loving her, he called it, and perhaps it was; that too.

He knew not whether to be cheered or dismayed, on coming skulking in, to find her not only up from her bed but downstairs, full-dressed for the saddle . . . for action. The gloves, the short split twill skirt, baring the black boots with their big elegantly-wicked silver Spanish spurs—all this could not for long distract his addled wits and anxious eyes from her face, almost unaltered since the morning, the dabs of raddle and powder doing nothing whatever to mask or mellow the ravaged, begrutten, *vicious* look, the look of one shaken to her very depths, holding herself together but by the mightiest strife of will. Busy buckling a shellbelt about her waist, with its holstered revolver, she seemed serenely unmindful of having only hours ago bidden him *Begone.*

"Cathal—" he blurted, the conventionally concerned spouse. "Are you sure you should be up?"

She affected amusement. "Oh, I'm a sick woman?" Having drawn, hefted, checked the revolver, she reholstered it. "I'm joining tonight's little social call on the good Gaunce. On *his,* if not quite *him.* Don't you fancy he'll appreciate the honor?"

"Oh, Cathal"—convention out the window, he was appalled, frantic—"no! Above all, not *now.*"

"Why? What's special about now? Life goes on. 'Though the world be lost, and the heavens fall'!" Her would-be mirth rang right over his head. He grasped at her—at straws:

"You're—you're upset; not yourself. *Nothing's* itself. It's—it's not the right time. Let things quieten down a bit—"

"Myself mostly? To the contrary, I find it's just the *right* time."

"At least let me"—nerving himself—"I'll come with you."

"Oh—to protect me?" She made a false show of stifling her scorn. "My . . . my resident Galahad?"

Torn between throwing his hands up in surrender and hanging his head in despair, Chance managed neither with conviction, though putting the feelings across all the same.

"Could I help it that Webb had been here before me?"

"Webb had been here before you. Oh, I like the way you put it! It could be said of more than one occasion, couldn't it?"

"For God's sake! Even Galahads need occasions, opportunities. I was as good a soldier as Webb, I wager. Even *he* always said *I* was the knight-errant. *Cathal"*—his plaint grew ever shriller, more feckless—"give me a *chance*—!"

"A chance? An occasion? I don't recall the particular occasions of Galahad and his sort"—the viciousness was resurfacing—"though I suspect your run-of-the-mill knight-errant would have found his marital honor occasion enough."

"My marital honor?" Blankly Chance stared. "It hasn't been *tried,* that I know of."

"Oh, you're not a wittol, then? I think that's the term for a *knowing* cuckold."

"What are you talking about? Don't twice-torture me!"

"Give you a chance? I give you your *choice:* Tag along tonight as my shadow—the man you told me you wouldn't be—if you want to go on earning my contempt. Or, if you want to win my esteem—and more than my esteem—then *kill him*!" She didn't trouble to name the "him." Incredible as he found it, the name was not needed, was a given. It was the verb that was needed, that pierced him, even as her eyes—those demoness-eyes. "Kill him. The other man who lay with your wife."

"Lay with you?" He could not speak the name himself, he found. "Years before I ever knew you, in any sense? But that's —that's madness! You can't mean it!"

Her laughter, at least, verged on the mad. "The husband the last to know, as ever! The *other* 'deceived' knew, the other woman; Candacy Ann knew. Why do you think she did what she did, shoved that ring in my face, all but slapped me with it? Because she *knew,* somehow she knew, knew her husband had been here, had renewed our 'knowledge' of each other, passed the night in my bed." Satisfiedly seeing the shock and pain play over his face in waves, devilesslike she gave the screw the final turn. "If that isn't enough for you, when he came here to see me only this morning—you asked him to come, didn't you, your *friend,* to come and plead for you?—when he came, it was to ask me, *beg* me, to leave you, forsake you. To run away with him."

Chance gripped a chair back, literally needing the support. He gaped at her, then away, shaking his head. "Could I but believe you were making it up! You women, you seem capable of malice no end. But, no, you're not making it up."

"'I am a woman'—as *she* said. I am malicious, oh yes—like *her*—but not mendacious too—like her."

"Malicious! That's far too weak a word for it. *Me,* kill *Webb?* Great God, you don't know what you're saying, asking." Chance eyed his scarred palm. "My blood-brother!"

"That didn't stop you on Bloody Island, as I heard it told. What odds," she challenged—"save that then the issue was your fiancée's honor, not just your wife's?"

"Oh, Cathal—! You hate him so much? He . . . hurt you so?"

"I leave you to be your own judge of that, and make your choice at leisure." She smiled wickedly as she drew on her riding gloves. "I'm taking Sable. I would tell you not to wait up for me; but I doubt you'll feel much like sleeping."

TWENTY-FOUR

Major General Starcross, still such in a shrinking officer corps, ever keen of his appearance, paid it yet keener mind on the last morning of his life, almost as if he knew, were dressing for his funeral. But he did not know, had not even a premonition. His head was too full of other things, more down-to-earth things: the busy day ahead, that day of worldlier obsequies, of the visiting Personages, of martial pomp and circumstance; full too of the day just past: of the latest attempt on his life, despite himself brought back as he made ready, what with Candacy Ann there by his side clucking mother-henlike as with ludicrous pains she combed the thick taffy not-quite-curls over the crease in his scalp, about which she'd learned only, after listening long to his laments on the skirmish's salient casuality his favorite hat, and noting the lowness of the hole through the crown. He had been riding home from a scheduled call on Chief Rayne, albeit—a detail *un*scheduled—not alone; escorted not just by Captain Coonce but by the chief himself and a quartet of his stouter, less-civilized attendants. Two of the half-dozen attackers were corpses; the rest had fled the field not in the finest of fettle. The Indians were left mourning a mount; the general mourning his hat. A tardily alarmed Candacy Ann mourned his furrowed scalp. To her alone did it seem to occur, if only on the surface: *They* were getting closer.

Along with this exploit to reflect on, Starcross had the somewhat less personally stimulating—indeed, personally appalling—incident of the nighttime burglary of one of the subagency offices, the blasting of a safe and the carrying off of whatever of value it had held, gold whether in the form of incriminating records or merely minted eagles. The agent was evasive, paradoxically so, wavering between suffering his vague loss in stoic silence and demanding restitution and blanket retribution.

To Starcross personally dismaying because it only added to the old personal worry, or complex of worries, crowding all the rest—mere would-be assassinations, waves of outlawry—into the crannies of his mind. For to him, and he feared not just to him, it meant that Cathal after all had *not* taken to her bed, unless in some symbolical sense; that her private pain, far from staying her from her perilous public course, was driving her deeper, farther along it. The gutwrenching conviction gripped him that the robbery, in its very foolhardiness, its impudence, were her gauntlet flung down to him, just *him,* her final spurning of his final supplication. Frantic to understand, to feel with her, he felt she must be feeling, now, much as *he* had felt with her revolver aimed at his midriff. A bullet might not make things right, but it would end them. Even if not quite ready to turn the weapon against herself, she seemed to be inviting—forcing—others to be turned against her; making them make away with herself for her.

And Chance—Starcross had seen no more of Chance, but had heard much, and none of it cheering. Chance seemed to be passing ever less time at home. Or at least was passing ever more of it in the stews outside the fort, in one or another of its dreggier doggeries, settings to match his ever seedier self—morally as well as otherwise seedy. He was drinking more and handling it worse. The unknowing laid his dissolution to the drink; Starcross knew the reverse to be the case. And he was keeping ever more questionable company—not only that of the Territory's "official" outlaws, the sullen Indians, the sullener ex-Confederates like himself, but alike that of the counter-outlaws, so to call them, the anti-guerrillas as they'd been known during the war; the likes, for one, of Uriel Purinton, the ex-everything, struggling, rather paradoxically, to fall back on his prewar trade of the law in this lawlessest of new lands, and consorting, professionally and otherwise, with its lawlessest spirits. Starcross, unlike Chance, had not himself run afoul Purinton since his turning up in the neighborhood; albeit he could fairly *feel* the man's bale for himself—amid all the other bales; but he had thrust him from mind with contempt.

Chance Buckhannon had gone crawling home toward morning, that first morning after the scarifying interview with his wife, fairly palsied with dread; only to find all serene and everyday on the surface: the horses in their stalls, the young bravoes, red or white, innocently abed alongside wives regular or provisional, his own wife in her—once *their*—bed, where he left her undisturbed, retreating to the other room to which he had already retreated in the fuller sense. The one anomaly, though damning enough, was the little ironbound chest casually abandoned on a table in the study, its hasp forced off, its contents, when he lifted the lid, fairly lighting the room as only gold could do. In appalled haste Chance closed the lid and made an effort, little more serious than hers, to stow the chest out of sight—his own, at least.

Meeting her later in the day, as-it-were but in passing, almost strangers, he did not even try taking things up with her where they had left them. If Cathal were bent on self-ruin he was powerless, clearly, to stop her; powerless in more ways than one. What could *he* do, whose sin was just that he had done nothing? She had told him; had given him his choice, his occasion. He could have her, her and her regard, her *love;* he could even save her, be her savior after all, turn her from her perditionward path; though in but one way, the unthinkablest way. Webb? *Kill* Webb? Another gage? Thirty paces—again? Or a shot from ambush? A stab in the back? As from the very thoughts themselves, hours ere nightfall Chance fled back to town, to his most frequented doggery—back, by hap, to the company of Uriel Purinton, with whom, surprisingly it was coming to seem, he had more than a little in common. And all of it having to do with Webb Starcross, the shadow over both their lives. "He leads a charmed life"—Chance awoke mid-carouse to the fact that his companion had long been harping on Starcross's latest hairbreadth escape—"always has."

"Yes." Chance could but agree, if on another level. "He has."

"His luck will run out one day."

A threat or just a prediction? drunkenly Chance puzzled. "I don't understand your loathing, Purinton. Webb hasn't oared into *your* life at its every twist and turn."

"No? My luck started going sour when I tried *telling* people about him at Brocksborough, him and that—" Purinton recognized what he was saying and caught himself. "But no! Just 'cause he had his fool's luck to *win,* I damned myself, not him." He fixed a fish-eye on Chance. "What's past understanding is your *not* loathing him. He's oared into your life right along."

At any other time Chance would have protested the implication, handily refuted it. But it was becoming necessary, urgent, for him to convince himself, *be* convinced, that somehow, yes, Webb Starcross had come between him and his once high destiny, had stood in his way at every crossroads of his life; that Cathal could be his, be really his at last, if the way were but cleared, the shadow but lifted. Chance, when he was himself, was far too generous a man to prove the old saw that the surest way to win a man's hate is to do him favors; but Chance was himself no longer. Or rather he was *two* selves, the old self appalled at the new one he was becoming; or, as Starcross had once noted, with the one briefly winning out over the other, devil over angel.

"But I *can't*—I can't do it." What he could not do had not been said, not in words; it was unnecessary. Chance's distaste fell from his distasteful companion to his scarred palm. "It's not just *this.* I just—*can't*. I could as easily kill myself."

"Christ—no wonder you rebels lost the war. Chivalry's dead and done, haven't you heard? Well, but even Bogan Dark fell for it in a sense, didn't he? Dark, the bushwhacker born! He couldn't just politely *waylay* the bastard. Well, by God, *I* could!" Purinton glowered, his bale seemingly shifting from the man of his talk to the maudlin one before him. "You can't do it for reasons of conscience maybe; mine are more practical." Grimly he looked away. "I've got to lay hold of some cash—above all if I *were* to do it. Sure and I'd have to light out of here like a shot."

"B-but what about Gaunce? I thought—"

"You thought wrong, whatever the hell you thought. Gaunce doesn't trust me—and likewise, I assure you. Just 'cause Dark fouled up, and I'd talked Dark up big—"

With seductive horror the image rose anew in Chance's half-sodden, half-mad mind of the golden eagles gleaming at him out of the little chest, paired with the far more precious image of a face. A face only waiting to smile on him, bestow its redemption. What were a few filched coins? What was *any*thing—?

This lofty exchange had taken place only a day or so before "the day," as already they were calling it, and afterwards would call it with far more reason. Starcross left his living quarters full of a sense of urgency, as if late for things of greater moment than the airy nothings that awaited him downstairs; weighed upon, even in his private disdain, by mindfulness of the Personages due to descend on him locustlike at some unknown early hour; of the troop units already on practice parade in the compound's far end, the civilians and even Indians gathered in greater than usual numbers the length and breadth of street and square in anticipation of a show. Candacy Ann trailed him to the door, still picking real or fancied lint from his splendor as he strode ahead, excitedly chattering of preparings yet to be made for her own part in the day, joining him on the grandstand, queening it over the evening banquet laid on for the cream of the Personages. Vaguely aware of repeating a placatory "Yes—yes," he crammed on his rakish, red-plumed campaign hat—his second-favorite, unriddled such hat—caught up his saber, and stepped out onto the stairway's landing, casting a half-unseeing look about at the day while fumblingly bringing the scabbard strap about his waist.

A report, sharp and muffled alike, followed at once by another like an echo, rent the stillness. Instantly sensible of heavy blows, if not of pain, Starcross reeled, eyes rushing out over the prospect below, the space between Headquarters House and its twin just nextdoor, with its colonnaded gallery. A quiet, peopleless, out-of-the-way space, though just off the busy street and compound. He saw the lone figure, saw the back of it at least, the reeking revolver still in its hand, rushing for the alley end of the passage, making for the mazes of stables and storage sheds.

Groping for the rail his off hand let go the scabbard, which slid off, went clattering away, leaving him with the bared blade in his right, handle-gripped as for action. And acting at once, acting all on reflex or instinct—perhaps in some clouded cranny of his mind was the notion of distracting, delaying the fleeing figure till others came, drawn by the reports; but there was no thought, no time for thought—he cocked his arm and launched the saber with every strand of his swordsman's skill and the last ounce of his strength. Instinct, skill, strength, all these; and yet to the very last, if not quite luck, something of the supernatural, the miraculous—so it would be called afterwards, in hushed tones of awe—hung over Webb Starcross. The heavy blade sliced through the intervening air as from the hand of a master of the knife-throwing art. The needle-sharp point caught the fleeing form in the back and not only went right through it but sent it staggering, stumbling against one of the wooden gallery pillars and left it there, pinned to the post like an entomological specimen to a board. Its arms made aimless, futile, struggling motions; but only for a moment.

The author of the uncanny deadly riposte, meanwhile, lost self-awareness; as-it-were his body went tumbling pellmell down the stairs without him. Following a vague, seemingly brief lapse he came back to his body to find it right-side-up at the foot—none the worse, wryly he mused, but for the loss of that hat, and of course the ruin of his best dress-jacket by those two little holes and their fast-spreading issue, like a new kind of buttons among the brass ones, those two little flowing wells of red. The world around him began to press in then, all cacophony and confusion: Candacy Ann, an embodied scream, pelting breakneck down the steps after him; officers from the office around the corner, and others, familiar and strange, from every compass point, drawn to the passage's mouth in mere puzzlement and then flooding forward into it in waxing concern, all talking at once, and at cross-purposes—and beyond, out on the road, the chance-bypassing horse-and-rider, halted as in spite of itself, familiar blooded black horse, and even-more-familiar, more-blooded rider, this time riding agee though seated as sure as a cavalryman, as at home in one saddle as another, her hair aflame under the defiant black-plumed hat, her paled face warped in a look of aghast denial, horrified disbelief; though less of disbelief than just of horror, all-too-believing.

The minutes following were worse than confusion—were sheer pandemonium: Candacy Ann crumpled atop him, wailing still, voice as feckless as the fumblings of her hands; the others, even the officers, milling around her like cattle; cries of *Doctor!* uttered and surprisingly soon answered, to however little avail. Only the dying man at the storm's eye seemed to know peace, and even he really only its shadow, his peace marred by the urgency of his last thoughts, of trying to put them into words, straining to sear them into her to whom they were addressed.

"Candacy Ann"—he gripped her arms, fought their flailings, fought her futile, barehanded fighting-back his lifeblood's flow; fought for her full attention, a hard enough fight at the best of times—"listen to me! The girl, Star—Candacy Ann, little Webb is her brother. And he must know it. They must know each other, if *she* will, if she'll have it. You must never deny it—*you,* at least, must never stand between them." With wandering wits though still daunting strength: "Promise me."

"Yes, Webb," she intoned, trancelike. "Anything! Just—"

"Promise! *Say* it!"

"I promise. What—what you said. Oh, Webb—! Oh, no, no!" Hands were gently tugging at her, urging her aside for Doctor Cripliver, hovering with his bag, hatless, tieless, coatless, his breakfast becrumbing his chin and shirtfront. For the moment their millings-about cleared the line-of-sight out to the street.

Yes, she was there still, frozen there on the horse, frozen in horror yet, but the horror already fading into despair. Just before the gap closed back up, the general smiled.

"Never mind, Doctor." And along with the choking words, blood came pouring through the beatific smile, soaking the beard, reddening the gold. "I have seen my Valkyrie."

The dazed doctor, who would tell and mull those last words for days to come, murmured words of his own, some would-be-reassuring incoherence; but the general's half-closed eyes already wore the glaze of death. The medic looked around the circle and shook his head; he turned his attention where it might avail: to Candacy Ann, who had collapsed altogether, literally and otherwise, on her husband's body, face buried in his bloody jacket, moaning softly now—keening, ghostlike. The officers were still barking orders at each other; and still gapers gathered: the visitors come for a show, for reflected limelight, and their callous hopes fulfilled beyond their wildest dreams; the residents, the dead general's friends and foes alike, trucially knotted not just in a circumspect ring around his mortal coil, somehow resplendent even in bloody death, but less circumspectly around his assassin, almost-offhandedly slain himself—saber-spitted like a joint of meat, hung up there on the post like a suit of old clothes.

"Did you ever see anything like that in your life?"

"If I wasn't seeing it, I wouldn't believe it."

They were, for the nonce, as in a whole other world, where the laws of nature were suspended. None noted, would have in any case, or found it strange, what with the strangeness that had pervaded the whole, first to last, that the woman on the horse was there no more, had gone up as in a puff of smoke; or perhaps had never been there at all. Nor did any seem to reflect that Webb Starcross, slaying his slayer, had silenced him.

Heads crooked, taking in the dead face. "Purinton."

"And so they got him after all, at last. It was bound to be, I reckon."

TWENTY-FIVE

"They have him laid out in the fort chapel, his body. The service is tomorrow."

Chance Buckhannon as it were threw in this news ahead of himself, to draw fire or test the temperature, or as an ice-breaking greeting to his wife, seeing her for the first time in—how long had it been? The atmosphere could scarcely have improved in the interval, he knew; but knew as well he couldn't stay away forever, stay *drunk* forever. Though no more had he opened his mouth, roused her out of her trance, there at the study table, than he heartily wished he might have; that he had held his peace, and left her to hers—to her what passed for peace.

For if he had left her—whenever, however long ago—left her a diamondback rattlesnake coiled to strike, it was to come back to find her a fire-breathing dragoness. Fire—that was what shot up at him, deigned to crackle about at him as he spoke.

"You. Where have you been hiding yourself? You should have stayed there." He all but looked for his hair to catch fire. Just because it was such an ordeal for him to look back at her, to face that ravaged, ravaging face, face what she had become, what he had helped to make her, he forced his own eyes on to the table there before her—only to find them fixed, in fascinated horror, on what lay there, there alongside the near-emptied whiskey bottle, the glass: the memorable heavy Toledo saber and its scabbard. His pointing finger, the exclamation that erupted from him, might have been for a coiled diamondback indeed.

"Where did you—where did *that* come from?"

"Oh, I do have *some* friends." Her haggard, witch's eyes went on withering him. "Who will do what I want, get me what I want, even without being asked." She seemed to find it obscurely amusing. "Without my quite knowing myself, even."

"Oh, Cathal—!" Well he knew the definition excluded himself, indeed was crafted just to exclude himself.

"The perfect memento." She touched the blade. "I'm trying to decide whether to stick it in your breast or my own, or both."

As if she'd indeed stuck it in his, a little more life seemed to bleed out of him. "Stick it in mine, if it will help, will please you." She, too, showed little life. They might have been plague victims apathetically comparing their symptoms. "Webb stuck it in Purinton. I can see I'm as contemptible to you as Purinton was to Webb. And I don't much want to go on living that way."

She let that point pass. "Webb stuck it in Purinton." Litany-like she repeated his remark, wringing the last savor from the significance. "Purinton will never speak."

"No. True to the grave, our Webb." Chance tried to be sardonic, callous; but he was near tears. "And beyond."

She went on rending his flesh, like a scavenger a wounded animal. "You won't even have to pay him the rest of his fee—I take it that was only the down payment they found in his room, a thousand of Gaunce's gold dollars. Isn't that amusing? Downright hilarious! They may even fancy Gaunce faked the robbery and paid the gold straight to Purinton, no middleman!"

Chance stared at her till their eyes met, then just shook his head. "How can you be so—so offhand about it?"

"Yes. I wonder myself." Yet she was more chiding than accusing, for the nonce; amused even as appalled. "You didn't hide the rest of the money much better than I. What an incompetent crew of constables they make, they at the fort, not even coming here to look! Or could it be too much of Webb's softheartedness, his soft spot, shall we call it, rubbed off? His officers revered him so. I wager, unlike those of Chievous's time, instead of vying for the honor of coming here to shoot it out with me, they're tossing it back and forth like a hot potato."

"You're mad." Chance squeezed his eyes shut. "Insane."

"Yes. I must be." All her venom resurged. "How else could I sit here looking at you, casually passing the time with you—you who bought the death of the man I loved, the *only* man I ever loved? The only man—*man*—I ever knew!"

He gaped; but his grief trumped both his shock and his sense of grievance. "I did what you wanted; what you asked."

Her laugh was macabre; grotesque. "How little you know of me; of any woman! For God's sake—if only you'd taken a horsewhip to me instead of heeding me! I might have respected you after all, a little." She bowed her head, and then threw it up in defiance. "Webb would have known better—I'm mad, you say; I *was*, at least—Webb wouldn't have humored a madwoman. Though of course I wouldn't have been a madwoman if it had been Webb—he wouldn't have had to horsewhip me."

"God Almighty! Purinton was right. My friend—my nemesis! I can't escape him." Chance spoke as to himself, as if all alone in the room—in the world. Alone with his grievance and his grief. "Even dead, he outshines me. Purinton should have warned me of *that.*" He brought his eyes into focus on her. "How little I know of women indeed, mad or no. Sometimes I think you're all mad." As in final appeal: "I took you at your word. Though it sickened me, I did what you wanted, *said* you wanted."

"Oh, but you *didn't;* you didn't even do that, even that much—that little." Having withered him with a look, she turned from him in disgust. "If you had, if you had repeated your escapade on Bloody Island, had even walked into his office and gunned him down—that I might have understood; I might have mustered an ounce of respect for you. But a hired assassin, a *Purinton,* for God's sake! You—I can't think of words adequate, things bad enough to call you. You who have slain the noblest man who ever drew breath!" She slumped over the table, shaking with silent sobs. "We have slain him between us."

"Yes," he agreed. "And you hate me for it; and I return the courtesy. I love you, Cathal—and I hate you. And I hate you more. I hate myself for what I did, and I hate you for putting me up to it. Only *you* could have done it, bewitched me into killing my friend, my best, my only friend. The noblest man, just as you say, worth a dozen of you, and more than a dozen of me."

"No—I don't hate you; you aren't worth it; but I can't bear the sight of you any longer. Go—get out, or I *will* stick this blade in you, *his* blade. Unless you can do for me first."

"Oh, I wouldn't ever kill you, certainly not for that reason, to save my own life. And you, you needn't bother. I'll—I'll go." As in the utter depths of despair, he turned for the door, giving only a brief glance back. "I'll spare you the trouble."

She should have known what he meant; no doubt did know, deep inside. But she was too self-immersed, too sunk in her own, her private pain, consciously to know but that he left the room, left her to it, took himself away with his own. When the shot came, distinct if muffled, as from farther than upstairs, from his room of exile, his purgatory, in spite of herself she started. And she might have wept, but that she was already worn out from her weeping, wept out. The new grief sobered her of the old. Sobered her even of the drink, shocked her to her sober self.

"'Nothing in his life became him like the leaving it,'" quoth she to herself; but then shook her head as if to clear it of such sentimentality, free it for more prosaic concerns.

Still, back up in her bedroom, she had the unprosaic feeling almost of a bride, going through the bridal motions, arraying herself for the great occasion with the same stern care as *he,* though with the difference that she *knew* the occasion, knew she was dressing, if not for her funeral, at least for the next thing to, the next thing before. She might have been going out as on any day, albeit her leave-taking of her daughter palpably was longer, more heartfelt. Buckchita, dutifully fetching the sidesaddled black horse around for her, might have looked with misgivings on the revolver, on the scabbarded saber buckled over her elegant velvet riding habit, on the whole berserker panoply of her; but he was too much the fatalist for misgivings, certainly too Indian to show them.

Others too might have looked with misgivings, though what struck them most was that she had never looked finer—not the late demoness of home but rather the queen of all she surveyed, regal under her plume. Funereally she lazed past Headquarters House, as if giving them every chance to spew forth and lay hands on her; but military reflexes worked more slowly than that. Before the Indian Agency office she dismounted, tethered the black, and swept inside, swept straight on past the clerks, whose reflexes too were slow. Caughlin Gaunce, as she stepped into his sanctum, closing the door after her, eased to his feet behind his desk, clearly more in surprise and uncertainty than in respect.

"Mrs. Buckhannon. . . ." It was not quite an exclamation.

"How does it feel, Mr. Gaunce"—blandly, if bluntly; conversational—"after getting away with all you've *done,* being blamed for the one thing you *didn't,* of which you're perfectly innocent? The irony! All the world thinks *you* hired the general's death; only you and I know better. I'm sure you know why *I* know."

Gaunce had sunk back into his seat, mechanically gesturing at another; but she went on standing. Grudging admiration stole into his look of wariness. He seemed to fancy he faced a kindred spirit, as unscrupulous—as venal—as himself.

"My golden eagles seem to have made quite a migration," he mused, in all candor, enjoying himself. "You still have the ones Uriel Purinton didn't live to collect, I take it."

"You'd like them back, would you? Well—why not?"

"The planting of the evidence? Sealing the case against me, the one accusation, amid all the valid ones, of which you grant I'm blameless?" He laughed without humor, and sobered at once. "Believe me, I regret the general's death—I regret having had to *wish* him dead. *Such* a man! Oh, a pure fool, of course, but a *man* withal. To kill his killer, and with fair supernatural powers, in his very death-throes! And all to shield the fair name of his beloved, who, as well he knew, really killed him!"

"I was sure you would have plumbed the truth, even though such motivations clearly are beyond your moneygrubbing reckoning." His indictment had left her unfazed—as her insults did him—she had so thoroughly indicted herself. "My husband shot himself this morning," conversationally. She had taken a turn about the room. When she faced him again, the revolver was in her hand. "The Territory is being cleansed."

The shot was unmistakable in the outer office; but those in it, in their eyeshades and sleeve protectors, were hardly the sort to dispute a figure holding a smoking revolver, even a woman—*this* woman above all. She was outside, not just well along the street but across it, the hitched black forsaken behind her, before the clutch of blue forms, swarmed out of Headquarters House like shy hornets, less likely drawn by the shot than only at last worked up to action after having seen her pass, riding in, ventured closer. Hesitant, if not quite cautious, the bareheaded, empty-handed, though still redoubtable men faced the lone woman, who might have been but paused midway through a shopping outing—the majestic, majestically-dressed woman beneath her proud black plume, incongruously armed as a cavalryman.

"Chivalry dies hard, doesn't it, gentlemen?" she greeted, all mock-cheer. "How long have you—and Webb—been sitting on evidence enough to lock me up, or hang me? I just shot that thief —that other thief." She nodded back at the Agency office. "I must *make* you do your duty, it seems. Well—why aren't you summoning troops? How many will it take, do you reckon?"

"Mrs. Buckhannon—Cathal—" Colonel Yulee took a hesitant step ahead of his fellows. "*He* wouldn't have wanted this."

"Webb? Oh, you're perfectly right, I'm sure." She turned dreamy. "We were one soul in two bodies, and yet somehow we were always at cross purposes. Fitting I should defy him even to the last." She shook herself back to reality, smiled. "Your next move is to assure me they won't hang me, even for murder. It'll be merely the madhouse or the like? Oh, don't fret. I won't shoot anybody else." She gestured behind her. "Just give me a few minutes to, shall we say, pay my respects?"

It was but half a question, and only then did it strike them that she stood square before the old white frame chapel. And even as they took in what she said—what she meant—she turned and stepped inside and closed the door behind her.

The scene had begun to garner attention. Among the gathering figures was that of the post chaplain, the Reverend Captain Yonderly. Apprized of the situation he stood with the rest, alike at-a-loss, gazing at the austere little meeting-house patinated and betraying its age; venerable, dating as it did from earliest, real-fort days, a very fort itself—the *keep*, as it were, more-than-spiritual. Forebodingly Yulee cast about at the collecting curious.

"News travels fast," he muttered.

"*Bad*, above all." Captain Coonce frowned, asked—asked himself: "Why do we *know* it's going to be bad?"

On this misgiving note they went on waiting, staring. "She should be coming out." Isham Klyce looked at his big pocket watch—a tic of nervousness more than a serious interest in the exact passage of time. "You don't suppose. . . ."

"She's not coming out." It was Eadred Coonce who first saw and pointed to the tendrils of smoke starting to seep out under the double chapel doors. "As we should have known—she's fooled us—fooled us again!" He was already racing forward, the rest on his heels. He tried the latch, but the doors moved not at all. "We won't break in either, not in time." Feckless lunges of their several shoulders confirmed him. "These are oak, made to be barred, made for just this sort of thing—assault. Siege."

"The rear—?" somebody straw-grasped.

"The same. And the windows—inside shutters, barred. Oh dear, dear God!" The Reverend Captain Yonderly wrung his hands. "It's *built*, oh yes; built to last, to *take* it; but *dry*—a very tinderbox. And the *oil!*" His despair grew with his alarm, overwhelmed it. "The lamps—they were filled only yesterday."

Klyce swung on a hovering sergeant. "The fire brigade—not that it'll do much good."

The next few hours were a mighty muddle in the memories of all. As impotent as the others, the officers stood, watched the soldier firemen straggle to the scene and blunder through their motions, milling like strangely inept satanic imps in the glare that grew not just with the fire itself but against the colorful crowning afternoon sky. The building soon had become a pyre, a torch, and there was little any could do but drench its neighbors and wait for the fire to burn itself out and then douse the ashes. In every head were images of what was being consumed.

"It's—it's like a Viking funeral." For the moment even Yonderly was pagan.

Yulee threw him a strange look. "That's just what it is."

As they backed on off across the street, fleeing the mounting heat, they caught sight of Candacy Ann, standing at the foot of the steps from her quarters, not far along, her baby son in her arms, her servants at her shoulder. Yulee hurried to her, told the tale briefly, delicately—it was almost an apology.

She headshook. "I don't think he would have minded."

In the others' distraction Candacy Ann was the first to notice the newcomer, though he was a commanding figure, instantly dominating the scene, a warrior fresh from battle, or warrior-god: not a big man in height, but broad, barrel-like, and big in some indefinable other way as well; old, yet indeterminately so, his gray hair and beard streaked as with rust; his one gray eye paired with a stark black patch. Incongruously he led gently by the hand a child: a little girl with ruddy streaks, not too unlike his own, in her pale hair, doubling its radiance. The manner of their coming was unclear. They were just *not* there, and then *there*.

Yulee noticed too, at last; noticed her notice. "General McQuaife." Though the stranger was in mufti—slouch-hat, badgeless gray coat—and Yulee was hatless, his hand rose in half-salute all the same. Still, he was long taking it in. He glanced about at the dying fire. "I sense you know what's just happened, sir. I regret to welcome you under such—sad circumstances."

The venerable general nodded politely, but his attention for the moment was still all for Candacy Ann. "Mrs. Starcross." He *did* half-salute, half doff his hat. "We met long ago."

"Yes, General." She smiled, if not at all socially; an infinitely sad smile. "Long, long ago. Another world."

"My deepest condolences, my dear." He caressed her hand. He was a good—a fine man."

"And *she* . . . oh, sir! What can I say?"

"And this is your son, and his." Heedless he stroked the head of the child, heedless alike, there in her arms, and then looked down at the other child close by his side. "And this, as I'm sure you know, is Star." His one gray eye came back up to her face, regarded it thoughtfully before going on: "Have they told you? Major Buckhannon took his own life—he too."

"No—but I'm not surprised. So many lives taken! Thank God *you've* come. To stay—?" anxiously.

"Don't despair, my dear. All is not lost. There are lives left." His eye took in the two as one. "There are the living."

"Yes." She thought it over. "Webb's last words were about them. I understand him now. He made me promise—that little Webb should know his sister, if *she* would have it." Almost tearfully she added, "That, alas, no longer applies."

"He will know her. And she would have had it, I think. She was . . . many things, but not mean-spirited."

They stood there together, silent, as in a trance, watching the fire crest then subside, the firemen fight their way into the fallen heaps of still flickering coals as if they would find life there, find aught to justify their peril, broadcasting water that seemed but to turn to steam on contact with the brands. Bit by bit, though, the fire died, less for their labors than for want of tinder.

The leather-helmeted Hadean specter that hove out of the smoke and crossed over proved to be but the mere-human fire captain, all sooty and singed-looking and grasping gingerly in his gloved hands an incongruous long object. Seemingly with ease recognizing the stranger's ascendancy, in years at least if not in some moral sense, he handed it to him, not his colonel, though it was the latter he duteously bespoke.

"The bodies are . . . consumed, sir—the oil. And this—it's hard to be sure, but I'd say she . . . used it just before the flames closed over them. Fell on it"—delicately—"and him."

Yulee shook his head. "What a woman! Was she mad, sir, or just—what? Devilish or divine? Hell or heaven?"

"A fine line to draw, sometimes," the general mused.

His heart full, only with effort, it seemed, did he at last look down at what he held: the storied saber, its sharkskin grip singed but otherwise intact, and immaculate—the fireman had wiped it clean. Yulee ever after told himself, though—surely the fire had taken some of the temper out of the steel.

How else explain it? Almost casually General McQuaife's gloved hands brought the blade down over his flexed knee and easily, cleanly broke it at the hilt, with strength more than an old man's—more than human. He offered Candacy Ann the shards: symbolically, not meaning her to take them now.

"For the boy, don't you think, my dear? Long ago I gave it to his grandfather, if in rather a different condition. But perhaps the time has come for the different condition—for plowshares, as it were." He hefted the shards. "It has an unhappy history; still, it's a story he should know, the boy. Should know his father never unsheathed it without reason or sheathed it without honor. He was, to say it again, a fine man, his father."

"You can say that?" Candacy Ann puzzled, painfully. "You're very generous, sir. After what he—her—"

"'I fell into the wiles from whence our lives may not escape,' he might have said. A fine—a magnificent man."

The thought seemed to echo in all their minds. It struck none as strange that it was the wife's lips that rounded it out.

"A man to match *her.*"

"Who only could? A man mad, too, in his way. Heaven and hell. Though I fear I ill repay *your* generosity."

"No no; it's all right, General." Candacy Ann half-laughed, as if at herself; self-amazed. "I told him I would even share him with her, would you believe it? And so I have. And I no longer mind." On impulse Candacy Ann drew the braided golden band from her finger and held it out to the general. "It was his mother's, Webb's. I think he would want *her* to have it, Star. It's another unhappy, unlucky piece; but, again, a story to be known."

"*Things* aren't unhappy or unlucky, my dear. Only mortals."

"What—what will become of her, General?"

The craggy old warrior-face smiled. "I read your thoughts. I am a trifle old and rough to settle down to child-rearing, oh aye, *girl*-child-rearing. I did ill enough before, when I was younger. Yes. Something—something—will have to be done."

"Perhaps . . . perhaps *I* could do it. Take her; adopt her. She deserves to bear her father's name."

"That's generous of you indeed, Mrs. Starcross."

"If you're willing—and she, of course. And if—"

"Are you quite sure, though?" Realistically he clarified, "You have small reason to love the child."

"On the contrary—you're wrong all around. I'm *not* generous. I'm just—ashamed. And I don't *not* love anybody any more. Our ranks are so thinned!" She thought it over. "Even *she,* even Cathal. It's myself I can't love, not her, her memory. What I did to her! And *he* knew, and he never threw it up to me. To salve my pride, I struck at hers, and in so doing I killed *him*—and her, and even Chance." Surrendering to tears: "I killed them all."

"No, my dear. Nothing is so simple. As sensibly say I struck the telling blow myself, years before you." He glanced across at the smoldering coals. "I kept them apart."

"And then *I* kept them apart, though. I stood between them. Isn't it strange, now I own it—*know* it, now that it's too late—he belonged to her, not me. Oh, if only—!"

"If only. If only we weren't human, my dear. *They* were; we mustn't lose sight of that. If there was something more than human about them, or less, it was after all just that human-all-too-humanness of the gods, whether of Olympus or Valhalla." The general sighed: "'The worst of them was their virtue.'"

"I think I know what you mean. It was their undoing, wasn't it, their virtue, their very—goodness? Their crime was love, loving each other. And the world does sometimes make it a crime. I did my share. But if theirs was a crime, so was mine."

"You're a remarkable woman, my dear. These children are very lucky." He looked back again toward the late funeral pyre. "Their undoing, yes. And yet perhaps alike their making. They were just too—well, not too *good* for the world, perhaps; just too *much* for it. They are better off where they are."

"Strange, though—it's as if it lives on, their love."

"Doesn't it?" General McQuaife looked down at the children, at his side and in her arms. "Doesn't yours?"

The End